THE LOEB CLASSICAL LIBRARY

FOUNDED BY JAMES LOEB, LL.D.

EDITED BY

E. H. WARMINGTON, M.A., F.R.HIST.SOC.

FORMER EDITORS

† T. E. PAGE, C.H., LITT.D.   † E. CAPPS, PH.D., LL.D.

† W. H. D. ROUSE, LITT.D.   L. A. POST, L.H.D.

OVID

I

HEROIDES AND AMORES

41

OVID

IN SIX VOLUMES
I
HEROIDES AND AMORES

WITH AN ENGLISH TRANSLATION BY

GRANT SHOWERMAN

PROFESSOR OF LATIN IN THE
UNIVERSITY OF WISCONSIN

CAMBRIDGE, MASSACHUSETTS
HARVARD   UNIVERSITY   PRESS
LONDON
WILLIAM   HEINEMANN   LTD
MCMLXXI

American ISBN 0–674–99045–5
British ISBN 0 434 99041 8

First printed 1914
Reprinted 1921, 1925, 1930, 1947
1955, 1958, 1963, 1971

Printed in Great Britain

CONTENTS

871
OVIDIUS

I

THE HEROIDES

OVID'S LIFE

Publius Ovidius Naso was born at Sulmo, a city
about ninety miles south-east of Rome, in the country
of the Paeligni, on March 20, 43 B.C., the year of
the second triumvirate, composed of Augustus,
Antony, and Lepidus, and the year of the proscription
and death of the Ciceros. His family had been of
equestrian rank for several generations.

Ovid's education was begun at Sulmo, and com-
pleted at Rome and Athens. In deference to his
father's wishes, he pursued, with his brother, the
rhetorical studies usual with the ambitious young
men of the time, expecting to enter upon a public
career ; but so fervent was his passion for literature,
and so irresistible his instinct for literary art—he
himself says that whatever he attempted to write
took the form of verse—that he found it impossible
to follow the profession of his father's preference.
He held, indeed, one or two minor offices in the
public service, but his chief interests were always
among the social and literary circles of the capital.
Among those with whom he was intimate were
Tibullus, who died when Ovid was twenty-four,
Propertius, and Aemilius Macer of Verona. Horace
and Virgil were his seniors by twenty-two and
twenty-seven years respectively ; he heard the
former recite, and says he merely saw Virgil, and
was probably well acquainted with neither.

OVID'S LIFE

At the age of nineteen, Ovid mourned the death of his only brother. The poet was three times married—twice with divorce as a hasty result, and the third time to a lady of one of the oldest and most respected families of Rome, the Fabii. The last union seems to have been based upon serious affection, or, at least, esteem, and remained unbroken to Ovid's death. A daughter, Perilla, is said to have been born of this marriage. In 8 A.D., the poet was suddenly banished by Augustus—without loss of property or citizenship, however—to Tomi, a distant town on the Black Sea, where he dragged out a miserable, though poetically productive, existence until his death in the year 18 at the age of sixty-one. The cause of his banishment is generally supposed to have had some connection with the scandalous conduct of the Emperor's granddaughter Julia.

Ovid's literary activities began at about his twentieth year, and extended over a period of nearly forty years. His works fall naturally into three groups : the amatory poems, consisting of the *Amores*, the *Heroides*, *De Medicamine Faciei*, *Ars Amatoria*, and *Remedia Amoris*, were the works of his youth ; in the following period appeared two poems, the *Fasti* and the *Metamorphoses*, which may be described as mythological ; and the final products of his pen, the *Tristia* and the *Epistulae ex Ponto*, came from Tomi, and were in the nature of laments. All of these poems have been preserved. The *Medea*, a Gigantomachy, a Panegyric of Augustus after his death, a Parody on Bad Authors, and a poem in the language of the Getae, may be mentioned among works which have been lost.

3

OVID'S LIFE

Though composed after the *Amores,* the *Heroides* are placed first in this volume because the *Amores* in their extant form were the result of a revision by the poet, who first published them in five books. The present tendency may be said to favour the assumption that the last six of the *Heroides,* in spite of suspicious irregularities in form and language, represent a reawakening of the poet's interest in this field at a period later than the appearance of the first fifteen—possibly during or shortly after his composition of the *Metamorphoses.*

MANUSCRIPTS, EDITIONS, AND TEXTUAL CRITICISM OF THE HEROIDES

The principal manuscripts of the *Heroides* are the following :—

1. Codex Parisinus 8242, formerly called Puteanus, of the eleventh century, corrected about the twelfth ; by universal consent the best manuscript. It contains the *Heroides* and the *Amores*, with omissions. Of the Heroides there is lacking: I ; II, 1–13 ; IV, 48–103 ; V, 97–end ; VI, 1–49 ; XV ; XVI, 39–142 ; XX, 176–end.

2. Codex Guelferbytanus, of the twelfth century, with a recension in the thirteenth ; of comparatively little value. XVII–XX are almost illegible. The first hand gave to XX, 194.

3. Codex Etonensis, of the eleventh century, but inferior to its contemporary, the Parisinus. It contains, with various other compositions, the *Heroides* up to VII, 157.

4. Schedae Vindobonenses, of the twelfth century, containing fragments of X–XX, omitting XV, and often serving to confirm the Parisinus.

5. Codex Francofurtanus, of the thirteenth century, the best authority for XV.

6. A mass of manuscripts of the thirteenth, four-teenth, and fifteenth centuries, all of which have been subjected to extensive alterations.

7. The Greek translation of Maximus Planudes, of the latter part of the thirteenth century, from a Latin manuscript resembling the Parisinus, and of considerable value in the parts omitted by it.

Two Editiones Principes of Ovid appeared in 1471 —one at Rome and one at Bologna, with independent texts. A Venetian edition was published in 1491, with commentary by Vossius.

The principal edition of recent times is that of Arthur Palmer, Oxford, 1898. It contains the Greek translation of Planudes. The introduction and por-tions of the commentary are by Louis C. Purser, who assumed the task of completing the work at Palmer's request a short time before his death in 1897. The text in Postgate's Corpus Poetarum Latinorum, Vol. I, 1894, is also Palmer's.

Other editors and critics may be mentioned as follows: A. Heinsius, Amsterdam, 1661; Bentley, 1662–1742; Heinsius-Burmann, Amsterdam, 1727; Van Lennep, Amsterdam, 1809: Loers, Cologne, 1829; Madvig, Emendationes Latinae, 1873; Mer-kel, 1876; Shuckburgh, Thirteen Epistles, London, 1879, corrected in 1885; Sedlmayer, Vienna, 1886; Ehwald, edition of Merkel, 1888; Housman, critical notes, Classical Review, 1897.

SIGNS AND ABBREVIATIONS

P = Parisinus.
G = Guelferbytanus.
E = Etonensis.
V = Vindobonensis.
F = Francofurtanus.
ω = the mass of MSS. of the thirteenth to fifteenth centuries.
ς = a few inferior MSS. of the thirteenth to fifteenth centuries.
Bent. = Bentley.
Hein. = Heinsius.
Burm. = Burmann.
Merk. = Merkel.
Sedl. = Sedlmayer.
Ehw. = Ehwald.
Pa. = Palmer.
Hous. = Housman.

IN APPRECIATION OF THE HEROIDES

THE *Heroides* are not a work of the highest order of genius. Their language, nearly always artificial, frequently rhetorical, and often diffuse, is the same throughout—whether from the lips of barbarian Medea or Sappho the poetess. The heroines and heroes who speak it are creatures from the world of legend, are not always warm flesh and blood, and rarely communicate their passions to us. The critic who cares more for the raising of a laugh than for the strict rendering of justice may with no great difficulty find room here for the exercise of his wit.

Yet the malicious critic of the *Heroides* will be hard to find; for they belong to the engaging sort of art which disarms criticism. Their theme, first of all, is the universal theme of love—and of woman's love—and of woman's love in straits. The heroines that speak to us from Ovid's page may lack in convincing quality, and may not stir our passions, but they are sufficiently real to win our sympathy, and to blind us for the moment to the faults of both themselves and their sponsor. Their language may be unvarying, and may border too much on the rhetorical, but it is full-flowing, clear, euphonious, and restful. It may be artificial, but its very artificiality is of charming quality.

IN APPRECIATION OF THE HEROIDES

What the *Heroides* lose by reason of being the portrayal of legendary characters in language removed from ordinary life they gain from their pleasant quality of style, and from their constant stimulation of literary reminiscence. They should not be judged as attempts at realistic art; their author did not aim at even naturalism. If we must choose, they should be judged on the basis of their connection rather with literature than with life.

Yet we need not choose; we may enjoy them as clever and genial treatments of literary themes enriched with enough of the warmly human to beget in the benevolent reader the illusion of life. Penelope, Briseis, Dido, and Helen no doubt interest us mainly as figures from Homer and Virgil, but even they possess qualities that give them semblance of reality: Penelope is faithful, Briseis forgiving, Dido filled with despair, and Helen with vanity. In Medea, Hypsipyle, Oenone, and Ariadne, there is a nearer approach to real passion. The wifely solicitude of Laodamia, the loving trustfulness of deserted Phyllis, and the mother's grief of Canace are still more warm with life. The stories of Acontius and Cydippe, and in greater degree of Hero and Leander, are so full of the romance of young love that we think of neither life nor letters, but simply enjoy the delightful tale. And, whatever else may be said of his heroines, in every one of them the poet has placed the most human of qualities—a heart submissive to the power of love. All the world loves a lover, and all the world has for a long time loved most of the *Heroides*.

P. OVIDI NASONIS HEROIDES

I

PENELOPE ULIXI

HANC tua Penelope lento tibi mittit, Ulixe—
 nil mihi rescribas tu tamen;[1] ipse veni!
Troia iacet certe, Danais invisa puellis;
 vix Priamus tanti totaque Troia fuit.
o utinam tum, cum Lacedaemona classe petebat,   5
 obrutus insanis esset adulter aquis!
non ego deserto iacuissem frigida lecto,
 non quererer tardos ire relicta dies;
nec mihi quaerenti spatiosam fallere noctem
 lassaret[2] viduas pendula tela manus.   10
Quando ego non timui graviora pericula veris?
 res est solliciti plena timoris amor.
in te fingebam violentos Troas ituros;
 nomine in Hectoreo pallida semper eram.
sive quis Antilochum narrabat ab hoste revictum,[3] 15
 Antilochus nostri causa timoris erat;

[1] tu tamen *Bent.*: at tamen *G. Often written* rescribas, tu
tamen ipse veni.   [2] lassaret ω : lassasset *G.*
 [3] ab hoste revictum *Hous.*: ab Hectore victum *MSS. con-
tradicts the fact.*

THE
HEROIDES OF P. OVIDIUS NASO

I

PENELOPE TO ULYSSES

THIS missive your Penelope sends to you, O Ulysses, slow of return that you are—yet write nothing back to me; yourself come! Troy, to be sure, is fallen, hated of the daughters of Greece; but scarcely were Priam and all Troy worth the price to me.[a] O would that then, when his ship was on the way to Lacedaemon, the adulterous lover had been overwhelmed by raging waters! Then had I not lain cold in my deserted bed, nor would now be left alone complaining of slowly passing days; nor would the hanging web be wearying now my widowed hands as I seek to beguile the hours of spacious night.

[11] When have I not feared dangers graver than the real? Love is a thing ever filled with anxious fear. It was upon you that my fancy ever told me the furious Trojans would rush; at mention of the name of Hector my pallor ever came. Did someone begin the tale of Antilochus laid low by the enemy, Antilochus was cause of my alarm; or,

---

[a] Homer is Ovid's direct source for this letter. Tennyson's *Ulysses* is of interest in connection with it.

For brief statements of the circumstances under which the heroines write their letters, and for proper names in general, consult the index.

sive Menoetiaden falsis cecidisse sub armis,
    flebam successu posse carere dolos.
sanguine Tlepolemus Lyciam tepefecerat hastam;
    Tlepolemi leto cura novata mea est.   20
denique, quisquis erat castris iugulatus Achivis,
    frigidius glacie pectus amantis erat.
Sed bene consuluit casto deus aequus amori.
    versa est in cineres sospite Troia viro.
Argolici rediere duces, altaria fumant;   25
    ponitur ad patrios barbara praeda deos.
grata ferunt nymphae pro salvis dona maritis;
    illi victa suis Troica fata canunt.
mirantur iustique senes trepidaeque puellae;
    narrantis coniunx pendet ab ore viri.   30
atque aliquis posita monstrat fera proelia mensa,
    pingit et exiguo Pergama tota mero:
" hac ibat Simois; haec est Sigeia tellus;
    hic steterat Priami regia celsa senis.
illic Aeacides, illic tendebat Ulixes;   35
    hic lacer admissos terruit Hector equos."
Omnia namque tuo senior te quaerere misso
    rettulerat nato Nestor, at ille mihi.
rettulit et ferro Rhesumque Dolonaque caesos,
    utque sit hic somno proditus, ille dolo.   40
ausus es,—o nimium nimiumque oblite tuorum!—
    Thracia nocturno tangere castra dolo
totque simul mactare viros, adiutus ab uno!
    at bene cautus eras et memor ante mei!

---

a Patroclus in the armour of Achilles.
b Tlepolemus was slain by Sarpedon, king of Lycia.
c The past rises vividly in her mind.

did he tell of how the son of Menoetius fell in armour not his own,[a] I wept that wiles could lack success. Had Tlepolemus with his blood made warm the Lycian spear,[b] in Tlepolemus' fate was all my care renewed. In short, whoever it was in the Argive camp that was pierced and fell, colder than ice grew the heart of her who loves you.

23 But good regard for me had the god who looks with favour upon chaste love. Turned to ashes is Troy, and my lord is safe. The Argolic chieftains have returned, our altars are a-smoke;[c] before the gods of our fathers is laid the barbarian spoil. The young wife comes bearing thank-offering for her husband saved; the husband sings of the fates of Troy that have yielded to his own. Righteous elder and trembling girl admire; the wife hangs on the tale that falls from her husband's lips. And someone about the board shows thereon the fierce combat, and with scant tracing of wine pictures forth all Pergamum : " Here flowed the Simois; this is the Sigeian land; here stood the lofty palace of Priam the ancient. Yonder tented the son of Aeacus; yonder, Ulysses; here, in wild course went the frightened steeds with Hector's mutilated corpse."

37 For the whole story was told your son, whom I sent to seek you; ancient Nestor told him, and he told me. He told as well of Rhesus' and Dolon's fall by the sword, how the one was betrayed by slumber, the other undone by guile. You had the daring—O too, too forgetful of your own !—to set wily foot by night in the Thracian camp, and to slay so many men, all at one time, and with only one to aid ! Ah yes, you were cautious, indeed, and ever gave *me*

13

usque metu micuere sinus, dum victor amicum   45
    dictus es Ismariis isse per agmen equis.
Sed mihi quid prodest vestris disiecta lacertis
    Ilios et, murus quod fuit, esse solum,
si maneo, qualis Troia durante manebam,
    virque mihi dempto fine carendus abest?   50
diruta sunt aliis, uni mihi Pergama restant,
    incola captivo quae bove victor arat.
iam seges est, ubi Troia fuit, resecandaque falce
    luxuriat Phrygio sanguine pinguis humus;
semisepulta virum curvis feriuntur aratris   55
    ossa, ruinosas occulit herba domos.
victor abes, nec scire mihi, quae causa morandi,
    aut in quo lateas ferreus orbe, licet!
Quisquis ad haec vertit peregrinam litora puppim,
    ille mihi de te multa rogatus abit,   60
quamque tibi reddat, si te modo viderit usquam,
    traditur huic digitis charta notata meis.
nos Pylon, antiqui Neleia Nestoris arva,
    misimus; incerta est fama remissa Pylo.
misimus et Sparten; Sparte quoque nescia veri.[1]   65
    quas habitas terras, aut ubi lentus abes?
utilius starent etiamnunc moenia Phoebi—
    irascor votis, heu, levis ipsa meis!
scirem ubi pugnares, et tantum bella timerem,
    et mea cum multis iuncta querela foret.   70

[1] vestri Bent.

---

[a] If this refers to Telemachus' journey, Ovid has forgotten his Homer, or disregards it; for in the *Odyssey* (2, 373) Telemachus goes without his mother's knowledge.

first thought! My heart leaped with fear at every word until I was told of your victorious riding back through the friendly lines of the Greeks with the coursers of Ismarus.

⁴⁷ But of what avail to me that Ilion has been scattered in ruin by your arms, and that what once was wall is now level ground—if I am still to remain such as I was while Troy endured, and must live to all time bereft of my lord? For others Pergamum has been brought low; for me alone it still stands, though the victor dwell within and drive there the plow with the ox he took as spoil. Now are fields of corn where Troy once was, and soil made fertile with Phrygian blood waves rich with harvest ready for the sickle; the half-buried bones of her heroes are struck by the curvèd share, and herbage hides from sight her ruined palaces. A victor, you are yet not here, nor am I let know what causes your delay, or in what part of the world hard-heartedly you hide.

⁵⁹ Whoso turns to these shores of ours his stranger ship is plied with many a question ere he go away, and into his hand is given the sheet writ by these fingers of mine, to render up should he but see you anywhere. We have sent to Pylos, the land of ancient Nestor, Neleus' son; the word brought back from Pylos was nothing sure.ᵃ We have sent to Sparta, too; Sparta also could tell us nothing true. In what lands are you abiding, or where do you idly tarry? Better for me, were the walls of Phoebus still standing in their place—ah me inconstant, I am wroth with the vows myself have made! Had they not fallen, I should know where you were fighting, and have only war to fear, and my plaint would be joined with that of many another.

quid timeam, ignoro—timeo tamen omnia demens,
    et patet in curas area lata meas.
quaecumque aequor habet, quaecumque pericula tellus,
    tam longae causas suspicor esse morae.
haec ego dum stulte metuo, quae vestra libido est, 75
    esse peregrino captus amore potes.
forsitan et narres, quam sit tibi rustica coniunx,
    quae tantum lanas non sinat esse rudes.
fallar, et hoc crimen tenues vanescat in auras,
    neve, revertendi liber, abesse velis !   80
Me pater Icarius viduo discedere lecto
    cogit et immensas increpat usque moras.
increpet usque licet—tua sum, tua dicar oportet ;
    Penelope coniunx semper Ulixis ero.
ille tamen pietate mea precibusque pudicis   85
    frangitur et vires temperat ipse suas.
Dulichii Samiique et quos tulit alta Zacynthos,
    turba ruunt in me luxuriosa proci,
inque tua regnant nullis prohibentibus aula ;
    viscera nostra, tuae dilacerantur opes.   90
quid tibi Pisandrum Polybumque Medontaque dirum
    Eurymachique avidas Antinoique manus
atque alios referam, quos omnis turpiter absens
    ipse tuo partis sanguine rebus alis ?
Irus egens pecorisque Melanthius actor edendi   95
    ultimus accedunt in tua damna pudor.

---

    a Rustica is frequent in the Heroides. It suggests "rustic,"
"countryfied," "simple," "homely," "unsophisticated,"
but may be rendered well by no single word.

But now, what I am to fear I know not—yet none
the less I fear all things, distraught, and wide
is the field lies open for my cares. Whatever
dangers the deep contains, whatever the land, sus-
picion tells me are cause of your long delay. While
I live on in foolish fear of things like these,
you may be captive to a stranger love—such are
the hearts of you men! It may be you even
tell how rustic^a a wife you have—one fit only to
dress fine the wool. May I be mistaken, and this
charge of mine be found slight as the breeze that
blows, and may it not be that, free to return, you
will to be away!

⁸¹ As for me—my father Icarius enjoins on me
to quit my widowed couch, and ever chides me
for my measureless delay. Let him chide on —
yours I am, yours must I be called ; Penelope,
the wife of Ulysses, ever shall I be. Yet is he
bent by my faithfulness and my chaste prayers,
and of himself abates his urgency. The men of
Dulichium and Samos, and they whom high
Zacynthus bore—a wanton throng—come pressing
about me, suing for my hand. In your own hall they
are masters, with none to say them nay ; my heart is
being torn, your substance spoiled. Why tell you
of Pisander, and of Polybus, and of Medon the
cruel, and of the grasping hands of Eurymachus and
Antinous, and of others, all of whom through
shameful absence you yourself are feeding fat with
store that was won at cost of your blood ? Irus the
beggar, and Melanthius, who drives in your flocks to
be consumed, are the crowning disgrace now added
to your ruin.

OVID

Tres sumus inbelles numero, sine viribus uxor
    Laertesque senex Telemachusque puer.
ille per insidias paene est mihi nuper ademptus,
    dum parat invitis omnibus ire Pylon.[1]   100
di, precor, hoc iubeant, ut euntibus ordine fatis
    ille meos oculos conprimat, ille tuos!
hac faciunt custosque boum longaevaque nutrix,
    Tertius inmundae cura fidelis harae;[2]
sed neque Laertes, ut qui sit inutilis armis,   105
    hostibus in mediis regna tenere potest—
Telemacho veniet, vivat modo, fortior aetas;
    nunc erat auxiliis illa tuenda patris[3]—
nec mihi sunt vires inimicos pellere tectis.
    tu citius venias, portus et ara tuis!   110
est tibi sitque, precor, natus, qui mollibus annis
    in patrias artes erudiendus erat.
respice Laerten; ut iam sua lumina condas,
    extremum fati sustinet ille diem.[4]
Certe ego, quae fueram te discedente puella,   115
    protinus ut venias, facta videbor anus.

II

Phyllis Demophoonti

Hospita, Demophoon, tua te Rhodopeia Phyllis
    ultra promissum tempus abesse queror.

---

[1] 99,100 *spurious Bent.*
[2] *Ehw. places* 103, 104 *after* 96 : hac *Tyrrell* ; hec *G E ω* :
huc *Bent.* : hinc *Merk.*

[97] We number only three, unused to war—a power-less wife ; Laertes, an old man ; Telemachus, a boy. He was of late all but waylaid and taken from me, while making ready, against the will of all of them, to go to Pylos. The gods grant, I pray, that our fated ends may come in due succession—that he be the one to close my eyes, the one to close yours ! To sustain our cause are the guardian of your cattle and the ancient nurse, and, as a third, the faithful ward of the unclean stye ; but neither Laertes, unable as he is to wield arms now, can sway the sceptre in the midst of our foes—Telemachus, in-deed, so he live on, will arrive at years of strength, but now should have his father's aid and guarding— nor have I strength to repel the enemy from our halls. Do you yourself make haste to come, haven and altar of safety for your own ! You have a son— and may you have him ever, is my prayer—who in his tender years should have been trained by you in his father's ways. Have regard for Laertes ; in the hope that you will come at last to close his eyes, he is withstanding the final day of fate.

[115] As for myself, who when you left my side was but a girl, though you should come straightway, I surely shall seem grown an aged dame.

II

PHYLLIS TO DEMOPHOON

I, YOUR Phyllis, who welcomed you to Rhodope, Demophoon, complain that the promised day is past,

---

[3] *Birt places* 107, 108 *after* 98 : *spurious Sedl. Schenkel.*
[4] 111–114 *spurious Bent.*

cornua cum lunae pleno semel orbe coissent,
　litoribus nostris ancora pacta tua est—
luna quater latuit, toto quater orbe recrevit;　　5
　nec vehit Actaeas Sithonis unda rates.
tempora si numeres — bene quae[1] numeramus
　　amantes—
non venit ante suam nostra querela diem.
Spes quoque lenta fuit; tarde, quae credita laedunt,
　credimus. invito nunc et amore noces.[2]　　10
saepe fui mendax pro te mihi, saepe putavi[3]
　alba procellosos vela referre Notos.
Thesea devovi, quia te dimittere nollet;
　nec tenuit cursus forsitan ille tuos.
interdum timui, ne, dum vada tendis ad Hebri,　　15
　mersa foret cana naufraga puppis aqua.
saepe deos[4] supplex, ut tu, scelerate, valeres,
　cum prece turicremis sum venerata sacris;
saepe, videns ventos caelo pelagoque faventes,
　ipsa mihi dixi: "si valet ille, venit."　　20
denique fidus amor, quidquid properantibus obstat,
　finxit, et ad causas ingeniosa fui.
at tu lentus abes; nec te iurata reducunt
　numina, nec nostro motus amore redis.
Demophoon, ventis et verba et vela dedisti;　　25
　vela queror reditu, verba carere fide.

[1] bene quae *E ω Plan.*: quae nos *G Merk.*
[2] *So G* : invita nunc et amante nocens *E.*
[3] putavi *E s Plan.*: notavi *G Merk.*
[4] deo *Pa. who omits* 18, 19.

a Attica.

and you not here. When once the horns of the
moon should have come together in full orb, our
shores were to expect your anchor—the moon has
four times waned, and four times waxed again to her
orb complete ; yet the Sithonian wave brings not the
ships of Acte.[a] Should you count the days—which
we count well who love—you will find my plaint
come not before its time.

⁹ Hope, too, has been slow to leave me ; we are
tardy in believing, when belief brings hurt. Even
now my love is loath to let me think you
wrong me. Oft have I been false to myself
in my defence of you; oft have I thought the
gusty breezes of the south were bringing back your
white sails. Theseus I have cursed, because
methought he would not let you go; yet mayhap
'tis not he that has stayed your course. At times
have I feared lest, while you were holding toward
the waters of the Hebrus, your craft had been
wrecked and engulfed in the foaming wave. Oft,
bending the knee in prayer that you fare well—ah,
wretched man!—have I venerated the gods with
prayer or with burning of holy incense ; oft, seeing
in sky and on sea that the winds were favouring,
have I said to myself : " If he do fare well, he is on
the way." In a word, all things soever that hinder
those in haste to come, my faithful love has tried to
image forth, and my wit has been fertile in thé
finding of causes. But you delay long your coming ;
neither do the gods by whom you swore bring you
back to me, nor does love of mine move your
return. Demophoon, to the winds you gave at once
both promised word and sails ; your sails, alas! have
not returned, your promised word has not been kept.

OVID

Dic mihi, quid feci, nisi non sapienter amavi?
  crimine te potui demeruisse meo.
unum in me scelus est, quod te, scelerate, recepi;
  sed scelus hoc meriti pondus et instar habet.   30
iura, fides ubi nunc, commissaque dextera dextrae,
  quique erat in falso plurimus ore deus?
promissus socios ubi nunc Hymenaeus in annos,
  qui mihi coniugii sponsor et obses erat?
per mare, quod totum ventis agitatur et undis,   35
  per quod saepe ieras, per quod iturus eras,
perque tuum mihi iurasti—nisi fictus et ille est—
  concita qui ventis aequora mulcet, avum,
per Venerem nimiumque mihi facientia tela—
  altera tela arcus, altera tela faces—   40
Iunonemque, toris quae praesidet alma maritis,
  et per taediferae mystica sacra deae.
si de tot laesis sua numina quisque deorum
  vindicet, in poenas non satis unus eris.
At laceras etiam puppes furiosa refeci—   45
  ut, qua desererer, firma carina foret!—
remigiumque dedi, quod me fugiturus haberes.
  heu! patior telis vulnera facta meis!
credidimus blandis, quorum tibi copia, verbis;
  credidimus generi nominibusque tuis;   50

²⁷ Tell me, what have I done, except not wisely
love?—and by the very fault I might well have
won you for my own. The one crime which may be
charged to me is that I took you, O faithless, to
myself; but this crime has all the weight and
seeming of good desert. The bonds that should
hold you, the faith that you swore, where are
they now?—and the pledge of the right hand you
placed in mine, and the talk of God that was ever on
your lying lips? Where now the bond of Hymen
promised for years of life together—promise that was
my warrant and surety for the wedded state? By
the sea, all tossed by wind and wave, over which you
had often gone, over which you were still to go; and
by your grandsire—unless he, too, is but a fiction—
by your grandsire, who calms the windwrought wave,
you swore to me; yes, and by Venus and the
weapons that wound me all too much—one weapon
the bow, the other the torch; and by Juno, the
kindly ward of the bridal bed; and by the mystical
rites of the goddess who bears the torch. Should
all the many gods you have wronged take vengeance
for the outrage to their sacred names, your single
life would not suffice.

⁴⁵ Yes, and more, in my madness I even refitted
your shattered ships—that the keel might be firm
by which I was left behind!—and gave you the
oars by which you were to fly from me. Ah me, my
pangs are from wounds wrought by weapons of my
own! I had faith in your wheedling words, and
you had good store of them; I had faith in your
lineage, and in the names it shows; I had faith

credidimus lacrimis—an et hae simulare docentur?
  hae quoque habent artes, quaque iubentur, eunt?
dis quoque credidimus. quo iam tot pignora nobis?
  parte satis potui qualibet inde capi.
Nec moveor, quod te iuvi portuque locoque—   55
  debuit haec meriti summa fuisse mei!
turpiter hospitium lecto cumulasse iugali
  paenitet, et lateri conseruisse latus.
quae fuit ante illam, mallem suprema fuisset
  nox mihi, dum potui Phyllis honesta mori.   60
speravi melius, quia me meruisse putavi;
  quaecumque ex merito spes venit, aequa venit.
Fallere credentem non est operosa puellam
  gloria. simplicitas digna favore fuit.
sum decepta tuis et amans et femina verbis.   65
  di faciant, laudis summa sit ista tuae!
inter et Aegidas, media statuaris in urbe,
  magnificus titulis stet pater ante suis.
cum fuerit Sciron lectus torvusque Procrustes
  et Sinis et tauri mixtaque forma viri   70
et domitae bello Thebae fusique bimembres
  et pulsata nigri regia caeca dei—
hoc tua post illos titulo signetur imago:

HIC EST, CUIUS AMANS HOSPITA CAPTA DOLO EST.

de tanta rerum turba factisque parentis   75
  sedit in ingenio Cressa relicta tuo.

---

^a Theseus.

in your tears—or can these also be taught to feign;
and are these also guileful, and ready to flow where
bidden? I had faith, too, in the gods by whom
you swore. To what end, pray, so many pledges of
faith to me? By any part of them, however slight,
I could have been ensnared.

⁵⁵ I am stirred by no regret that I aided you with
haven and abiding-place—only, this should have
been the limit of my kindness! Shamefully to
have added to my welcome of the guest the favours
of the marriage-bed is what I repent me of—to have
pressed your side to my own. The night before
that night I could wish had been the last for me,
while I still could have died Phyllis the chaste. I
had hope for a better fate, for I thought it my
desert; the hope—whatever it be—that is grounded
in desert, is just.

⁶³ To beguile a trustful maid is glory but cheaply
earned; my simple faith was worthy of regard. I was
deceived by your words—I, who loved and was a
woman. May the gods grant that this be your
crowning praise! In the midst of your city, even
among the sons of Aegeus, go let yourself be statued,
and let your mighty father ᵃ be set there first, with
record of his deeds. When men shall have read
of Sciron, and of grim Procrustes, and of Sinis, and
of the mingled form of bull and man, and of Thebes
brought low in war, and of the rout of the two-
framed Centaurs, and of the knocking at the gloomy
palace of the darksome god—after all these, under
your own image let be inscribed these words:

THIS IS HE WHOSE WILES BETRAYED THE HOSTESS
THAT LOVED HIM.

Of all the great deeds in the long career of your
sire, nothing has made impress upon your nature but

OVID

quod solum excusat, solum miraris in illo ;
　　heredem patriae, perfide, fraudis agis.
illa—nec invideo—fruitur meliore marito
　　inque capistratis tigribus alta sedet ;　　　　80
at mea despecti fugiunt conubia Thraces,
　　quod ferar externum praeposuisse meis.
atque aliquis "iam nunc doctas eat," inquit, "Athenas;
　　armiferam Thracen qui regat, alter erit.
exitus acta probat." careat successibus, opto,　　85
　　quisquis ab eventu facta notanda putat !
at si nostra tuo spumescant aequora remo,
　　iam mihi, iam dicar consuluisse meis—
sed neque consului, nec te mea regia tanget
　　fessaque Bistonia membra lavabis aqua !　　90
Illa meis oculis species abeuntis inhaeret,
　　cum premeret portus classis itura meos.
ausus es amplecti colloque infusus amantis
　　oscula per longas iungere pressa moras
cumque tuis lacrimis lacrimas confundere nostras, 95
　　quodque foret velis aura secunda, queri
et mihi discedens suprema dicere voce :
　　" Phylli, fac expectes Demophoonta tuum !"
Expectem, qui me numquam visurus abisti ?
　　expectem pelago vela negata meo ? [1]　　　　100

　　[1] *So G ω* : negante data *Pa.*: velane gatata meo *P.*

　　[a] After Theseus' desertion of her, Ariadne was wedded to
Bacchus, whose tigers and car she drives.

26

the leaving of his Cretan bride. The only deed
that draws forth his excuse, that only you admire in
him; you act the heir to your father's guile, per-
fidious one. She—and with no envy from me—
enjoys now a better lord, and sits aloft behind
her bridled tigers [a]; but me, the Thracians whom
I scorned will not now wed, for rumour declares I
set a stranger before my countrymen. And some-
one says: "Let her now away to learned Athens;
to rule in armour-bearing Thrace another shall be
found. The event proves well the wisdom of her
course." Let him come to naught, I pray, who
thinks the deed should be condemned from its
result. Ah, but if our seas should foam beneath
your oar, then should I be said to have counselled
well for myself, then well for my countrymen; but I
have neither counselled well, nor will my palace feel
your presence more, nor will you bathe again your
wearied limbs in the Bistonian wave!

[91] Ever to my sight clings that vision of you as
you went, what time your ships were riding the
waters of my harbour, all ready to depart. You dared
embrace me, and, with arms close round the neck of
her who loved you, to join your lips to mine in
long and lingering kisses, to mingle with my tears
your own, to complain because the breeze was
favouring to your sails, and, as you left my side, to
say for your last words: "Phyllis, remember well,
expect your own Demophoon!"

[99] And am I to expect, when you went forth with
thought never to see me more? Am I to expect the
sails denied return to my seas? And yet I do

OVID

et tamen expecto—redeas modo serus amanti,
  ut tua sit solo tempore lapsa fides!
Quid precor infelix? te iam tenet altera coniunx
  forsitan et, nobis qui male favit, amor;
utque tibi excidimus, nullam, puto, Phyllida nosti. 105
  ei mihi! si, quae sim Phyllis et unde, rogas—
quae tibi, Demophoon, longis erroribus acto
  Threicios portus hospitiumque dedi,
cuius opes auxere meae, cui dives egenti
  munera multa dedi, multa datura fui; 110
quae tibi subieci latissima regna Lycurgi,
  nomine femineo vix satis apta regi,
qua patet umbrosum Rhodope glacialis ad Haemum,
  et sacer admissas exigit Hebrus aquas,
cui mea virginitas avibus libata sinistris 115
  castaque fallaci zona recincta manu!
pronuba Tisiphone thalamis ululavit in illis,
  et cecinit maestum devia carmen avis;
adfuit Allecto brevibus torquata colubris,
  suntque sepulcrali lumina mota face! 120
Maesta tamen scopulos fruticosaque litora calco
  quaeque patent oculis litora[1] lata meis.
sive die laxatur humus, seu frigida lucent
  sidera, prospicio, quis freta ventus agat;
et quaecumque procul venientia lintea vidi, 125
  protinus illa meos auguror esse deos.

¹ litora *MSS.*: aequora *Aldus Pa.*

ᵃ A Fury, instead of Juno, patroness of marriage.

expect—ah, return only, though late, to her who loves you, and prove your promise false only for the time that you delay!

103 Why entreat, unhappy that I am? It may be you are already won by another bride, and feel for her the love that favoured me but ill; and since I have fallen from out your life, I feel you know Phyllis no more. Ah me! if you ask who I, Phyllis, am, and whence—I am she, Demophoon, who, when you had been driven far in wanderings on the sea, threw open to you the havens of Thrace and welcomed you as guest, you, whose estate my own raised up, to whom in your need I in my plenty gave many gifts, and would have given many still; I am she who rendered to you the broad, broad realms of Lycurgus, scarce meet to be ruled in a woman's name, where stretches icy Rhodope to Haemus with its shades, and sacred Hebrus drives his headlong waters forth—to you, on whom mid omens all sinister my maiden innocence was first bestowed, and whose guileful hand ungirdled my chaste. zone! Tisiphone was minister at that bridal, with shrieks,*a* and the bird that shuns the light chanted her mournful note; Allecto was there, with little serpents coiled about her neck, and the lights that waved were torches of the tomb!

121 Heavy in soul, none the less do I tread the rocks and the thicket-covered strand, where'er the sea view opens broad before my eyes. Whether by day the soil is loosed by warmth, or whether constellations coldly shine, I look ever forth to see what wind doth sweep the straits; and whatever sails I see approaching from afar, straightway I augur them the answer to my prayers. I rush forth to

OVID

in freta procurro, vix me retinentibus undis,
  mobile qua primas porrigit aequor aquas.
quo magis accedunt, minus et minus utilis adsto ;
  linquor et ancillis excipienda cado.   130
Est sinus, adductos modice falcatus in arcus ;
  ultima praerupta cornua mole rigent.
hinc mihi suppositas inmittere corpus in undas
  mens fuit ; et, quoniam fallere pergis, erit.
ad tua me fluctus proiectam litora portent,   135
  occurramque oculis intumulata tuis !
duritia ferrum ut superes adamantaque teque,
  "non tibi sic," dices, " Phylli, sequendus eram !"
saepe venenorum sitis est mihi ; saepe cruenta
  traiectam gladio morte perire iuvat.   140
colla quoque, infidis quia se nectenda lacertis
  praebuerunt, laqueis inplicuisse iuvat.
stat nece matura tenerum pensare pudorem.
  in necis electu parva futura mora est.
Inscribere meo causa invidiosa sepulcro.   145
  aut hoc aut simili carmine notus eris :

Phyllida Demophoon leto dedit hospes amantem ;
  ille necis causam praebuit, ipsa manum.

the waters, scarce halted by the waves where first
the sea sends in its mobile tide. The nearer the
sails advance, the less and less the strength that
bears me up; my senses leave me, and I fall, to be
caught up by my handmaids' arms.

¹³¹ There is a bay, whose bow-like lines are
gently curved to sickle shape ; its outmost horns
rise rigid and in rock-bound mass. To throw myself
hence into the waves beneath has been my mind ;
and, since you still pursue your faithless course, so
shall it be. Let the waves bear me away, and cast
me up on your shores, and let me meet your eyes
untombed ! Though in hardness you be more than
steel, than adamant, than your very self, you shall
say : " Not so, Phyllis, should I have been followed
by thee ! " Oft do I long for poison ; oft with the
sword would I gladly pierce my heart and pour
forth my blood in death. My neck, too, because
once offered to the embrace of your false arms, I
could gladly ensnare in the noose. My heart is
fixed to die before my time, and thus make amends
to tender purity. In the choosing of my death there
shall be but small delay.

¹⁴⁵ On my tomb shall you be inscribed the hate-
ful cause of my death. By this, or by some similar
verse, shall you be known :

DEMOPHOON 'TWAS SENT PHYLLIS TO HER DOOM ;
    HER GUEST WAS HE, SHE LOVED HIM WELL.
HE WAS THE CAUSE THAT BROUGHT HER DEATH TO
    PASS ;
    HER OWN THE HAND BY WHICH SHE FELL.

OVID

III

Briseis Achilli

Quam legis, a rapta Briseide littera venit,
    vix bene barbarica Graeca notata manu.
quascumque adspicies, lacrimae fecere lituras ;
    sed tamen et lacrimae pondera vocis habent.
Si mihi pauca queri de te dominoque viroque   5
    fas est, de domino pauca viroque querar.
non, ego poscenti quod sum cito tradita regi,
    culpa tua est—quamvis haec quoque culpa tua est ;
nam simul Eurybates me Talthybiusque vocarunt,
    Eurybati data sum Talthybioque comes.   10
alter in alterius iactantes lumina vultum
    quaerebant taciti, noster ubi esset amor.
differri potui ; poenae mora grata fuisset.
    ei mihi ! discedens oscula nulla dedi ;
at lacrimas sine fine dedi rupique capillos—   15
    infelix iterum sum mihi visa capi !
Saepe ego decepto volui custode reverti,
    sed, me qui timidam prenderet,[1] hostis erat.
si progressa forem, caperer ne nocte timebam,
    quamlibet ad Priami munus itura nurum.   20
Sed data sim, quia danda fui—tot noctibus absum
    nec repetor ; cessas, iraque lenta tua est.

               [1] redderet *Ehw.*

---

    [a] Briseis was a captive from Lyrnesus, in Mysia. Iliad IX
is the basis of this letter.
    [b] Agamemnon forced Achilles to give up Briseis. Achilles
having refused to aid the Greeks, Agamemnon sent an embassy
to him, but the offended warrior scorned his advances.

III

BRISEIS TO ACHILLES

FROM stolen Briseis is the writing you read, scarce charactered in Greek by her barbarian hand.[a] Whatever blots you shall see, her tears have made; but tears, too, have none the less the weight of words.

[5] If 'tis right for me to utter brief complaint of you, my master and my beloved, of you, my master and my beloved, will I utter brief complaint. That I was all too quickly delivered over to the king at his demand is not your fault—yet this, too, is your fault; for as soon as Eurybates and Talthybius came to ask for me, to Eurybates was I given over, and to Talthybius, to go with them.[b] Each, casting eyes into the face of other, inquired in silence where now was the love between us. My going might have been deferred; a stay of my pain would have eased my heart. Ah me! I had to go, and with no farewell kiss; but tears without end I shed, and rent my hair—miserable me, I seemed a second time to suffer the captive's fate!

[17] Oft have I wished to elude my guards and return to you; but the enemy was there, to seize upon a timid girl. Should I have gone far, I feared I should be taken in the night, and delivered over a gift to some one of the ladies of Priam's sons.

[21] But grant I was given up because I must be given—yet all these nights I am absent from your side, and not demanded back; you delay, and your

ipse Menoetiades tum, cum tradebar, in aurem
    " quid fles ? hic parvo tempore,"[a] dixit, " eris."
Nec repetisse parum; pugnas, ne reddar, Achille! 25
    i nunc et cupidi nomen amantis habe !
venerunt ad te Telamone et Amyntore nati—
    ille gradu propior sanguinis, ille comes—
Laertaque satus, per quos comitata redirem.
    auxerunt blandas grandia dona preces :   30
viginti fulvos operoso ex aere lebetas,
    et tripodas septem pondere et arte pares ;
addita sunt illis auri bis quinque talenta,
    bis sex adsueti vincere semper equi,
quodque supervacuum est, forma praestante puellae 35
    Lesbides, eversa corpora capta domo,
cumque tot his—sed non opus est tibi coniuge—
       coniunx
    ex Agamemnoniis una puella tribus.
si tibi ab Atride pretio redimenda fuissem,
    quae dare debueras, accipere illa negas !   40
qua merui culpa fieri tibi vilis, Achille ?
    quo levis a nobis tam cito fugit amor ?
An miseros tristis fortuna tenaciter urget,
    nec venit inceptis mollior hora malis ?[1]
diruta Marte tuo Lyrnesia moenia vidi—   45
    et fueram patriae pars ego magna meae ;
vidi consortes pariter generisque necisque
    tres cecidisse—tribus, quae mihi, mater erat ;
vidi, quantus erat, fusum tellure cruenta
    pectora iactantem sanguinolenta virum.   50

---

[1] malis *Lehrs Hous. Plan.*: meis *MSS.*

---

[a] Patroclus.

anger is slow. Menoetius' son himself,[a] at the time I was delivered up, whispered into my ear: "Why do you weep? But a short time," he said, "will you be here."

²⁵ And not to have claimed me back is but a slight thing; you even oppose my being restored, Achilles. Go now, deserve the name of an eager lover! There came to you the sons of Amyntor and Telamon—the one near in degree of blood, the other a comrade—and Laertes' son; in company of these I was to return. Rich presents lent weight to their wheedling prayers: twenty ruddy vessels of wrought bronze, and tripods seven, equal in weight and workmanship; added to these, of gold twice five talents, twice six coursers ever wont to win, and—what there was no need of! —Lesbian girls surpassing fair, maids taken when their home was overthrown; and with all these —though of a bride you have no need—as bride, one of the daughters three of Agamemnon. What you must have given had you had to buy me back from Atrides with a price, that you refuse as a gift! What have I done that I am held thus cheap by you, Achilles? Whither has fled your light love so quickly from me?

⁴³ Or can it be that a gloomy fortune still weighs the wretched down, and a gentler hour comes not when woes have once begun? The walls of Lyrnesus I have seen laid in ruin by your soldier band—I, who myself had been great part of my father's land; I have seen fall three who were partners alike in birth and in death—and the three had the mother who was mine; I have seen my wedded lord stretched all his length upon the gory ground, heaving in agony

tot tamen amissis te conpensavimus unum ;
    tu dominus, tu vir, tu mihi frater eras.
tu mihi, iuratus per numina matris aquosae,
    utile dicebas ipse fuisse capi—
scilicet ut, quamvis veniam dotata, repellas   55
    et mecum fugias quae tibi dantur opes !
quin etiam fama est, cum crastina fulserit Eos,
    te dare nubiferis lintea velle Notis.
Quod scelus ut pavidas miserae mihi contigit aures,
    sanguinis atque animi pectus inane fuit.   60
ibis et—o miseram !—cui me, violente,[1] relinquis ?
    quis mihi desertae mite levamen erit ?
devorer ante, precor, subito telluris hiatu
    aut rutilo missi fulminis igne cremer,
quam sine me Phthiis canescant aequora remis,   65
    et videam puppes ire relicta tuas !
si tibi iam reditusque placent patriique Penates,
    non ego sum classi sarcina magna tuae.
victorem captiva sequar, non nupta maritum ;
    est mihi, quae lanas molliat, apta manus.   70
inter Achaeiadas longe pulcherrima matres
    in thalamos coniunx ibit eatque tuos,
digna nurus socero, Iovis Aeginaeque nepote,
    cuique senex Nereus prosocer esse velit.
nos humiles famulaeque tuae data pensa trahemus, 75
    et minuent plenos stamina nostra colos.

[1] tu lente *Bent.*

---

[a] Peleus, son of Aeacus, son of Jupiter and Aegina.
[b] Thetis, mother of Achilles, was daughter of Nereus.

his bloody breast. For so many lost to me I still had only you in recompense; you were my master, you my husband, you my brother. You swore to me by the godhead of your seaborn mother, and yourself said that my captive's lot was gain—yes, that though I come to you with dowry, you may thrust me back, scorning with me the wealth that is tendered you! Nay, 'tis even said that when to-morrow's dawn shall have shone forth, you mean to unfurl your linen sails to the cloud-bringing winds of the south.

[59] When the monstrous tale fell on my wretched and terror-stricken ears, the blood went from my breast, and with it my senses fled. You are going— ah me, wretched!—and to whom do you leave me, O hardened of heart? Who shall afford me gentle solace, left behind? May I be swallowed up, I pray, in sudden yawning of the earth, or consumed by the ruddy fire of careering thunderbolt, e'er that, without me, the seas foam white with Phthian oars, and I am left behind to see your ships fare forth! If it please you now to return to the hearth of your fathers, I am no great burden to your fleet. As captive let me follow my captor, not as wife my wedded lord; I have a hand well skilled to dress the wool. The most beauteous by far among the women of Achaea will come to the marriage-chamber as your bride—and may she come! —a bride worthy of her lord's father,[a] the grandchild of Jove and Aegina, and one whom ancient Nereus would welcome as his grandson's bride.[b] As for me, I shall be a lowly slave of yours and spin off the given task, and the full distaff shall grow slender at the drawing of my threads. Only let not your lady

37

exagitet ne me tantum tua, deprecor, uxor—
  quae mihi nescio quo non erit aequa modo—
neve meos coram scindi patiare capillos
  et leviter dicas : " haec quoque nostra fuit."   80
vel patiare licet, dum ne contempta relinquar—
  hic mihi vae ! miserae concutit ossa metus.
Quid tamen expectas ? Agamemnona paenitet irae,
  et iacet ante tuos Graecia maesta pedes.
vince animos iramque tuam, qui cetera vincis !   85
  quid lacerat Danaas inpiger Hector opes ?
arma cape, Aeacide, sed me tamen ante recepta,
  et preme turbatos Marte favente viros !
propter me mota est, propter me desinat ira,
  simque ego tristitiae causa modusque tuae.   90
nec tibi turpe puta precibus succumbere nostris ;
  coniugis Oenides versus in arma prece est.
res audita mihi, nota est tibi. fratribus orba
  devovit nati spemque caputque parens.
bellum erat ; ille ferox positis secessit ab armis   95
  et patriae rigida mente negavit opem.
sola virum coniunx flexit. felicior illa !
  at mea pro[1] nullo pondere verba cadunt.
nec tamen indignor nec me pro coniuge gessi
  saepius in domini serva vocata torum.   100
me quaedam, memini, dominam captiva vocabat.
  " servitio," dixi, " nominis addis onus."
Per tamen ossa viri subito male tecta sepulcro,
  semper iudiciis ossa verenda meis ;

[1] pro ! *Madv.*

---

[a] The story of Meleager, who slew his mother Althea's
brother, and was cursed by her. Refusing to aid his country
in the war that followed the killing of the Calydonian boar,
he was turned from his purpose by his wife Cleopatra.

be harsh with me, I pray—for in some way I feel
she will not be kind—and suffer her not to tear my
hair before your eyes, while you lightly say of me:
"She, too, once was mine." Or, suffer it even so,
if only I am not despised and left behind—this is
the fear, ah woe is wretched me, that shakes my
very bones!

83 What do you still await? Agamemnon repents
him of his wrath, and Greece lies prostrate in
affliction at your feet. Subdue your own angry
spirit, you who subdue all else! Why does eager
Hector still harry the Danaan lines? Seize up your
armour, O child of Aeacus—yet take me back first
—and with the favour of Mars rout and overwhelm
their ranks. For me your anger was stirred, through
me let it be allayed; and let me be both the cause
and the measure of your gloomy wrath. Nor think
it unseemly for you to yield to prayer of mine; by
the prayer of his wedded wife was the son of Oeneus
roused to arms.[a] 'Tis only a tale to me, but to you
well known. Reft of her brothers, a mother cursed
the hope and head of her son. There was war;
in fierce mood he laid down his arms and stood
apart, and with unbending purpose refused his country
aid. Only the wife availed to bend her husband.
The happier she!—for my words have no weight,
and fall for naught. And yet I am not angered, nor
have I borne myself as wife because oft summoned,
a slave, to share my master's bed. Some captive
woman once, I mind me, called me mistress. "To
slavery," I replied, "you add a burden in that
name."

103 None the less, by the bones of my wedded lord,
ill covered in hasty sepulture bones ever to be

perque trium fortes animas, mea numina, fratrum, 105
    qui bene pro patria cum patriaque iacent;
perque tuum nostrumque caput, quae iunximus una,
    perque tuos enses, cognita tela meis—
nulla Mycenaeum sociasse cubilia mecum
    iuro; fallentem deseruisse velis! 110
si tibi nunc dicam: "fortissime, tu quoque iura
    nulla tibi sine me gaudia facta!" neges.
at Danai maerere putant—tibi plectra moventur,
    te tenet in tepido mollis amica sinu!
et quisquam[1] quaerit, quare pugnare recuses? 115
    pugna nocet, citharae noxque Venusque iuvant.
tutius est iacuisse toro, tenuisse puellam,
    Threiciam digitis increpuisse lyram,
quam manibus clipeos et acutae cuspidis hastam,
    et galeam pressa sustinuisse coma. 120
Sed tibi pro tutis insignia facta placebant,
    partaque bellando gloria dulcis erat.
an tantum dum me caperes, fera bella probabas,
    cumque mea patria laus tua victa iacet?
di melius! validoque, precor, vibrata lacerto 125
    transeat Hectoreum Pelias hasta latus!
mittite me, Danai! dominum legata rogabo
    multaque mandatis oscula mixta feram.
plus ego quam Phoenix, plus quam facundus Ulixes,
    plus ego quam Teucri, credite, frater agam. 130

---

[1] *So G*: si quisquam (quisquis?) *P*: et si quis *ω*: et quis-
quis *s*: si quis nunc quaerat *or* si quis forte roget *Bent.*

---

[a] Because Orpheus was a Thracian.
[b] Ajax. The three were the delegation sent by Agamem-
non to offer to make amends.

40

held sacred in my eyes; and by the brave souls of
my three brothers, to me now spirits divine, who
died well for their country, and lie well with it
in death; and by your head and mine, which we
have laid each to each; and by your sword, weapon
well known to my kin—I swear that the Mycenaean
has shared no couch with me; if I prove false,
wish never to see me more! If now I should say
to you: "Most valiant one, do you swear also that
you have tasted no joys apart from me!" you
would refuse. Yes, the Danai think you are
mourning for me—but you are wielding the plectrum,
and a tender mistress holds you in her warm
embrace! And does anyone ask wherefore do you
refuse to fight? Because the fight brings danger;
while the zither, and night, and Venus, bring
delight. Safer is it to lie on the couch, to clasp a
sweetheart in your arms, to tinkle with your fingers
the Thracian [a] lyre, than to take in hand the shield,
and the spear with sharpened point, and to sustain
upon your locks the helmet's weight.

[121] Once the deed of renown, rather than safety,
was your pleasure, and glory won in warring was
sweet to you. Or can it be that you favoured fierce
war only till you could make me captive, and that your
praise lies dead, o'ercome together with my native
land? Ye gods forfend! and may the spéar of
Pelion go quivering from your strong arm to pierce
the side of Hector! Send me, O Danai! I
will be ambassadress and supplicate my lord, and
carry many kisses mingled with my message. I shall
achieve more than Phoenix, believe me, more than
eloquent Ulysses, more than Teucer's brother! [b] It

OVID

est aliquid, collum solitis tetigisse lacertis,
   praesentisque oculos admonuisse sinu.[1]
sis licet inmitis matrisque ferocior undis,
   ut taceam, lacrimis conminuere meis.
Nunc quoque—sic omnes Peleus pater inpleat
     annos,   135
   sic eat auspiciis Pyrrhus ad arma tuis !—
respice sollicitam Briseida, fortis Achille,
   nec miseram lenta ferreus ure mora !
aut, si versus amor tuus est in taedia nostri,
   quam sine te cogis vivere, coge mori !   140
utque facis, coges. abiit corpusque colorque;
   sustinet hoc animae spes tamen una tui.
qua si destituor, repetam fratresque virumque—
   nec tibi magnificum femina iussa mori.
cur autem iubeas? stricto pete corpora ferro; 145
   est mihi qui fosso pectore sanguis eat.
me petat ille tuus, qui, si dea passa fuisset,
   ensis in Atridae pectus iturus erat !
A, potius serves nostram, tua munera, vitam !
   quod dederas hosti victor, amica rogo.   150
perdere quos melius possis, Neptunia praebent
   Pergama; materiam caedis ab hoste pete.
me modo, sive paras inpellere remige classem,
   sive manes, domini iure venire iube !

              [1] sinu *G E ω*; sinus *s*: suis *P.*

will avail something to have touched your neck with the accustomed arms, to have seen you and stirred your recollection by the sight of my bosom. Though you be cruel, though more savage than your mother's waves, even should I keep silence you will be broken by my tears.

¹³⁵ Even now—so may Peleus your father fill out his tale of years, so may Pyrrhus take up arms with fortune as good as yours!—have regard for anxious Briseis, brave Achilles, and do not hard-heartedly torment a wretched maid with long drawn out delay! Or, if your love for me has turned to weariness, compel the death of her whom you compel to live without you! And, as you now are doing, you will compel it. Gone is my flesh, and gone my colour; what spirit I still have is but sustained by hope in you. If I am left by that, I shall go to rejoin my brothers and my husband—and 'twill be no boast for you to have bid a woman die. And more, why should you bid me die? Draw the steel and plunge it in my body; I have blood to flow when once my breast is pierced. Let me be stricken with that sword of yours, which, had the goddess not said nay, would have made its way into the heart of Atreus' son!

¹⁴⁹ Ah, rather save my life, the gift you gave me! What you gave, when victor, to me your foe, I ask now from you as your friend. Those whom 'twere better you destroyed, Neptunian Pergamum affords; for matter for your sword, go seek the foe. Only, whether you make ready to speed on with the oar your ships, or whether you remain, O, by your right as master, bid me come!

OVID

IV

Phaedra Hippolyto

Quam nisi tu dederis, caritura est ipsa, salutem
　　mittit Amazonio Cressa puella viro.
perlege, quodcumque est—quid epistula lecta nocebit?
　　te quoque in hac aliquid quod iuvet esse potest;
his arcana notis terra pelagoque feruntur.　　　　　5
　　inspicit acceptas hostis ab hoste notas.
Ter tecum conata loqui ter inutilis haesit
　　lingua, ter in primo destitit ore sonus.
qua licet et sequitur, pudor est miscendus amori;
　　dicere quae puduit, scribere iussit amor.　　　10
quidquid Amor iussit, non est contemnere tutum;
　　regnat et in dominos ius habet ille deos.
ille mihi primo dubitanti scribere dixit:
　　" scribe! dabit victas ferreus ille manus."
adsit et, ut nostras avido fovet igne medullas,　　15
　　figat sic animos in mea vota tuos!
Non ego nequitia socialia foedera rumpam;
　　fama—velim quaeras—crimine nostra vacat.
venit amor gravius, quo serius—urimur intus;
　　urimur, et caecum pectora vulnus habent.　　　20

44

IV

Phaedra to Hippolytus

With wishes for the welfare which she herself, unless you give it her, will ever lack, the Cretan maid greets the hero whose mother was an Amazon. Read to the end, whatever is here contained—what shall reading of a letter harm? In this one, too, there may be something to pleasure you; in these characters of mine, secrets are borne over land and sea. Even foe looks into missive writ by foe.

7 Thrice making trial of speech with you, thrice hath my tongue vainly stopped, thrice the sound failed at first threshold of my lips. Wherever modesty may attend on love, love should not lack in it; with me, what modesty forbade to say, love has commanded me to write. Whatever Love commands, it is not safe to hold for naught; his throne and law are over even the gods who are lords of all. 'Twas he who spoke to me when first I doubted if to write or no: "Write; the iron-hearted one will yield his hand." Let him aid me, then, and, just as he heats my marrow with his avid flame, so may he transfix your heart that it yield to my prayers!

17 It will not be through wanton baseness that I shall break my marriage-bond; my name—and you may ask—is free from all reproach. Love has come to me, the deeper for its coming late—I am burning with love within; I am burning, and my breast has an unseen wound. As the first bearing of the yoke

45

OVID

scilicet ut teneros laedunt iuga prima iuvencos,
    frenaque vix patitur de grege captus equus,
sic male vixque subit primos rude pectus amores,
    sarcinaque haec animo non sedet apta meo.
ars fit, ubi a teneris crimen condiscitur annis ;   25
    quae[1] venit exacto tempore, peius amat.
tu nova servatae carpes libamina famae,
    et pariter nostrum fiet uterque nocens.
est aliquid, plenis pomaria carpere ramis,
    et tenui primam delegere ungue rosam.   30
si tamen ille prior, quo me sine crimine gessi,
    candor ab insolita labe notandus erat,
at bene successit, digno quod adurimur igni ;
    peius adulterio turpis adulter obest.
si mihi concedat Iuno fratremque virumque,   35
    Hippolytum videor praepositura Iovi!
Iam quoque—vix credes—ignotas mutor in artes ;
    est mihi per saevas impetus ire feras.
iam mihi prima dea est arcu praesignis adunco
    Delia ; iudicium subsequor ipsa tuum.   40
in nemus ire libet pressisque in retia cervis
    hortari celeris per iuga summa canes,
aut tremulum excusso iaculum vibrare lacerto,
    aut in graminea ponere corpus humo.
saepe iuvat versare leves in pulvere currus   45
    torquentem frenis ora fugacis equi ;
nunc feror, ut Bacchi furiis Eleleides[2] actae,
    [3] quaeque sub Idaeo tympana colle movent,

---

[1] cui *Hein. Bent.*   [2] Elelegides *P* : Eleides/ *s.*
[3] 48–103 *lost from P.*

galls the tender steer, and as the rein is scarce
endured by the colt fresh taken from the drove, so
does my untried heart rebel, and scarce submit to
the first restraints of love, and the burden I undergo
does not sit well upon my soul. Love grows to be
but an art, when the fault is well learned from
tender years; she who yields her heart when the
time for love is past, has a fiercer passion. You
will reap the fresh first-offerings of purity long
preserved, and both of us will be equal in our guilt.
'Tis something to pluck fruit from the orchard with
full-hanging branch, to cull with delicate nail the
first rose. If nevertheless the white and blameless
purity in which I have lived before was to be marked
with unwonted stain, at least the fortune is kind
that burns me with a worthy flame; worse than
forbidden love is a lover who is base. Should
Juno yield me him who is at once her brother
and her lord, methinks I should prefer Hippolytus
to Jove.

[37] Now too—you will scarce believe it—I am
changing to pursuits I did not know; I am stirred
to go among wild beasts. The goddess first for me
now is the Delian, known above all for her curvèd
bow; it is your choice that I myself now follow.
My pleasure leads me to the wood, to drive the
deer into the net, and to urge on the fleet hound
over the highest ridge, or with arm shot forth to let
fly the quivering spear, or to lay my body upon the
grassy ground. Oft do I delight to whirl the light
car in the dust of the course, twisting with the
rein the mouth of the flying steed; now again
I am borne on, like daughters of the Bacchic cry
driven by the frenzy of their god, and those who

aut quas semideae Dryades Faunique bicornes
    numine contactas attonuere suo.   50
namque mihi referunt, cum se furor ille remisit,
    omnia ; me tacitam conscius urit amor.
Forsitan hunc generis fato reddamus amorem,
    et Venus ex tota gente tributa petat.
Iuppiter Europen—prima est ea gentis origo—   55
    dilexit, tauro dissimulante deum.
Pasiphae mater, decepto subdita tauro,
    enixa est utero crimen onusque suo.
perfidus Aegides, ducentia fila secutus,
    curva meae fugit tecta sororis ope.   60
en, ego nunc, ne forte parum Minoia credar,
    in socias leges ultima gentis eo !
hoc quoque fatale est : placuit domus una duabus ;
    me tua forma capit, capta parente soror.
Thesides Theseusque duas rapuere sorores—   65
    ponite de nostra bina tropaea domo !
Tempore quo nobis inita est Cerealis Eleusin,
    Gnosia me vellem detinuisset humus !
tunc mihi praecipue, nec non tamen ante, placebas ;
    acer in extremis ossibus haesit amor.   70
candida vestis erat, praecincti flore capilli,
    flava verecundus tinxerat ora rubor,
quemque vocant aliae vultum rigidumque trucemque,
    pro rigido Phaedra iudice fortis erat.
sint procul a nobis iuvenes ut femina compti !—   75
    fine coli modico forma virilis amat.

---

[a] The votaries of Cybele, Great Mother of the Gods.
[b] The gods caused the animal to see in her his own kind.
[c] The story of the Minotaur and the Labyrinth.

shake the timbrel at the foot of Ida's ridge,[a] or
those whom Dryad creatures half-divine and Fauns
two-horned have touched with their own spirit
and driven distraught. For they tell me of all these
things when that madness of mine has passed
away; and I keep silence, conscious 'tis love that
tortures me.

[53] It may be this love is a debt I am paying,
due to the destiny of my line, and that Venus is
exacting tribute of me for all my race. Europa—
this is the first beginning of our line—was loved
of Jove ; a bull's form disguised the god. Pasiphaë
my mother, victim of the deluded bull,[b] brought forth
in travail her reproach and burden. The faithless
son of Aegeus followed the guiding thread, and
escaped from the winding house through the aid my
sister gave.[c] Behold, now I, lest I be thought
too little a child of Minos' line, am the latest of
my stock to come under the law that rules us all!
This, too, is fateful, that one house has won us both ;
your beauty has captured my heart, my sister's
heart was captured by your father. Theseus' son
and Theseus have been the undoing of sisters
twain—rear ye a double trophy at our house's fall!

[67] That time I went to Eleusis, the city of Ceres,
would that the Gnosian land had held me back! It
was then you pleased me most, and yet you had
pleased before ; piercing love lodged in my deepest
bones. Shining white was your raiment, bound round
with flowers your locks, the blush of modesty had
tinged your sun-browned cheeks, and, what others
call a countenance hard and stern, in Phaedra's eye
was strong instead of hard. Away from me with your
young men arrayed like women !—beauty in a man

te tuus iste rigor positique sine arte capilli
  et levis egregio pulvis in ore decet.
sive ferocis equi luctantia colla recurvas,
  exiguo flexos miror in orbe pedes ;   80
seu lentum valido torques hastile lacerto,
  ora ferox in se versa lacertus habet,
sive tenes lato venabula cornea ferro.
  denique nostra iuvat[1] lumina, quidquid agis.
Tu modo duritiam silvis depone iugosis ;   85
  non sum militia[2] digna perire tua.
quid iuvat incinctae studia exercere Dianae,
  et Veneri numeros eripuisse suos ?
quod caret alterna requie, durabile non est ;
  haec reparat vires fessaque membra novat.   90
arcus—et arma tuae tibi sunt imitanda Dianae—
  si numquam cesses tendere, mollis erit.
clarus erat silvis Cephalus, multaeque per herbas
  conciderant illo percutiente ferae ;
nec tamen Aurorae male se praebebat amandum.   95
  ibat ad hunc sapiens a sene diva viro.
saepe sub ilicibus Venerem Cinyraque creatum
  sustinuit positos quaelibet herba duos.
arsit et Oenides in Maenalia Atalanta ;
  illa ferae spolium pignus amoris habet.   100
nos quoque iam primum turba numeremur in ista !
  si Venerem tollas, rustica silva tua est.
ipsa comes veniam, nec me latebrosa movebunt
  saxa neque obliquo dente timendus aper.

---

[1] iuvat *E ω Plan.* : iuvas *ω vulg.*
[2] materia *MSS.* : militia *Pa.*: materias digna vigore tuo
Bent.: duritia *Faber.*

---

[a] Tithonus.   [b] Adonis.

would fain be striven for in measure. That hardness
of feature suits you well, those locks that fall without
art, and the light dust upon your handsome face.
Whether you draw rein and curb the resisting neck
of your spirited steed, I look with wonder at your
turning his feet in circle so slight; whether with
strong arm you hurl the pliant shaft, your gallant
arm draws my regard upon itself, or whether you
grasp the broad-headed cornel hunting-spear. To say
no more, my eyes delight in whatsoe'er you do.

[85] Do you only lay aside your hardness upon the
forest ridges; I am no fit spoil for your campaign.
What use to you to practise the ways of girded
Diana, and to have stolen from Venus her own
due? That which lacks its alternations of repose
will not endure; this is what repairs the strength
and renews the wearied limbs. The bow—and you
should imitate the weapons of your Diana—if you
never cease to bend it, will grow slack. Renowned
in the forest was Cephalus, and many were the wild
beasts that had fallen on the sod at the piercing
of his stroke; yet he did not ill in yielding himself
to Aurora's love. Oft did the goddess sagely go to
him, leaving her aged spouse.[a] Many a time beneath
the ilex did Venus and he[b] that was sprung of Cinyras
recline, pressing some chance grassy spot. The son
of Oeneus, too, took fire with love for Maenalian
Atalanta; she has the spoil of the wild beast as the
pledge of his love. Let us, too, be now first
numbered in that company! If you take away love,
the forest is but a rustic place. I myself will come
and be at your side, and neither rocky covert shall
make me fear, nor the boar dreadful for the side-
stroke of his tusk.

Aequora bina suis obpugnant fluctibus isthmon, 105
  et tenuis tellus audit utrumque mare.
hic tecum Troezena colam, Pittheia regna;
  iam nunc est patria gratior illa mea.
tempore abest aberitque diu Neptunius heros;
  illum Pirithoi detinet ora sui. 110
praeposuit Theseus—nisi si[1] manifesta negamus—
  Pirithoum Phaedrae Pirithoumque tibi.
sola nec haec ad nos iniuria venit ab illo;
  in magnis laesi rebus uterque sumus.
ossa mei fratris clava perfracta trinodi 115
  sparsit humi; soror est praeda relicta feris.
prima securigeras inter virtute puellas
  te peperit, nati digna vigore parens;
si quaeras, ubi sit—Theseus latus ense peregit,
  nec tanto mater pignore tuta fuit. 120
at ne nupta quidem taedaque accepta iugali—
  cur, nisi ne caperes regna paterna nothus?
addidit et fratres ex me tibi, quos tamen omnis
  non ego tollendi causa, sed ille fuit.
o utinam nocitura tibi, pulcherrime rerum, 125
  in medio nisu viscera rupta forent!
i nunc, sic meriti lectum reverere parentis—
  quem fugit et factis abdicat ipse suis!
Nec, quia privigno videar coitura noverca,
  terruerint animos nomina vana tuos. 130

<hr>

[1] nisi si *Hein.*: nisi *P*: nisi nos *Gω*.

<hr>

[a] The king of the Lapithae, Theseus' companion on the
expedition to Hades, aided by him in the war against the
Centaurs.
  [b] Antiope, sister of Hippolyte, is here meant; but the
usual story made Hippolyte Theseus' mother.
  [c] Palmer makes Hippolytus the antecedent of *quem*.

[105] There are two seas that on either side assail an isthmus with their floods, and the slender land hears the waves of both. Here with you will I dwell, in Troezen's land, the realm of Pittheus; yon place is dearer to me now than my own native soil. The hero son of Neptune is absent now, in happy hour, and will be absent long; he is kept by the shores of his dear Pirithous.[a] Theseus—unless, indeed, we refuse to own what all may see—has come to love Pirithous more than Phaedra, Pirithous more than you. Nor is that the only wrong we suffer at his hand; there are deep injuries we both have had from him. The bones of my brother he crushed with his triple-knotted club and scattered o'er the ground; my sister he left at the mercy of wild beasts. The first in courage among the women[b] of the battle-axe bore you, a mother worthy of the vigour of her son; if you ask where she is—Theseus pierced her side with the steel, nor did she find safety in the pledge of so great a son. Yes, and she was not even wed to him and taken to his home with the nuptial torch—why, unless that you, a bastard, should not come to your father's throne? He has bestowed brothers on you, too, from me, and the cause of rearing them all as heirs has been not myself, but he. Ah, would that the bosom which was to work you wrong, fairest of men, had been rent in the midst of its throes! Go now, reverence the bed of a father who thus deserves of you—the bed[c] which he neglects and is disowning by his deeds.

[129] And, should you think of me as a stepdame who would mate with her husband's son, let empty names fright not your soul. Such old-fashioned

ista vetus pietas, aevo moritura futuro,
  rustica Saturno regna tenente fuit.
Iuppiter esse pium statuit, quodcumque iuvaret,
  et fas omne facit fratre marita soror.
illa coit firma generis iunctura catena,   135
  inposuit nodos cui Venus ipsa suos.
nec labor est celare—licet; pete munus ab illa;[1]
  cognato poterit nomine culpa tegi.
viderit amplexos aliquis, laudabimur ambo;
  dicar privigno fida noverca meo.   140
non tibi per tenebras duri reseranda mariti
  ianua, non custos decipiendus erit;
ut tenuit domus una duos, domus una tenebit;
  oscula aperta dabas, oscula aperta dabis;
tutus eris mecum laudemque merebere culpa,   145
  tu licet in lecto conspiciare meo.
tolle moras tantum properataque foedera iunge—
  qui mihi nunc saevit, sic tibi parcat Amor!
non ego dedignor supplex humilisque precari.
  heu! ubi nunc fastus altaque verba? iacent! 150
et pugnare diu nec me submittere culpae
  certa fui—certi siquid haberet amor;
victa precor genibusque tuis regalia tendo
  bracchia! quid deceat, non videt ullus amans.
depuduit, profugusque pudor sua signa reliquit.[2]   155
    Da veniam fassae duraque corda doma!
quod mihi sit genitor, qui possidet aequora, Minos,
  quod veniant proavi fulmina torta manu,

---

[1] licet pete munus ab illa *MSS.*: licet ; pete munus ! ab illa
Ehw.: licet ; peccemus, amorem *Pa. Sedl.*: celare virum ;
pete munus ab illo *Bent.*: celare ; licet ; pete munus ab ipsa
Madv.: etc.   [2] relinquit *P s.*

regard for virtue was rustic even in Saturn's reign, and doomed to die in the age to come. Jove fixed that virtue was to be in whatever brought us pleasure; and naught is wrong before the gods since sister was made wife by brother. That bond of kinship only holds close and firm in which Venus herself has forged the chain. Nor need you fear the trouble of concealment—it will be easy; ask the aid of Venus! Through her our fault will be covered under name of kinship. Should someone see us embrace, we both shall meet with praise; I shall be called a faithful stepdame to the son of my lord. No portal of a dour husband will need unbolting for you in the darkness of night; there will be no guard to be eluded; as the same roof has covered us both, the same will cover us still. Your wont has been to give me kisses unconcealed, your wont will be still to give me kisses unconcealed. You will be safe with me, and will earn praise by your fault, though you be seen upon my very couch. Only, away with tarrying, and make haste to bind our bond—so may Love be merciful to you, who is bitter to me now! I do not disdain to bend my knee and humbly make entreaty. Alas! where now are my pride, my lofty words? Fallen! I was resolved—if there was aught love could resolve —both to fight long and not to yield to fault; but I am overcome. I pray to you, to clasp your knees I extend my queenly arms. Of what befits, no one who loves takes thought. My modesty has fled, and as it fled it left its standards behind.

[156] Forgive me my confession, and soften your hard heart! That I have for sire Minos, who rules the seas, that from my ancestor's hand comes hurled the

quod sit avus radiis frontem vallatus acutis,
    purpureo tepidum qui movet axe diem—   160
nobilitas sub amore iacet! miserere priorum
    et, mihi si non vis parcere, parce meis!
est mihi dotalis tellus Iovis insula, Crete—
    serviat Hippolyto regia tota meo!
Flecte, ferox,[1] animos! potuit corrumpere taurum 165
    mater; eris tauro saevior ipse truci?
per Venerem, parcas, oro, quae plurima mecum est!
    sic numquam, quae te spernere possit, ames;
sic tibi secretis agilis dea saltibus adsit,
    silvaque perdendas praebeat alta feras;   170
sic faveant Satyri montanaque numina Panes,
    et cadat adversa cuspide fossus aper;
sic tibi dent Nymphae, quamvis odisse puellas
    diceris, arentem quae levet unda sitim!
Addimus his precibus lacrimas quoque; verba
    precantis   175
    perlegis et lacrimas finge videre meas!

V

OENONE PARIDI [2]

PERLEGIS? an coniunx prohibet nova? perlege—
    non est
    ista Mycenaea littera facta manu!

---

[1] ferox *P s*: feros *P₂ ω vulg.*
[2] *Introductory couplets found in V–XII, XVII, XX, XXI,
are omitted by Plan. and condemned by Pa. Merk. et al.*

56

lightning-stroke, that the front of my grandsire, he who moves the tepid day with gleaming chariot, is crowned with palisade of pointed rays—what of this, when my noble name is prostrate under love? Have pity on those who have gone before, and, if me you will not spare, O spare my line! To my dowry belongs the Cretan land, the isle of Jove—let my whole court be slaves to my Hippolytus!

165 Bend, O cruel one, your spirit! My mother could pervert the bull; will you be fiercer than a savage beast? Spare me, by Venus I pray, who is chiefest with me now. So may you never love one who will spurn you; so may the agile goddess wait on you in the solitary glade to keep you safe, and the deep forest yield you wild beasts to slay; so may the Satyrs be your friends, and the mountain deities, the Pans, and may the boar fall pierced in full front by your spear; so may the Nymphs—though you are said to loathe womankind—give you the flowing water to relieve your parching thirst!

175 I mingle with these prayers my tears as well. The words of her who prays, you are reading; her tears, imagine you behold!

V

Oenone to Paris

WILL you read my letter through? or does your new wife forbid? Read—this is no letter writ by Mycenaean hand![a] It is the fountain-nymph Oenone

---

[a] She taunts Paris with fear of Agamemnon and Menelaus.

OVID

Pegasis Oenone, Phrygiis celeberrima silvis,
  laesa queror de te, si sinis, ipsa meo.
Quis deus opposuit nostris sua numina votis?   5
  ne tua permaneam, quod mihi crimen obest?
leniter, ex merito quidquid patiare, ferendum est;
  quae venit indigno poena, dolenda venit.
Nondum tantus eras, cum te contenta marito
  edita de magno flumine nympha fui.   10
qui nunc Priamides—absit reverentia vero!—
  servus eras; servo nubere nympha tuli!
saepe greges inter requievimus arbore tecti,
  mixtaque cum foliis praebuit herba torum;
saepe super stramen faenoque iacentibus alto   15
  defensa est humili cana pruina casa.
quis tibi monstrabat saltus venatibus aptos,
  et tegeret catulos qua fera rupe suos?
retia saepe comes maculis distincta tetendi;
  saepe citos egi per iuga longa canes.   20
incisae servant a te mea nomina fagi,
  et legor OENONE falce notata tua,[1]
et quantum trunci, tantum mea nomina crescunt.   25
  crescite et in titulos surgite recta meos!
popule, vive, precor, quae consita margine ripae
  hoc in rugoso cortice carmen habes:

CUM PARIS OENONE POTERIT SPIRARE RELICTA,
  AD FONTEM XANTHI VERSA RECURRET AQUA.   30

---

[1] *vv.* 23, 24 *omitted as spurious Merk.* :
      populus est, memini, pluviali consita rivo,
      est in qua nostri littera scripta memor.
"*there is a poplar, I mind me, planted on the banks of c
stream, on which is written the legend that recalls our memory.*"

writes, well-known to the Phrygian forests—wronged, and with complaint to make of you, you my own, if you but allow.

⁵ What god has set his will against my prayers? What guilt stands in my way, that I may not remain your own? Softly must we bear whatever suffering is our desert; the penalty that comes without deserving brings us dole.

⁹ Not yet so great were you when I was content to wed you—I, the nymph-daughter of a mighty stream. You who are now a son of Priam—let not respect keep back the truth!—were then a slave; I deigned to wed a slave—I, a nymph! Oft among our flocks have we reposed beneath the sheltering trees, where mingled grass and leaves afforded us a couch; oft have we lain upon the straw, or on the deep hay in a lowly hut that kept the hoar-frost off. Who was it pointed out to you the coverts apt for the chase, and the rocky den where the wild beast hid away her cubs? Oft have I gone with you to stretch the hunting-net with its wide mesh; oft have I led the fleet hounds over the long ridge. The beeches still conserve my name carved on them by you, and I am read there OENONE, charactered by your blade; and the more the trunks, the greater grows my name. Grow on, rise high and straight to make my honours known! O poplar, ever live, I pray, that art planted by the marge of the stream and hast in thy seamy bark these verses:

IF PARIS' BREATH SHALL FAIL NOT, ONCE OENONE HE
    DOTH SPURN,
THE WATERS OF THE XANTHUS TO THEIR FOUNT SHALL
    BACKWARD TURN.

OVID

Xanthe, retro propera, versaeque recurrite lymphae !
    sustinet Oenonen deseruisse Paris.
Illa dies fatum miserae mihi dixit, ab illa
    pessima mutati coepit amoris hiemps,
qua Venus et Iuno sumptisque decentior armis   35
    venit in arbitrium nuda Minerva tuum.
attoniti micuere sinus, gelidusque cucurrit,
    ut mihi narrasti, dura per ossa tremor.
consului—neque enim modice terrebar—anusque
    longaevosque senes.   constitit esse nefas.   40
Caesa abies, sectaeque trabes, et classe parata
    caerula ceratas accipit unda rates.
flesti discedens—hoc saltim parce negare ! [1]
    miscuimus lacrimas maestus uterque suas ;   46
non sic adpositis vincitur vitibus ulmus,
    ut tua sunt collo bracchia nexa meo.
a, quotiens, cum te vento quererere teneri,
    riserunt comites—ille secundus erat !   50
oscula dimissae quotiens repetita dedisti !
    quam vix sustinuit dicere lingua " vale " !
Aura levis rigido pendentia lintea malo
    suscitat, et remis eruta canet aqua.
prosequor infelix oculis abeuntia vela,   55
    qua licet, et lacrimis umet harena meis,
utque celer venias, virides Nereidas oro—
    scilicet ut venias in mea damna celer !

[1] *vv. 44, 45 omitted as spurious Merk. :*
        praeterito magis est iste pudendus amor.
    et flesti et nostros vidisti flentis ocellos.
"*the love that holds you now is more to your shame than th
one of yore.   You both wept and you saw my weeping eyes.*"

60

O Xanthus, backward haste; turn, waters, and flow again to your fount! Paris has deserted Oenone, and endures it.

³³ That day spoke doom for wretched me, on that day did the awful storm of changèd love begin, when Venus and Juno, and unadornèd Minerva, more comely had she borne her arms, appeared before you to be judged. My bosom leaped with amaze as you told me of it, and a chill tremor rushed through my hard bones. I took counsel—for I was no little terrified—with grandams and long-lived sires. 'Twas clear to us all that evil threatened me.

⁴¹ The firs were felled, the timbers hewn; your fleet was ready, and the deep-blue wave received the waxèd crafts. Your tears fell as you left me— this, at least, deny not! We mingled our weeping, each a prey to grief; the elm is not so closely clasped by the clinging vine as was my neck by your embracing arms. Ah, how oft, when you complained that you were kept by the wind, did your comrades smile!—that wind was favouring. How oft, when you had taken your leave of me, did you return to ask another kiss! How your tongue could scarce endure to say "Farewell!"

⁵³ A light breeze stirs the sails that hang idly from the rigid mast, and the water foams white with the churning of the oar. In wretchedness I follow with my eyes the departing sails as far as I may, and the sand is humid with my tears; that you may swiftly come again, I pray the sea-green daughters of Nereus—yes, that you may swiftly come to my undoing! Expected to return in answer to my

votis ergo meis alii rediture redisti?
   ei mihi, pro dira paelice blanda fui!   60
Adspicit inmensum moles nativa profundum—
   mons fuit; aequoreis illa resistit aquis.
hinc ego vela tuae cognovi prima carinae,
   et mihi per fluctus impetus ire fuit.
dum moror, in summa fulsit mihi purpura prora— 65
   pertimui; cultus non erat ille tuus.
fit propior terrasque cita ratis attigit aura;
   femineas vidi corde tremente genas.
non satis id fuerat— quid enim furiosa morabar?—
   haerebat gremio turpis amica tuo!   70
tunc vero rupique sinus et pectora planxi,
   et secui madidas ungue rigente genas,
inplevique sacram querulis ululatibus Iden
   illuc has lacrimas in mea saxa tuli.
sic Helene doleat desertaque coniuge ploret,   75
   quaeque prior nobis intulit, ipsa ferat!
Nunc tibi conveniunt, quae te per aperta sequantur
   aequora legitimos destituantque viros;
at cum pauper eras armentaque pastor agebas,
   nulla nisi Oenone pauperis uxor erat.   80
non ego miror opes, nec me tua regia tangit
   nec de tot Priami dicar ut una nurus—
non tamen ut Priamus nymphae socer esse recuset,
   aut Hecubae fuerim dissimulanda nurus;

vows, have you returned for the sake of another?
Ah me, 'twas for the sake of a cruel rival that my
persuasive prayers were made!

⁶¹ A mass of native rock looks down upon the
unmeasured deep—a mountain it really is; it stays
the billows of the sea. From here I was the first to
spy and know the sails of your bark, and my heart's
impulse was to rush through the waves to you.
While I delayed, on the highest of the prow I saw
the gleam of purple—fear seized upon me; that was
not the manner of your garb. The craft comes
nearer, borne on a freshening breeze, and touches
the shore; with trembling heart I have caught the
sight of a woman's face. And this was not enough
—why was I mad enough to stay and see?—in your
embrace that shameless woman clung! Then
indeed did I rend my bosom and beat my breast,
and with the hard nail furrowed my streaming
cheeks, and filled holy Ida with wailing cries of
lamentation; yonder to the rocks I love I bore my
tears. So may Helen's grief be, and so her lamenta-
tion, when she is deserted by her love; and what
she was first to bring on me may she herself
endure!

⁷⁷ Your pleasure now is in jades who follow you
over the open sea, leaving behind their lawful-
wedded lords; but when you were poor and
shepherded the flocks, Oenone was your wife, poor
though you were, and none else. I am not dazzled by
your wealth, nor am I touched by thought of your
palace, nor would I be called one of the many wives
of Priam's sons—yet not that Priam would disdain
a nymph as wife to his son, or that Hecuba
would have to hide her kinship with me; I am

dignaque sum et cupio fieri matrona potentis ;   85
    sunt mihi, quas possint sceptra decere, manus.
nec me, faginea quod tecum fronde iacebam,
    despice ; purpureo sum magis apta toro.
Denique tutus amor meus est ; tibi nulla parantur
    bella, nec ultrices advehit unda rates.   90
Tyndaris infestis fugitiva reposcitur armis ;
    hac venit in thalamos dote superba tuos.
quae si sit Danais reddenda, vel Hectora fratrem,
    vel cum Deiphobo Polydamanta roga ;
quid gravis Antenor, Priamus quid suadeat ipse,   95
    consule, quis aetas longa magistra fuit ! [1]
turpe rudimentum, patriae praeponere raptam.
    causa pudenda tua est ; iusta vir arma movet.
Nec tibi, si sapias, fidam promitte Lacaenam,
    quae sit in amplexus tam cito versa tuos.   100
ut minor Atrides temerati foedera lecti
    clamat et externo laesus amore dolet,
tu quoque clamabis.   nulla reparabilis arte
    laesa pudicitia est ; deperit illa semel.
ardet amore tui ?   sic et Menelaon amavit.   105
    nunc iacet in viduo credulus ille toro.
felix Andromache, certo bene nupta marito !
    uxor ad exemplum fratris habenda fui ;
tu levior foliis, tum cum sine pondere suci
    mobilibus ventis arida facta volant ;   110

---

[1] *From* 97 *to* VI, 49 *are missing in* P.

[a] Of his career as a prince, after his recognition.

worthy of being, and I desire to be, the matron of a puissant lord ; my hands are such as the sceptre could well beseem. Nor despise me because once I pressed with you the beechen frond ; I am better suited for the purpled marriage-bed.

[89] Remember, too, my love can bring no harm ; it will beget you no wars, nor bring avenging ships across the wave. The Tyndarid run-away is now demanded back by an enemy under arms ; this is the dower the dame brings proudly to your marriage-chamber. Whether she should be rendered back to the Danai, ask Hector your brother, if you will, or Deiphobus and Polydamas ; take counsel with grave Antenor, find out what Priam's self persuades, whose long lives have made them wise. 'Tis but a base beginning,[a] to prize a stolen mistress more than your native land. Your case is one that calls for shame ; just are the arms her lord takes up.

[99] Think not, too, if you are wise, that the Laconian will be faithful—she who so quickly turned to your embrace. Just as the younger Atrides cries out at the violation of his marriage-bed, and feels his painful wound from the wife who loves another, you too will cry. By no art may purity once wounded be made whole ; 'tis lost, lost once and for all. Is she ardent with love for you ? So, too, she loved Menelaus. He, trusting fool that he was, lies now in a deserted bed. Happy Andromache, well wed to a constant mate ! I was a wife to whom you should have clung after your brother's pattern ; but you—are lighter than leaves what time their juice has failed, and dry they flutter in the shifting breeze ; you have less weight than

et minus est in te quam summa pondus arista,
  quae levis adsiduis solibus usta riget.
Hoc tua—nam recolo—quondam germana canebat,
  sic mihi diffusis vaticinata comis :
" quid facis, Oenone? quid harenae semina
    mandas?   115
  non profecturis litora bubus aras.
Graia iuvenca venit, quae te patriamque domumque
  perdat ! io prohibe ! Graia iuvenca venit !
dum licet, obscenam ponto demergite [1] puppim !
  heu !   quantum Phrygii sanguinis illa vehit ! " 120
Dixerat ; in cursu famulae rapuere furentem ;
  at mihi flaventes diriguere comae.
a, nimium miserae vates mihi vera fuisti—
  possidet, en, saltus illa [2] iuvenca meos !
sit facie quamvis insignis, adultera certe est ;   125
  deseruit socios hospite capta deos.
illam de patria Theseus—nisi nomine fallor—
  nescio quis Theseus abstulit ante sua.
a iuvene et cupido credatur reddita virgo ?
  unde hoc conpererim tam bene, quaeris ? amo. 130
vim licet appelles et culpam nomine veles ;
  quae totiens rapta est, praebuit ipsa rapi.
at manet Oenone fallenti casta marito—
  et poteras falli legibus ipse tuis !
Me Satyri celeres—silvis ego tecta latebam—   135
  quaesierunt rapido, turba proterva, pede
cōrnigerumque caput pinu praecinctus acuta
  Faunus in inmensis, qua tumet Ida, iugis.

---

[1] dimergite *s* : di mergite *E s Hein.*
[2] Graia *G Merk.* : illa *E ω Plan.*

---

[a] Cassandra.
[b] Theseus and Pirithous had carried away Helen in her
early youth.

66

the tip of the spear of grain, burned light and crisp by ever-shining suns.

[113] This, once upon a time—for I call it back to mind—your sister[a] sang to me, with locks let loose, foreseeing what should come: "What art thou doing, Oenone? Why commit seeds to sand? Thou art ploughing the shores with oxen that will accomplish naught. A Greek heifer is on the way, to ruin thee, thy home-land, and thy house! Ho, keep her far! A Greek heifer is coming! While yet ye may, sink in the deep the unclean ship! Alas, how much of Phrygian blood it hath aboard!"

[121] She ceased to speak; her slaves seized on her as she madly ran. And I—my golden locks stood stiffly up. Ah, all too true a prophetess you were to my poor self—she has them, lo, the heifer has my pastures! Let her seem how fair soever of face, none the less she surely is a jade; smitten with a stranger, she left behind her marriage-gods. Theseus—unless I mistake the name—one Theseus, even before, had stolen her away from her father's land.[b] Is it to be thought she was rendered back a maid, by a young man and eager? Whence have I learned this so well? you ask. I love. You may call it violence, and veil the fault in the word; yet she who has been so often stolen has surely lent herself to theft. But Oenone remains chaste, false though her husband prove—and, after your own example, she might have played you false.

[135] Me, the swift Satyrs, a wanton rout with nimble foot, used to come in quest of—where I would lie hidden in covert of the wood—and Faunus, with hornèd head girt round with sharp pine needles, where Ida swells in boundless ridges. Me, the

67

me fide conspicuus Troiae munitor amavit,
  admisitque meas ad sua dona manus.[1]   146
quaecumque herba potens ad opem radixque
    medendo [2]
  utilis in toto nascitur orbe, mea est.
me miseram, quod amor non est medicabilis herbis !
  deficior prudens artis ab arte mea.   150
Quod nec graminibus tellus fecunda creandis   153
  nec deus, auxilium tu mihi ferre potes.
et potes, et merui—dignae miserere puellae !   155
  non ego cum Danais arma cruenta fero—
sed tua sum tecumque fui puerilibus annis
  et tua, quod superest temporis, esse precor!

VI

HYPSIPYLE IASONI

LITORA Thessaliae reduci tetigisse carina
  diceris auratae vellere dives ovis.
gratulor incolumi, quantum sinis ; hoc tamen ipsum [3]
  debueram scripto certior [4] esse tuo.
nam ne pacta tibi praeter mea regna redires,   5
  cum cuperes, ventos non habuisse potes ;
quamlibet adverso signetur epistula vento.
  Hypsipyle missa digna salute fui.

  [1] vv. 140–145, 151, 152 condemned Merk:

    ille meae spolium virginitatis habet,   140
     id quoque luctando ; rupi tamen ungue capillos,
      oraque sunt digitis aspera facta meis ;
    nec pretium stupri gemmas aurumque poposci :
      turpiter ingenuum munera corpus emunt ;
    ipse, ratus dignam, medicas mihi tradidit artes 145
    ipse repertor opis vaccas pavisse Pheraeas   151
      fertur et a nostro saucius igne fuit.

builder of Troy, well known for keeping faith, loved, and let my hands into the secret of his gifts. Whatever herb potent for aid, whatever root that is used for healing grows in all the world, is mine. Alas, wretched me, that love may not be healed by herbs! Skilled in an art, I am left helpless by the very art I know.

[153] The aid that neither earth, fruitful in the bringing forth of herbs, nor a god himself, can give, you have the power to bestow on me. You can bestow it, and I have merited—have pity on a deserving maid! I come with no Danai, and bear no bloody armour—but I am yours, and I was your mate in childhood's years, and yours through all time to come I pray to be!

VI

HYPSIPYLE TO JASON

You are said to have touched the shores of Thessaly with safe-returning keel, rich in the fleece of the golden ram. I speak you well for your safety —so far as you give me chance; yet of this very thing I should have been informed by message of your own. For the winds might have failed you, even though you longed to see me, and kept you from returning by way of the realms I pledged you;[a] but a letter may be written, howe'er adverse the wind. Hypsipyle deserved the sending of a greeting.

[a] As her marriage portion.

---

[2] medendo *Ehw.*: medendi *MSS.* : medenti *Hein.*
[3] ipsum *Plan. s* : ipso *G ω* : ipsa *Hein. Ehw.*
[4] *So the MSS.*: debuerat . . . certius *Pa.*

Cur mihi fama prior de te quam littera venit :
　　isse sacros Martis sub iuga panda boves,　　　10
seminibus iactis segetes adolesse virorum
　　inque necem dextra non eguisse tua,
pervigilem spolium pecudis servasse draconem,
　　rapta tamen forti vellera fulva manu ?
haec ego si possem timide credentibus "ista　　15
　　ipse mihi scripsit" dicere, quanta forem !
Quid queror officium lenti cessasse mariti ?
　　obsequium, maneo si tua, grande tuli !
barbara narratur venisse venefica tecum,
　　in mihi promissi parte recepta tori.　　　20
credula res amor est ; utinam temeraria dicar
　　criminibus falsis insimulasse virum !
nuper ab Haemoniis hospes mihi Thessalus oris
　　venerat, et tactum vix bene limen erat,
"Aesonides," dixi, "quid agit meus ? " ille pudore 25
　　haesit in opposita lumina fixus humo.
protinus exilui tunicisque a pectore ruptis
　　"vivit ? an," exclamo, "me quoque fata vocant ? "
"vivit," ait.　timidum quod amat[1] ; iurare coegi.
　　vix mihi teste deo credita vita tua est.　　　30
Utque animus rediit, tua facta requirere coepi.
　　narrat aenipedes Martis arasse boves,
vipereos dentes in humum pro semine iactos,
　　et subito natos arma tulisse viros—

---

[1] timidum quod amat *E s Shuckburgh Hous.* : timidumque
mihi *G s* : timidus timidum *Pa.*

⁹ Why was it rumour brought me tidings of you, rather than lines from your hand?—tidings that the sacred bulls of Mars had received the curving yoke; that at the scattering of the seed there sprang forth the harvest of men, who for their doom had no need of your right arm; that the spoil of the ram, the deep-gold fleece the unsleeping dragon guarded, had nevertheless been stolen away by your bold hand. Could I say to those who are slow to credit these reports, "He has written me this with his own hand," how proud should I be!

¹⁷ But why complain that my lord has been slow in his duty? I shall think myself treated with all indulgence, so I remain yours. A barbarian poisoner, so the story goes, has come with you, admitted to share the marriage-couch you promised me. Love is quick to believe; may it prove that I am hasty, and have brought a groundless charge against my lord! Only now from Haemonian borders came a Thessalian stranger to my gates. Scarce had he well touched the threshold, when I cried, "How doth my lord, the son of Aeson?" Speechless he stood in embarrassment, his eyes fixed fast upon the ground. I straight leaped up, and rent the garment from my breast. "Lives he?" I cried, "or must fate call me too?" "He lives," was his reply. Full of fears is love; I made him say it on his oath. Scarce with a god to witness could I believe you living.

³¹ When calm of mind returned, I began to ask of your fortunes. He tells me of the brazenfooted oxen of Mars, how they ploughed, of the serpent's teeth scattered upon the ground in way of seed, of men sprung suddenly forth and bearing

OVID

terrigenas po̅pulos civili Marte peremptos   35
  inplesse aetatis fata diurna suae.
devictus serpens.   iterum, si vivat Iason,
  quaerimus ; alternant spesque timorque fidem.[1]
Singula dum narrat, studio cursuque loquendi
  detegit ingenio vulnera nostra suo.   40
heu ! ubi pacta fidës ?   ubi conubialia iura
  faxque sub arsuros dignior ire rogos ?
non ego sum furto tibi cognita ; pronuba Iuno
  adfuit et sertis tempora vinctus Hymen.
at mihi nec Iuno, nec Hymen, sed tristis Erinys   45
  praetulit.infaustas sanguinolenta faces.
Quid mihi cum Minyis, quid cum Dodonide [2] pinu ?
  quid tibi cum patria, navita Tiphy, mea ?
non erat hic aries villo spectabilis aureo,
  nec senis Aeetae regia Lemnos erat.   50
certa fui primo—sed me mala fata trahebant—
  hospita feminea pellere castra manu ;
Lemniadesque viros, nimium quoque, vincere norunt.
  milite tam forti causa [3] tuenda fuit !
Urbe virum vidi, tectoque animoque recepi !   55
  hic tibi bisque aestas bisque cucurrit hiemps.
tertia messis erat, cum tu dare vela coactus
  inplesti lacrimis talia verba tuis :
"abstrahor, Hypsipyle ; sed dent modo fata recursus,
  vir tuus hinc abeo, vir tibi semper ero.   60

[1] vv. 31–38 *spurious Merk. Pa.*: 31–36 *defended Hous.*
[2] Dodonide *Plan.*: Tritonide *MSS.*
[3] causa *Merk. Pa.*: vita $P_2 G E \omega Plan.$: fortuna P_1.

[a] The Argo, with whose building Dodona in Thessaly had to do.
[b] The women of Lemnos had once slain all the men in the island as a measure of revenge against their husbands, who had taken Thracian women in their stead.

7 2

arms—earth-born peoples slain in combat with their fellows, filling out the fates of their lives in the space of a day. He tells of the dragon overcome. Again I ask if Jason lives; hope and fear bring trust and mistrust by turns.

³⁹ While part by part he tells the tale, such, in the rushing eagerness of his speech, is his unconscious art that he lays bare my wounds. Alas! where is the faith that was promised me? Where the bonds of wedlock, and the marriage torch, more fit to set ablaze my funeral pile? I was not made acquaint with you in stealthy wise; Juno was there to join us when we were wed, and Hymen, his temples bound with wreaths. And yet neither Juno nor Hymen, but gloomy Erinys, stained with blood, carried before me the unhallowed torch.

⁴⁷ What had I with the Minyae, or Dodona's pine?ᵃ What had you with my native land, O helmsman Tiphys? There was here no ram, sightly with golden fleece, nor was Lemnos the royal home of old Aeëtes. I was resolved at first—but my ill fate drew me on—to drive out with my women's band the stranger troop; the women of Lemnos know—yea, even too well—how to vanquish men.ᵇ I should have let a soldiery so brave defend my cause.

⁵⁵ But I looked on the man in my city; I welcomed him under my roof and into my heart! Here twice the summer fled for you, here twice the winter. It was the third harvest when you were compelled to set sail, and with your tears poured forth such words as these: "I am sundered from thee, Hypsipyle; but so the fates grant me return, thine own I leave thee now, and thine own will I ever be.

quod tamen e nobis gravida celatur in alvo,
  vivat, et eiusdem simus uterque parens ! "
Hactenus, et lacrimis in falsa cadentibus ora
  cetera te memini non potuisse loqui.
Ultimus e sociis sacram conscendis in Argon.   65
  illa volat ; ventus concava vela tenet ;
caerula propulsae subducitur unda carinae ;
  terra tibi, nobis adspiciuntur aquae.
in latus omne patens turris circumspicit undas ;
  huc feror, et lacrimis osque sinusque madent.   70
per lacrimas specto, cupidaeque faventia menti
  longius adsueto lumina nostra vident.
adde preces castas inmixtaque vota timori—
  nunc quoque te salvo persoluenda mihi.
Vota ego persolvam ?   votis Medea fruetur !   75
  cor dolet, atque ira mixtus abundat amor.
dona feram templis, vivum quod Iasona perdo ?
  hostia pro damnis concidat icta meis ?
Non equidem secura fui semperque verebar,
  ne pater Argolica sumeret urbe nurum.   80
Argolidas timui—nocuit mihi barbara paelex !
  non expectata vulnus ab hoste tuli.
nec facie meritisque placet, sed carmina novit
  diraque cantata pabula falce metit.
illa reluctantem cursu [1] deducere lunam   85
  nititur et tenebris abdere solis equos ;

---

[1] cursu *P E ω* : curru *s Hein.*

---

[a] Built at the instigation of Athena.

74

What lieth heavy in thy bosom from me—may it come to live, and may we both share in its parentage ! ''

⁶³ Thus did you speak ; and with tears streaming down your false face I remember you could say no more.

⁶⁵ You are the last of your band to board the sacred Argo.ᵃ It flies upon its way ; the wind bellies out the sail ; the dark-blue wave glides from under the keel as it drives along ; your gaze is on the land, and mine is on the sea. There is a tower that looks from every side upon the waters round about ; thither I betake myself, my face and bosom wet with tears. Through my tears I gaze ; my eyes are gracious to my eager heart, and see farther than their wont. Add thereto pure-hearted prayers, and vows mingled with fears—vows which I must now fulfil, since you are safe.

⁷⁵ And am I to absolve these vows—vows but for Medea to enjoy ? My heart is sick, and surges with mingled wrath and love. Am I to bear gifts to the shrines because Jason lives, though mine no more ? Is a victim to fall beneath the stroke for the loss that has come to me ?

⁷⁹ No, I never felt secure ; but my fear was ever that your sire would look to an Argolic city for a bride to his son. 'Twas the daughters of Argolis I feared—yet my ruin has been a barbarian jade ! The wound I feel is not from the foe whence I thought to see it come. Her charm for you is neither in her beauty nor her merit ; but you are made hers by the incantations she knows, by the enchanted blade with which she garners the baneful herb. She strives with the reluctant moon, to bring it down from its course in the skies, and makes hide away in shadows

illa refrenat aquas obliquaque flumina sistit ;
  illa loco silvas vivaque saxa movet.
per tumulos errat passis discincta capillis
  certaque de tepidis colligit ossa rogis.   90
devovet absentis simulacraque cerea figit,
  et miserum tenuis in iecur urget acus—
et quae nescierim melius.   male quaeritur herbis
  moribus et forma conciliandus amor.
Hanc potes amplecti thalamoque relictus in uno   95
  inpavidus somno nocte silente frui ?
scilicet ut tauros, ita te iuga ferre coegit
  quaque feros anguis, te quoque mulcet ope.
adde, quod adscribi factis procerumque tuisque
  se facit,[1] et titulo coniugis uxor obest.   100
atque aliquis Peliae de partibus acta venenis
  inputat et populum, qui sibi credat, habet :
" non haec Aesonides, sed Phasias Aeetine
  aurea Phrixeae terga revellit ovis."
non   probat   Alcimede   mater   tua — consule
  matrem—   105
  non pater, a gelido cui venit axe nurus.
illa sibi a Tanai Scythiaeque paludibus udae
  quaerat et a patria Phasidis usque virum !
Mobilis Aesonide vernaque incertior aura,
  cur tua polliciti pondere verba carent ?   110
vir meus hinc ieras, vir non meus inde redisti.
  sim reducis coniunx, sicut euntis eram !

---

[1] facit P_1 E s, *Ehw.*: f̤a̤v̤e̤t̤ P : favet G *Merk.*

the steeds of the sun; she reins the waters in, and
stays the down-winding stream; she charms life into
trees and rocks, and moves them from their place.
Among sepulchres she stalks, ungirded, with hair
flowing loose, and gathers from the yet warm funeral
pyre the appointed bones. She vows to their doom
the absent, fashions the waxen image, and into its
wretched heart drives the slender needle—and other
deeds 'twere better not to know. Ill sought by
herbs is love that should be won by virtue and
by beauty.

[95] A woman like this can you embrace? Can you
be left in the same chamber with her and not feel
fear, and enjoy the slumber of the silent night?
Surely, she must have forced you to bear the yoke,
just as she forced the bulls, and has you subdued
by the same means she uses with fierce dragons.
Add that she has her name writ in the record of
your own and your heroes' exploits, and the wife
obscures the glory of the husband. And someone
of the partisans of Pelias imputes your deeds to her
poisons, and wins the people to believe: "This fleece
of gold from the ram of Phrixus the son of Aeson did
not seize away, but the Phasian girl, Aeëtes' child."
Your mother Alcimede—ask counsel of your mother
—favours her not, nor your sire, who sees his son's
bride come from the frozen north. Let her seek for
herself a husband—from the Tanais, from the marshes
of watery Scythia, even from her own land of Phasis!

[109] O changeable son of Aeson, more uncertain
than the breezes of springtime, why lack your words
the weight a promise claims? My own you went
forth hence; my own you have not returned. Let
me be your wedded mate now you are come back,

si te nobilitas generosaque nomina tangunt—
    en, ego Minoo nata Thoante feror!
Bacchus avus; Bacchi coniunx redimita corona   115
    praeradiat stellis signa minora suis.
dos tibi Lemnos erit, terra ingeniosa colenti;
    me quoque dotalis [1] inter habere potes.
Nunc etiam peperi; gratare ambobus, Iason!
    dulce mihi gravidae fecerat auctor onus.   120
felix in numero quoque sum prolemque gemellam,
    pignora Lucina bina favente dedi.
si quaeris, cui sint similes, cognosceris illis.
    fallere non norunt; cetera patris habent.
legatos quos paene dedi pro matre ferendos;   125
    sed tenuit coeptas saeva noverca vias.
Medeam timui: plus est Medea noverca;
    Medeae faciunt ad scelus omne manus.
Spargere quae fratris potuit lacerata per agros
    corpora, pignoribus parceret illa meis?   130
hanc, hanc,[2] o demens Colchisque ablate venenis,
    diceris Hypsipyles praeposuisse toro!
turpiter illa virum cognovit adultera virgo;
    me tibi teque mihi taeda pudica dedit.
prodidit illa patrem; rapui de clade Thoanta.   135
    deseruit Colchos; me mea Lemnos habet.

---

[1] dotales *Salmasius*: quoque //////, *with* l *and* s *visible* P:
quod tales G *s*: res tales *many* MSS.
[2] hanc hanc *Pa.*: hanc P: hanc tamen G ω.

---

[a] Nebrophonus and Euneus, according to Apollodorus;
according to Hyginus, Euneus and Deiphilus.
[b] So Medea had done with Absyrtus, to delay her father's
pursuit of Jason and herself.
[c] She had saved her father from the general massacre of
the men of Lemnos.

as I was when you set forth! If noble blood and generous lineage move you—lo, I am known as daughter of Minoan Thoas! Bacchus was my grandsire; the bride of Bacchus, with crown-encircled brow, outshines with her stars the lesser constellations. Lemnos will be my marriage portion, land kindly-natured to the husbandman; and me, too, you will possess among the subjects my dowry brings.

¹¹⁹ And now, too, I have brought forth; rejoice for us both, Jason! Sweet was the burden that I bore— its author had made it so. I am happy in the number, too, for by Lucina's kindly favour I have brought forth twin offspring, a pledge for each of us.[a] If you ask whom they resemble, I answer, yourself is seen in them. The ways of deceit they know not; for the rest, they are like their father. I almost gave them to be carried to you, their mother's ambassadors; but thought of the cruel stepdame turned me back from the path I would have trod. 'Twas Medea I feared. Medea is more than a stepdame; the hands of Medea are fitted for any crime.

¹²⁹ Would she who could tear her brother limb from limb and strew him o'er the fields be one to spare my pledges?[b] Such is she, such the woman, O madman swept from your senses by the poisons of Colchis, for whom you are said to have slighted the marriage-bed with Hypsipyle! Base and shameless was the way that maid became your bride; but the bond that gave me to you, and you to me, was chaste. She betrayed her sire; I rescued from death my father Thoas.[c] She deserted the Colchians; my Lemnos has me still. What matters aught, if sin is

79

Quid refert, scelerata piam si vincet et ipso
  crimine dotata est emeruitque virum ?
Lemniadum facinus culpo, non miror, Iason ;
  quamlibet infirmis ipse [1] dat arma dolor.   140
dic age, si ventis, ut oportuit, actus iniquis
  intrasses portus tuque comesque meos,
obviaque exissem fetu comitante gemello—
  hiscere nempe tibi terra roganda fuit !—
quo vultu natos, quo me, scelerate, videres ?   145
  perfidiae pretio qua nece dignus eras ?
ipse quidem per me tutus sospesque fuisses—
  non quia tu dignus, sed quia mitis ego.
paelicis ipsa meos inplessem sanguine vultus,
  quosque veneficiis abstulit illa suis !   150
Medeae Medea forem ! quodsi quid ab alto
  iustus adest votis Iuppiter ipse [2] meis,
quod gemit Hypsipyle, lecti quoque subnuba nostri
  maereat et leges sentiat ipsa suas ;
utque ego destituor coniunx materque duorum,   155
  a totidem natis orba sit illa viro !
nec male parta diu teneat peiusque relinquat—
  exulet et toto quaerat in orbe fugam !
quam fratri germana fuit miseroque parenti
  filia, tam natis, tam sit acerba viro !   160

---

[1] ipse P_2: iste *Madv.*
[2] ipse *the MSS.*: illa *Hein. Bent. Pa.*

to be set before devotion, and she has won her husband with the very crime she brought him as her dower?

[139] The vengeful deed of the Lemnian women I condemn, Jason, I do not marvel at it; passion itself drives the weak, however powerless, to take up arms. Come, say, what if, driven by unfriendly gales, you had entered my harbours, as 'twere fitting you had done, you and your companion, and I had come forth to meet you with my twin babes—surely you must have prayed earth to yawn for you— with what countenance could you have gazed upon your children, O wretched man, with what countenance upon me? What death would you not deserve as the price of your perfidy? And yet you yourself would have met with safety and protection at my hands—not that you deserved, but that I was merciful. But as for your mistress—with my own hand I would have dashed my face with her blood, and your face, that she stole away with her poisonous arts! I would have been Medea to Medea!

[151] But if in any way just Jupiter himself from on high attends to my prayers, may the woman who intrudes upon my marriage-bed suffer the woes in which Hypsipyle groans, and feel the lot she herself now brings on me; and as I am now left alone, wife and mother of two babes, so may she one day be reft of as many babes, and of her husband! Nor may she long keep her ill-gotten gains, but leave them in worse hap—let her be an exile, and seek a refuge through the entire world! A bitter sister to her brother, a bitter daughter to her wretched sire, may she be as bitter to her children, and as bitter to her husband! When she shall have no hope more of

OVID

cum mare, cum terras consumpserit, aera temptet ;

    erret inops, exspes, caede cruenta sua !

haec ego, coniugio fraudata Thoantias oro.

    vivite, devoto nuptaque virque toro !

VII

Dido Aeneae

Sic ubi fata vocant, udis abiectus in herbis

    ad vada Maeandri concinit albus olor.

Nec quia te nostra sperem prece posse moveri,

    adloquor—adverso movimus ista deo ;

sed merita et famam corpusque animumque

      pudicum   5

    cum male perdiderim, perdere verba leve est.

Certus es ire tamen miseramque relinquere Didon,

    atque idem venti vela fidemque ferent ?

certus es, Aenea, cum foedere solvere naves,

    quaeque ubi sint nescis, Itala regna sequi ?   10

nec nova Carthago, nec te crescentia tangunt

    moenia nec sceptro tradita summa tuo ?

facta fugis, facienda petis ; quaerenda per orbem

    altera, quaesita est altera terra tibi.

---

[a] The song preceding death.

[b] Ovid has the fourth book of the *Aeneid* in mind as he
composes this letter.

refuge by the sea or by the land, let her make trial
of the air; let her wander, destitute, bereft of hope,
stained red with the blood of her murders! This
fate do I, the daughter of Thoas, cheated of my
wedded state, in prayer call down upon you. Live
on, a wife and husband, accursed in your bed!

VII

DIDO TO AENEAS

THUS, at the summons of fate, casting himself down
amid the watery grasses by the shallows of Maeander,
sings the white swan.[a]

3 Not because I hope you may be moved by
prayer of mine do I address you—for with God's
will adverse I have begun the words you read; but
because, after wretched losing of desert, of reputa-
tion, and of purity of body and soul, the losing of
words is a matter slight indeed.

7 Are you resolved none the less to go, and to
abandon wretched Dido,[b] and shall the same winds
bear away from me at once your sails and your
promises? Are you resolved, Aeneas, to break at
the same time from your moorings and from your
pledge, and to follow after the fleeting realms of
Italy, which lie you know not where? and does new-
founded Carthage not touch you, nor her rising walls,
nor the sceptre of supreme power placed in your
hand? What is achieved, you turn your back
upon; what is to be achieved, you ever pursue.
One land has been sought and gained, and ever
must another be sought, through the wide world.

ut terram invenias, quis eam tibi tradet haben-
    dam? 15
  quis sua non notis arva tenenda dabit?
alter habendus amor tibi restat et altera Dido ; [1]
  quamque iterum fallas altera danda fides.
quando erit, ut condas instar Carthaginis urbem
  et videas populos altus ab arce tuos? 20
omnia ut eveniant, nec te tua vota morentur,
  unde tibi, quae te sic amet, uxor erit?
Uror, ut inducto ceratae sulpure taedae,
  ut pia fumosis addita tura focis. [2]
Aeneas oculis semper vigilantis inhaeret; 25
  Aenean animo noxque diesque refert.
ille quidem male gratus et ad mea munera surdus,
  et quo, si non sim stulta, carere velim ;
non tamen Aenean, quamvis male cogitat, odi,
  sed queror infidum questaque peius amo. 30
parce, Venus, nurui, durumque amplectere fratrem,
  frater Amor, castris militet ille tuis !
aut ego, quem [3] coepi—neque enim dedignor—amare,
  materiam curae praebeat ille meae !
Fallor, et ista mihi falso iactatur imago ; 35
  matris ab ingenio dissidet ille suae.
te lapis et montes innataque rupibus altis
  robora, te saevae progenuere ferae,

---

[1] *So* s *Burm.*: alter amor tibi est habendus et *P* : a. a. t. et
exstat habendus *G E* s : a. a. tibi restat? habendast altera
Dido ? *Birt Ehw.*

[2] *vv.* 24, 25 *defended by Hous., condemned by Pa. Ehw.*

[3] quem ω *early editions* : quae *P G E* s *Plan.*

Yet, even should you find the land of your desire, who will give it over to you for your own? Who will deliver his fields to unknown hands to keep? A second love remains for you to win, and a second Dido; a second pledge to give, and a second time to prove false. When will it be your fortune, think you, to found a city like to Carthage, and from the citadel on high to look down upon peoples of your own? Should your every wish be granted, even should you meet with no delay in the answering of your prayers, whence will come the wife to love you as I?

²³ I am all ablaze with love, like torches of wax tipped with sulphur, like pious incense placed on smoking altar-fires. Aeneas my eyes cling to through all my waking hours; Aeneas is in my heart through the night and through the day. 'Tis true he is an ingrate, and unresponsive to my kindnesses, and were I not fond I should be willing to have him go; yet, however ill his thought of me, I hate him not, but only complain of his faithlessness, and when I have complained I do but love more madly still. Spare, O Venus, the bride of thy son; lay hold of thy hard-hearted brother, O brother Love, and make him to serve in thy camp! Or make him to whom I have let my love go forth—I first, and with never shame for it—yield me himself, the object of my care!

³⁵ Ah, vain delusion! the fancy that flits before my mind is not the truth; far different his heart from his mother's. Of rocks and mountains were you begotten, and of the oak sprung from the lofty cliff, of savage wild beasts, or of the sea—such a sea as even now

aut mare, quale vides agitari nunc quoque ventis,
 quo tamen adversis fluctibus ire paras. 40
quo fugis? obstat hiemps. hiemis mihi gratia prosit
 adspice, ut eversas concitet Eurus aquas!
quod tibi malueram, sine me debere procellis;
 iustior est animo ventus et unda tuo.
Non ego sum tanti—quid non censeris inique?— 45
 ut pereas, dum me per freta longa fugis.
exerces pretiosa odia et constantia magno,
 si, dum me careas, est tibi vile mori.
iam venti ponent, strataque aequaliter unda
 caeruleis Triton per mare curret equis. 50
tu quoque cum ventis utinam mutabilis esses!
 et, nisi duritia robora vincis, eris.
quid, si nescires, insana quid aequora possunt?
 expertae totiens quam[1] male credis aquae!
ut, pelago suadente etiam, retinacula solvas, 55
 multa tamen latus tristia pontus habet.
nec violasse fidem temptantibus aequora prodest;
 perfidiae poenas exigit ille locus,
praecipue cum laesus amor, quia mater Amorum
 nuda Cytheriacis edita fertur aquis. 60
Perdita ne perdam, timeo, noceamve nocenti,
 neu bibat aequoreas naufragus hostis aquas.
vive, precor! sic te melius quam funere perdam.
 tu potius leti causa ferere mei.

[1] quam *s Merk.*

you look upon, tossed by the winds, on which you are none the less making ready to sail, despite the threatening floods. Whither are you flying? The tempest rises to stay you. Let the tempest be my grace! Look you, how Eurus tosses the rolling waters! What I had preferred to owe to you, let me owe to the stormy blasts; wind and wave are juster than your heart.

⁴⁵ I am not worth enough—ah, why do I not wrongly rate you?—to have you perish flying from me over the long seas. 'Tis a costly and a dear-bought hate that you indulge if, to be quit of me, you account it cheap to die. Soon the winds will fall, and o'er the smooth-spread waves will Triton course with cerulean steeds. O that you too were changeable with the winds!—and, unless in hardness you exceed the oak, you will be so. What could you worse, if you did not know of the power of raging seas? How ill to trust the wave whose might you have so often felt! Even should you loose your cables at the persuasion of calm seas, there are none the less many woes to be met on the vasty deep. Nor is it well for those who have broken faith to tempt the billows. Yon is the place that exacts the penalty for faithlessness, above all when 'tis love has been wronged; for 'twas from the sea, in Cytherean waters, so runs the tale, that the mother of the Loves, undraped, arose.

⁶¹ Undone myself, I fear lest I be the undoing of him who is my undoing, lest I bring harm to him who brings harm to me, lest my enemy be wrecked at sea and drink the waters of the deep. O live; I pray it! Thus shall I see you worse undone than by death. You shall rather be reputed the cause of my own doom. Imagine, pray, imagine

finge, age, te rapido—nullum sit in omine
    pondus !—   65
  turbine deprendi ; quid tibi mentis erit ?
protinus occurrent falsae periuria linguae,
    et Phrygia Dido fraude coacta mori ;
coniugis ante oculos deceptae stabit imago
    tristis et effusis sanguinolenta comis.   70
quid tanti est ut tum " merui ! concedite ! " dicas,
    quaeque cadent, in te fulmina missa putes ?
Da breve saevitiae spatium pelagique tuaeque ;
    grande morae pretium tuta futura via est.
nec mihi tu curae ; puero parcatur Iulo !   75
  te satis est titulum mortis habere meae.
quid puer Ascanius, quid di meruere[1] Penates ?
  ignibus ereptos obruet unda deos ?
sed neque fers tecum, nec, quae mihi, perfide, iactas,
    presserunt umeros sacra paterque tuos.   80
omnia mentiris, neque enim tua fallere lingua
  incipit a nobis, primaque plector ego.
si quaeras, ubi sit formosi mater Iuli—
  occidit a duro sola relicta viro !
haec mihi narraras—sat me monuere ![2] merentem 85
  ure ; minor culpa poena futura mea est.
Nec mihi mens dubia est, quin te tua numina
    damnent.
  per mare, per terras septima iactat hiemps.

[1] *So G ω vulg.*: quid meruere *P* : quid commeruere *Pa.*
[2] at me novere *E ω*: at me movere *Merk. Pa.*: di me
monuere *Madv.*: sat me monuere *Hous.*

---

    [a] Another name for Ascanius, the son of Aeneas.

that you are caught—may there be nothing in the
omen!—in the sweeping of the storm; what will be
your thoughts? Straight will come rushing to your
mind the perjury of your false tongue, and Dido
driven to death by Phrygian faithlessness; before
your eyes will appear the features of your deceived
wife, heavy with sorrow, with hair streaming, and
stained with blood. What now can you gain to
recompense you then, when you will have to say:
"'Tis my desert; forgive me, ye gods!" when you
will have to think that whatever thunderbolts fall
were hurled at you?

73 Grant a short space for the cruelty of the sea,
and for your own, to subside; your safe voyage
will be great reward for waiting. Nor is it
you for whom I am anxious; only let the little
Iulus[a] be spared! For you, enough to have the
credit for my death. What has little Ascanius
done, or what your Penates, to deserve ill fate?
Have they been rescued from fire but to be over-
whelmed by the wave? Yet neither are you bearing
them with you; the sacred relics which are your
pretext never rested on your shoulders, nor did
your father. You are false in everything—and I
am not the first your tongue has deceived, nor am
I the first to feel the blow from you. Do you ask
where the mother of pretty Iulus is?—she perished,
left behind by her unfeeling lord! This was the
story you told me—yes, and it was warning enough
for me! Burn me; I deserve it! The punishment
will be less than befits my fault.

87 And my mind doubts not that you, too, are
under condemnation of your gods. Over sea and
over land you are now for the seventh winter being

fluctibus eiectum tuta statione recepi
   vixque bene audito nomine regna dedi.   90
his tamen officiis utinam contenta fuissem,
   et mihi concubitus fama sepulta foret!
illa dies nocuit, qua nos declive sub antrum
   caeruleus subitis conpulit imber aquis.
audieram vocem; nymphas ululasse putavi—   95
   Eumenides fatis signa dedere meis!
Exige, laese pudor, poenas! violate Sychaei [1] . . . .
   ad quas, me miseram, plena pudoris eo.
est mihi marmorea sacratus in aede Sychaeus—
   oppositae frondes velleraque alba tegunt.   100
hinc ego me sensi noto quater ore citari;
   ipse sono tenui dixit " Elissa, veni! "
Nulla mora est, venio, venio tibi debita coniunx;
   sum tamen admissi tarda pudore mei.
da veniam culpae! decepit idoneus auctor;   105
   invidiam noxae detrahit ille meae.
diva parens seniorque pater, pia sarcina nati,
   spem mihi mansuri rite dedere viri.[2]
si fuit errandum, causas habet error honestas;
   adde fidem, nulla parte pigendus erit.   11(
Durat in extremum vitaeque novissima nostrae
   prosequitur fati, qui fuit ante, tenor.
occidit internas coniunx mactatus ad aras,
   et sceleris tanti praemia frater habet;

             [1] *Lacuna.*   [2] tori *G Merk.*

---

         [a] Dido's husband in Tyre.

tossed. You were cast ashore by the waves and I received you to a safe abiding-place; scarce knowing your name, I gave to you my throne. Yet would I had been content with these kindnesses, and that the story of our union were buried! That dreadful day was my ruin, when sudden downpour of rain from the deep-blue heaven drove us to shelter in the lofty grot. I had heard a voice; I thought it a cry of the nymphs—'twas the Eumenides sounding the signal for my doom!

[97] Exact the penalty of me, O purity undone!—the penalty due Sychaeus.[a] To absolve it now I go—ah me, wretched that I am, and overcome with shame! Standing in shrine of marble is an image of Sychaeus I hold sacred—in the midst of green fronds hung about, and fillets of white wool. From within it four times have I heard myself called by a voice well known; 'twas he himself crying in faintly sounding tone: "Elissa, come!"

[103] I delay no longer, I come; I come thy bride, thine own by right; I am late, but 'tis for shame of my fault confessed. Forgive me my offence! He was worthy who caused my fall; he draws from my sin its hatefulness. That his mother was divine and his aged father the burden of a loyal son gave hope he would remain my faithful husband. If 'twas my fate to err, my error had honourable cause; so only he keep faith, I shall have no reason for regret.

[111] The lot that was mine in days past still follows me in these last moments of life, and will pursue to the end. My husband fell in his blood before the altars in his very house, and my brother possesses the fruits of the monstrous crime; myself am driven

exul agor cineresque viri patriamque relinquo,   115
 et feror in duras hoste sequente vias.
adplicor ignotis fratrique elapsa fretoque
 quod tibi donavi, perfide, litus emo.
urbem constitui lateque patentia fixi
 moenia finitimis invidiosa locis.   120
bella tument ; bellis peregrina et femina temptor,
 vixque rudis portas urbis et arma paro.
mille procis placui, qui me coiere querentes
 nescio quem thalamis praeposuisse suis.
quid dubitas vinctam Gaetulo tradere Iarbae ?   125
 praebuerim sceleri bracchia nostra tuo.
est etiam frater, cuius manus inpia possit
 respergi nostro, sparsa cruore viri.
pone deos et quae tangendo sacra profanas !
 non bene caelestis inpia dextra colit.   130
si tu cultor eras elapsis igne futurus,
 paenitet elapsos ignibus esse deos.
Forsitan et gravidam Didon, scelerate, relinquas,
 parsque tui lateat corpore clausa meo.
accedet fatis matris miserabilis infans,   135
 et nondum nato[1] funeris auctor eris,
cumque parente sua frater morietur Iuli,
 poenaque conexos auferet una duos.
" Sed iubet ire deus."   vellem, vetuisset adire,
 Punica nec Teucris pressa fuisset humus !   14

---

[1] nato *Hein.*: nati *Pa.*

into exile, compelled to leave behind the ashes
of my lord and the land of my birth. Over hard
paths I fly, and my enemy pursues. I land on shores
unknown; escaped from my brother and the sea, I
purchase the strand that I gave, perfidious man, to
you. I establish a city, and lay about it the found-
ations of wide-reaching walls that stir the jealousy
of neighbouring realms. Wars threaten; by wars,
a stranger and a woman, I am assailed; hardly can
I rear rude gates to the city and make ready my
defence. A thousand suitors cast fond eyes on me,
and have joined in the complaint that I preferred
the hand of some stranger love. Why do you not
bind me forthwith, and give me over to Gaetulian
Iarbas? I should submit my arms to your shameful
act. There is my brother, too, whose impious hand
could be sprinkled with my blood, as it is already
sprinkled with my lord's. Lay down those gods and
sacred things; your touch profanes them! It is
not well for an impious right hand to worship
the dwellers in the sky. If 'twas fated for you to
worship the gods that escaped the fires, the gods
regret that they escaped the fires.

¹³³ Perhaps, too, it is Dido soon to be mother,
O evil-doer, whom you abandon now, and a part
of your being lies hidden in myself. To the fate
of the mother will be added that of the wretched
babe, and you will be the cause of doom to your yet
unborn child; with his own mother will Iulus'
brother die, and one fate will bear us both away
together.

¹³⁹ "But you are bid to go—by your god!" Ah,
would he had forbidden you to come; would
Punic soil had never been pressed by Teucrian

93

hoc duce nempe deo ventis agitaris iniquis
　　et teris in rapido tempora longa freto ?
Pergama vix tanto tibi erant repetenda labore,
　　Hectore si vivo quanta fuere forent.
non patrium Simoenta petis, sed Thybridas
　　undas—　　　　　　　　　　　　　　　　145
　　nempe ut pervenias, quo cupis, hospes eris ;
utque latet vitatque tuas abstrusa carinas,
　　vix tibi continget terra petita seni.
Hos potius populos in dotem, ambage remissa,
　　accipe et advectas Pygmalionis opes.　　　150
Ilion in Tyriam transfer felicius urbem
　　resque loco[1] regis sceptraque sacra tene !
si tibi mens avida est belli, si quaerit Iulus,
　　unde suo partus Marte triumphus eat,
quem superet, nequid desit, praebebimus hos-
　　tem ;　　　　　　　　　　　　　　　　155
　　hic pacis leges, hic locus arma capit.
tu modo, per matrem fraternaque tela, sagittas,
　　perque fugae comites, Dardana sacra, deos—
sic superent, quoscumque tua de gente reportas,
　　Mars ferus et damni sit modus ille tui,　　160
Ascaniusque suos feliciter inpleat annos,
　　et senis Anchisae molliter ossa cubent !—
parce, precor, domui, quae se tibi tradit habendam !
　　quod crimen dicis praeter amasse meum ?
non ego sum Phthias magnisque oriunda Mycenis,[a] 16[5]
　　nec steterunt in te virque paterque meus.

---

[1] *So Pa.*: inque loco P_2 *over an erasure G E s* : iamqu[e]
locum *Ehw.*: *etc.*

---

[a] The home of Achilles.

feet! Is this, forthsooth, the god under whose
guidance you are tossed about by unfriendly winds,
and pass long years on the surging seas? 'Twould
scarce require such toil to return again to Perga-
mum, were Pergamum still what it was while Hector
lived. 'Tis not the Simois of your fathers you seek,
but the waves of Tiber—and yet, forsooth, should
you arrive at the place you wish, you will be but
a stranger; and the land of your quest so hides
from your sight, so draws away from contact with
your keels, that 'twill scarce be your lot to reach
it in old age.

[149] Cease, then, your wanderings! Choose rather
me, and with me my dowry—these peoples of mine,
and the wealth of Pygmalion I brought with me.
Transfer your Ilion to the Tyrian town, and give
it thus a happier lot; enjoy the kingly state, and
the sceptre's right divine. If your soul is eager
for war, if Iulus must have field for martial
prowess and the triumph, we shall find him foes
to conquer, and naught shall lack; here there is
place for the laws of peace, here place, too, for
arms. Do you only, by your mother I pray, and by
the weapons of your brother, his arrows, and by
the divine companions of your flight, the gods of
Dardanus—so may those rise above fate whom you
are saving from out your race, so may that cruel war
be the last of misfortunes to you, and so may
Ascanius fill happily out his years, and the bones of
old Anchises rest in peace!—do you only spare the
house which gives itself without condition into your
hand. What can you charge me with but love?
I am not of Phthia,[a] nor sprung of great Mycenae,
nor have I had a husband and a father who have

si pudet uxoris, non nupta, sed hospita dicar ;
   dum tua sit, Dido quidlibet esse feret.
Nota mihi freta sunt Afrum plangentia litus ;
   temporibus certis dantque negantque viam.   170
cum dabit aura viam, praebebis carbasa ventis ;
   nunc levis eiectam continet alga ratem.
tempus ut observem, manda mihi ; serius ibis,
   nec te, si cupies, ipsa manere sinam.
et socii requiem poscunt, laniataque classis   175
   postulat exiguas semirefecta moras ;
pro meritis et siqua tibi debebimus ultra,[1]
   pro spe coniugii tempora parva peto—
dum freta mitescunt et amor, dum tempore et usu
   fortiter edisco tristia posse pati.   180
Si minus, est animus nobis effundere vitam ;
   in me crudelis non potes esse diu.
adspicias utinam, quae sit scribentis imago !
   scribimus, et gremio Troicus ensis adest,
perque genas lacrimae strictum labuntur in
      ensem,   185
   qui iam pro lacrimis sanguine tinctus erit.
quam bene conveniunt fato tua munera nostro !
   instruis inpensa nostra sepulcra brevi.
nec mea nunc primum feriuntur pectora telo ;
   ille locus saevi vulnus amoris habet.   190
Anna soror, soror Anna, meae male conscia culpae,
   iam dabis in cineres ultima dona meos.

[1] ultro P.

stood against you. If you shame to have me your
wife, let me not be called bride, but hostess;
so she be yours, Dido will endure to be what
you will.

¹⁶⁹ Well do I know the seas that break upon
African shores; they have their times of granting
and denying the way. When the breeze permits,
you shall give your canvas to the gale; now the
light seaweed detains your ship by the strand.
Entrust me with the watching of the skies; you
shall go later, and I myself, though you desire it,
will not let you to stay. Your comrades, too, de-
mand repose, and your shattered fleet, but half
refitted, calls for a short delay; by your past kind-
nesses, and by that other debt I still, perhaps, shall
owe you, by my hope of wedlock, I ask for a little
time—while the sea and my love grow calm, while
through time and wont I learn the strength to
endure my sorrows bravely.

¹⁸¹ If you yield not, my purpose is fixed to pour
forth my life; you can not be cruel to me for long.
Could you but see now the face of her who writes
these words! I write, and the Trojan's blade is
ready in my lap. Over my cheeks the tears
roll, and fall upon the drawn steel—which soon
shall be stained with blood instead of tears. How
fitting is your gift in my hour of fate! You furnish
forth my death at a cost but slight. Nor does
my heart now for the first time feel a weapon's
thrust; it already bears the wound of cruel
love.

¹⁹¹ Anna my sister, my sister Anna, wretched
sharer in the knowledge of my fault, soon shall you
give to my ashes the last boon. Nor when I have

nec consumpta rogis inscribar Elissa Sychaei,
  hoc tamen in tumuli marmore carmen erit :

PRAEBUIT AENEAS ET CAUSAM MORTIS ET ENSEM ;   195
  IPSA SUA DIDO CONCIDIT USA MANU.

VIII

HERMIONE ORESTI

1 PYRRHUS Achillides, animosus imagine patris,   3
  inclusam contra iusque piumque tenet.
quod potui, renui, ne non invita tenerer ;   5
  cetera femineae non valuere manus.
" quid facis, Aeacide ? non sum sine vindice," dixi :
  " haec tibi sub domino est, Pyrrhe, puella suo ! "
surdior ille freto clamantem nomen Orestis
  traxit inornatis in sua tecta comis.   10
quid gravius capta Lacedaemone serva tulissem,
  si raperet Graias barbara turba nurus ?
parcius Andromachen vexavit Achaia victrix,
  cum Danaus Phrygias ureret ignis opes.
At tu, cura mei si te pia tangit, Oreste,   15
  inice non timidas in tua iura manus !

---

1 vv. 1, 2 *spurious, but given in Ald. Burm.: see note to* V, *title.*

---

  a A legal allusion : a *vindex* was one who undertook the
defence of a person seized for debt.
  b Andromache's son Astyanax was thrown from the wall

been consumed upon the pyre, shall my inscription read : ELISSA, WIFE OF SYCHAEUS ; yet there shall be on the marble of my tomb these lines :

FROM AENEAS CAME THE CAUSE OF HER DEATH, AND FROM HIM THE BLADE ; FROM THE HAND OF DIDO HERSELF CAME THE STROKE BY WHICH SHE FELL.

VIII

HERMIONE TO ORESTES

PYRRHUS, Achilles' son, in self-will the image of his sire, holds me in durance against every law of earth and heaven. All that lay in my power I have done—I have refused consent to be held ; farther than that my woman's hands could not avail. "What art thou doing, son of Aeacus ? I lack not one to take my part ! " [a] I cried. "This is a woman, I tell thee, Pyrrhus, who has a master of her own ! " Deafer to me than the sea as I shrieked out the name of Orestes, he dragged me with hair all disarrayed into his palace. What worse my lot had Lacedaemon been taken and I been made a slave, carried away by the barbarian rout with the daughters of Greece ? Less misused by the victorious Achaeans was Andromache herself, what time the Danaän fire consumed the wealth of Phrygia.[b]

15 But do you, if your heart is touched with any natural care for me, Orestes, lay claim to your right with no timid hand. What ! should anyone

of Troy, and she became the prize of Pyrrhus (also called Neoptolemus). She was afterwards given by him to Helenus.

an siquis rapiat stabulis armenta reclusis,
  arma feras,[1] rapta coniuge lentus eris ?
sit socer exemplo nuptae repetitor ademptae,
  cui pia militiae causa puella fuit !   20
si socer ignavus vidua stertisset in aula,
  nupta foret Paridi mater, ut ante fuit.
Nec tu mille rates sinuosaque vela pararis
  nec numeros Danai militis—ipse veni !
sic quoque eram repetenda tamen, nec turpe
    marito   25
  aspera pro caro bella tulisse toro.
quid, quod avus nobis idem Pelopeius Atreus,
  et, si non esses vir mihi, frater eras.
vir, precor, uxori, frater succurre sorori !
  instant officio nomina bina tuo.   30
Me tibi Tyndareus, vita gravis auctor et annis,
  tradidit ; arbitrium neptis habebat avus.
at pater Aeacidae promiserat inscius acti ;
  plus quoque, qui prior est ordine, posset [2] avus.
cum tibi nubebam, nulli mea taeda nocebat ;   35
  si iungar Pyrrho, tu mihi laesus eris.
et pater ignoscet nostro Menelaus amori—
  succubuit telis praepetis ipse dei.
quem sibi permisit, genero concedet amorem ;
  proderit exemplo mater amata suo.   40
tu mihi, quod matri pater est ; quas egerat olim
  Dardanius partis advena, Pyrrhus agit.

  [1] feras *P* : feres *s*.
  [2] posset *P G* ω : possit *s and early editions* : pollet *Bent.*

  _____

              [a] *Frater* is often so used.

break open your pens and steal away your herds,
would you resort to arms? and when your wife is
stolen away will you be slow to move? Let your
father-in-law Menelaus be your example, he who
demanded back the wife taken from him, and had in
a woman righteous cause for war. Had he been
spiritless, and drowsed in his deserted halls, my
mother would still be wed to Paris, as she was before.

²³ Yet make not ready a thousand ships with
bellying sails, and hosts of Danaän soldiery—yourself come! Yet even thus I might well have been
sought back, nor is it unseemly for a husband to
have endured fierce combat for love of his marriage-bed. Remember, too, the same grandsire is ours,
Atreus, Pelops' son, and, were you not husband to
me, you would still be cousin.ᵃ Husband, I entreat,
succour your wife; brother, your sister! Both bonds
press you on to your duty.

³¹ I was given to you by Tyndareus, weighty
of counsel both for his life and for his years; the
grandsire was arbiter of the grandchild's fate. But
my father, it might be said, had promised me to
Aeacus' son, not knowing this; yet my grandsire,
who is first in order, should also be first in power.
When I was wed to you, my union brought harm
to none; if I wed with Pyrrhus, I shall deal
a wound to you. My father Menelaus, too, will
pardon our love—he himself succumbed to the darts
of the wingèd god. The love he allowed himself,
he will concede to his daughter's chosen; my
mother, loved by him, will aid with her precedent.
You are to me what my sire is to my mother, and
the part which once the Dardanian stranger played,
Pyrrhus now plays. Let him be endlessly proud

OVID

ille licet patriis sine fine superbiat actis ;
  et tu, quae referas facta parentis, habes.
Tantalides omnis ipsumque regebat Achillem.   45
  hic pars militiae ; dux erat ille ducum.
tu quoque habes proavum Pelopem Pelopisque paren-
      tem ;
  si melius numeres, a Iove quintus eris.
Nec virtute cares.   arma invidiosa tulisti,
  sed tibi—quid faceres ?—induit illa pater.[1]   50
materia vellem fortis meliore fuisses ;
  non lecta est operi, sed data causa tuo.
hanc tamen inplesti ; iuguloque Aegisthus aperto
  tecta cruentavit, quae pater ante tuus.
increpat Aeacides laudemque in crimina vertit—   55
  et tamen adspectus sustinet ille meos.
rumpor, et ora mihi pariter cum mente tumescunt,
  pectoraque inclusis ignibus usta dolent.
Hermione coram quisquamne obiecit Oresti,
  nec mihi sunt vires, nec ferus ensis adest ?   60
flere licet certe ; flendo defundimus iram,
  perque sinum lacrimae fluminis instar eunt.
has solas habeo semper semperque profundo ;
  ument incultae fonte perenne genae.
Num generis fato, quod nostros errat in annos,   65
  Tantalides matres apta rapina sumus ?

---

[1] *So Hous.*: Sed tu quid faceres ? *others.*

---

[a] Jupiter, Tantalus, Pelops, Atreus, Agamemnon, Orestes
—really sixth.
[b] During Agamemnon's absence, Aegisthus won Clytem-
nestra's heart, and the two compassed the king's death.
After seven years of reigning, Aegisthus and Clytemnestra
were slain by her son Orestes.

because of his father's deeds; you, too, have a sire's achievements of which to boast. The son of Tantalus was ruler over all, over Achilles himself. The one was but a part of the soldier band; the other was chief of chiefs. You, too, have ancestors—Pelops, and the father of Pelops; should you care to count more closely, you could call yourself fifth from Jove.[a]

[49] Nor are you without your prowess. The arms you wielded were hateful—but what were you to do?—your father placed them in your hand. I could wish that fortune had given you more excellent matter for courage; but the cause that called forth your deed was not chosen — it was fixed. The call you none the less obeyed; and the pierced throat of Aegisthus stained with blood the dwelling your father's blood had reddened before.[b] The son of Aeacus assails your name, and turns your praise to blame—and yet shrinks not before my gaze. I burst with anger, and my face swells with passion no less than my heart, and my breast burns with the pains of pent-up wrath. Has anyone in hearing of Hermione said aught against Orestes, and have I no strength, and no keen sword at hand? I can weep, at least. In weeping I let pour forth my ire, and over my bosom course the tears like a flowing stream. These only I still have, and still do I let them gush; my cheeks are wet and unsightly from their never-ending fount.

[65] Can it be some fate has come upon our house and pursued it through the years even to my time, that we Tantalid women are ever victims ready to the ravisher's hand? I shall not rehearse the lying

OVID

non ego fluminei referam mendacia cygni
    nec querar in plumis delituisse Iovem.
qua duo porrectus longe freta distinet Isthmos,
    vecta peregrinis Hippodamia rotis ; [1]   70
Taenaris Idaeo trans aequora ab hospite rapta   73
    Argolicas pro se vertit in arma manus.
vix equidem memini, memini tamen. omnia luctus, 75
    omnia solliciti plena timoris erant ;
flebat avus Phoebeque soror fratresque gemelli,
    orabat superos Leda suumque Iovem.
ipsa ego, non longos etiamtunc scissa capillos,
    clamabam : " sine me, me sine, mater, abis ? "   80
nam coniunx aberat ! ne non Pelopeia credar,
    ecce, Neoptolemo praeda parata fui !
Pelides utinam vitasset Apollinis arcus !
    damnaret nati facta proterva pater ;
nec quondam placuit nec nunc placuisset Achilli   85
    abducta viduum coniuge flere virum.
quae mea caelestis iniuria fecit iniquos,
    quodve mihi miserae sidus obesse querar ?
parva mea sine matre fui, pater arma ferebat,
    et duo cum vivant, orba duobus eram.   90
non tibi blanditias primis, mea mater, in annis
    incerto dictas ore puella tuli ;
non ego captavi brevibus tua colla lacertis
    nec gremio sedi sarcina grata tuo.
non cultus tibi cura mei, nec pacta marito   95
    intravi thalamos matre parante novos.

[1] 71, 72 *spurious Pa* :
        Castori Amyclaeo et Amyclaeo Polluci
         reddita Mopsopia Taenaris urbe soror ;

---

  [a] The story of Leda and the swan.   [b] Pelops won her
in the race with Oenomaus, her father, whose death he com-
passed by tampering with Oenomaus' charioteer Myrtilus.
  [c] Apollo directed the arrow of Paris which wounded
Achilles in the heel, his only vulnerable part.

words of the swan upon the stream, nor complain of
Jove disguised in plumage.[a] Where the sea is
sundered in two by the far-stretched Isthmus,
Hippodamia [b] was borne away in the car of the
stranger; she of Taenarus, stolen away across the
seas by the stranger-guest from Ida, roused to arms
in her behalf all the men of Argos. I scarcely
remember, to be sure, yet remember I do. All was
grief, everywhere anxiety and fear; my grandsire
wept, and my mother's sister Phoebe, and the twin
brothers, and Leda fell to praying the gods above, and
her own Jove. As for myself, tearing my locks, not
yet long, I began to cry aloud: " Mother, will you go
away, and will you leave me behind ? " For her lord
was gone. Lest I be thought none of Pelops' line, lo,
I too have been left a ready prey for Neoptolemus!

[83] Would that Peleus' son had escaped the bow of
Apollo ! [c] The father would condemn the son for
his wanton deed; 'twas not of yore the pleasure of
Achilles, nor would it be now his pleasure, to see
a widowed husband weeping for his stolen wife.
What wrong have I done that heaven's hosts are
against me ? or what constellation shall I complain is
hostile to my wretched self ? In my childhood I had
no mother; my father was ever in the wars—though
the two were not dead, I was reft of both. You
were not near in my first years, O my mother, to
receive the caressing prattle from the tripping
tongue of the little girl; I never clasped about your
neck the little arms that would not reach, and never
sat, a burden sweet, upon your lap. I was not
reared and cared for by your hand; and when I was
promised in wedlock I had no mother to make ready
the new chamber for my coming. I went out to

OVID

obvia prodieram reduci tibi—vera fatebor—
  nec facies nobis nota parentis erat!
te tamen esse Helenen, quod eras pulcherrima, sensi;
  ipsa requirebas, quae tua nata foret!   100
Pars haec una mihi, coniunx bene cessit Orestes;
  is quoque, ni pro se pugnat, ademptus erit.
Pyrrhus habet captam reduce et victore parente—
  hoc munus! nobis [1] diruta Troia dedit!
cum tamen altus equis Titan radiantibus instat,   105
  perfruor infelix liberiore malo;
nox ubi me thalamis ululantem et acerba gementem
  condidit in maesto procubuique toro,
pro somno lacrimis oculi funguntur obortis,
  quaque licet, fugio sicut ab hoste viro.   110
saepe malis stupeo rerumque oblita locique
  ignara tetigi Scyria membra manu,
utque nefas sensi, male corpora tacta relinquo
  et mihi pollutas credor habere manus.
saepe Neoptolemi pro nomine nomen Orestis   115
  exit, et errorem vocis ut omen amo.
Per genus infelix iuro generisque parentem,
  qui freta, qui terras et sua regna quatit;
per patris ossa tui, patrui mihi, quae tibi debent,
  quod se sub tumulo fortiter ulta iacent—   12(
aut ego praemoriar primoque exstinguar in aevo,
  aut ego Tantalidae Tantalis uxor ero!

  [1] *So G* s *Merk. Pa.*: et minus a nobis *P*: munus et hc
nobis s *Plan.*: munus et a! nobis *Ehw.*

106

meet you when you came back home—what I shall
say is truth—and the face of my mother was unknown
to me! That you were Helen I none the less knew,
because you were most beautiful; but you—you had
to ask who your daughter was!

¹⁰¹ This one favour of fortune has been mine—to
have Orestes for my wedded mate; but he, too, will
be taken from me if he does not fight for his own.
Pyrrhus holds me captive, though my father is
returned and a victor—this is the boon brought me
by the downfall of Troy! Yet my unhappy soul has
the comfort, when Titan is urging aloft his radiant
steeds, of being more free in its wretchedness; but
when the dark of night has fallen and sent me to my
chamber with wails and lamentation for my bitter lot,
and I have stretched myself prostrate on my sorrowful
bed, then springing tears, not slumber, is the service
of mine eyes, and in every way I can I shrink from
my mate as from a foe. Oft I am distraught
with woe; I lose sense of where I am and what my
fate, and with witless hand have touched the body of
him of Scyrus; but when I have waked to the awful
act, I draw my hand from the base contact, and look
upon it as defiled. Oft, instead of Neoptolemus the
name of Orestes comes forth, and the mistaken
word is a treasured omen.

¹¹⁷ By our unhappy line I swear, and by the parent
of our line, he who shakes the seas, the land, and
his own realms on high; by the bones of your father,
uncle to me, which owe it to you that bravely
avenged they lie beneath their burial mound—either
shall die before my time and in my youthful years be
blotted out, or I, a Tantalid, shall be the wife of him
sprung from Tantalus!

OVID

IX

Deianira Herculi

Gratulor Oechaliam titulis accedere nostris;
    victorem victae succubuisse queror.
fama Pelasgiadas subito pervenit in urbes
    decolor et factis infitianda tuis,
quem numquam Iuno seriesque inmensa laborum   5
    fregerit, huic Iolen inposuisse iugum.
hoc velit Eurystheus, velit hoc germana Tonantis,
    laetaque sit vitae labe noverca tuae;
at non ille velit, cui nox—sic creditur—una
    non tanta,[1] ut tantus conciperere, fuit.   10
Plus tibi quam Iuno, nocuit Venus: illa premendo
    sustulit, haec humili [2] sub pede colla tenet.
respice vindicibus pacatum viribus orbem,
    qua latam Nereus caerulus ambit humum.
se tibi pax terrae, tibi se tuta aequora debent;   15
    inplesti meritis solis utramque domum.
quod te laturum est, caelum prius ipse tulisti;
    Hercule supposito sidera fulsit Atlans.
quid nisi notitia est misero quaesita pudori,
    si cumulus stupri facta priora notat?   2·

---

[1] tanta *s Iahn Loers van Lennep* : tanti *P G ω.*
[2] humilis *P G ω Bent. Ehw.*

---

[a] The *Trachiniae* of Sophocles dramatizes the Deiani
story, and Apollodorus contains it. See also Ovid, *Metar*
ix. 1–273, and Seneca, *Hercules Oetaeus.*
[b] Who imposed the twelve labours on Hercules at t
instigation of Juno.

IX

Deianira to Hercules

^a I RENDER thanks that Oechalia has been added to the list of our honours; but that the victor has yielded to the vanquished, I complain. The rumour has suddenly spread to all the Pelasgian cities—a rumour unseemly, to which your deeds should give the lie—that on the man whom Juno's unending series of labours has never crushed, on him Iole has placed her yoke. This would please Eurystheus,^b and it would please the sister of the Thunderer; stepdame^c that she is, she would gladly know of the stain upon your life; but 'twould give no joy to him for whom, so 'tis believed, a single night did not suffice for the begetting of one so great.

¹¹ More than Juno, Venus has been your bane. The one, by crushing you down, has raised you up; the other has your neck beneath her humbling foot. Look but on the circle of the earth made peaceful by your protecting strength, wherever the blue waters of Nereus wind round the broad land. To you is owing peace upon the earth, to you safety on the seas; you have filled with worthy deeds both abodes of the sun.^d The heaven that is to bear you, yourself once bore; Hercules bent to the load of the stars when Atlas was their stay. What have you gained but to spread the knowledge of your wretched shame, if a final act of baseness blots your former deeds? Can it be you that men say

---

^c Jupiter was the father of Hercules by Alcmene.
^d Farthest east and west.

tene ferunt geminos pressisse tenaciter angues,
    cum tener in cunis iam Iove dignus eras?
coepisti melius quam desinis; ultima primis
    cedunt; dissimiles hic vir et ille puer.
quem non mille ferae, quem non Stheneleius
      hostis,   25
    non potuit Iuno vincere, vincit amor.
At bene nupta feror, quia nominer Herculis uxor,
    sitque socer, rapidis qui tonat altus equis.
quam male inaequales veniunt ad aratra iuvenci,
    tam premitur magno coniuge nupta minor.   30
non honor est sed onus species laesura ferentis;
    siqua voles apte nubere, nube pari.
vir mihi semper abest, et coniuge notior hospes,
    monstraque terribiles persequiturque feras.
ipsa domo vidua votis operata pudicis   35
    torqueor, infesto ne vir ab hoste cadat;
inter serpentes aprosque avidosque leones
    iactor et haesuros terna per ora canes.
me pecudum fibrae simulacraque inania somni
    omniaque arcana nocte petita movent.   40
aucupor infelix incertae murmura famae,
    speque timor dubia spesque timore cadit.
mater abest queriturque deo placuisse potenti,
    nec pater Amphitryon nec puer Hyllus adest;
arbiter Eurystheus irae Iunonis iniquae   45
    sentitur nobis iraque longa deae.

clutched tight the serpents twain while a tender babe in the cradle, already worthy of Jove ? You began better than you end ; your last deeds yield to your first ; the man you are and the child you were are not the same. He whom not a thousand wild beasts, whom not the Stheneleian foe, whom not Juno could overcome, love overcomes.

²⁷ Yet I am said to be well mated, because I am called the wife of Hercules, and because the father of my lord is he who thunders on high with impetuous steeds. As the ill-mated steer yoked miserably at the plough, so fares the wife who is less than her mighty lord. It is not honour, but mere fair-seeming, and brings dole to us who bear the load ; would you be wedded happily, wed your equal. My lord is ever absent from me—he is better known to me as guest than husband—ever pursuing monsters and dreadful beasts. I myself, at home and widowed, am busied with chaste prayers, in torment lest my husband fall by the savage foe ; with serpents and with boars and ravening lions my imaginings are full, and with hounds three-throated hard upon the prey. The entrails of slain victims stir my fears, the idle images of dreams, and the omen sought in the mysterious night. Wretchedly I catch at the uncertain murmurs of the common talk ; my fear is lost in wavering hope, my hope again in fear. Your mother is away, and laments that she ever pleased the potent god, and neither your father Amphitryon is here, nor your son Hyllus ; the acts of Eurystheus, the instrument of Juno's unjust wrath, and the long-continued anger of the goddess—I am the one to feel.

OVID

Haec mihi ferre parum? peregrinos addis amores,
  et mater de te quaelibet esse potest.
non ego Partheniis temeratam vallibus Augen,
  nec referam partus, Ormeni nympha, tuos ;   50
non tibi crimen erunt, Teuthrantia turba, sorores,
  quarum de populo nulla relicta tibi est.
una, recens crimen, referetur adultera nobis,
  unde ego sum Lydo facta noverca Lamo.
Maeandros, terris totiens errator in isdem,   55
  qui lassas in se saepe retorquet aquas,
vidit in Herculeo suspensa monilia collo
  illo, cui caelum sarcina parva fuit.
non puduit fortis auro cohibere lacertos,
  et solidis gemmas opposuisse toris ?   60
nempe sub his animam pestis Nemeaea lacertis
  edidit, unde umerus tegmina laevus habet !
ausus es hirsutos mitra redimire capillos !
  aptior Herculeae populus alba comae.
nec te Maeonia lascivae more puellae   65
  incingi zona dedecuisse pudet ?[1]
non tibi succurrit crudi Diomedis imago,
  efferus humana qui dape pavit equas ?
si te vidisset cultu Busiris in isto,
  huic victor victo[2] nempe pudendus eras.   70
detrahat Antaeus duro redimicula collo,
  ne pigeat molli succubuisse viro.
Inter Ioniacas calathum tenuisse puellas
  diceris et dominae pertimuisse minas.

[1] pudet *P G ω* : putas *s Burm.* : pputes *Leidensis* : patet *Pa.*
[2] Hic /// victor victo *P* ; huic *ω* : victori victo . . . erat *Pa.*

---

[a] There were fifty of them, and their father Thespiu
wished for fifty grandchildren by Hercules.

[b] Hercules was the lover of Omphale, or Iardanis (v. 103
queen of Lydia, sold to her by Hermes as a slave.

⁴⁷ Is this too little for me to endure? You add
to it your stranger loves, and whoever will may
be by you a mother. I will say nothing of Auge
betrayed in the vales of Parthenius, or of thy travail,
nymph sprung of Ormenus; nor will I charge
against you the daughters of Teuthras' son, the
throng of sisters from whose number none was
spared by you.^a But there is one love—a fresh
offence of which I have heard—a love by which
I am made stepdame to Lydian Lamus.^b The
Meander, so many times wandering in the same
lands, who oft turns back upon themselves his
wearied waters, has seen hanging from the neck of
Hercules—the neck which found the heavens but
slight burden—bejewelled chains! Felt you no
shame to bind with gold those strong arms, and to
set the gem upon that solid brawn? Ah, to think
'twas these arms that crushed the life from the
Nemean pest, whose skin now covers your left side!
You have not shrunk from binding your shaggy hair
with a woman's turban! More meet for the locks
of Hercules were the white poplar. And for you to
disgrace yourself by wearing the Maeonian zone,
like a wanton girl—feel you no shame for that?
Did there come to your mind no image of savage
Diomede, fiercely feeding his mares on human meat?
Had Busiris seen you in that garb, he whom you
vanquished would surely have reddened for such a
victor as you. Antaeus would tear from the hard
neck the turban-bands, lest he feel shame at having
succumbed to an unmanly foe.

⁷³ They say that you have held the wool-basket
among the girls of Ionia, and been frightened at
our mistress' threats. Do you not shrink, Alcides,

113

non fugis, Alcide, victricem mille laborum   75
  rasilibus calathis inposuisse manum,
crassaque robusto deducis pollice fila,
  aequaque formosae pensa rependis erae?
a, quotiens digitis dum torques stamina duris,
  praevalidae fusos conminuere manus!   80
ante pedes dominae[1] . . . .
  factaque narrabas dissimulanda tibi—   84
scilicet inmanes elisis faucibus hydros   85
  infantem caudis involuisse manum,
ut Tegeaeus aper cupressifero Erymantho
  incubet et vasto pondere laedat humum.
non tibi Threiciis adfixa penatibus ora,
  non hominum pingues caede tacentur equae;   90
prodigiumque triplex, armenti dives Hiberi
  Geryones, quamvis in tribus unus erat;
inque canes totidem trunco digestus ab uno
  Cerberos inplicitis angue minante comis;
quaeque redundabat fecundo vulnere serpens   95
  fertilis et damnis dives ab ipsa suis;
quique inter laevumque latus laevumque lacertum
  praegrave conpressa fauce pependit onus;
et male confisum pedibus formaque bimembri
  pulsum Thessalicis agmen equestre iugis.   100
Haec tu Sidonio potes insignitus amictu
  dicere?   non cultu lingua retenta silet?
se quoque nympha tuis ornavit Iardanis armis
  et tulit a capto nota tropaea viro.

[1] 81, *half of* 82, *and* 83, *spurious*, Merk. Pa.
      crederis infelix scuticae tremefactus habenis
        ante pedes dominae pertimuisse minas . . .
      eximias pompas, inmania semina laudum.

114

from laying to the polished wool-basket the hand
that triumphed over a thousand toils; do you draw
off with stalwart thumb the coarsely spun strands,
and give back to the hand of a pretty mistress the
just portion she weighed out? Ah, how often,
while with dour finger you twisted the thread, have
your too strong hands crushed the spindle! Before
your mistress' feet . . . . and told of the deeds of
which you should now say naught—of enormous
serpents, throttled and coiling their lengths about
your infant hand; how the Tegeaean boar has his
lair on cypress-bearing Erymanthus, and afflicts the
ground with his vast weight. You do not omit the
skulls nailed up in Thracian homes, nor the mares
made fat with the flesh of slain men; nor the triple
prodigy, Geryones, rich in Iberian cattle, who was
one in three; nor Cerberus, branching from one
trunk into a three-fold dog, his hair inwoven with
the threatening snake; nor the fertile serpent that
sprang forth again from the fruitful wound, grown
rich from her own hurt; nor him whose mass
hung heavy between your left side and left arm as
your hand clutched his throat; nor the equestrian
array that put ill trust in their feet and dual form,
confounded by you on the ridges of Thessaly.

[101] These deeds can you recount, gaily arrayed in
a Sidonian gown? Does not your dress rob from
our tongue all utterance? The nymph-daughter
of Iardanus [a] has even tricked herself out in your
arms, and won famous triumphs from the vanquished

[a] Omphale.

i nunc, tolle animos et fortia gesta recense ;   105
   quo [1] tu non esses, iure vir illa fuit.
qua tanto minor es, quanto te, maxime rerum,
   quam quos vicisti, vincere maius erat.
illi procedit rerum mensura tuarum—
   cede bonis ; heres laudis amica tuae.   110
o pudor ! hirsuti costis exuta leonis
   aspera texerunt vellera molle latus !
falleris et nescis—non sunt spolia illa leonis,
   sed tua, tuque feri victor es, illa tui.
femina tela tulit Lernaeis atra venenis,   115
   ferre gravem lana vix satis apta colum,
instruxitque manum clava domitrice ferarum,
   vidit et in speculo coniugis arma sui !
Haec tamen audieram ; licuit non credere famae,
   et venit ad sensus mollis ab aure dolor—   120
ante meos oculos adducitur advena paelex,
   nec mihi, quae patior, dissimulare licet !
non sinis averti ; mediam captiva per urbem
   invitis oculis adspicienda venit.
nec venit incultis captarum more capillis,   125
   fortunam vultu fassa decente [2] suam ;
ingreditur late lato spectabilis auro,
   qualiter in Phrygia tu quoque cultus eras.
dat vultum populo sublimis ut [3] Hercule victo ;
   Oechaliam vivo stare parente putes.   13(

[1] quo *Pa.*: quem P_1 : quod P_2 G ω : quom *Madv.*
[2] *So van Lennep* : vultu fassa tegente *P.*
[3] *So early editions, Plan* : sublime sub Hercule victo P G α

---

[a] Iole.

hero. Go now, puff up your spirit and recount your brave deeds done; she has proved herself a man by a right you could not urge. You are as much less than she, O greatest of men, as it was greater to vanquish you than those you vanquished. To her passes the full measure of your exploits—yield up what you possess; your mistress is heir to your praise. O shame, that the rough skin stripped from the flanks of the shaggy lion has covered a woman's delicate side! You are mistaken, and know it not— that spoil is not from the lion, but from you; you are victor over the beast, but she over you. A woman has borne the darts blackened with the venom of Lerna, a woman scarce strong enough to carry the spindle heavy with wool; a woman has taken in her hand the club that overcame wild beasts, and in the mirror gazed upon the armour of her lord!

[119] These things, however, I had only heard; I could distrust men's words, and the pain hit on my senses softly, through the ear—but now my very eyes must look upon a stranger-mistress [a] led before them, nor may I now dissemble what I suffer! You do not allow me to turn away; the woman comes a captive through the city's midst, to be looked upon by my unwilling eyes. Nor comes she after the manner of captive women, with hair unkempt, and with becoming countenance that tells to all her lot; she strides along, sightly from afar in plenteous gold, apparelled in such wise as you yourself in Phrygia. She looks straight out at the throng, with head held high, as if 'twere she had conquered Hercules; you might think Oechalia standing yet, and her father yet alive. Perhaps you

OVID

forsitan et pulsa Aetolide Deianira
  nomine deposito paelicis uxor erit,
Eurytidosque Ioles atque Aonii [1] Alcidae
  turpia famosus corpora iunget Hymen.
mens fugit admonitu, frigusque perambulat artus,   135
  et iacet in gremio languida facta manus.
Me quoque cum multis, sed me sine crimine amasti.
  ne pigeat, pugnae bis tibi causa fui.
cornua flens legit ripis Achelous in udis
  truncaque limosa tempora mersit aqua ;   140
semivir occubuit in lotifero Eueno [2]
  Nessus, et infecit sanguis equinus aquas.
sed quid ego haec refero ?   scribenti nuntia venit
  fama, virum tunicae tabe perire meae.
ei mihi ! quid feci ? quo me furor egit aman-
    tem ?   145
  inpia quid dubitas Deianira mori ?
An tuus in media coniunx lacerabitur Oeta,
  tu sceleris tanti causa superstes eris ?
siquid adhuc habeo facti, cur Herculis uxor
  credar, coniugii mors mea pignus erit !   150
tu quoque cognosces in me, Meleagre, sororem !
  inpia quid dubitas Deianira mori ?
Heu devota domus !   solio sedet Agrios alto ;
  Oenea desertum nuda senecta premit.
exulat ignotis Tydeus germanus in oris ;   155
  alter fatali vivus in igne fuit ;

[1] atque Aonii *Bent. Merk.*: et insanii *P* : insani *G*.
[2] lotifero *Bent.*: Eueno *Hein.*: letiferoque veneno *G* : i
lorifero eueneno *Guelf.* 3 : in letifero Eueno *Hein. Burm. etc.*

[a] His poisoned blood is in the robe she sends to Hercules
[b] Agrius drove out Oeneus his brother after Meleager'
death.
[c] By Oeneus, for slaying a brother.
[d] Meleager perished when his mother Althea, in reveng
118

will even drive away Aetolian Deianira, and her rival
will lay aside the name of mistress, and be made
your wife. Iole, the daughter of Eurytus, and
Aonian Alcides will be basely joined in shameful
bonds of Hymen. My mind fails me at the thought,
a chill sweeps through my frame, and my hand lies
nerveless in my lap.

[137] Me, too, you have possessed among your many
loves—but me with no reproach. Regret it not—
twice you have fought for the sake of me. In tears
Achelous gathered up his horns on the wet banks of
his stream, and bathed in its clayey tide his mutilated
brow; the half-man Nessus sank down in lotus-
bearing Euenus, tingeing its waters with his equine
blood.[a] But why am I reciting things like these?
Even as I write comes rumour to me saying my
lord is dying of the poison from my cloak. Alas
me! what have I done? Whither has madness
driven me in my love? O wicked Deianira, why
hesitate to die?

[147] Shall thy lord be torn to death on midmost
Oeta, and shalt thou, the cause of the monstrous
deed, remain alive? If I have yet done aught to win
the name of wife of Hercules, my death shall be the
pledge of our union. Thou, Meleager, shalt also
see in me a sister of thine own! O wicked Deianira,
why hesitate to die?

[153] Alas, for my devoted house! Agrius sits on
the lofty throne;[b] Oeneus is reft of all, and
barren old age weighs heavy on him. Tydeus my
brother is exiled on an unknown shore;[c] my second
brother's life hung on the fateful fire;[d] our mother

---

[*] his slaying her brother, finally burned the brand on
whose preservation the Fates had said his life depended.

exegit ferrum sua per praecordia mater.
　inpia quid dubitas Deianira mori ?
Deprecor hoc unum per iura sacerrima lecti,
　ne videar fatis insidiata tuis.　　　　　　　　160
Nessus, ut est avidum percussus harundine pectus,
　" hic," dixit, " vires sanguis amoris habet."
inlita Nesseo misi tibi texta veneno.
　inpia quid dubitas Deianira mori ?
Iamque vale, seniorque pater germanaque Gorge,　165
　et patria et patriae frater adempte tuae,
et tu lux oculis hodierna novissima nostris,
　virque—sed o possis !—et puer Hylle, vale !

X

ARIADNE THESEO

MITIUS inveni quam te genus omne ferarum ;
　credita non ulli quam tibi peius eram.
quae legis, ex illo, Theseu, tibi litore mitto
　unde tuam sine me vela tulere ratem,
in quo me somnusque meus male prodidit et tu,　　
　per facinus somnis insidiate meis.
Tempus erat, vitrea quo primum terra pruina
　spargitur et tectae fronde queruntur aves.
incertum vigilans a somno languida movi
　Thesea prensuras semisupina manus—　　　　　1

drove the steel through her own heart. O wicked Deianira, why hesitate to die?

159 This one thing I deprecate, by the most sacred bonds of our marriage-bed—that I seem to have plotted for your doom. Nessus, stricken with the arrow in his lustful heart, "This blood," he said, "has power over love." The robe of Nessus, saturate with poisonous gore, I sent to you. O wicked Deianira, why hesitate to die?

165 And now, fare ye well, O aged father, and O my sister Gorge, and O my native soil, and brother taken from thy native soil, and thou, O light that shinest to-day, the last to strike upon mine eyes; and thou my lord, O fare thou well—would that thou couldst!—and Hyllus, thou my son, farewell to thee!

X

ARIADNE TO THESEUS

GENTLER than you I have found every race of wild beasts; to none of them could I so ill have trusted as to you. The words you now are reading, Theseus, I send you from that shore from which the sails bore off your ship without me, the shore on which my slumber, and you, so wretchedly betrayed me—you, who wickedly plotted against me as I slept.

7 'Twas the time when the earth is first besprinkled with crystal rime, and songsters hid in the branch begin their plaint. Half waking only, languid from sleep, I turned upon my side and put forth hands to clasp my Theseus—he was not

nullus erat! referoque manus iterumque retempto,
    perque torum moveo bracchia—nullus erat!
excussere metus somnum; conterrita surgo,
    membraque sunt viduo praecipitata toro.
protinus adductis sonuerunt pectora palmis,   15
    utque erat e somno turbida, rapta coma est.
Luna fuit; specto, siquid nisi litora cernam.
    quod videant oculi, nil nisi litus habent.
nunc huc, nunc illuc, et utroque sine ordine, curro;
    alta puellares tardat harena pedes.   20
interea toto clamanti [1] litore "Theseu!"
    reddebant nomen concava saxa tuum,
et quotiens ego te, totiens locus ipse vocabat.
    ipse locus miserae ferre volebat opem.
Mons fuit—apparent frutices in vertice rari;   25
    hinc [2] scopulus raucis pendet adesus aquis.
adscendo—vires animus dabat—atque ita late
    aequora prospectu metior alta meo.
inde ego—nam ventis quoque sum crudelibus usa—
    vidi praecipiti carbasa tenta Noto.   30
ut vidi haut dignam [3] quae me vidisse putarem,
    frigidior glacie semianimisque fui.
nec languere diu patitur dolor; excitor illo,
    excitor et summa Thesea voce voco.
"quo fugis?" exclamo; "scelerate revertere
    Theseu!   35
    flecte ratem! numerum non habet illa suum!"

[1] clamanti *s Plan.*: clamati//// *P*: clamanti in (
clamavi *V s Bent.*: clamavi in *Ehw.*
[2] hinc *G Burm.*: nunc *P V*: hic, huic *s.*
[3] *So Hous.*: aut vidi a///uam quae me *P*: aut vidi a
tamquam quae me *G.*

there! I drew back my hands, a second time I made essay, and o'er the whole couch moved my arms—he was not there! Fear struck away my sleep; in terror I arose, and threw myself headlong from my abandoned bed. Straight then my palms resounded upon my breasts, and I tore my hair, all disarrayed as it was from sleep.

¹⁷ The moon was shining; I bend my gaze to see if aught but shore lies there. So far as my eyes can see, naught do they find but shore. Now this way, and now that, and ever without plan, I course; the deep sand stays my girlish feet. And all the while I cried out "Theseus!" along the entire shore, and the hollow rocks sent back your name to me; as often as I called out for you, so often did the place itself call out your name. The very place felt the will to aid me in my woe.

²⁵ There was a mountain, with bushes rising here and there upon its top; a cliff hangs over from it, gnawed into by deep-sounding waves. I climb its slope—my spirit gave me strength—and thus with prospect broad I scan the billowy deep. From there —for I found the winds cruel, too—I beheld your sails stretched full by the headlong southern gale. As I looked on a sight methought I had not deserved to see, I grew colder than ice, and life half left my body. Nor does anguish allow me long to lie thus quiet; it rouses me, it stirs me up to call on Theseus with all my voice's might. "Whither dost fly?" I cry aloud. "Come back, O wicked Theseus! Turn about thy ship! She hath not all her crew!"

Haec ego ; quod voci deerat, plangore replebam ;
   verbera cum verbis mixta fuere meis.
si non audires, ut saltem cernere posses,
   iactatae late signa dedere manus ;   40
candidaque inposui longae velamina virgae—
   scilicet oblitos admonitura mei !
iamque oculis ereptus eras.   tum denique flevi ;
   torpuerant molles ante dolore genae.
quid potius facerent, quam me mea lumina flerent, 45
   postquam desieram [1] vela videre tua ?
aut ego diffusis erravi sola capillis,
   qualis ab Ogygio concita Baccha deo,
aut mare prospiciens in saxo frigida sedi,
   quamque lapis sedes, tam lapis ipsa fui.   50
saepe torum repeto, qui nos acceperat ambos,
   sed non acceptos exhibiturus erat,
et tua, quae possum pro te, vestigia tango
   strataque quae membris intepuere tuis.
incumbo, lacrimisque toro manante profusis,   55
   " pressimus," exclamo, " te duo—redde duos !
venimus huc ambo ; cur non discedimus ambo ?
   perfide, pars nostri, lectule, maior ubi est ? "
Quid faciam ? quo sola ferar ? vacat insula cultu.
   non hóminum video, non ego facta boum.   60
omne latus terrae cingit mare ; navita nusquam,
   nulla per ambiguas puppis itura vias.
finge dari comitesque mihi ventosque ratemque—
   quid sequar ? accessus terra paterna negat.

      [1] desieram *P ω* : desierant *s Plan.* : desierat *G.*

[37] Thus did I cry, and what my voice could not avail, I filled with beating of my breast; the blows I gave myself were mingled with my words. That you at least might see, if you could not hear, with might and main I sent you signals with my hands ; and upon a long tree-branch I fixed my shining veil—yes, to put in mind of me those who had forgotten ! And now you had been swept beyond my vision. Then at last I let flow my tears ; till then my tender eyeballs had been dulled with pain. What better could my eyes do than weep for me, when I had ceased to see your sails ? Alone, with hair loose flying, I have either roamed about, like to a Bacchant roused by the Ogygian god, or, looking out upon the sea, I have sat all chilled upon the rock, as much a stone myself as was the stone I sat upon. Oft do I come again to the couch that once received us both, but was fated never to show us together again, and touch the imprint left by you—'tis all I can in place of you !—and the stuffs that once grew warm beneath your limbs. I lay me down upon my face, bedew the bed with pouring tears, and cry aloud : "We were two who pressed thee—give back two ! We came to thee both together ; why do we not depart the same ? Ah, faithless bed—the greater part of my being, oh, where is he ?

[59] What am I to do ? Whither shall I take myself—I am alone, and the isle untilled. Of human traces I see none ; of cattle, none. On every side the land is girt by sea ; nowhere a sailor, no craft to make its way over the dubious paths. And suppose I did find those to go with me, and winds, and ship—yet where am I to go ?

ut rate felici pacata per aequora labar,   65
    temperet ut ventos Aeolus—exul ero!
non ego te, Crete centum digesta per urbes,
    adspiciam, puero cognita terra Iovi!
at pater et tellus iusto regnata parenti
    prodita sunt facto, nomina cara, meo,   70
cum tibi, ne victor tecto morerere recurvo,
    quae regerent passus, pro duce fila dedi,
cum mihi dicebas: "per ego ipsa pericula iuro,
    te fore, dum nostrum vivet uterque, meam."
Vivimus, et non sum, Theseu, tua—si modo vivit 75
    femina periuri fraude sepulta viri.
me quoque, qua fratrem, mactasses, inprobe, clava;
    esset, quam dederas, morte soluta fides.
nunc ego non tantum, quae sum passura, recordor,
    sed quaecumque potest ulla relicta pati.   80
occurrunt animo pereundi mille figurae,
    morsque minus poenae quam mora mortis habet.
iam iam venturos aut hac aut suspicor illac,
    qui lanient avido viscera dente, lupos.
quis scit an et[1] fulvos tellus alat ista leones? 85
    forsitan et saevas tigridas insula habet.[2]
et freta dicuntur magnas expellere phocas!
    quis vetat et gladios per latus ire meum?
Tantum ne religer dura captiva catena,
    neve traham serva grandia pensa manu,   90

[1] Quis scit an *made to change places with* forsitan et, *for the sake of syntax Hous.*
[2] saevas tigridas insula habet *G*: trigides insula habent *P*: et saevam tigrida Dia ferat *editor of E.*

[a] Her aid to Theseus in his slaying of the Minotaur her brother, and his escape from the Labyrinth.

My father's realm forbids me to approach. Grant
I do glide with fortunate keel over peaceful seas,
that Aeolus tempers the winds—I still shall be an
exile! 'Tis not for me, O Crete composed of the
hundred cities, to look upon thee, land known to
the infant Jove! No, for my father and the land
ruled by my righteous father—dear names!—were
betrayed by my deed [a] when, to keep you, after your
victory, from death in the winding halls, I gave into
your hand the thread to direct your steps in place of
guide—when you said to me: "By these very perils
of mine, I swear that, so long as both of us shall live,
thou shalt be mine!"

75 We both live, Theseus, and I am not yours!—
if indeed a woman lives who is buried by the treason
of a perjured mate. Me, too, you should have
slain, O false one, with the same bludgeon that slew
my brother; then would the oath you gave me
have been absolved by my death. Now, I ponder
over not only what I am doomed to suffer, but all
that any woman left behind can suffer. There
rush into my thought a thousand forms of perishing,
and death holds less of dole for me than the delay
of death. Each moment, now here, now there, I
look to see wolves rush on me, to rend my vitals
with their greedy fangs. Who knows but that this
shore breeds, too, the tawny lion? Perchance the
island harbours the savage tiger as well. They say,
too, that the waters of the deep cast up the mighty
seal! And who is to keep the swords of men from
piercing my side?

89 But I care not, if I am but not left captive
in hard bonds, and not compelled to spin the
long task with servile hand—I, whose father is

cui pater est Minos, cui mater filia Phoebi,
    quodque magis memini, quae tibi pacta fui !
si mare, si terras porrectaque litora vidi,
    multa mihi terrae, multa minantur aquae.
caelum restabat—timeo simulacra deorum !   95
    destituor rapidis praeda cibusque feris ;
sive colunt habitantque viri, diffidimus illis—
    externos didici laesa timere viros.
Viveret Androgeos utinam ! nec facta luisses
    inpia funeribus, Cecropi terra, tuis ;   100
nec tua mactasset nodoso stipite, Theseu,
    ardua parte virum dextera, parte bovem ;
nec tibi, quae reditus monstrarent, fila dedissem,
    fila per adductas saepe recepta manus.
non equidem miror, si stat victoria tecum,   105
    strataque Cretaeam belua planxit[1] humum.
non poterant figi praecordia ferrea cornu ;
    ut te non tegeres, pectore tutus eras.
illic tu silices, illic adamanta tulisti,
    illic qui silices, Thesea, vincat, habes.   110
Crudeles somni, quid me tenuistis inertem ?
    aut semel aeterna nocte premenda fui.
vos quoque crudeles, venti, nimiumque parati
    flaminaque in lacrimas officiosa meas.
dextera crudelis, quae me fratremque necavit,   115
    et data poscenti, nomen inane, fides !

---

[1] planxit *Bent*.: stravit *P G*₂ *Plan*.: texit *G*₁ *Merk*.:
pressit *s Sedl*.: tinxit *ω Burm*.

---

[a] Androgeos, Ariadne's brother, was accidentally killed at
Athens.

Minos, whose mother the child of Phoebus, and who
—what memory holds more close—was promised
bride to you! When I have looked on the sea, and
on the land, and on the wide-stretching shore, I
know many dangers threaten me on land, and
many on the waters. The sky remains—yet there I
fear visions of the gods! I am left helpless, a prey
to the maws of ravening beasts; and if men dwell in
the place and keep it, I put no trust in them—my
hurts have taught me fear of stranger-men.

[99] O, that Androgeos were still alive, and that
thou, O Cecropian land, hadst not been made to
atone for thy impious deeds with the doom of thy
children! [a] and would that thy upraised right hand,
O Theseus, had not slain with knotty club him
that was man in part, and in part bull; and I had
not given thee the thread to show the way of thy
return—thread oft caught up again and passed
through the hands led on by it. I marvel not—ah,
no!—if victory was thine, and the monster smote
with his length the Cretan earth. His horn could not
have pierced that iron heart of thine; thy breast
was safe, even didst thou naught to shield thy-
self. There barest thou flint, there barest thou
adamant; there hast thou a Theseus harder than
any flint!

[111] Ah, cruel slumbers, why did you hold me
thus inert? Or, better had I been weighed down
once for all by everlasting night. You, too, were
cruel, O winds, and all too well prepared, and you
breezes, eager to start my tears. Cruel the right
hand that has brought me and my brother to our
death, and cruel the pledge—an empty word—that
you gave at my demand! Against me conspiring

in me iurarunt somnus ventusque fidesque;
    prodita sum causis una puella tribus!
Ergo ego nec lacrimas matris moritura videbo,
    nec, mea qui digitis lumina condat, erit?   120
spiritus infelix peregrinas ibit in auras,
    nec positos artus unguet amica manus?
ossa superstabunt volucres inhumata marinae?
    haec sunt officiis digna sepulcra meis?
ibis Cecropios portus patriaque receptus,   125
    cum steteris turbae [1] celsus in ore [2] tuae
et bene narraris letum taurique virique
    sectaque per dubias saxea tecta vias,
me quoque narrato sola tellure relictam!
    non ego sum titulis subripienda tuis.   130
nec pater est Aegeus, nec tu Pittheidos Aethrae
    filius; auctores saxa fretumque tui! [3]
Di facerent, ut me summa de puppe videres;
    movisset vultus maesta figura tuos!
nunc quoque non oculis, sed, qua potes, adspice
      mente   135
    haerentem scopulo, quem vaga pulsat aqua.
adspice demissos lugentis more capillos
    et tunicas lacrimis sicut ab imbre gravis.
corpus, ut inpulsae segetes aquilonibus, horret,
    litteraque articulo pressa tremente labat.   140
non te per meritum, quoniam male cessit, adoro;
    debita sit facto gratia nulla meo.
sed ne poena quidem! si non ego causa salutis,
    non tamen est, cur sis tu mihi causa necis.

[1] turbae *G ω* : turbes P₃ : urbis *P₂ s* : urbes P₁.
[2] in ore *G₁ Jahn Merk. Ehw.* : in aure *P₁* : in arce *P₂ V s* :
urbis . . . arce *Pa.*
[3] *vv.* 131, 132 *after* 110 *Birt Ehw.*

were slumber, wind, and treacherous pledge—treason three-fold against one maid!

[119] Am I, then, to die, and, dying, not behold my mother's tears; and shall there be no one's finger to close my eyes? Is my unhappy soul to go forth into stranger-air, and no friendly hand compose my limbs and drop on them the unguent due? Are my bones to lie unburied, the prey of hovering birds of the shore? Is this the entombment due to me for my kindnesses? You will go to the haven of Cecrops; but when you have been received back home, and have stood in pride before your thronging followers, gloriously telling the death of the man-and-bull, and of the halls of rock cut out in winding ways, tell, too, of me, abandoned on a solitary shore—for I must not be stolen from the record of your honours! Neither is Aegeus your father, nor are you the son of Pittheus' daughter Aethra; they who begot you were the rocks and the deep!

[133] Ah, I could pray the gods that you had seen me from the high stern; my sad figure had moved your heart! Yet look upon me now—not with eyes, for with them you cannot, but with your mind—clinging to a rock all beaten by the wandering wave. Look upon my locks, let loose like those of one in grief for the dead, and on my robes, heavy with tears as if with rain. My body is a-quiver like standing corn struck by the northern blast, and the letters I am tracing falter beneath my trembling hand. 'Tis not for my desert—for that has come to naught—that I entreat you now; let no favour be due for my service. Yet neither let me suffer for it! If I am not the cause of your deliverance, yet neither is it right that you should cause my death.

Has tibi plangendo lugubria pectora lassas   145
    infelix tendo trans freta longa manus ;
hos tibi—qui superant—ostendo maesta capillos !
    per lacrimas oro, quas tua facta movent—   150
flecte ratem, Theseu, versoque relabere vento !
    si prius occidero, tu tamen ossa feres !

XI

CANACE MACAREO

SIQUA tamen caecis errabunt scripta lituris,
    oblitus a dominae caede libellus erit.
dextra tenet calamum, strictum tenet altera ferrum,
    et iacet in gremio charta soluta meo.
haec est Aeolidos fratri scribentis imago ;   5
    sic videor duro posse placere patri.
Ipse necis cuperem nostrae spectator adesset,
    auctorisque oculis exigeretur opus !
ut ferus est multoque suis truculentior Euris,
    spectasset siccis vulnera nostra genis.   10
scilicet est aliquid, cum saevis vivere ventis ;
    ingenio populi convenit ille sui.
ille Noto Zephyroque et Sithonio Aquiloni
    imperat et pinnis, Eure proterve, tuis.
imperat heu ! ventis, tumidae non imperat irae,   15
    possidet et vitiis regna minora suis.

[145] These hands, wearied with beating of my sorrowful breast, unhappy I stretch toward you over the long seas; these locks—such as remain—in grief I bid you look upon! By these tears I pray you—tears moved by what you have done—turn about your ship, reverse your sail, glide swiftly back to me! If I have died before you come, 'twill yet be you who bear away my bones!

XI

CANACE TO MACAREUS

IF aught of what I write is yet blotted deep and escapes your eye, 'twill be because the little roll has been stained by its mistress' blood. My right hand holds the pen, a drawn blade the other holds, and the paper lies unrolled in my lap. This is the picture of Aeolus' daughter writing to her brother; in this guise, it seems, I may please my hard-hearted sire.

[7] I would he himself were here to view my end, and the deed were done before the eyes of him who orders it! Fierce as he is, far harsher than his own east-winds, he would look dry-eyed upon my wounds. Surely, something comes from a life with savage winds; his temper is like that of his subjects. It is Notus, and Zephyrus, and Sithonian Aquilo, over whom he rules, and over thy pinions, wanton Eurus. He rules the winds, alas! but his swelling wrath he does not rule, and the realms of his possession are less wide than his faults. Of what

quid iuvat admotam per avorum nomina caelo
   inter cognatos posse referre Iovem?
num minus infestum, funebria munera, ferrum
   feminea teneo, non mea tela, manu?   20
O utinam, Macareu, quae nos commisit in unum,
   venisset leto serior hora meo!
cur umquam plus me, frater, quam frater amasti,
   et tibi, non debet quod soror esse, fui?
ipsa quoque incalui, qualemque audire solebam,   25
   nescio quem sensi corde tepente deum.
fugerat ore color; macies adduxerat artus;
   sumebant minimos ora coacta cibos;
nec somni faciles et nox erat annua nobis,
   et gemitum nullo laesa dolore dabam.   30
nec, cur haec facerem, poteram mihi reddere causam
   nec noram, quid amans esset; at illud eram.
Prima malum nutrix animo praesensit anili;
   prima mihi nutrix "Aeoli," dixit, "amas!"
erubui, gremioque pudor deiecit ocellos;   35
   haec satis in tacita signa fatentis erant.
iamque tumescebant vitiati pondera ventris,
   aegraque furtivum membra gravabat onus.
quas mihi non herbas, quae non medicamina nutrix
   attulit audaci supposuitque manu,   40
ut penitus nostris—hoc te celavimus unum—
   visceribus crescens excuteretur onus!
a, nimium vivax admotis restitit infans
   artibus et tecto tutus ab hoste fuit!

avail for me through my grandsires' names to reach even to the skies, to be able to number Jove among my kin ? Is there less deadliness in the blade—my funeral gift !—that I hold in my woman's hand, weapon not meet for me ?

²¹ Ah, Macareus, would that the hour that made us two as one had come after my death ! Oh why, my brother, did you ever love me more than brother, and why have I been to you what a sister should not be ? I, too, was inflamed by love ; I felt some god in my glowing heart, and knew him from what I used to hear he was. My colour had fled from my face ; wasting had shrunk my frame ; I scarce took food, and with unwilling mouth ; my sleep was never easy, the night was a year for me, and I groaned, though stricken with no pain. Nor could I render myself a reason why I did these things ; I did not know what it was to be in love—yet in love I was.

³³ The first to perceive my trouble, in her old wife's way, was my nurse ; she first, my nurse, said : " Daughter of Aeolus, thou art in love ! " I blushed, and shame bent down my eyes into my bosom ; I said no word, but this was sign enough that I confessed. And presently there grew apace the burden of my wayward bosom, and my weakened frame felt the weight of its secret load. What herbs and what medicines did my nurse not bring to me, applying them with bold hand to drive forth entirely from my bosom—this was the only secret we kept from you—the burden that was increasing there ! Ah, too full of life, the little thing withstood the arts employed against it, and was kept safe from its hidden foe !

OVID

Iam noviens erat orta soror pulcherrima Phoebi, 45
    denaque [1] luciferos Luna movebat equos.
nescia, quae faceret subitos mihi causa dolores,
    et rudis ad partus et nova miles eram.
nec tenui vocem. " quid," ait, " tua crimina prodis ?"
    oraque clamantis conscia pressit anus. 50
quid faciam infelix ? gemitus dolor edere cogit,
    sed timor et nutrix et pudor ipse vetant.
contineo gemitus elapsaque verba reprendo
    et cogor lacrimas conbibere ipsa meas.
mors erat ante oculos, et opem Lucina negabat— 55
    et grave, si morerer, mors quoque crimen erat—
cum super incumbens scissa tunicaque comaque
    pressa refovisti pectora nostra tuis,
et mihi " vive, soror, soror o carissima," aisti ;
    " vive nec unius corpore perde duos ! 60
spes bona det vires ; fratri nam nupta futura es.[2]
    illius, de quo mater, et uxor eris."
Mortua, crede mihi, tamen ad tua verba revixi :
    et positum est uteri crimen onusque mei.
quid tibi grataris ? media sedet Aeolus aula ; 65
    crimina sunt oculis subripienda patris.
frugibus [3] infantem ramisque albentis olivae
    et levibus vittis sedula celat anus,
fictaque sacra facit dicitque precantia verba ;
    dat populus sacris, dat pater ipse viam. 70
iam prope limen erat—patrias vagitus ad auris
    venit, et indicio proditur ille suo !

[1] nonaque *P s Ehw.*: denaque *others*: pronaque *Bent.*
[2] *So G ω Merk.*: fratri es nam nuptura *P₂*: fratris nam
nupta futura es *Pα.*: germano nupta futura es *Ehw.*
[3] frugibus *P* : frondibus *G V Plan.*

136

⁴⁵ And now for the ninth time had Phoebus'
fairest sister risen, and for the tenth time the
moon was driving on her light-bearing steeds. I
knew not what caused the sudden pangs in me;
to travail I was unused, a soldier new to the service.
I could not keep from groans. "Why betray thy
fault?" said the ancient dame who knew my
secret, and stopped my crying lips. What shall I
do, unhappy that I am? The pains compel my groans,
but fear, the nurse, and shame itself forbid. I repress
my groans, and try to take back the words that slip
from me, and force myself to drink my very tears.
Death was before my eyes; and Lucina denied
her aid—death, too, were I to die, would fasten upon
me heavy guilt—when leaning over me, you tore
my robe and my hair away, and warmed my bosom
back to life with the pressure of your own, and said:
"Live, sister, sister O most dear; live, and do not
be the death of two beings in one! Let good hope
give thee strength; for now thou shalt be thy
brother's bride. He who made thee mother will
also make thee wife."

⁶³ Dead that I am, believe me, yet at your words
I live again, and have brought forth the reproach
and burden of my womb. But why rejoice? In the
midst of the palace hall sits Aeolus; the sign of my
fault must be removed from my father's eyes. With
fruits and whitening olive-branches, and with light
fillets, the careful dame attempts to hide the babe,
and makes pretence of sacrifice, and utters words of
prayer; the people give way to let her pass, my father
himself gives way. She is already near the threshold
—my father's ears have caught the crying sound, and
the babe is lost, betrayed by his own sign! Aeolus

eripit infantem mentitaque sacra revelat
    Aeolus ; insana regia voce sonat.
ut mare fit tremulum, tenui cum stringitur aura,   75
    ut quatitur tepido fraxina virga [1] Noto,
sic mea vibrari pallentia membra videres ;
    quassus ab inposito corpore lectus erat.
inruit et nostrum vulgat clamore pudorem,
    et vix a misero continet ore manus.   80
ipsa nihil praeter lacrimas pudibunda profudi ;
    torpuerat gelido lingua retenta metu.
Iamque dari parvum canibusque avibusque nepotem
    iusserat, in solis destituique locis.
vagitus dedit ille miser—sensisse putares—   85
    quaque suum poterat voce rogabat avum.
quid mihi tunc animi credis, germane, fuisse—
    nam potes ex animo colligere ipse tuo—
cum mea me coram silvas inimicus in altas
    viscera montanis ferret edenda lupis ?   90
exierat thalamo ; tunc demum pectora plangi
    contigit inque meas unguibus ire genas.
Interea patrius vultu maerente satelles
    venit et indignos edidit ore sonos :
" Aeolus hunc ensem mittit tibi " — tradidit
        ensem—   95
    " et iubet ex merito scire, quid iste velit."
scimus, et utemur violento fortiter ense ;
    pectoribus condam dona paterna meis.
his mea muneribus, genitor, conubia donas ?
    hac tua dote, pater, filia dives erit ?   100

[1] *The usual MSS. reading* : fraxinçieş virga *P* : fraxinus
icta *Pa.*

catches up the child and reveals the pretended sacrifice ; the whole palace resounds with his maddened cries. As the sea is set a-trembling when a light breeze passes o'er, as the ashen branch is shaken by the tepid breeze from the south, so might you have seen my blanching members quiver ; the couch was a-quake with the body that lay upon it. He rushes in and with cries makes known my shame to all, and scarce restrains his hand from my wretched face. Myself in my confusion did naught but pour forth tears ; my tongue had grown dumb with the icy chill of fear.

[83] And now he had ordered his little grandchild thrown to the dogs and birds, to be abandoned in some solitary place. The hapless babe broke forth in wailings—you would have thought he understood —and with what utterance he could entreated his grandsire. What heart do you think was mine then, O my brother—for you can judge from your own— when the enemy before my eyes bore away to the deep forests the fruit of my bosom to be devoured by mountain wolves? My father had gone out of my chamber ; then at length could I beat my breasts and furrow my cheeks with the nail.

[93] Meanwhile with sorrowful air came one of my father's guards, and pronounced these shameful words : " Aeolus sends this sword to you "—he handed me the sword—" and bids you know from your desert what it may mean." I do know, and shall bravely make use of the violent blade ; I shall bury in my breast my father's gift. Is it presents like this, O my sire, you give me on my marriage ? With this dowry from you, O father, shall your daughter be made rich ? Take away afar, deluded

OVID

tolle procul, decepte, faces, Hymenaee, maritas
    et fuge turbato tecta nefanda pede !
ferte faces in me quas fertis, Erinyes atrae,
    et meus ex isto luceat igne rogus !
nubite felices Parca meliore sorores,   105
    amissae memores sed tamen este mei !
Quid puer admisit tam paucis editus horis ?
    quo laesit facto vix bene natus avum ?
si potuit meruisse necem, meruisse putetur—
    a, miser admisso plectitur ille meo !   110
nate, dolor matris, rapidarum [1] praeda ferarum.
    ei mihi ! natali dilacerate tuo ;
nate, parum fausti miserabile pignus amoris—
    haec tibi prima dies, haec tibi summa fuit.
non mihi te licuit lacrimis perfundere iustis,   115
    in tua non tonsas ferre sepulcra comas ;
non super incubui, non oscula frigida carpsi.
    diripiunt avidae viscera nostra ferae.
Ipsa quoque infantis cum vulnere prosequar umbras
    nec mater fuero dicta nec orba diu.   120
tu tamen, o frustra miserae sperate sorori,
    sparsa, precor, nati collige membra tui,
et refer ad matrem socioque inpone sepulcro,
    urnaque nos habeat quamlibet arta duos !
vive memor nostri, lacrimasque in vulnera funde, 125
    neve reformida corpus amantis amans.
tu, rogo,[2] dilectae nimium mandata sororis
    perfer ; mandatum persequar ipsa patris !

---

[1] rabidarum s *Bent.*
[2] tura rogo placitae . . . tu fer *Pa.*

Hymenaeus, thy wedding-torches, and fly with frightened foot from these nefarious halls! Bring for me the torches ye bear, Erinyes dark, and let my funeral pyre blaze bright from the fires ye give! Wed happily under a better fate, O my sisters, but yet remember me though lost!

[107] What crime could the babe commit, with so few hours of life? With what act could he, scarce born, do harm to his grandsire? If it could be he deserved his death, let it be judged he did—ah, wretched child, it is my fault he suffers for! O my son, grief of thy mother, prey of the ravening beasts, ah me! torn limb from limb on thy day of birth; O my son, miserable pledge of my unhallowed love—this was the first of days for thee, and this for thee the last. Fate did not permit me to shed o'er thee the tears I owed, nor to bear to thy tomb the shorn lock; I have not bent o'er thee, nor culled the kiss from thy cold lips. Greedy wild beasts are rending in pieces the child my womb put forth.

[119] I, too, shall follow the shades of my babe— shall deal myself the stroke—and shall not long have been called or mother or bereaved. Do thou, nevertheless, O hoped for in vain by thy wretched sister, collect, I entreat, the scattered members of thy son, and bring them again to their mother to share her sepulchre, and let one urn, however scant, possess us both! O live, and forget me not; pour forth thy tears upon my wounds, nor shrink from her thou once didst love, and who loved thee! Do thou, I pray, fulfil the behests of the sister thou didst love too well; the behest of my father I shall myself perform!

OVID

XII

Medea Iasoni

At tibi Colchorum, memini, regina vacavi,
　　ars mea cum peteres ut tibi ferret opem.
tunc quae dispensant mortalia fata [1] sorores
　　debuerant fusos evoluisse meos.
tum potui Medea mori bene! quidquid ab illo　　　　5
　　produxi vitam [2] tempore, poena fuit.
Ei mihi! cur umquam iuvenalibus acta lacertis
　　Phrixeam petiit Pelias arbor ovem?
cur umquam Colchi Magnetida vidimus Argon,
　　turbaque Phasiacam Graia bibistis aquam?　　　10
cur mihi plus aequo flavi placuere capilli
　　et decor et linguae gratia ficta tuae?
aut, semel in nostras quoniam nova puppis harenas
　　venerat audacis attuleratque viros,
isset anhelatos non praemedicatus in ignes　　　　15
　　inmemor Aesonides oraque adusta boum;
semina iecisset,[3] totidemque et [4] semina et hostes,
　　ut caderet cultu cultor ab ipse suo!
quantum perfidiae tecum, scelerate, perisset,
　　dempta forent capiti quam mala multa meo!　　20

---

[1] fata *G ω*: facta *P*: fila *s Hein. Pa.*　　　[2] vitae *ω.*
[3] iecisset *P G*: sensisset *s*: sevisset *Hein. Merk. Pa.*
[4] totidemque et *P*: totidem quod *G*: quot *Pa.*

---

[a] Medea begins suddenly, as if in answer to a refusal of
Jason to listen to her plea.
　　Euripides wrote a *Medea*, and was followed by Ennius,

XII

MEDEA TO JASON

AND yet[a] for you, I remember, I the queen of Colchis could find time, when you besought that my art might bring you help. Then was the time when the sisters who pay out the fated thread of mortal life should have unwound for aye my spindle. Then could Medea have ended well! Whatever of life has been lengthened out for me from that time forth has been but punishment.

[7] Ah me! why was the ship from the forests of Pelion ever driven over the seas by strong young arms in quest of the ram of Phrixus?[b] Why did we Colchians ever cast eye upon Magnesian Argo, and why did your Greek crew ever drink of the waters of the Phasis? Why did I too greatly delight in those golden locks of yours, in your comely ways, and in the false graces of your tongue? Yet delight too greatly I did—else, when once the strange craft had been beached upon our sands and brought us her bold crew, all unanointed would the unremembering son of Aeson have gone forth to meet the fires exhaled from the flame-scorched nostrils of the bulls; he would have scattered the seeds—as many as the seeds were the enemy, too—for the sower himself to fall in strife with his own sowing! How much perfidy, vile wretch, would have perished with you, and how many woes been averted from my head!

Accius, and Ovid himself, whose play is lost, and Seneca. In this letter Ovid draws from Euripides and Apollonius Rhodius, *Argonautica* III and IV.   [b] See Index.

Est aliqua ingrato meritum exprobrare voluptas.
    hac fruar ; haec de te gaudia sola feram.
iussus inexpertam Colchos advertere puppim
    intrasti patriae regna beata meae.
hoc illic Medea fui, nova nupta quod hic est ;   25
    quam pater est illi, tam mihi dives erat.
hic Ephyren bimarem, Scythia tenus ille nivosa
    omne tenet, Ponti qua plaga laeva iacet.
Accipit hospitio iuvenes Aeeta Pelasgos,
    et premitis pictos, corpora Graia, toros.   30
tunc ego te vidi, tunc coepi scire, quis esses ;
    illa fuit mentis prima ruina meae.
et vidi et perii ; nec notis ignibus arsi,
    ardet ut ad magnos pinea taeda deos.
et formosus eras, et me mea fata trahebant ;   35
    abstulerant oculi lumina nostra tui.
perfide, sensisti—quis enim bene celat amorem ?
    eminet indicio prodita flamma suo.
Dicitur interea tibi lex ut dura ferorum
    insolito premeres vomere colla boum.   40
Martis erant tauri plus quam per cornua saevi,
    quorum terribilis spiritus ignis erat ;
aere pedes solidi praetentaque naribus aera,
    nigra per adflatus haec quoque facta suos.
semina praeterea populos genitura iuberis   45
    spargere devota lata per arva manu,
qui peterent natis secum tua corpora telis ;
    illa est agricolae messis iniqua suo.

---

^a Corinth.

THE HEROIDES XII

²¹ 'Tis some pleasure to reproach the ungrateful with favours done. That pleasure I will enjoy; that is the only delight I shall win from you. Bidden to turn the hitherto untried craft to the shores of Colchis, you set foot in the rich realms of my native land. There I, Medea, was what here your new bride is; as rich as her sire is, so rich was mine. Hers holds Ephyre,ᵃ washed by two seas; mine, all the country which lies along the left strand of the Pontus e'en to the snows of Scythia.

²⁹ Aeëtes welcomes to his home the Pelasgian youths, and you rest your Greek limbs upon the pictured couch. Then 'twas that I saw you, then began to know you; that was the first impulse to the downfall of my soul. I saw you, and I was undone; nor did I kindle with ordinary fires, but like the pine-torch kindled before the mighty gods. Not only were you noble to look upon, but my fates were dragging me to doom; your eyes had robbed mine of their power to see. Traitor, you saw it—for who can well hide love? Its flame shines forth its own betrayer.

³⁹ Meanwhile the condition is imposed that you press the hard necks of the fierce bulls at the unaccustomed plow. To Mars the bulls belonged, raging with more than mere horns, for their breathing was of terrible fire; of solid bronze were their feet, wrought round with bronze their nostrils, made black, too, by the blasts of their own breath. Besides this, you are bidden to scatter with obedient hand over the wide fields the seeds that should beget peoples to assail you with weapons born with themselves; a baneful harvest, that, to its own husbandman. The eyes of the guardian that

lumina custodis succumbere nescia somno,
  ultimus est aliqua decipere arte labor.   50
Dixerat Aeetes ; maesti consurgitis omnes,
  mensaque purpureos deserit alta toros.
quam tibi tunc longe regnum dotale Creusae
  et socer et magni nata Creontis erat ?
tristis abis ; oculis abeuntem prosequor udis,   55
  et dixit tenui murmure lingua : " vale ! "
ut positum tetigi thalamo male saucia lectum,
  acta est per lacrimas nox mihi, quanta fuit ;
ante oculos taurique meos segetesque nefandae,
  ante meos oculos pervigil anguis erat.   60
hinc amor, hinc timor est ; ipsum timor auget
    amorem.
  mane erat, et thalamo cara recepta soror[a]
disiectamque comas adversaque [1] in ora iacentem
  invenit, et lacrimis omnia plena meis.
orat opem Minyis. alter petit, alter habebit ; [2]   65
  Aesonio iuveni quod rogat illa, damus.
Est nemus et piceis et frondibus ilicis atrum ;
  vix illuc radiis solis adire licet.
sunt in eo—fuerant certe—delubra Dianae ;
  aurea barbarica stat dea facta manu.   70
noscis ? an exciderunt mecum loca ? venimus illuc.
  orsus es infido sic prior ore loqui :
" ius tibi et arbitrium nostrae fortuna salutis
  tradidit, inque tua est vitaque morsque manu.

---

[1] adversaque *P G ω Merk Ehw.*: aversaque *V s Burm. Sedl.*
[2] So *P₂ Sedl.*: petit altera et altera habebit *P₂ G s Burm.*:
petit altera et altera habebat *ω Jahn.*

---

[a] Chalciope.

know not yielding to sleep—by some art to elude them is your final task.

[51] Aeëtes had spoken; in gloom you all rise up, and the high table is removed from the purple-spread couches. How far away then from your thought were Creusa's dowry-realm, and the daughter of great Creon, and Creon the father of your bride! With foreboding you depart; and as you go my moist eyes follow you, and in faint murmur comes from my tongue: "Fare thou well!" Laying myself on the ordered couch within my chamber, grievously wounded, in tears I passed the whole night long; before my eyes appeared the bulls and the dreadful harvest, before my eyes the un-sleeping serpent. On the one hand was love, on the other, fear; and fear increased my very love. Morning came, and my dear sister,[a] admitted to my chamber, found me with loosened hair and lying prone upon my face, and everywhere my tears. She implores aid for your Minyae. What one asks, another is to receive; what she petitions for the Aesonian youth, I grant.

[67] There is a grove, sombre with pine-trees and the fronds of the ilex; into it scarce can the rays of the sun find way. There is in it—there was, at least—a shrine to Diana, wherein stands the goddess, a golden image fashioned by barbaric hand. Do you know the place? or have places fallen from your mind along with me? We came to the spot. You were the first to speak, with those faithless lips, and these were your words: "To thy hand fortune has committed the right of choosing or not my deliverance, and in thy hand are the ways of life and death for me. To have power to ruin

perdere posse sat est, siquem iuvet ipsa potestas ; 75
    sed tibi servatus gloria maior ero.
per mala nostra precor, quorum potes esse levamen,
    per genus, et numen cuncta videntis avi,
per triplicis vultus arcanaque sacra Dianae,
    et si forte aliquos gens habet ista deos— 80
o virgo, miserere mei, miserere meorum ;
    effice me meritis tempus in omne tuum !
quodsi forte virum non dedignare Pelasgum—
    sed mihi tam faciles unde meosque deos ?—
spiritus ante meus tenues vanescat in auras 85
    quam thalamo nisi tu nupta sit ulla meo !
conscia sit Iuno sacris praefecta maritis,
    et dea marmorea cuius in aede sumus ! ''
Haec animum—et quota pars haec sunt !—movere
    puellae
    simplicis, et dextrae dextera iuncta meae. 90
vidi etiam lacrimas—an pars est fraudis[1] in illis ?
    sic cito sum verbis capta puella tuis.
iungis et aeripedes inadusto corpore tauros
    et solidam iusso vomere findis humum.
arva venenatis pro semine dentibus inples ; 95
    nascitur et gladios scutaque miles habet.
ipsa ego, quae dederam medicamina, pallida sedi,
    cum vidi subitos arma tenere viros ;
donec terrigenae, facinus mirabile, fratres
    inter se strictas conseruere manus. 100

[1] a! pars est *L. Mueller* : an et ars est *Sedl.*: an et est pars *some of the early editions.*

148

is enough, if anyone delight in power for itself; but to save me will be greater glory. By our misfortunes, which thou hast power to relieve, I pray, by thy line, and by the godhead of thy all-seeing grandsire the sun, by the three-fold face and holy mysteries of Diana, and by the gods of that race of thine—if so be gods it have—by all these, O maiden, have pity upon me, have pity on my men; be kind to me and make me thine for ever! And if it chance thou dost not disdain a Pelasgian suitor—but how can I hope the gods will be so facile to my wish?—may my spirit vanish away into thin air before another than thou shall come a bride to my chamber! My witness be Juno, ward of the rites of wedlock, and the goddess in whose marble shrine we stand!"

[89] Words like these—and how slight a part of them is here!—and your right hand clasped with mine, moved the heart of the simple maid. I saw even tears—or was there in the tears, too, part of your deceit? Thus quickly was I ensnared, girl that I was, by your words. You yoke together the bronze-footed bulls with your body unharmed by their fire, and cleave the solid mould with the share, as you were bid. The ploughed fields you sow full with envenomed teeth in place of seed; and there rises out of the earth, with sword and shield, a warrior band. Myself, the giver of the charmèd drug, sat pallid there at sight of men all suddenly arisen and in arms; until the earth-born brothers—O deed most wonderful!—drew arms and came to the grapple each with each.

OVID

Insopor ecce vigil [1] squamis crepitantibus horrens
    sibilat et torto pectore verrit humum !
dotis opes ubi erant ? ubi erat tibi regia coniunx,
    quique maris gemini distinet Isthmos aquas ?
illa ego, quae tibi sum nunc denique barbara
       facta,   105
    nunc tibi sum pauper, nunc tibi visa nocens,
flammea subduxi medicato lumina somno,
    et tibi, quae raperes, vellera tuta dedi.
proditus est genitor, regnum patriamque reliqui ;
    munus, in exilio quod licet esse, tuli !   110
virginitas facta est peregrini praeda latronis ;
    optima cum cara matre relicta soror.
At non te fugiens sine me, germane, reliqui !
    deficit hoc uno littera nostra loco.
quod facere ausa mea est, non audet scribere
       dextra.   115
    sic ego, sed tecum, dilaceranda fui.
nec tamen extimui—quid enim post illa timerem ?—
    credere me pelago, femina iamque nocens.
numen ubi est ? ubi di ? meritas subeamus in alto,
    tu fraudis poenas, credulitatis ego !   120
Compressos utinam Symplegades elisissent,
    nostraque adhaererent ossibus ossa tuis ;
aut nos Scylla rapax canibus mersisset [2] edendos—
    debuit ingratis Scylla nocere viris ;
quaeque vomit totidem fluctus totidemque resor-
       bet,   125
    nos quoque Trinacriae supposuisset aquae !

---

[1] *So* P_1 G_1 *Merk.*: Pervigil ecce draco P_2 ω *Burm.*: insuper
ecce vigil *Hein.*: insopor ecce draco *Pa.*
[2] mersisset *Pa.*: misisset *MSS.*

---

    [a] The dismemberment of her brother Absyrtus.

[101] Then, lo and behold! all a-bristle with rattling scales, comes the unsleeping sentinel, hissing and sweeping the ground with winding belly. Where then was your rich dowry? Where then your royal consort, and the Isthmus that sunders the waters of two seas? I, the maiden who am now at last become a barbarian in your eyes, who now am poor, who now seem baneful—I closed the lids of the flame-like eyes in slumber wrought by my drug, and gave into your hand the fleece to steal away unharmed. I betrayed my sire, I left my throne and my native soil; the reward I get is leave to live in exile! My maidenly innocence has become the spoil of a pirate from overseas; beloved mother and best of sisters I have left behind.

[113] But thee, O my brother, I did not leave behind as I fled! In this one place my pen fails. Of the deed my right hand was bold enough to do,[a] it is not bold enough to write. So I, too, should have been torn limb from limb—but with thee! And yet I did not fear—for what, after that, could I fear?— to trust myself to the sea, woman though I was, and now with guilt upon me. Where is heavenly justice? Where the gods? Let the penalty that is our due overtake us on the deep—you for your treachery, me for my trustfulness!

[121] Would the Symplegades had caught and crushed us out together, and that my bones were clinging now to yours; or Scylla the ravening submerged us in the deep to be devoured by her dogs —fit were it for Scylla to work woe to ingrate men! And she who spews forth so many times the floods, and sucks them so many times back in again—would she had brought us, too, beneath the Trinacrian

OVID

sospes ad Haemonias victorque reverteris urbes ;
    ponitur ad patrios aurea lana deos.
Quid referam Peliae natas pietate nocentes
    caesaque virginea membra paterna manu ?   130
ut culpent alii, tibi me laudare necesse est,
    pro quo sum totiens esse coacta nocens.
ausus es—o, iusto desunt sua verba dolori !—
    ausus es " Aesonia," dicere, " cede domo ! "
iussa domo cessi natis comitata duobus   135
    et, qui me sequitur semper, amore tui.
ut subito nostras Hymen cantatus ad aures
    venit, et accenso lampades igne micant,
tibiaque effundit socialia carmina vobis,
    at mihi funerea flebiliora tuba,   140
pertimui, nec adhuc tantum scelus esse putabam ;
    sed tamen in toto pectore frigus erat.
turba ruunt et " Hymen," clamant, " Hymenaee ! "
    frequenter—
    quo propior vox haec, hoc mihi peius erat.
diversi flebant servi lacrimasque tegebant—   145
    quis vellet tanti nuntius esse mali ?
me quoque, quidquid erat, potius nescire iuvabat ;
    sed tamquam scirem, mens mea tristis erat,
cum minor e pueris iussus [1] studioque videndi
    constitit ad geminae limina prima foris.   150
" hinc" [2] mihi " mater, abi ! [3] pompam pater,"
    inquit, " Iason
    ducit et adiunctos aureus urget equos ! "

[1] iussus *P G Plan.*: lassus *Pa.*
[2] hic *s Hein.*   [3] abi *P* : adi *Ehw.*

---

[a] At the persuasion of Medea, who wished to avenge Jason, they attempted the rejuvenation of their father by dismembering and boiling him in a supposed magic cauldron.
[b] They were still in the palace. Palmer, who reads *lassus* and *abi*, pictures Medea and her son in the street.

wave! Yet unharmed and victorious you return to Haemonia's towns, and the golden fleece is laid before your fathers' gods.

[129] Why rehearse the tale of Pelias' daughters, by devotion led to evil deeds—of how their maiden hands laid knife to the members of their sire?[a] I may be blamed by others, but you perforce must praise me—you, for whom so many times I have been driven to crime. Yet you have dared—O, fit words fail me for my righteous wrath!—you have dared to say : " Withdraw from the palace of Aeson's line!" At your bidding I have withdrawn from your palace, taking with me our two children, and— what follows me evermore—my love for you. When, all suddenly, there came to my ears the chant of Hymen, and to my eyes the gleam of blazing torches, and the pipe poured forth its notes, for you a wedding-strain, but for me a strain more tearful than the funeral trump, I was filled with fear; I did not yet believe such monstrous guilt could be; but all my breast none the less grew chill. The throng pressed eagerly on, crying " Hymen, O Hymen-aeus!" in full chorus—the nearer the cry, for me the more dreadful. My slaves turned away and wept, seeking to hide their tears—who would be willing messenger of tidings so ill? Whatever it was, 'twas better, indeed, that I not know; but my heart was heavy, as if I really knew, when the younger of the children, at my bidding, and eager for the sight, went and stood at the outer threshold of the double door. "Here, mother, come out!"[b] he cries to me. "A procession is coming, and my father Jason leading it. He's all in gold, and driving a team of horses!" Then straight I rent my cloak

153

protinus abscissa planxi mea pectora veste,
 tuta nec a digitis ora fuere meis.
ire animus mediae suadebat in agmina turbae   155
 sertaque conpositis demere rapta comis;
vix me continui, quin sic laniata capillos
 clamarem "meus est!" iniceremque manus.
Laese pater, gaude! Colchi gaudete relicti!
 inferias umbrae fratris habete mei;   160
deseror amissis regno patriaque domoque
 coniuge, qui nobis omnia solus erat!
serpentis igitur potui taurosque furentes;
 unum non potui perdomuisse virum,
quaeque feros pepuli doctis medicatibus ignes,   165
 non valeo flammas effugere ipsa meas.
ipsi me cantus herbaeque artesque relinquunt;
 nil dea, nil Hecates sacra potentis agunt.
non mihi grata dies; noctes vigilantur amarae,
 et tener a misero pectore somnus abit.[1]   170
quae me non possum, potui sopire draconem;
 utilior cuivis quam mihi cura mea est.
quos ego servavi, paelex amplectitur artus,
 et nostri fructus illa laboris habet.
Forsitan et, stultae dum te iactare maritae   175
 quaeris et iniustis auribus apta loqui,
in faciem moresque meos nova crimina fingas.
 rideat et vitiis laeta sit illa meis!
rideat et Tyrio iaceat sublimis in ostro—
 flebit et ardores vincet adusta meos!   180
dum ferrum flammaeque aderunt sucusque veneni,
 hostis Medeae nullus inultus erit!

---

[1] *So Pa.*: nec ten//ra misero pectore somnus habet *P* :
nec tener ah miserae pectora somnus habet *or* alit *Hein.*

---

[a] Creusa and her father will really be consumed in the fire,
with the palace.

and beat my breast and cried aloud, and my cheeks were at the mercy of my nails. My heart impelled me to rush into the midst of the moving throng, to tear off the wreaths from my ordered locks; I scarce could keep from crying out, thus with hair all torn, " He is mine!" and laying hold on you.

159 Ah, injured father, rejoice! Rejoice, ye Colchians whom I left! Shades of my brother, receive in my fate your sacrifice due; I am abandoned; I have lost my throne, my native soil, my home, my husband—who alone for me took the place of all! Dragons and maddened bulls, it seems, I could subdue; a man alone I could not; I, who could beat back fierce fire with wise drugs, have not the power to escape the flames of my own passion. My very incantations, herbs, and arts abandon me; naught does my goddess aid me, naught the sacrifice I make to potent Hecate. I take no pleasure in the day; my nights are watches of bitterness, and gentle sleep is far departed from my wretched soul. I, who could charm the dragon to sleep, can bring none to myself; my effort brings more good to any one else soever than to me. The limbs I saved, a wanton now embraces; 'tis she who reaps the fruit of my toil.

175 Perhaps, too, when you wish to make boast to your stupid mate and say what will pleasure her unjust ears, you will fashion strange slanders against my face and against my ways. Let her make merry and be joyful over my faults! Let her make merry, and lie aloft on the Tyrian purple—she shall weep, and the flames [a] that consume her will surpass my own! While sword and fire are at my hand, and the juice of poison, no foe of Medea shall go unpunished!

Quodsi forte preces praecordia ferrea tangunt,
    nunc animis audi verba minora meis!
tam tibi sum supplex, quam tu mihi saepe fuisti, 185
    nec moror ante tuos procubuisse pedes.
si tibi sum vilis, communis respice natos;
    saeviet in partus dira noverca meos.
et nimium similes tibi sunt, et imagine tangor,
    et quotiens video, lumina nostra madent.   190
per superos oro, per avitae lumina flammae,
    per meritum et natos, pignora nostra, duos—
redde torum, pro quo tot res insana reliqui;
    adde fidem dictis auxiliumque refer!
non ego te inploro contra taurosque virosque,   195
    utque tua serpens victa quiescat ope;
te peto, quem merui, quem nobis ipse dedisti,
    cum quo sum pariter facta parente parens.
Dos ubi sit, quaeris?   campo numeravimus illo,
    qui tibi laturo vellus arandus erat.   200
aureus ille aries villo spectabilis alto
    dos mea, quam, dicam si tibi "redde!" neges.
dos mea tu sospes; dos est mea Graia iuventus!
    i nunc, Sisyphias, inprobe, confer opes!
quod vivis, quod habes nuptam socerumque
    potentis,   205
    hoc ipsum, ingratus quod potes esse, meum est.
quos equidem actutum—sed quid praedicere poenam
    attinet? ingentis parturit ira minas.

[183] But if it chance my entreaties touch a heart of iron, list now to my words—words too humble for my proud soul! I am as much a suppliant to you as you have often been to me, and I hesitate not to cast myself at your feet. If I am cheap in your eyes, be kind to our common offspring; a hard stepdame will be cruel to the fruitage of my womb. Their resemblance to you is all too great, and I am touched by the likeness; and as often as I see them, my eyes drop tears. By the gods above, by the light of your grandsire's beams, by my favours to you, and by the two children who are our mutual pledge—restore me to the bed for which I madly left so much behind; be faithful to your promises, and come to my aid as I came to yours! I do not implore you to go forth against bulls and men, nor ask your aid to quiet and overcome a dragon; it is you I ask for,—you, whom I have earned, whom you yourself gave to me, by whom I became a mother, as you by me a father.

[199] Where is my dowry, you ask? On the field I counted it out—that field which you had to plough before you could bear away the fleece. The famous golden ram, sightly for deep flock, is my dowry— the which, should I say to you "Restore it!" you would refuse to render up. My dowry is yourself— saved; my dowry is the band of Grecian youth! Go now, wretch, compare with that your wealth of Sisyphus! That you are alive, that you take to wife one who, with the father she brings you, is of kingly station, that you have the very power of being ingrate—you owe to me. Whom, hark you, I will straight—but what boots it to foretell your penalty? My ire is in travail with mighty threats. Whither

quo feret ira, sequar ! facti fortasse pigebit—
   et piget infido consuluisse viro.   210
viderit ista deus, qui nunc mea pectora versat !
   nescio quid certe mens mea maius agit !

XIII

Laudamia Protesilao.

Mittit et optat amans, quo mittitur, ire salutem
   Haemonis Haemonio Laudamia[1] viro.
Aulide te fama est vento retinente morari.
   a, me cum fugeres, hic ubi ventus erat?
tum freta debuerant vestris obsistere remis ;   5
   illud erat saevis utile tempus aquis.
oscula plura viro mandataque plura dedissem ;
   et sunt quae volui dicere multa tibi.
raptus es hinc praeceps, et qui tua vela vocaret,
   quem cuperent nautae, non ego, ventus erat ; 10
ventus erat nautis aptus, non aptus amanti.
   solvor ab amplexu, Protesilae, tuo,
linguaque mandantis verba inperfecta reliquit ;
   vix illud potui dicere triste " vale ! "
Incubuit Boreas abreptaque vela tetendit,   15
   iamque meus longe Protesilaus erat.
dum potui spectare virum, spectare iuvabat,
   sumque tuos oculos usque secuta meis ;

---

      [1] Laudamia *G ω* : Laudomia *P V*.

---

   [a] Homer, *Il.* ii. 695 ff., refers to the story of Protesilaus,
and Euripides uses it in his *Protesilaus*. Compare also
Hyginus, *Fab.* ciii.
   [b] With the rest of the Greek fleet, which was under divine

my ire leads, will I follow. Mayhap I shall repent
me of what I do—but I repent me, too, of regard for
a faithless husband's good. Be that the concern of
the god who now embroils my heart! Something
portentous, surely, is working in my soul!

XIII

LAODAMIA TO PROTESILAUS

GREETINGS and health Haemonian Laodamia sends
her Haemonian lord,[a] and desires with loving heart
they go where they are sent.

[3] Report says you are held at Aulis by the wind.[b]
Ah, when you were leaving me behind, where then
was this wind? Then should the seas have risen
to stay your oars; that was the fitting time for
the floods to rage. I could have given my lord
more kisses and laid upon him more behests; and
many are the things I wished to say to you. But
you were swept headlong hence; and the wind that
invited forth your sails was one your seamen longed
for, not I; it was a wind suited to seamen, not to
one who loved. I must needs loose myself from
your embrace, Protesilaus, and my tongue leave half
unsaid what I would enjoin; scarce had I time to
say that sad "Farewell!"

[15] Boreas came swooping down, seized on and
stretched your sails, and my Protesilaus soon was far
away. As long as I could gaze upon my lord, to
gaze was my delight, and I followed your eyes ever

displeasure because Agamemnon had killed a stag in the
grove of Diana.

ut te non poteram, poteram tua vela videre,
  vela diu vultus detinuere meos.   20
at postquam nec te nec vela fugacia vidi,
  et quod spectarem nil nisi pontus erat,
lux quoque tecum abiit, tenebrisque exanguis
    obortis
  succiduo dicor procubuisse genu.
vix socer Iphiclus, vix me grandaevus Acastus,   25
  vix mater gelida maesta refecit aqua ;
officium fecere pium, sed inutile nobis.
  indignor miserae non licuisse mori !
Ut rediit animus, pariter rediere dolores.
  pectora legitimus casta momordit amor.   30
nec mihi pectendos cura est praebere capillos,
  nec libet aurata corpora veste tegi.
ut quas pampinea tetigisse Bicorniger hasta,
  creditur, huc illuc, qua furor egit, eo.
conveniunt matres Phylaceides [1] et mihi clamant : 35
  " Indue regales, Laudamia, sinus !"
scilicet ipsa geram saturatas murice vestes,
  bella sub Iliacis moenibus ille geret ?
ipsa comas pectar, galea caput ille premetur ?
  ipsa novas vestes, dura vir arma feret ?   40
qua [2] possum, squalore tuos imitata labores
  dicar, et haec belli tempora tristis agam.
Dyspari Priamide, damno formose tuorum,
  tam sis hostis iners, quam malus hospes eras !

---

[1] phylaceides $P_2\omega$: phyleides P_1 : phylleides *Hein.*
Phyllos was a well known town in Thessaly.
[2] Qua P_1 : quo $P_2\omega$.

---

[a] The bacchic frenzy.

with my own; when I could no longer see you, I
still could see your sails, and long your sails detained
my eyes. But after I descried no more either you
or your flying sails, and what my eyes rested on was
naught but only sea, the light, too, went away with
you, the darkness rose about me, my blood retreated,
and with failing knee I sank, they say, upon the
ground. Scarce your sire Iphiclus, scarce mine, the
aged Acastus, scarce my mother, stricken with grief,
could bring me back to life with water icy-cold.
They did their kindly task, but it had no profit for
me. 'Tis shame I had not in my misery the right
to die!

[29] When consciousness returned, my pain returned
as well. The wifely love I bore you has torn at my
faithful heart. I care not now to let my hair be
dressed, nor does it pleasure me to be arrayed in
robes of gold. Like those whom he of the two
horns is believed to have touched with his vine-
leafed rod, hither and thither I go, where madness
drives.[a] The matrons of Phylace gather about, and
cry to me: " Put on thy royal robes, Laodamia ! "
Shall I, then, go clad in stuffs that are saturate with
costly purple, while my lord goes warring under the
walls of Ilion? Am I to dress my hair, while his
head is weighed down by the helm? Am I to wear
new apparel while my lord wears hard and heavy
arms? In what I can, they shall say I imitate your
toils—in rude attire; and these times of war I will
pass in gloom.

[43] Ill-omened Paris, Priam's son, fair at cost of
thine own kin, mayst thou be as inert a foe as
thou wert a faithless guest! Would that either

aut te Taenariae faciem culpasse maritae,   45
    aut illi vellem displicuisse tuam !
tu, qui pro rapta nimium, Menelae, laboras,
    ei mihi, quam multis flebilis ultor eris !
di, precor, a nobis omen removete sinistrum,
    et sua det Reduci vir meus arma Iovi !   50
sed timeo, quotiens subiit miserabile bellum ;
    more nivis lacrimae sole madentis eunt.
Ilion et Tenedos Simoisque et Xanthus et Ide
    nomina sunt ipso paene timenda sono.
nec rapere ausurus, nisi se defendere posset,   55
    hospes erat ; vires noverat ille suas.
venerat, ut fama est, multo spectabilis auro
    quique suo Phrygias corpore ferret opes,
classe virisque potens, per quae fera bella geruntur—
    et sequitur regni pars quotacumque sui ?   60
his ego te victam, consors Ledaea gemellis,
    suspicor ; haec Danais posse nocere puto.[1]
Hectora, quisquis is est, si sum tibi cara, caveto ;   65
    signatum memori pectore nomen habe !
hunc ubi vitaris, alios vitare memento
    et multos illic Hectoras esse puta ;
et facito ut dicas, quotiens pugnare parabis :
    "parcere me iussit Laudamia sibi."   70
si cadere Argolico fas est sub milite Troiam,
    te quoque non ullum vulnus habente cadat !
pugnet et adversos tendat Menelaus in hostis ;[2]
    hostibus e mediis nupta petenda viro est.   76

---

[1] 63, 64 *spurious Pa.* :
    Hectora nescio quem timeo : Paris Hectora dixit
      ferrea sanguinea bella movere manu ;
[2] 74, 75 *spurious Merk. Pa.* :
    ut rapiat Paridi quam Paris ante sibi
    inruat et causa quem vicit, vincat et armis :

thou hadst seen fault in the face of the Taenarian
wife, or she had taken no pleasure in thine ! Thou,
Menelaus, who dost grieve o'ermuch for the stolen
one, ah me, how many shall shed tears for thy
revenge ! Ye gods, I pray, keep from us the sinister
omen, and let my lord hang up his arms to Jove-of-
Safe-Return ! But I am fearful as oft as the
wretched war comes to my thoughts ; my tears come
forth like snow that melts beneath the sun. Ilion
and Tenedos and Simois and Xanthus and Ida are
names to be feared from their very sound. Nor would
the stranger have dared the theft if he had not power
to defend himself ; his own strength he well knew.
He arrived, they say, sightly in much gold, bearing
upon his person the wealth of Phrygia, and potent
in ships and men, with which fierce wars are fought
—and how great a part of his princely power came
with him ? With means like these were you over-
come, I suspect, O Leda's daughter, sister to the
Twins ; these are the things I feel may be working
the Danaäns woe.

⁶⁵ Of Hector, whoe'er he be, if I am dear to you,
be ware ; keep his name stamped in ever mindful
heart ! When you have shunned him, remember to
shun others ; think that many Hectors are there ;
and see that you say, as oft as you make ready for
the fight : " Laodamia bade me spare herself." If it
be fated Troy shall fall before the Argolic host, let
it also fall without your taking a single wound ! Let
Menelaus battle, let him press to meet the foe ; to
seek the wife from the midst of the foe is the

causa tua est dispar ; tu tantum vivere pugna,
   inque pios dominae posse redire sinus.
Parcite, Dardanidae, de tot, precor, hostibus uni,
   ne meus ex illo corpore sanguis eat !   80
non est quem deceat nudo concurrere ferro,
   saevaque in oppositos pectora ferre viros ;
fortius ille potest multo, quam pugnat, amare.
   bella gerant alii ; Protesilaus amet !
Nunc fateor—volui revocare, animusque ferebat ; 85
   substitit auspicii lingua timore mali.
cum foribus velles ad Troiam exire paternis,
   pes tuus offenso limine signa dedit.
ut vidi, ingemui, tacitoque in pectore dixi :
   " signa reversuri sint, precor, ista viri ! "   90
haec tibi nunc refero, ne sis animosus in armis ;
   fac, meus in ventos hic timor omnis eat !
Sors quoque nescio quem fato designat iniquo,
   qui primus Danaum Troada tangat humum.
infelix, quae prima virum lugebit ademptum !   95
   di faciant, ne tu strenuus esse velis !
inter mille rates tua sit millensima puppis,
   iamque fatigatas ultima verset aquas !
hoc quoque praemoneo : de nave novissimus exi ;
   non est, quo properas, terra paterna tibi.   100
cum venies, remoque move veloque carinam
   inque tuo celerem litore siste gradum !
Sive latet Phoebus seu terris altior exstat,
   tu mihi luce dolor, tu mihi nocte venis,

husband's part. Your case is not the same; do you fight merely to live, and to return to your faithful queen's embrace.

79 O ye sons of Dardanus, spare, I pray, from so many foes at least one, lest my blood flow from that body! He is not one it befits to engage with bared steel in the shock of battle, to present a savage breast to the opposing foe; his might is greater far in love than on the field. Let others go to the wars; let Protesilaus love!

85 I confess now, I would have called you back, and my spirit strove; but my tongue stood still for fear of evil auspice. When you would fare forth from your paternal doors to Troy, your foot, stumbling upon the threshold, gave ill sign. At the sight I groaned, and in my secret heart I said: "May this, I pray, be omen that my lord return!" Of this I tell you now, lest you be too forward with your arms. See you make this fear of mine all vanish to the winds!

93 There is a prophecy, too, that marks someone for an unjust doom—the first of the Danaäns to touch the soil of Troy. Unhappy she who first shall weep for her slain lord! The gods keep you from being too eager! Among the thousand ships let yours be the thousandth craft, and the last to stir the already wearied wave! This, too, I warn you of: be last to leave your ship; the land to which you haste is not your father's soil. When you return, then speed your keel with oar and sail at once, and on your own shore stay your hurried pace.

103 Whether Phoebus be hid, or high above the earth he rise, you are my care by day, you come to me in the night; and yet more by night than in the

nocte tamen quam luce magis—nox grata
    puellis   105
  quarum suppositus colla lacertus habet.
aucupor in lecto mendaces caelibe somnos;
  dum careo veris gaudia falsa iuvant.
Sed tua cur nobis pallens occurrit imago?
  cur venit a labris [1] multa querela tuis?   110
excutior somno simulacraque noctis adoro;
  nulla caret fumo Thessalis ara meo;
tura damus lacrimamque super, qua sparsa relucet,
  ut solet adfuso surgere flamma mero. [a]
quando ego, te reducem cupidis amplexa lacertis, 115
  languida laetitia solvar ab ipsa mea?
quando erit, ut lecto mecum bene iunctus in uno
  militiae referas splendida facta tuae?
quae mihi dum referes, quamvis audire iuvabit,
  multa tamen capies oscula, multa dabis.   120
semper in his apte narrantia verba resistunt;
  promptior est dulci lingua referre mora.
Sed cum Troia subit, subeunt ventique fretumque;
  spes bona sollicito victa timore cadit.
hoc quoque, quod venti prohibent exire carinas, 125
  me movet—invitis ire paratis aquis.
quis velit in patriam vento prohibente reverti?
  a patria pelago vela vetante datis!
ipse suam non praebet iter Neptunus ad urbem.
  quo ruitis? vestras quisque redite domos!   130
quo ruitis, Danai? ventos audite vetantis!
  non subiti casus, numinis ista mora est.

[1] a labris *Birt. Sedl. Jackson* (*Trans. Camb. Phil. Soc. I,*
p. 377 *n.*).

---

[a] The final flare when the fire at the altar is quenched.

light of day—night is welcome to women beneath whose necks an embracing arm is placed. I, in my widowed couch, can only court a sleep with lying dreams; while true joys fail me, false ones must delight.

[109] But why does your face, all pale, appear before me? Why from your lips comes many a complaint? I shake slumber from me, and pray to the apparitions of night; there is no Thessalian altar without smoke of mine; I offer incense, and let fall upon it my tears, and the flame brightens up again as when wine has been sprinkled o'er.[a] When shall I clasp you, safe returned, in my eager arms, and lose myself in languishing delight? When will it be mine to have you again close joined to me on the same couch, telling me your glorious deeds in the field? And while you are telling them, though it delight to hear, you will snatch many kisses none the less, and will give me many back. The words of well-told tales meet ever with such stops as this; more ready for report is the tongue refreshed by sweet delay.

[123] But when Troy rises in my thoughts, I think of the winds and sea; fair hope is overcome by anxious fear, and falls. This, too, moves me, that the winds forbid your keels to fare forth—yet you make ready to sail despite the seas. Who would be willing to return homeward with the wind saying nay? Yet you trim sail to leave your homes, though the sea forbids! Neptune himself will open up no way for you against his own city. Whither your headlong course? Return ye all to your own abodes! Whither your headlong course, O Danaäns? Heed the winds that say you nay! No sudden chance, but God himself, sends

quid petitur tanto nisi turpis adultera bello?
  dum licet, Inachiae vertite vela rates!
sed quid ago? revoco? revocaminis omen abesto, 135
  blandaque conpositas aura secundet aquas !
Troasin invideo, quae sic lacrimosa suorum
  funera conspicient, nec procul hostis erit.
ipsa suis manibus forti nova nupta marito
  inponet galeam Dardanaque arma dabit. 140
arma dabit, dumque arma dabit, simul oscula
    sumet—
  hoc genus officii dulce duobus erit—
producetque virum, dabit et mandata reverti
  et dicet: "referas ista fac arma Iovi!"
ille ferens dominae mandata recentia secum 145
  pugnabit caute respicietque domum.
exuet haec reduci clipeum galeamque resolvet,
  excipietque suo corpora lassa sinu.
Nos sumus incertae ; nos anxius omnia cogit,
  quae possunt fieri, facta putare timor. 150
dum tamen arma geres diverso miles in orbe,
  quae referat vultus est mihi cera tuos ;
illi blanditias, illi tibi debita verba
  dicimus, amplexus accipit illa meos.
crede mihi, plus est, quam quod videatur,
    imago ; 155
  adde sonum cerae, Protesilaus erit.
hanc specto teneoque sinu pro coniuge vero,
  et, tamquam possit verba referre, queror.

that delay of yours. What is your quest in so great a war but a shameful wanton? While you may, reverse your sails, O ships of Inachus! But what am I doing? Do I call you back? Far from me be the omen of calling back; may caressing gales second a peaceful sea!

[137] I envy the women who dwell in Troy, who will thus behold the tearful fates of them they love, with the foe not far away. With her own hand the newly wedded bride will set the helmet upon her valiant husband's head, and give into his hands the Dardanian arms. She will give him his arms, and the while she gives him arms will receive his kisses— a kind of office sweet to both—and will lead her husband forth, and lay on him the command to return, and say: "See that you bring once more those arms to Jove!" He, bearing fresh in mind with him the command of his mistress, will fight with caution, and be mindful of his home. When safe returned, she will strip him of his shield, unloose his helm, and receive to her embrace his wearied frame.

[149] But we are left uncertain; we are forced by anxious fear to fancy all things befallen which may befall. None the less, while you, a soldier in a distant world, will be bearing arms, I keep a waxen image to give back your features to my sight; it hears the caressing phrase, it hears the words of love that are yours by right, and it receives my embrace. Believe me, the image is more than it appears; add but a voice to the wax, Protesilaus it will be. On this I look, and hold it to my heart in place of my real lord, and complain to it, as if it could speak again.

Per reditus corpusque tuum, mea numina, iuro,
    perque pares animi coniugiique faces,[1]   160
me tibi venturam comitem, quocumque vocaris,   163
    sive—quod heu! timeo—sive superstes eris.
ultima mandato claudetur epistula parvo :
    si tibi cura mei, sit tibi cura tui !

XIV

HYPERMESTRA LYNCEO

MITTIT Hypermestra de tot modo fratribus uni—
    cetera nuptarum crimine turba iacet.
clausa domo teneor gravibusque coercita vinclis ;
    est mihi supplicii causa fuisse piam.
quod manus extimuit iugulo demittere ferrum,   5
    sum rea ; lauderer, si scelus ausa forem.
esse ream praestat, quam sic placuisse parenti ;
    non piget inmunes caedis habere manus.
me pater igne licet, quem non violavimus, urat,
    quaeque aderant sacris, tendat in ora faces ;   10
aut illo iugulet, quem non bene tradidit ensem,
    ut, qua non cecidit vir nece, nupta cadam—
non tamen, ut dicant morientia " paenitet ! " ora,
    efficiet.   non est, quam piget esse piam.
paeniteat sceleris Danaum saevasque sorores ;   15
    hic solet eventus facta nefanda sequi.

---

[1] 161, 162 *spurious Pa.* :
      perque, quod ut videam canis albere capillis,
      quod tecum possis ipse referre, caput.

[159] By thy return and by thyself, who art my god, I swear, and by the torches alike of our love and our wedding-day, I will come to be thy comrade whithersoever thou dost call, whether that which, alas, I fear, shall come to pass, or whether thou shalt still survive. The last of my missive, ere it close, shall be the brief behest : if thou carest ought for me, then care thou for thyself !

XIV

HYPERMNESTRA TO LYNCEUS

HYPERMNESTRA sends this letter to the one brother left of so many but now alive—the rest of the company lie dead by the crime of their brides. Kept close in the palace am I, bound with heavy chains; and the cause of my punishment is that I was faithful. Because my hand shrank from driving into your throat the steel, I am charged with crime; I should be praised, had I but dared the deed. Better be charged with crime than thus to have pleased my sire ; I feel no regret at having hands free from the shedding of blood. My father may burn me with the flame [a] I would not violate, and hold to my face the torches that shone at my marriage rites ; or he may lay to my throat the sword he falsely gave me, so that I, the wife, may die the death my husband did not die—yet he will not bring my dying lips to say " I repent me ! " She is not faithful who regrets her faith. Let repentance for crime come to Danaus and my cruel sisters ; this is the wonted event that follows on wicked deeds.

[a] Of the marriage-altar.

OVID

Cor pavet admonitu temeratae sanguine noctis,
    et subitus dextrae praepedit ossa tremor.
quam tu caede putes fungi potuisse mariti,
    scribere de facta non sibi caede timet !   20
Sed tamen experiar.   modo facta crepuscula terris ;
    ultima pars lucis primaque noctis erat.
ducimur Inachides magni sub tecta Pelasgi,
    et socer armatas accipit ipse nurus.
undique conlucent praecinctae lampades auro ;   25
    dantur in invitos inpia tura focos ;
vulgus "Hymen, Hymenaee!" vocant. fugit ille
      vocantis ;
    ipsa Iovis coniunx cessit ab urbe sua !
ecce, mero dubii, comitum clamore frequentes,
    flore novo madidas inpediente comas,   30
in thalamos laeti—thalamos, sua busta !—feruntur
    strataque corporibus funere digna premunt.
Iamque cibo vinoque graves somnoque iacebant,
    securumque quies alta per Argos erat—
circum me gemitus morientum audire videbar ;   35
    et tamen audibam,[1] quodque verebar erat.
sanguis abit, mentemque calor corpusque relinquit,
    inque novo iacui frigida facta toro.
ut leni Zephyro graciles vibrantur aristae,
    frigida populeas ut quatit aura comas,   40
aut sic, aut etiam tremui magis. ipse iacebas,
    quaeque tibi dederam, vina [2] soporis erant.

    [1] audibam *P Burm.*: audieram *s G?*: auditum *s.*
    [2] vina *P G V ω*: plena *Pa.*

---

    [a] Inachus, Io, Epaphus, Libya, Belus, Danaus—was their
descent.   [b] King of Argos.   [c] Aegyptus.

[17] My heart is struck with fear at remembrance of that night profaned with blood, and sudden trembling fetters the bones of my right hand. She you think capable of having compassed her husband's death fears even to write of murder done by hands not her own!

[21] Yet I shall essay to write. Twilight had just settled on the earth; it was the last part of day and the first of night. We daughters of Inachus[a] are escorted beneath the roof of great Pelasgus,[b] and our husbands' father[c] himself receives the armed brides of his sons. On every side shine bright the lamps girt round with gold; unholy incense is scattered on unwilling altar-fires; the crowd cry "Hymen, Hymenaeus!" The god shuns their cry; Jove's very consort has withdrawn from the city of her choice! Then, look you, confused with wine, they come in rout amidst the cries of their companions; with fresh flowers in their dripping locks, all joyously they burst into the bridal chambers —the bridal chambers, their own tombs!—and with their bodies press the couches that deserve to be funeral beds.

[33] And now, heavy with food and wine they lay in sleep, and deep repose had settled on Argos, free from care—when round about me I seemed to hear the groans of dying men; nay, I heard indeed, and what I feared was true. My blood retreated, warmth left my body and soul, and on my newly-wedded couch all chill I lay. As the gentle zephyr sets a-quiver the slender stalk of grain, as wintry breezes shake the poplar leaves, even thus—yea, even more—did I tremble. Yourself lay quiet; the wine I had given you was the wine of sleep.

Excussere metum violenti iussa parentis ;
  erigor et capio tela tremente manu.
non ego falsa loquar : ter acutum sustulit ensem, 45
  ter male sublato reccidit ense manus.
admovi iugulo—sine me tibi vera fateri !—
  admovi iugulo tela paterna tuo ;
sed timor et pietas crudelibus obstitit ausis,
  castaque mandatum dextra refugit opus. 50
purpureos laniata sinus, laniata capillos
  exiguo dixi talia verba sono :
" saevus, Hypermestra, pater est tibi ; iussa parentis
  effice ; germanis sit comes iste suis !
femina sum et virgo, natura mitis et annis ; 55
  non faciunt molles ad fera tela manus.
quin age, dumque iacet, fortis imitare sorores—
  credibile est caesos omnibus esse viros !
si manus haec aliquam posset committere caedem,
  morte foret dominae sanguinolenta suae. 60
hanc meruere necem patruelia regna tenendo ;
  cum sene nos inopi turba vagamur inops.[1]
finge viros meruisse mori—quid fecimus ipsae ?
  quo mihi commisso non licet esse piae ?
quid mihi cum ferro ? quo bellica tela puellae ? 65
  aptior est digitis lana colusque meis."
Haec ego ; dumque queror, lacrimae sua verba se-
    quuntur
  deque meis oculis in tua membra cadunt.
dum petis amplexus sopitaque bracchia iactas,
  paene manus telo saucia facta tua est. 70

---

[1] 114 *placed here by Hous. who omits* 62 *and* 113, *fabricated
to accommodate the misplaced* 114.

[43] Thought of my violent father's mandates struck away my fear. I rise, and clutch with trembling hand the steel. I will not tell you aught untrue : thrice did my hand raise high the piercing blade, and thrice, having basely raised it, fell again. I brought it to your throat—let me confess to you the truth !—I brought my father's weapon to your throat; but fear and tenderness kept me from daring the cruel stroke, and my chaste right hand refused the task enjoined. Rending the purple robes I wore, rending my hair, I spoke with scant sound such words as these : " A cruel father, Hypermnestra, thine ; perform thy sire's command, and let thy husband there go join his brethren ! A woman am I, and a maid, gentle in nature and in years ; my tender hands ill suit fierce weapons. But come, while he lies there, do like as thy brave sisters—it well may be that all have slain their husbands ! Yet had this hand power to deal out murder at all, it would be bloody with the death of its own mistress. They have deserved this end for seizing on their uncle's realms ; we, helpless band, must wander in exile with our aged, helpless sire. Yet suppose our husbands have deserved to die— what have we done ourselves ? What crime have I committed that I must not be free from guilt ? What have swords to do with me ? What has a girl to do with the weapons of war ? More suited to my hands are the distaff and the wool."

[67] Thus I to myself ; and while I utter my complaint, my tears follow forth the words that start them, and from my eyes fall down upon your body. While you grope for my embrace and toss your slumbrous arms, your hand is almost wounded by

iamque patrem famulosque patris lucemque timebam
    expulerunt somnos haec mea dicta tuos:
"surge age, Belide, de tot modo fratribus unus!
    nox tibi, ni properas, ista perennis erit!"
territus exsurgis; fugit omnis inertia somni;   75
    adspicis in timida fortia tela manu.
quaerenti causam "dum nox sinit, effuge!" dixi.
    dum nox atra sinit, tu fugis, ipsa moror.
Mane erat, et Danaus generos ex caede iacentis
    dinumerat. summae criminis unus abes.   80
fert male cognatae iacturam mortis in uno
    et queritur facti sanguinis esse parum.
abstrahor a patriis pedibus, raptamque capillis—
    haec meruit pietas praemia!—carcer habet.
Scilicet ex illo Iunonia permanet ira   85
    cum bos ex homine est, ex bove facta dea.
at satis est poenae teneram mugisse puellam
    nec, modo formosam, posse placere Iovi.
adstitit in ripa liquidi nova vacca parentis,
    cornuaque in patriis non sua vidit aquis,   90
conatoque queri mugitus edidit ore
    territaque est forma, territa voce sua.
quid furis, infelix? quid te miraris in umbra?
    quid numeras factos ad nova membra pedes?
illa Iovis magni paelex metuenda sorori   95
    fronde levas nimiam caespitibusque famem,

---

[a] Belus, Aegyptus, Lynceus.
[b] The story of Io, daughter of the river Inachus.

my blade. And now fear of my father seized on me, and of my father's minions, and of the light of dawn; I drove away your sleep with these words of mine: " Rise up, away, O child of Belus,[a] the one brother left of so many but now alive! This night, unless you haste, will be forever night to you!" In terror you arise; all sleep's dulness flies away; you behold the strenuous weapon in my timorous hand. You ask the cause. "While night permits," I answer, "fly!" While the dark night permits, you fly, and I remain.

[79] 'Twas early morn, and Danaus counted o'er his sons-in-law that lay there slain. You alone lack to make the crime complete. He bears ill the loss of a single kinsman's death, and complains that too little blood was shed. I am seized by the hair, and dragged from my father's feet—such reward my love for duty won!—and thrust in gaol.

[85] Clear it is that Juno's wrath endures from the time the mortal maid became a heifer, and the heifer became a goddess.[b] Yet it is punishment enough that the tender maid was a lowing beast, and, but now so fair, could not retain Jove's love. On the banks of her sire's stream the new-created heifer stood, and in the parental waters beheld the horns that were not her own; with mouth that tried to complain, she gave forth only lowings; she felt terror at her form, and terror at her voice. Why rage, unhappy one? Why gaze at thyself in the water's shadow? Why count the feet thou hast for thy new-created frame? Thou art the mistress of great Jove, that rival to be dreaded by his sister—and must quiet thy fierce hunger with the leafy branch and grassy turf, drink at the spring, and gaze

OVID

fonte bibis spectasque tuam stupefacta figuram
    et, te ne feriant, quae geris, arma, times,
quaeque modo, ut posses etiam Iove digna videri,
    dives eras, nuda nuda recumbis humo.   100
per mare, per terras cognataque flumina curris ;
    dat mare, dant amnes, dat tibi terra viam.
quae tibi causa fugae ? quid tu freta longa pererras ?
    non poteris vultus effugere ipsa tuos.
Inachi, quo properas ? eadem sequerisque fu-
    gisque ;   105
    tu tibi dux comiti, tu comes ipsa duci.
Per septem Nilus portus emissus in aequor
    exuit insana paelicis ora bove.
ultima quid referam, quorum mihi cana senectus
    auctor ? dant anni, quod querar, ecce, mei.   110
bella pater patruusque gerunt ; regnoque domoque
    pellimur ; eiectos ultimus orbis habet.
de fratrum populo pars exiguissima restat.   115
    quique dati leto, quaeque dedere, fleo ;
nam mihi quot fratres, totidem periere sorores.
    accipiat lacrimas utraque turba meas !
en, ego, quod vivis, poenae cruciando reservor ;
    quid fiet sonti, cum rea laudis agar   120
et consanguineae quondam centensima turbae
    infelix uno fratre manente cadam ?
At tu, siqua piae, Lynceu,[1] tibi cura sororis,
    quaeque tibi tribui munera, dignus habes,

[1] *The name preserved only by Plan.*

---

[a] Oceanus, father of all streams, was father of Inachus,
Io's father.
[b] The scholiast to Euripides' *Hec.* 886 says Lynceus
avenged his brothers by slaying the guilty wives.

astonied on thine image there, and fear lest the arms thou bearest may wound thyself! Thou, who but now wert rich, so rich as to seem worthy even of Jove, liest naked upon the naked ground. Over seas, and lands, and kindred *a* streams dost thou course; the sea opens a way for thee, and the rivers, and the land. What is the cause of thy flight? Why dost thou wander over the long seas? Thou wilt not be able to fly from thine own features. Child of Inachus, whither dost thou haste? Thou followest and fliest—the same; thou art thyself guide to thy companion, thou art companion to thy guide!

[107] The Nile, let flow to the sea through seven mouths, strips from the maddened heifer the features loved of Jove. Why talk of far-off things, told me by hoary eld? My own years, look you, give me matter for lament. My father and my uncle are at war; we are driven from our realms and from our home; we are cast away to the farthest parts of earth. Of the number of the brothers but a scantest part remains. For those who were done to death, and for those who did the deed, I weep; as many brothers as I have lost, so many sisters also have I lost.*b* Let both their companies receive my tears! Lo, I, because you live, am kept for the torments of punishment; but what shall be the fate of guilt, when I am charged with crime for deeds of praise, and fall, unhappy that I am, once the hundredth member of a kindred throng, of whom one brother only now remains?

[123] But do thou, O Lynceus, if thou carest aught for thy sister, and art worthy of the gift I rendered thee, come bear me aid; or, if it please thee, abandon

OVID

vel fer opem, vel dede neci defunctaque vita   125
    corpora furtivis insuper adde rogis,
et sepeli lacrimis perfusa fidelibus ossa,
    sculptaque sint titulo nostra sepulcra brevi :
" exul Hypermestra, pretium pietatis iniquum,
    quam mortem fratri depulit, ipsa tulit."   130
Scribere plura libet, sed pondere lapsa catenae
    est manus, et vires subtrahit ipse timor.

XV

SAPPHO PHAONI [1]

ECQUID, ut adspecta est studiosae littera dextrae,
    Protinus est oculis cognita nostra tuis—
an, nisi legisses auctoris nomina Sapphus,
    hoc breve nescires unde movetur opus ?
Forsitan et quare mea sint alterna requiras   5
    carmina, cum lyricis sim magis apta modis.
flendus amor meus est—elegiae [2] flebile carmen ;
    non facit ad lacrimas barbitos ulla meas.
Uror, ut indomitis ignem exercentibus Euris
    fertilis accensis messibus ardet ager.   10
arva, Phaon, celebras diversa Typhoidos Aetnae ;
    me calor Aetnaeo non minor igne tenet.

---

[1] *This epistle is not in P, G, or any MS. earlier than P*
or G, and is not in Plan. In the MSS. which do contain it,
it is either annexed or prefixed to the whole. Hein. placed it
after XIV because of the presence of some verses from it in that
position in two MSS. of excerpts from a ninth or tenth century
archetype.
    The Sappho-Phaon story seems to have been well known by

me to death, and, when my body is done with life, lay it in secret on the funeral pile, and bury my bones moistened with faithful tears, and let my sepulchre be graved with this brief epitaph: "Exiled Hypermnestra, as the unjust price of her wifely deed, has herself endured the death she warded from her brother!"

131 I would write more; but my hand falls with the weight of my chains, and very fear takes away my strength.

XV

SAPPHO TO PHAON

TELL me, when you looked upon the characters from my eager right hand, did your eye know forthwith whose they were—or, unless you had read their author's name, Sappho, would you fail to know whence these brief words come?

5 Perhaps, too, you may ask why my verses alternate, when I am better suited to the lyric mode. I must weep, for my love — and elegy is the weeping strain; no lyre is suited to my tears.

9 I burn—as burns the fruitful acre when its harvests are ablaze, with untamed east-winds driving on the flame. The fields you frequent, O Phaon, lie far away, by Typhoean Aetna; and I—heat not less than the fires of Aetna preys on me. Nor can I

---

the fourth century B.C. *The authorship of this letter has been disputed, but it is generally conceded to be Ovid's.*

2 elegiae *Pa.*: elegi *many MSS.*: elegeia *or* elegia *s.*

nec mihi, dispositis quae iungam carmina nervis,
    proveniunt ; vacuae carmina mentis opus !
nec me Pyrrhiades Methymniadesve puellae,   15
    nec me Lesbiadum cetera turba iuvant.
vilis Anactorie, vilis mihi candida Cydro ;
    non oculis grata est Atthis, ut ante, meis,
atque aliae centum, quas hic sine crimine amavi ;
    inprobe, multarum quod fuit, unus habes.   20
Est in te facies, sunt apti lusibus anni—
    o facies oculis insidiosa meis !
sume fidem et pharetram—fies manifestus Apollo ;
    accedant capiti cornua—Bacchus eris !
et Phoebus Daphnen, et Gnosida Bacchus amavit, 25
    nec norat lyricos illa vel illa modos ;
at mihi Pegasides blandissima carmina dictant ;
    iam canitur toto nomen in orbe meum.
nec plus Alcaeus, consors patriaeque lyraeque,
    laudis habet, quamvis grandius ille sonet.   30
si mihi difficilis formam natura negavit,
    ingenio formae damna repende [1] meae.
sum brevis, at nomen, quod terras inpleat omnes,
    est mihi ; mensuram nominis ipsa fero.
candida si non sum, placuit Cepheia Perseo   35
    Andromede, patriae fusca colore suae.
et variis albae iunguntur saepe columbae,
    et niger a viridi turtur amatur ave.
si, nisi quae facie poterit te digna videri,
    nulla futura tua est, nulla futura tua est.   40

        [1] rependo *the MSS.*: repende *Bent.*

---

    a The parrot. Compare *Amores* II. vi. 16.

fashion aught of song to suit the well-ordered
string; songs are the labour of minds care-free!
Neither the maids of Pyrrha charm me now, nor
they of Methymna, nor all the rest of the throng of
Lesbian daughters. Naught is Anactorie to me,
naught Cydro, the dazzling fair; my eyes joy not in
Atthis as once they did, nor in the hundred other
maids I loved here to my reproach; unworthy one,
the love that belonged to many maids you alone
possess.

²¹ You have beauty, and your years are apt for
life's delights—O beauty that lay in ambush for my
eyes! Take up the lyre and quiver—you will be
Apollo manifest; let horns but spring on your head
—you will be Bacchus! Phoebus loved Daphne, and
Bacchus, too, loved the Gnosian maid, and neither
one nor other knew the lyric mode; yet for me
the daughters of Pegasus dictate sweetest songs;
my name is already sung abroad in all the earth.
Not greater is the praise Alcaeus wins, the sharer in
my homeland and in my gift of song, though a
statelier strain he sounds. If nature, malign to me,
has denied the charm of beauty, weigh in the stead
of beauty the genius she gave. I am slight of
stature, yet I have a name fills every land; the
measure of my name is my real height. If I am
not dazzling fair, Cepheus' Andromeda was fair
in Perseus' eyes, though dusky with the hue of her
native land. Besides, white pigeons oft are mated
with those of different hue, and the black turtle-
dove, too, is loved by the bird of green.ᵃ If none
shall be yours unless deemed worthy of you for
her beauty's sake, then none shall be yours at
all.

OVID

At mea cum legerem, sat iam[1] formosa videbar ;
  unam iurabas usque decere loqui.
cantabam, memini—meminerunt omnia amantes—
  oscula cantanti tu mihi rapta dabas.
haec quoque laudabas, omnique a parte place-
      bam—   45
  sed tum praecipue, cum fit amoris opus.
tunc te plus solito lascivia nostra iuvabat,
  crebraque mobilitas aptaque verba ioco,
et quod, ubi amborum fuerat confusa voluptas,
  plurimus in lasso corpore languor erat.   50
Nunc tibi Sicelides veniunt nova praeda puellae.
  quid mihi cum Lesbo ? Sicelis esse volo.
o[2] vos erronem tellure remittite vestra,
  Nisiades matres Nisiadesque nurus,
nec vos decipiant blandae mendacia linguae !   55
  quae dicit vobis, dixerat ante mihi.
tu quoque, quae montes celebras, Erycina, Sicanos—
  nam tua sum—vati consule, diva, tuae !
an gravis inceptum peragit fortuna tenorem
  et manet in cursu semper acerba suo ?   60
sex mihi natales ierant, cum lecta parentis
  ante diem lacrimas ossa bibere meas.
arsit iners[3] frater meretricis captus amore
  mixtaque cum turpi damna pudore tulit ;
factus inops agili peragit freta caerula remo,   65
  quasque male amisit, nunc male quaerit opes.

[1] So *Hous.*: legeres etiam *Pa.*
[2] O vos *F s* : at vos, nec vos, neu vos *s* : aut vos *Bent.*
[3] inops *the MSS.*: iners *Ouden. Pa.*: inops *of 65 caused the
corruption.*

---

[a] The Parian Marble says that Sappho really was exiled
and went to Sicily. Her troubles were of a political nature.

⁴¹ Yet, when I read you my songs, I seemed already beautiful enough; you swore 'twas I alone whom speech forever graced. I would sing to you, I remember—for lovers remember all—and while I sang you stole kisses from me. My kisses too you praised, and I pleased in every way—but then above all when we wrought at the task of love. Then did my playful ways delight you more than your wont— the quick embrace, the jest that gave spice to our sport, and, when the joys of both had mingled into one, the deep, deep languor in our wearied frames.

⁵¹ Now new prey is yours—the maids of Sicily. What is Lesbos now to me? I would I were a Sicilian maid.ᵃ Ah, send me back my wanderer, ye Nisaean matrons and Nisaean maids, nor let the lies of his bland tongue deceive you! What he says to you, he had said before to me. Thou too, Erycina, who dost frequent the Sicanian mountains—for I am thine—protect thy singer, O lady! Can it be my grievous fortune will hold the ways it first began, and ever remain bitter in its course? Six natal days had passed for me, when I gathered the bones of my father, dead before his time, and let them drink my tears. My untaught brother was caught in the flame of harlot love, and suffered loss together with foul shame; reduced to need, he roams the dark blue seas with agile oar, and the wealth he cast away by evil means once more by evil means he seeks.ᵇ As for me, because I often warned

ᵇ Probably as a pirate. He ransomed the courtesan Rhodopis from Egypt, and was reproved by Sappho in a poem.

OVID

me quoque, quod monui bene multa fideliter, odit ;
   hoc mihi libertas, hoc pia lingua dedit.
et tamquam desint, quae me sine fine fatigent,
   accumulat curas filia parva meas.   70
Ultima tu nostris accedis causa querelis.
   non agitur vento nostra carina suo.
ecce, iacent collo sparsi sine lege capilli,
   nec premit articulos lucida gemma meos ;
veste tegor vili, nullum est in crinibus aurum,   75
   non Arabum noster dona capillus habet.
cui colar infelix, aut cui placuisse laborem ?
   ille mei cultus unicus auctor abest.
molle meum levibusque cor est violabile telis,
   et semper causa est, cur ego semper amem— 80
sive ita nascenti legem dixere Sorores
   nec data sunt vitae fila severa meae,
sive abeunt studia in mores, artisque magistra
   ingenium nobis molle Thalia facit.
quid mirum, si me primae lanuginis aetas   85
   abstulit, atque anni quos vir amare potest ?
hunc ne pro Cephalo raperes, Aurora, timebam—
   et faceres, sed te prima rapina tenet !
hunc si conspiciat quae conspicit omnia Phoebe,
   iussus erit somnos continuare Phaon ;   90
hunc Venus in caelum curru vexisset eburno,
   sed videt et Marti posse placere suo.
o nec adhuc iuvenis, nec iam puer, utilis aetas,
   o decus atque aevi gloria magna tui,
huc ades inque sinus, formose, relabere nostros ! 95
   non ut ames oro, verum ut amere sinas.
Scribimus, et lacrimis oculi rorantur obortis ;
   adspice, quam sit in hoc multa litura loco !

---

^a Cleis.

186

him well and faithfully, he hates me; this has my candour brought me, this my duteous tongue. And as if there were lack of things to weary me endlessly, a little daughter ^a fills the measure of my cares.

⁷¹ Last cause of all are you for my complaint. My craft is not impelled by a propitious gale. Lo, see, my hair lies scattered in disorder about my neck, my fingers are laden with no sparkling gems; I am clad in garment mean, no gold is in the strands of my hair, my locks are scented with no gifts of Araby. For whom should I adorn myself, or whom should I strive to please? He, the one cause for my adornment, is gone. Tender is my heart, and easily pierced by the light shaft, and there is ever cause why I should ever love—whether at my birth the Sisters declared this law and did not spin my thread of life with austere strand, or whether tastes change into character, and Thalia, mistress of my art, is making my nature soft. What wonder if the age of first down has carried me away, and the years that stir men's love? Lest thou steal him in Cephalus' place, I ever feared, Aurora—and so thou wouldst do, but that thy first prey holds thee still. Him should Phoebe behold, who beholds all things, 'twill be Phaon she bids continue in his sleep; him Venus would have carried to the skies in her ivory car, but that she knows he might charm even her Mars. O neither yet man nor still boy—meet age for charm—O ornament and great glory of thy time, O hither come; sail back again, O beauteous one, to my embrace! I do not plead for thee to love, but to let thyself be loved.

⁹⁷ I write, and my eyes let fall the springing tears like drops of dew; look, how many a blot obscures

si tam certus eras hinc ire, modestius isses,
　　et [1] modo dixisses " Lesbi puella, vale ! "　　　100
non tecum lacrimas, non oscula nostra tulisti ;
　　denique non timui, quod dolitura fui.
nil de te mecum est nisi tantum iniuria ; nec tu,
　　admoneat quod te, pignus amantis habes.
non mandata dedi, neque enim mandata dedissem 105
　　ulla, nisi ut nolles inmemor esse mei.
per tibi—qui numquam longe discedat !—amorem,
　　perque novem iuro, numina nostra, deas,
cum mihi nescio quis " fugiunt tua gaudia " dixit,
　　nec me flere diu, nec potuisse loqui !　　　　　110
et lacrimae deerant oculis et verba palato,
　　adstrictum gelido frigore pectus erat.
postquam se dolor invenit, nec pectora plangi
　　nec puduit scissis exululare comis,
non aliter, quam si nati pia mater adempti　　　115
　　portet ad exstructos corpus inane rogos.
gaudet et e nostro crescit maerore Charaxus
　　frater, et ante oculos itque reditque meos,
utque pudenda mei videatur causa doloris,
　　" quid dolet haec ? certe filia vivit ! " ait.　　120
non veniunt in idem pudor atque amor. omne videbat
　　vulgus ; eram lacero pectus aperta sinu.
Tu mihi cura, Phaon ; te somnia nostra reducunt—
　　somnia formoso candidiora die.
illic te invenio, quamvis regionibus absis ;　　　125
　　sed non longa satis gaudia somnus habet
saepe tuos nostra cervice onerare lacertos,
　　saepe tuae videor supposuisse meos ;

　　　　　[1] et modo ω : et michi F : si modo s.

this place! If you were so resolved to leave my side, you could have gone in more becoming wise. You might at least have said to me: "O Lesbian mistress, fare you well!" You did not take with you my tears, you did not take my kisses; indeed, I felt no fear of the pangs I was to suffer. You have left me nothing, nothing except my wrong; and you—you have no token of my love to put you in mind of me. I gave you no behests—nor would I have given any, save not to be unmindful of me. O by our love—and may it never far depart!— and by the heavenly Nine who are my deities, I swear to you, when someone said to me: "Your joys are flying from you!" for a long time I could not weep, and could not speak! Tears failed my eyes, and words my tongue; my breast was fast frozen with icy chill. After my grief had found itself, I felt no shame to beat my breast, and rend my hair, and shriek, not otherwise than when the loving mother of a son whom death has taken bears to the high-built funeral pile his empty frame. Joy swells my brother Charaxus' heart as he sees my woe; he passes before my eyes, and passes again; and, purposing to make the cause of my grief appear immodest, he says: "Why does she grieve? Surely her daughter lives!" Modesty and love are not at one. There was no one did not see me; yet I rent my robe and laid bare my breast.

[123] You, Phaon, are my care; you, my dreams bring back to me—dreams brighter than the beauteous day. In them I find you, though in space you are far away; but not long enough are the joys that slumber gives. Often I seem with the burden of my neck to press your arms, often to place beneath

oscula cognosco, quae tu committere linguae
 aptaque consueras accipere, apta dare. 130
blandior interdum verisque simillima verba
 eloquor, et vigilant sensibus ora meis.
ulteriora pudet narrare, sed omnia fiunt,
 et iuvat, et siccae [1] non licet esse mihi.
At cum se Titan ostendit et omnia secum, 135
 tam cito me somnos destituisse queror ;
antra nemusque peto, tamquam nemus antraque
  prosint—
 conscia deliciis illa fuere meis.
illuc mentis inops, ut quam furialis Enyo [2]
 attigit, in collo crine iacente feror. 140
antra vident oculi scabro pendentia tofo,
 quae mihi Mygdonii marmoris instar erant ;
invenio silvam, quae saepe cubilia nobis
 praebuit et multa texit opaca coma—
sed non invenio dominum silvaeque meumque. 145
 vile solum locus est ; dos erat ille loci.
cognovi pressas noti mihi caespitis herbas ;
 de nostro curvum pondere gramen erat.
incubui tetigique locum, qua parte fuisti ;
 grata prius lacrimas conbibit herba meas. 150
quin etiam rami positis lugere videntur
 frondibus, et nullae dulce queruntur aves ;
sola virum non ulta pie maestissima mater
 concinit Ismarium Daulias ales Ityn.
ales Ityn, Sappho desertos cantat amores— 155
 hactenus ; ut media cetera nocte silent.
Est nitidus vitroque magis perlucidus omni
 fons sacer—hunc multi numen habere putant—

---

 [1] siccae *F* : sine te *ω*.
 [2] Enyo *F* : erictho, ericto, eritho, hericto, enio, en o,
erinnis *s*.

your neck my arms. I recognize the kisses—close
caresses of the tongue—which you were wont to
take and wont to give. At times I fondle you, and
utter words that seem almost the waking truth, and
my lips keep vigil for my senses. Further I blush
to tell, but all takes place ; I feel the delight, and
cannot rule myself.

135 But when Titan shows his face and lights up
all the earth, I complain that sleep has deserted me
so soon ; I make for the grots and the wood, as
if the wood and the grots could aid me—those
haunts were in the secret of my joys. Thither in
frenzied mood I course, like one whom the madden-
ing Enyo has touched, with hair flying loose about
my neck. My eyes behold the grots, hanging
with rugged rock—grots that to me were like
Mygdonian marble ; I find the forest out which oft
afforded us a couch to lie upon, and covered us with
thick shade from many leaves—but I find not the
lord both of the forest and myself. The place is but
cheap ground ; he was the dower that made it rich.
I have recognised the pressed-down grass of the
turf I knew so well ; the sod was hollowed from our
weight. I have laid me down and touched the spot,
the place you rested in ; the grass I once found
gracious has drunk my tears. Nay, even the
branches have laid aside their leafage, and no birds
warble their sweet complaint ; only the Daulian
bird, most mournful mother who wreaked unholy
vengeance on her lord, laments in song Ismarian
Itys. The bird sings of Itys, Sappho sings of love
abandoned—that is all ; all else is silent as midnight.

157 There is a sacred spring, bright and more
transparent than any crystal—many think a spirit

quem supra ramos expandit aquatica lotos,
    una nemus ; tenero caespite terra viret.   160
hic ego cum lassos posuissem flebilis [1] artus,
    constitit ante oculos Naias una meos.
constitit et dixit : " quoniam non ignibus aequis
    ureris, Ambracia est terra petenda tibi.
Phoebus ab excelso, quantum patet, adspicit
    aequor—   165
    Actiacum populi Leucadiumque vocant.
hinc se Deucalion Pyrrhae succensus amore
    misit, et inlaeso corpore pressit aquas.
nec mora, versus amor fugit [2] lentissima Pyrrhae
    pectora, Deucalion igne levatus erat.   170
hanc legem locus ille tenet.   pete protinus altam
    Leucada nec saxo desiluisse time ! "
Ut monuit, cum voce abiit ; ego territa surgo,
    nec lacrimas oculi continuere mei.[3]
ibimus, o nymphe, monstrataque saxa petemus ;   175
    sit procul insano victus amore timor !
quidquid erit, melius quam nunc erit ! aura, subito ;
    et mea non magnum corpora pondus habent.
tu quoque, mollis Amor, pennas suppone cadenti,
    ne sim Leucadiae mortua crimen aquae !   180
inde chelyn Phoebo, communia munera, ponam,
    et sub ea versus unus et alter erunt :

GRATA LYRAM POSUI TIBI, PHOEBE, POETRIA SAPPHO :
    CONVENIT ILLA MIHI, CONVENIT ILLA TIBI.

[1] fletibus *s*.
[2] fugit *F s* : tetigit *ω Hein.*: figit *s De Vries*.
[3] *So F* : nec gravidae lacrimas continuere genae *others*.

192

dwells therein—above which a watery lotus spreads
its branches wide, a grove all in itself; the earth is
green with tender turf. Here I had laid my wearied
limbs and given way to tears, when there stood
before my eyes a Naiad. She stood before me, and
said : "Since thou art burning with unrequited flame;
Ambracia is the land thou needs must seek. There
Phoebus from on high looks down on the whole
wide stretch of sea—of Actium, the people call it, and
Leucadian. From here Deucalion, inflamed with
love for Pyrrha, cast himself down, and struck the
waters with body all unharmed. Without delay,
his passion was turned from him, and fled from his
tenacious breast, and Deucalion was freed from the
fires of love. This is the law of yonder place. Go
straightway seek the high Leucadian cliff, nor from it
fear to leap!"

¹⁷³ Her warning given, she ceased her speech, and
vanished ; in terror I arose, and my eyes could not
keep back their tears. I shall go, O nymph, to seek
out the cliff thou toldst of ; away with fear—my
maddening passion casts it out. Whatever shall be,
better 'twill be than now ! Breeze, come—bear me
up ; my limbs have no great weight. Do thou, too,
tender Love, place thy pinions beneath me, lest I
die and bring reproach on the Leucadian wave !
Then will I consecrate to Phoebus my shell, our
common boon, and under it shall be writ one verse,
and a second :

SAPPHO THE SINGER, O PHOEBUS, HATH GRATEFULLY
BROUGHT THEE A ZITHER :
TOKEN WELL SUITED TO ME, TOKEN WELL SUITED TO
THEE.

Cur tamen Actiacas miseram me mittis ad oras,　185
　　cum profugum possis ipse referre pedem?
tu mihi Leucadia potes esse salubrior unda;
　　et forma et meritis tu mihi Phoebus eris.
an potes, o scopulis undaque ferocior omni,[1]
　　si moriar, titulum mortis habere meae?　190
at quanto melius iungi mea pectora tecum
　　quam poterant saxis praecipitanda dari!
haec sunt illa, Phaon, quae tu laudare solebas,
　　visaque sunt totiens ingeniosa tibi.
nunc vellem facunda forem! dolor artibus obstat, 195
　　ingeniumque meis substitit omne malis.
non mihi respondent veteres in carmina vires;
　　plectra dolore tacent, muta dolore lyra est.
Lesbides aequoreae, nupturaque nuptaque proles,
　　Lesbides, Aeolia nomina dicta lyra,　200
Lesbides, infamem quae me fecistis amatae,[2]
　　desinite ad citharas turba venire meas!
abstulit omne Phaon, quod vobis ante placebat,
　　me miseram, dixi quam modo paene "meus!"
efficite ut redeat; vates quoque vestra redibit.　205
　　ingenio vires ille dat, ille rapit.
Ecquid ago precibus, pectusve agreste movetur?
　　an[3] riget, et Zephyri verba caduca ferunt?
qui mea verba ferunt, vellem tua vela referrent;
　　hoc te, si saperes, lente, decebat opus.　210
sive redis, puppique tuae votiva parantur[4]
　　munera, quid laceras pectora nostra mora?

　　　[1] omni *F*: illa *s*.
　　　[2] amatae *F*: amare *others*: amore *Baehrens*.
　　　[3] an *Pa.*: A! *Baehrens*: piget *F*.
　　　[4] parantur *s*: paramus *Fω*.

[185] Yet why do you send me to the shores of Actium, unhappy that I am, when you yourself could turn back your wandering steps? You can better help my state than the Leucadian wave; both in beauty and in kindness you will be a Phoebus to me. Or, if I perish, O more savage than any cliff or wave, can you endure the name of causing my death? But how much better for my bosom to be pressed to yours than headlong to be hurled from the rocks!— the bosom, Phaon, of her whom you were wont to praise, and who so often seemed to you to have the gift of genius. Would I were eloquent now! Grief stops my art, and all my genius is halted by my woes. My old-time power in song will not respond to the call; my plectrum for grief is silent; mute for grief is my lyre. Lesbian daughters of the wave, ye who are to wed and ye already wed, ye Lesbian daughters, whose names have been sung to the Aeolian lyre, ye Lesbian daughters whom I have loved to my reproach, cease thronging to me more to hear my shell! Phaon has swept away all that ye loved before—ah, wretched me, how nearly I came then to saying "my Phaon"! Accomplish his return; your singer, too, will then return. My genius had its powers from him; with him they were swept away.

[207] But do my prayers accomplish aught, or is his churl's heart moved? or is it cold and hard, and do the zephyrs bear away my idly falling words? Would that the winds that bear away my words might bring your sails again; this deed were fitting for you, tardy one, had you a feeling breast. If you intend return, and are making for your stern the votive gift, why tear my heart with delay? Weigh

solve ratem! Venus orta mari mare praestat amanti.
  aura dabit cursum ; tu modo solve ratem!
ipse gubernabit residens in puppe Cupido ;   215
  ipse dabit tenera vela legetque manu.
sive iuvat longe fugisse Pelasgida Sapphon—
  non tamen invenies, cur ego digna fugi—
hoc saltem miserae crudelis epistula dicat,
  ut mihi Leucadiae fata petantur aquae !   220

XVI

PARIS HELENAE [1]

HANC tibi Priamides mitto, Ledaea, salutem,
  quae tribui sola te mihi dante potest.
Eloquar, an flammae non est opus indice notae,
  et plus quam vellem iam meus extat amor ?
ille quidem lateat malim, dum tempora dentur   5
  laetitiae mixtos non habitura metus,
sed male dissimulo ; quis enim celaverit ignem,
  lumine qui semper proditur ipse suo ?
si tamen expectas, vocem quoque rebus ut addam—
  uror ! habes animi nuntia verba mei.   10

---

[1] *Of Epistles* xvi.–xxi. *Palmer says :* "*I hold very strongly
the view* (1) *that they were not written by Ovid ;* (2) *that they
were all, except* 16. 39–142, 21. 13 *ad fin., written by the same
author ;* (3) *that that author lived in the early silver age, about
the epoch of Persius or Petronius.*" *For him, proofs of non-
Ovidian authorship lie in form, metre, and diction. Purser's
view, however, Introd. to Palmer, p. xxxii. has gained ground :*

THE HEROIDES XVI

anchor! Venus who rose from the sea makes way
on the sea for the lover. The wind will speed you
on your course; do you but weigh anchor! Cupid
himself will be helmsman, sitting upon the stern;
himself with tender hand will spread and furl the
sail. But if your pleasure be to fly afar from
Pelasgian Sappho—and yet you will find no cause for
flying from me—ah, at least let a cruel letter tell
me this in my misery, that I may seek my fate in
the Leucadian wave!

XVI

Paris to Helen

I, son of Priam, send you, Leda's daughter, this
wish for welfare—welfare that can fall to me through
your gift alone.

³ Shall I speak, or is there no need to tell of
a flame already known, and is my love already
clearer than I could wish? I should indeed prefer
to keep it hid, until the time came when my joy
could be unmixed with fears, but I can ill disguise;
for who could conceal a fire that ever betrays itself
by its own light? If, none the less, you look for me
to add word to fact—I am on fire with love! There
you have the words that bring the message of my

"*These Epistles, neither in matter nor in language, appear to
offer a sufficient number of anomalies to make it necessary to
disallow their Ovidian authorship. They probably formed a
separate volume,* Epistles (Second Series), *written some years
after the others, when Ovid was not so punctilious with regard
to his metre as he was in his earlier works, and when he had
acquired a greater diffuseness of style.*"

parce, precor, fasso nec vultu cetera duro
  perlege, sed formae conveniente tuae.
Iamdudum gratum est, quod epistula nostra recepta
  spem facit, hoc recipi me quoque posse modo.
quae rata sit, nec te frustra promiserit, opto,   15
  hoc mihi quae suasit, mater Amoris, iter;
namque ego divino monitu—ne nescia pecces—
  advehor, et coepto non leve numen adest.
praemia magna quidem, sed non indebita, posco;
  pollicita est thalamo te Cytherea meo.   20
hac duce Sigeo dubias a litore feci
  longa PheBooklea per freta puppe vias.
illa dedit faciles auras ventosque secundos—
  in mare nimirum ius habet orta mari.
perstet et ut pelagi, sic pectoris adiuvet aestum;   25
  deferat in portus et mea vota suos.
Attulimus flammas, non hic invenimus, illas.
  hae mihi tam longae causa fuere viae,
nam neque tristis hiemps neque nos huc appulit
      error;
  Taenaris est classi terra petita meae.   30
nec me crede fretum merces portante carina
  findere—quas habeo, di tueantur opes!
nec venio Graias veluti spectator ad urbes—
  oppida sunt regni divitiora mei.
te peto, quam pepigit lecto Venus aurea nostro;   35
  te prius optavi, quam mihi nota fores.

heart. Pardon, I entreat, my having confessed, and do not read the rest with face that is hard, but with one that suits your beauty.

[18] Long now have I had cheer, for your welcoming my letter begets the hope that I also may be like-wise welcomed. What the mother of Love, who persuaded me to this journey, has fixed upon, I deeply hope may be, and that she has not promised you to me in vain; for at divine behest—lest you sin unawares—I sail hither, and no slight godhead favours my undertaking. The prize I seek in-deed is great, but I ask naught that is not my due; you have been promised for my marriage-chamber by her of Cythera. With her for pilot, from the Sigean strand I have sailed in Phere-clean stern the dubious paths of the far-stretching flood. It is she who has given me gentle breeze and favouring wind—of a surety she has dominion over the sea, for she rose from the sea. May she still favour me, and calm my heart's tide as she calmed the wave's; and bring my vows to their desired haven.

[27] My passion for you I have brought; I did not find it here. It is that which was the cause of so long a voyage, for neither gloomy storm has driven me hither, nor a wandering course; Taenaris is the land toward which my ships were steered. Nor think I cleave the seas with a keel that carries merchandise—what goods I have, may the gods only keep for me! Nor am I come as one to see the sights of Grecian towns—the cities of my own realm are wealthier. It is you I come for—you, whom golden Venus has promised for my bed; you were my heart's desire before you were known to me. I

ante tuos animo vidi quam lumine vultus;
    prima tulit vulnus nuntia fama tui.[1]
Nec tamen est mirum,[2] si, sicut oportet, ab arcu
    missilibus telis eminus ictus amo.   40
sic placuit fatis; quae ne convellere temptes,
    accipe cum vera dicta relata fide.
matris adhuc utero partu remorante tenebar;
    iam gravidus iusto pondere venter erat.
illa sibi ingentem[3] visa est sub imagine somni   45
    flammiferam pleno reddere ventre facem.
territa consurgit metuendaque noctis opacae
    visa seni Priamo; vatibus ille refert.
arsurum Paridis vates canit Ilion igni—
    pectoris, ut nunc est, fax fuit illa mei!   50
Forma vigorque animi, quamvis de plebe videbar,
    indicium tectae nobilitatis erat.
est locus in mediis nemorosae vallibus Idae
    devius et piceis ilicibusque frequens,
qui nec ovis placidae nec amantis saxa capellae   55
    nec patulo tardae carpitur ore bovis.
hinc ego Dardaniae muros excelsaque tecta
    et freta prospiciens arbore nixus eram—
ecce! pedum pulsu visa est mihi terra moveri—
    vera loquar veri vix habitura fidem—   60

---

[1] *So Hous.*: mihi vultus *V*: fuit vultus *P ω*: prima mihi
vulnus nuntia fama tulit *Pa*.
[2] 39–142 *are in Cod. Pal. and the Pauline Fragment:
missing elsewhere and in Plan.*   [3] urgentis *Pa*.

---

[a] Of 39–142, Palmer says: " The question of authorship
of these verses is bound up with that of the authorship of
21. 13–248. Their date has been a subject of much discussion:
many critics have held that they were written so late as the

beheld your features with my soul ere I saw them
with my eyes; rumour, that told me of you, was the
first to deal my wound.

³⁹ Yet [a] it is not strange if I am prey to love, as 'tis
fitting I should be, stricken by darts that were sped
from far. Thus have the fates decreed; and lest you
try to say them nay, listen to words told faithfully and
true. I was still in my mother's bosom, tardy of
birth; her womb already was duly heavy with its
load. It seemed to her in the vision of a dream that
she put forth from her full womb a mighty flaming
torch. In terror she rose up, and told the dread
vision of opaque night to ancient Priam; he told it
to his seers. One of the seers sang that Ilion would
burn with the fire of Paris—that was the torch of
my heart, as now has come to pass!

⁵¹ My beauty and my vigour of mind, though I
seemed from the common folk, were the sign of
hidden nobility. There is a place in the woody
vales of midmost Ida, far from trodden paths and
covered over with pine and ilex, where never grazes
the placid sheep, nor the she-goat that loves the
cliff, nor the wide-mouthed, slowly-moving kine.
From here, reclining against a tree, I was looking
forth upon the walls and lofty roofs of the Dardanian
city, and upon the sea, when lo! it seemed to me
that the earth trembled beneath the tread of feet—
I shall speak true words, though they will scarce
have credit for truth—and there appeared and stood

revival of letters . . . Internal evidence seems to point to a
date not more than a generation later than that of the com-
position of the Epistles 16–21 : and the general correctness of
the versification speaks for an author with an instinctive, not
an acquired, feeling for Ovidian verse."

constitit ante oculos actus velocibus alis
    Atlantis magni Pleionesque nepos—
fas vidisse fuit, fas sit mihi visa referre !—
    inque dei digitis aurea virga fuit ;
tresque simul divae, Venus et cum Pallade Iuno,   65
    graminibus teneros inposuere pedes.
obstipui, gelidusque comas erexerat horror,
    cum mihi " pone metum !" nuntius ales ait,
" arbiter es formae ; certamina siste dearum ;
    vincere quae forma digna sit una duas ! "   70
neve recusarem, verbis Iovis imperat et se
    protinus aetheria tollit in astra via.
Mens mea convaluit, subitoque audacia venit,
    nec timui vultu quamque notare meo.
vincere erant omnes dignae iudexque querebar   75
    non omnes causam vincere posse suam.
sed tamen ex illis iam tunc magis una placebat,
    hanc esse ut scires, unde movetur amor.
tantaque vincendi cura est ; ingentibus ardent
    iudicium donis sollicitare meum.   80
regna Iovis coniunx, virtutem filia iactat ;
    ipse potens dubito fortis an esse velim.
dulce Venus risit ; " nec[1] te, Pari, munera tangant
    utraque suspensi plena timoris ! " ait ;
" nos dabimus, quod ames, et pulchrae filia Ledae 85
    ibit in amplexus pulchrior illa tuos ! "
dixit, et ex aequo donis formaque probata
    victorem caelo rettulit illa pedem.

[1] nec *MSS.*; ne *Bent.*

before my eyes, propelled on pinions swift, the grandchild of mighty Atlas and Pleione—it was allowed me to see, and may it be allowed to speak of what I saw!—and in the fingers of the god was a golden wand. And at the self-same time, three goddesses—Venus, and Pallas, and with her Juno—set tender feet upon the sward. I was mute, and chill tremors had raised my hair on end, when " Lay aside thy fear ! " the winged herald said to me ; " thou art the arbiter of beauty ; put an end to the strivings of the goddesses ; pronounce which one deserves for her beauty to vanquish the other two ! " And, lest I should refuse, he laid command on me in the name of Jove, and forthwith through the paths of ether betook him toward the stars.

[73] My heart was reassured, and on a sudden I was bold, nor feared to turn my face and observe them each. Of winning all were worthy, and I who was to judge lamented that not all could win. But, none the less, already then one of them pleased me more, and you might know it was she by whom love is inspired. Great is their desire to win; they burn to sway my verdict with wondrous gifts. Jove's consort loudly offers thrones, his daughter, might in war ; I myself waver, and can make no choice between power and the valorous heart. Sweetly Venus smiled : " Paris, let not these gifts move thee, both of them full of anxious fear ! " she says ; " my gift shall be of love, and beautiful Leda's daughter, more beautiful than her mother, shall come to thy embrace." She said, and with her gift and beauty equally approved, retraced her way victorious to the skies.

Interea—credo versis ad prospera fatis—
    regius adgnoscor per rata signa puer.   90
laeta domus nato post tempora longa recepto est,
    addit et ad festos hunc quoque Troia diem.
utque ego te cupio, sic me cupiere puellae;
    multarum votum sola tenere potes!
nec tantum regum natae petiere ducumque,   95
    sed nymphis etiam curaque amorque fui.
quam super Oenones faciem mirarer?[1] in orbe
    nec Priamo est a te dignior ulla nurus.
sed mihi cunctarum subeunt fastidia, postquam
    coniugii spes est, Tyndari, facta tui.   100
te vigilans oculis, animo te nocte videbam,
    lumina cum placido victa sopore iacent.
quid facies praesens, quae nondum visa placebas?
    ardebam, quamvis hic procul ignis erat,
nec potui debere mihi spem longius istam,   105
    caerulea peterem quin mea vota via.
Troia caeduntur Phrygia pineta securi
    quaeque erat aequoreis utilis arbor aquis;
ardua proceris spoliantur Gargara silvis,
    innumerasque mihi longa dat Ida trabes.   110
fundatura citas flectuntur robora naves,
    texitur et costis panda carina suis.
addimus antennas et vela sequentia malo;[2]
    accipit et pictos puppis adunca deos;
qua tamen ipse vehor, comitata Cupidine parvo   115
    sponsor coniugii stat dea picta tui.[3]

[1] So *Pa.*: quas super Oenones-faciem mirabar *Ehw.*: quas
. . . Oenonen facies *MSS.*: mutarer *Cod. Pal.*: imitarer
Paul. Frag.   [2] malo *Pa.*: malos *MSS.*: malis *Ehw.*
[3] tui *Bent.*: sui *MSS.*

THE HEROIDES XVI

[89] Meanwhile—I suppose because fate had turned to prosper me—I am found by well approved signs to be a child of the royal line. The son, after long time, is taken back to his home, the house is glad, and Troy adds this day, too, to its festivals. And as I long for you, so women have longed for me; alone, you can possess the object of many women's prayers! And not only have the daughters of princes and chieftains sought me, but even the nymphs have felt for me the cares of love. Whose beauty was I to admire more than Oenone's?—after you, the world contains none more fit than she to be bride to Priam's son. But I am weary of all of them, Tyndaris, since hope was made mine of winning you. It was you that filled my vision as I waked, and you my soul saw in the night, when eyes lie overcome in peaceful slumber. What will you be face to face, you who won me yet unseen? I was fired with love, though here, far away, was the flame. I could not longer cheat myself of the hope of you, but started on the dark blue path to seek the object of my vows.

[107] The Trojan groves of pine are felled by the Phrygian axe, and whatsoever tree will serve on the billowy seas; the steeps of Gargara are spoiled of their lofty woods, and far-stretched Ida gives up to me unnumbered beams. The oak is bent to make the frame for the speedy ship, and the curving keel is woven with the ribbèd sides. We add the yards, and the sails that hang to the mast; the hook-shaped stern, too, receives its painted gods; on the one which carries me stands painted—and, with her, tiny Cupid—the goddess who is sponsor for your wedding me. After the last hand has been laid

205

inposita est factae postquam manus ultima classi,
    protinus Aegaeis ire lubebat [1] aquis—
at pater et genetrix inhibent mea vota rogando
    propositumque pia [2] voce morantur iter;   120
et soror, effusis ut erat, Cassandra, capillis,
    cum vellent nostrae iam dare vela rates,
" quo ruis?" exclamat, " referes incendia tecum !
    quanta per has nescis flamma petatur aquas !"
vera fuit vates; dictos invenimus ignes,   125
    et ferus in molli pectore flagrat amor !
Portubus egredior, ventisque ferentibus usus
    applicor in terras, Oebali nympha, tuas.
excipit hospitio vir me tuus—hoc quoque factum
    non sine consilio numinibusque deum !   130
ille quidem ostendit, quidquid Lacedaemone tota
    ostendi dignum conspicuumque fuit;
sed mihi laudatam cupienti cernere formam
    lumina nil aliud quo caperentur erat.
ut vidi, obstipui praecordiaque intima sensi   135
    attonitus curis intumuisse novis.
his similes vultus, quantum reminiscor, habebat
    venit in arbitrium cum Cytherea meum.
si tu venisses pariter certamen in illud,
    in dubium Veneris palma futura fuit !   140
magna quidem de te rumor praeconia fecit,
    nullaque de facie nescia terra tua est;
nec tibi par usquam Phrygia nec solis ab ortu
    inter formosas altera nomen habet !
Credis et hoc nobis?—minor est tua gloria vero,   145
    famaque de forma paene maligna tua est;

---

[1] lubebat *N. Hein.*: iubebat *Paul. Frag.*: iubebar *Cod. Pal.*.
[2] pia *N. Hein.*: viae *MSS.*

to the ships, and all is complete, forthwith I am eager
to sail the Aegean main—but my father and lady
mother hold me back from my purpose with their
prayers, and with fond words delay the journey I
propose. My sister Cassandra, too, all as she was,
with hair let loose, when my vessels were eager now
to spread the sail, cried out : " Whither thy head-
long course ? Thou wilt bring conflagration back
with thee ! How great the flames thou seekest over
these waters, thou dost not know ! " A truthful
prophetess was she ; I have found the fires of which
she spoke, and flames of fierce love rage in my
helpless breast !

[127] I sail forth from the harbour, and with favour-
ing winds disembark upon your shores, O nymph of
Oebalus' line. Your lord receives me as befits a
guest—this, too, an act not without the counsel
and approval of the gods ! He showed me, of
course, whatever in all Lacedaemon was worthy to
be shown and sightly to be seen ; but I was eager
to behold your much-praised charms, and there
was nothing else by which my eyes could be held.
When I did look on them, I was astonished, mute,
and felt new cares swelling big in my inmost breast.
Features like those, as near as I recall, were
Cytherea's own when she came to be judged by
me. If you had come to that contest together with
her, the palm of Venus would have come in doubt !
Fame has indeed made great heralding of you, and
there is no land that knows not of your beauty ; no
other among fair women has a name like yours—
nowhere in Phrygia, nor from the rising of the sun !

[145] Will you believe me when I say this, too ?—
your glory is less than the truth, and fame has all

plus hic invenio, quam quod promiserat illa,
    et tua materia gloria victa sua est.
ergo arsit merito, qui noverat omnia, Theseus,
    et visa es tanto digna rapina viro,   150
more tuae gentis nitida dum nuda palaestra
    ludis et es nudis femina mixta viris.
quod rapuit, laudo ; miror, quod reddidit umquam.
    tam bona constanter praeda tenenda fuit.
ante recessisset caput hoc cervice cruenta,   155
    quam tu de thalamis abstraherere meis.
tene manus umquam nostrae dimittere vellent ?
    tene meo paterer vivus abire sinu ?
si reddenda fores, aliquid tamen ante tulissem,
    nec Venus ex toto nostra fuisset iners.   160
vel mihi virginitas esset libata, vel illud
    quod poterat salva virginitate rapi.
Da modo te, quae sit Paridis constantia, nosces ;
    flamma rogi flammas finiet una meas.
praeposui regnis ego te, quae maxima quondam 165
    pollicita est nobis nupta sororque Iovis ;
dumque tuo possem circumdare bracchia collo,
    contempta est virtus Pallade dante mihi.
nec piget, aut umquam stulte legisse videbor ;
    permanet in voto mens mea firma suo.   170
spem modo ne nostram fieri patiare caducam,
    deprecor, o tanto digna labore peti !

---

[a] Theseus and Pirithous carried her off, and Castor and
Pollux rescued her.

but maligned your charms; I find more here than the goddess promised me, and your glory is exceeded by its cause. And so Theseus rightly felt love's flame, for he was acquaint with all your charms, and you seemed fit spoil for the great hero to steal away,[a] when, after the manner of your race, you engaged in the sports of the shining palaestra, a nude maid mingled with nude men. His stealing you away, I commend; my marvel is that he ever gave you back. So fine a spoil should have been kept with constancy. Sooner would this head have left my bloody neck than you have been dragged from marriage-chamber of mine. One like you, would ever these hands of mine be willing to let go? One like you, would I, alive, allow to leave my embrace? If you must needs have been rendered up, I should first at least have taken some pledge from you; my love for you would not have been wholly for naught. Either your virgin flower I should have plucked, or taken what could be stolen without hurt to your virgin state.

[163] Only give yourself to me, and you shall know of Paris' constancy; the flame of the pyre alone will end the flames of my love. I have placed you before the kingdoms which greatest Juno, bride and sister of Jove, once promised me; so I could only clasp my arms about your neck, I have held but cheap the prowess that Pallas would bestow. And I have no regret, nor shall I ever seem in my own eyes to have made a foolish choice; my mind is fixed and persists in its desire. I only pray, O worthy to be sought with such great toils! that you will not allow my hopes to fall to earth. I am

non ego coniugium generosae degener opto,
   nec mea, crede mihi, turpiter uxor eris.
Pliada, si quaeres, in nostra gente Iovemque   175
   invenies, medios ut taceamus avos;
sceptra parens Asiae, qua nulla beatior ora est,
   finibus inmensis vix obeunda, tenet.
innumeras urbes atque aurea tecta videbis,
   quaeque suos dicas templa decere deos.   180
Ilion adspicies firmataque turribus altis
   moenia, Phoebeae structa canore lyrae.
quid tibi de turba narrem numeroque virorum?
   vix populum tellus sustinet illa suum.
occurrent denso tibi Troades agmine matres,   185
   nec capient Phrygias atria nostra nurus.
o quotiens dices: "quam pauper Achaia nostra est!"
   una domus quaevis urbis habebit opes.
Nec mihi fas fuerit Sparten contemnere vestram;
   in qua tu nata es, terra beata mihi est.   190
parca sed est Sparte, tu cultu divite digna;
   ad talem formam non facit iste locus.
hanc faciem largis sine fine paratibus uti
   deliciisque decet luxuriare novis.
cum videas cultus nostra de gente virorum,   195
   qualem Dardanias credis habere nurus?
da modo te facilem, nec dedignare maritum,
   rure Therapnaeo nata puella, Phrygem.
Phryx erat et nostro genitus de sanguine, qui nunc
   cum dis potando nectare miscet aquas.   200

---

   [a] Electra, mother of Dardanus, son of Jove.
   [b] Apollo with his music caused the walls to rise for
Laomedon.

no seeker after marriage ties with the nobly born,
while myself of lowly line, nor will you find it
disgrace, believe me, to be my wife. A Pleiad,[a] if
you will search, you will find in our line, and a Jove,
to say naught of our ancestry since their time;
my father wields the sceptre over Asia, land than
which none other has more wealth, with bounds
immense, scarce to be traversed. Unnumbered cities
and golden dwellings you will see, and temples
you would say fit well their gods. Ilion you will
look upon, and its walls made strong with lofty
towers, reared to the tunefulness of Phoebus' lyre.[b]
Why tell you of our thronging multitudes of men?
Scarce does that land sustain the dwellers in it.
In dense line the Trojan women will press forward
to meet you, and our palace halls will scarce contain
the daughters of Phrygia. Ah, how often will you
say: "How poor is our Achaia!" One house-
hold, any one you choose, will show a city's
wealth.

[189] And yet let me not presume to look down upon
your Sparta; the land in which you were born is
rich for me. But a niggard land is Sparta, and you
deserve keeping in wealth; with fairness such as
yours this place is not in accord. Beauty like
yours it befits to enjoy rich adornment without end,
and to wanton in ever new delights. When you
look on the garb of the men of our race, what
garb, think you, must be that of the daughters of
Dardanus? Only be compliant, and do not disdain
a Phrygian for your lord, you who were born in rural
Therapnae. A Phrygian, and born of our blood, was
he who now is with the gods, and mingles water with
the nectar for their drinking. A Phrygian was

OVID

Phryx erat Aurorae coniunx, tamen abstulit illum
    extremum noctis quae dea finit iter.
Phryx etiam Anchises, volucrum cui mater Amorum
    gaudet in Idaeis concubuisse iugis.
nec, puto, conlatis forma Menelaus et annis [1]   205
    iudice te nobis anteferendus erit.
non dabimus certe socerum tibi clara fugantem
    lumina, qui trepidos a dape vertat equos ;
nec Priamo pater est soceri de caede cruentus
    et qui Myrtoas crimine signat aquas ;   210
nec proavo Stygia nostro captantur in unda
    poma, nec in mediis quaeritur umor aquis.
Quid tamen hoc refert, si te tenet ortus ab illis,
    cogitur huic domui Iuppiter esse socer ?
heu facinus ! totis indignus noctibus ille   215
    te tenet amplexu perfruiturque tuo ;
at mihi conspiceris posita vix denique mensa,
    multaque quae laedant hoc quoque tempus habet.
hostibus eveniant convivia talia nostris,
    experior posito qualia saepe mero !   220
paenitet hospitii, cum me spectante lacertos
    inponit collo rusticus iste tuo.
rumpor et invideo—quidni tamen omnia narrem ?—
    membra superiecta cum tua veste fovet.
oscula cum vero coram non dura daretis,   225
    ante oculos posui pocula sumpta meos ;
lumina demitto cum te tenet artius ille,
    crescit et invito lentus in ore cibus.

[1] annis *P* : armis *G ω.*

---

[a] Tithonus, son of Laomedon.
[b] Referring to Atreus and his serving to Thyestes his own
sons.

Aurora's mate;[a] yet he was carried away by the goddess who sets the last bound to the advance of night. A Phrygian, too, Anchises, with whom the mother of the wingèd loves rejoices to consort on Ida's ridge. Nor do I think that Menelaus, when you compare our beauty and our years, will find higher place in your esteem than I. I shall at least not give you a father-in-law who puts to flight the clear beams of the sun, and turns away from the feast his affrighted steeds;[b] nor has Priam a sire who is stained with blood from the murder of his bride's father, or who marks the Myrtoan waters with his crime;[c] nor does ancestor of mine catch at fruits in the Stygian wave, or seek for water in the midst of waters.[d]

[213] Yet what avails me this, if one sprung from them possesses you, and Jove perforce is father-in-law to this house?[e] Ah, crime! Throughout whole nights that unworthy husband possesses you, enjoying your embrace; but I—I look on you only when at last the board is laid, and even this time brings many things that pain. May our enemies have such repasts as often I endure when the wine has been set before us! I regret my being a guest, when before my eyes that rustic lays his arms about your neck. I burst with anger and envy—for why should I not tell everything?—when he lays his mantle over your limbs to keep you warm. But when you openly give him tender kisses, I take up my goblet and hold it before my eyes; when he holds you closely pressed, I let my gaze fall, and the dull food

[c] Pelops, who compassed the death of Oenomaus in the famous race.   [d] Tantalus.

[e] Menelaus' wife was daughter of Jove and Leda.

saepe dedi gemitus; et te—lasciva!—notavi
   in gemitu risum non tenuisse meo.   230
saepe mero volui flammam compescere, at illa
   crevit, et ebrietas ignis in igne fuit,
multaque ne videam, versa cervice recumbo;
   sed revocas oculos protinus ipsa meos.
Quid faciam, dubito; dolor est meus illa videre,   235
   sed dolor a facie maior abesse tua.
qua licet et possum, luctor celare furorem;
   sed tamen apparet dissimulatus amor.
nec tibi verba damus; sentis mea vulnera, sentis!
   atque utinam soli sint ea nota tibi!   240
a, quotiens lacrimis venientibus ora reflexi,
   ne causam fletus quaereret ille mei!
a, quotiens aliquem narravi potus amorem,
   ad vultus referens singula verba tuos,
indiciumque mei ficto sub nomine feci!   245
   ille ego, si nescis, verus amator eram.
quin etiam, ut possem verbis petulantius uti,
   non semel ebrietas est simulata mihi.
Prodita sunt, memini, tunica tua pectora laxa
   atque oculis aditum nuda dedere meis—   250
pectora vel puris nivibus vel lacte tuamque
   complexo matrem candidiora Iove.
dum stupeo visis—nam pocula forte tenebam—
   tortilis a digitis excidit ansa meis.
oscula si natae dederas, ego protinus illa   255
   Hermiones tenero laetus ab ore tuli.

grows big within my unwilling mouth. Many a time
I have let forth groans; and you—ah, mischief that
you are!—I have marked you unable to keep from
laughing when I groaned. Oft I would have quenched
the flame of love in wine, but it grew instead, and
drinking was but fire upon the fire. That I may
miss the sight of much, I recline with head turned
from you; but you yourself straightway recall my
eyes again.

²³⁵ What I shall do, I know not; I suffer when
I look upon these things, but I suffer more when I
lack the sight of your face. In whatever way I
am allowed and have the power, I struggle to conceal
my madness; but none the less the love I cover up
appears. And I am not deceiving you; you are
aware what wounds are mine—you are aware! And
would that they were known to you alone! Ah,
how often at the coming of my tears I have turned
away my face, lest that man should ask the reasons
why I wept! Ah, how often, when in wine, I have
told the tale of some amour, speaking straight to
your face each single word, and have given you hint
of myself under the made-up name! I was the real
lover—if you do not know. Nay, indeed, that I
might be able to use more froward speech, not once
alone have I feigned I was in wine.

²⁴⁹ Your bosom once, I remember, was betrayed
by your robe; it was loose, and left your charms bare
to my gaze—breasts whiter than pure snows, or milk,
or Jove when he embraced your mother. While I
sat in ecstasy at the sight—I chanced to have my
goblet in hand—the twisted handle fell from my
fingers. If you had bestowed kisses on your child
Hermione, I forthwith snatched them with joy from

OVID

et modo cantabam veteres resupinus amores,
    et modo per nutum signa tegenda dabam,
et comitum primas, Clymenen Aethramque, tuarum
    ausus sum blandis nuper adire sonis,   260
quae mihi non aliud, quam formidare, locutae
    orantis medias deseruere preces.
Di facerent, pretium magni certaminis esses,
    teque suo posset victor habere toro !—
ut tulit Hippomenes Schoeneida praemia cursus, 265
    venit ut in Phrygios Hippodamia sinus,
ut ferus Alcides Acheloia cornua fregit,
    dum petit amplexus, Deianira, tuos.
nostra per has leges audacia fortiter isset,
    teque mei scires esse laboris opus.   270
nunc mihi nil superest nisi te, formosa, precari,
    amplectique tuos, si patiare, pedes.
o decus, o praesens geminorum gloria fratrum,
    o Iove digna viro, ni Iove nata fores,
aut ego Sigeos repetam te coniuge portus,   275
    aut hic Taenaria contegar exul humo !
non mea sunt summa leviter destricta[1] sagitta
    pectora ; descendit vulnus ad ossa meum !
hoc mihi—nam repeto—fore, ut a caeleste sagitta
    figar, erat verax vaticinata soror.   280
parce datum fatis, Helene, contemnere amorem—
    sic habeas faciles in tua vota deos !
Multa quidem subeunt ; sed coram ut plura loquamur,
    excipe me lecto nocte silente tuo.

[1] So *Hous.*

her tender lips. And now I would sing of old amours, lying careless on my back; and again I would nod, making signs I should have kept hid. The first of your companions, Clymene and Aethra, I lately ventured to approach with flattering words; who said naught else than that they were afraid, and left me in the midst of my entreaties.

263 Ah, might the gods make you the prize in a mighty contest, and let the victor have you for his couch!—as Hippomenes bore off, the prize of his running, Schoeneus' daughter, as Hippodamia came to Phrygian embrace, as fierce Hercules broke the horns of the Achelous while aspiring to thy embraces, Deianira. My daring would have boldly made its way in the face of conditions such as these, and you would know well how to be the object of my toils. Now nothing is left me but to entreat you, beauteous one, and to embrace your feet, so you suffer it. O honour, O present glory of the twin brethren, O worthy of Jove to husband were you not the child of Jove—either I shall return to the haven of Sigeum with you as my bride, or here, an exile, be covered with Taenarian earth! It is not slightly that my breast has been pierced, only by the arrow's point; my wound is deep—to the very bones! This—for I recall it—was what my truthful sister prophesied—that I should be transfixed by a heavenly dart. Do not, O Helen, despise a love ordained by fate—so may you find the gods gracious to your prayers!

283 Many things indeed come to my mind; but, that we may say more face to face, welcome me to your couch in the silent night. Or do you feel

an pudet et metuis Venerem temerare maritam   285
  castaque legitimi fallere iura tori ?
a, nimium simplex Helene, ne rustica dicam,
  hanc faciem culpa posse carere putas ?
aut faciem mutes aut sis non dura, necesse est ;
  lis est cum forma magna pudicitiae.   290
Iuppiter his gaudet, gaudet Venus aurea furtis ;
  haec tibi nempe patrem furta dedere Iovem.
vix fieri, si sunt vires in semine morum,[1]
  et Iovis et Ledae filia, casta potes.
casta tamen tum sis, cum te mea Troia tenebit,   295
  et tua sim, quaeso, crimina solus ego.
nunc ea peccemus quae corriget hora iugalis,
  si modo promisit non mihi vana Venus !
Sed tibi et hoc suadet rebus, non voce, maritus,
  neve sui furtis hospitis obstet, abest.   300
non habuit tempus, quo Cresia regna videret,
  aptius—o mira calliditate virum !
"res, et ut [2] Idaei mando tibi," dixit iturus,
  "curam pro nobis hospitis, uxor, agas."
neclegis absentis, testor, mandata mariti !   305
  cura tibi non est hospitis ulla tui.
huncine tu speras hominem sine pectore dotes
  posse satis formae, Tyndari, nosse tuae ?
falleris—ignorat ; nec, si bona magna putaret,
  quae tenet, externo crederet illa viro.   310
ut te nec mea vox nec te meus incitet ardor,
  cogimur ipsius commoditate frui—
aut erimus stulti, sic ut superemus et ipsum,
  si tam securum tempus abibit iners.

---

[1] morum *Merk.* : amorum *P G V Plan.* : avorum *s N*
Hein.

[2] *So Madv.* : esset et *P G V* : esset ut *G* : ivit et *s* : is
" sed et " *Pa.*

shame and fear to violate your wedded love, and
to be false to the chaste bonds of a lawful bed? Ah,
too simple—nay, too rustic—Helen! do you think
that beauty of yours can be free from fault? Either
you must change your beauty, or you must needs
not be hard; fairness and modesty are mightily
at strife. Jove's delight, and the delight of Venus,
are in stealthy sins like these; such stealthy sins,
indeed, gave you Jove for sire. If power over char-
acter be in the seed, it scarce can be that you, the
child of Jove and Leda, will remain chaste. Be
chaste, nevertheless—but when my Troy shall hold
you; and let your guilt, I beg, be with me alone.
Let our sin now be one the hour of marriage will
correct—if only what Venus promised me is not in
vain!

²⁹⁹ But even your husband presses you on to this—
by deed, if not by word. That his guest may find no
bar to theft, he absents himself. He could find
no time more suited for him to see the realms
of Crete—O husband marvellously shrewd! "I
enjoin upon you in my stead the care of my affairs,
and of our guest from Ida," he said, making ready
to depart. I call you to witness; you neglect the
injunction of your absent lord; you are not caring
for your guest at all. Do you hope, Tyndaris, that
so senseless a man as this can know well the riches
of your beauty? You are deceived—he does not
know; if he thought great the possessions that he
holds, he would not entrust them to an outlander.
Though neither my words should move you, nor my
ardour, I am driven to take the advantage he himself
gives—or I shall be foolish, even to surpassing him, if
I let so safe a time go idly by. Almost with his own

paene suis ad te manibus deducit amantem ;   315
   utere mandatis simplicitate viri !
Sola iaces viduo tam longa nocte cubili ;
   in viduo iaceo solus et ipse toro.
te mihi meque tibi communia gaudia iungant ;
   candidior medio nox erit illa die.   320
tunc ego iurabo quaevis tibi numina meque
   adstringam verbis in sacra vestra [1] meis ;
tunc ego, si non est fallax fiducia nostra,
   efficiam praesens, ut mea regna petas.
si pudet et metuis ne me videare secuta,   325
   ipse reus sine te criminis huius ero ;
nam sequar Aegidae factum fratrumque tuorum.
   exemplo tangi non propiore potes.
te rapuit Theseus, geminas Leucippidas illi ;
   quartus in exemplis adnumerabor ego.   330
Troia classis adest armis instructa virisque ;
   iam facient celeres remus et aura vias.
ibis Dardanias ingens regina per urbes,
   teque novam credet vulgus adesse deam,
quaque feres gressus, adolebunt cinnama flammae, 335
   caesaque sanguineam victima planget humum.
dona pater fratresque et cum genetrice sorores
   Iliadesque omnes totaque Troia dabit.
ei mihi ! pars a me vix dicitur ulla futuri.
   plura feres, quam quae littera nostra refert.   340
Nec tu rapta time, ne nos fera bella sequantur,
   concitet et vires Graecia magna suas.

       [1] *So Pa.*: sacra iura ω : tua iura *Ehw.*

hands he has brought your lover to you; profit by the behests of your artless lord!

³¹⁷ You lie alone through the long night in a companionless couch; in a companionless bed I, too, lie alone. Let mutual delights join you to me, and me to you; brighter than mid of day will that night be. Then I will swear to you by whatever gods you choose, and bind myself by my oath to observe the rites of your choice; then, if confidence does not beguile me, with a plea in person I will make you wish to seek my realms. If you feel shame and fear lest you seem to have followed me, I myself will meet this charge without you; for I will imitate the deed of Aegeus' son and of your brothers. You can be touched by no examples nearer than these. Theseus stole you away, and they the twin daughters of Leucippus; I shall be counted fourth among such examples. The Trojan fleet is ready, equipped with arms and men; soon oar and breeze will make swift our way. Like a great queen you will make your progress through the Dardanian towns, and the common crowd will think a new goddess come to earth; wherever you advance your steps, flames will consume the cinnamon, and the slain victim will strike the bloody earth. My father and my brothers and my sisters, with their mother, and all the daughters of Ilion, and Troy entire, will bring you gifts. Ah me! I am telling you scarce any part of what will be. You will receive more than my letter tells.

³⁴¹ And do not fear lest, if you are stolen away, fierce wars will follow after us, and mighty Greece will rouse her strength. Of so many who have been

tot prius abductis ecqua est repetita per arma?
　　crede mihi, vanos res habet ista metus.
nomine ceperunt Aquilonis Erechthida Thraces, 345
　　et tuta a bello Bistonis ora fuit;
Phasida puppe nova vexit Pagasaeus Iason,
　　laesa neque est Colcha Thessala terra manu.
te quoque qui rapuit, rapuit Minoida Theseus;
　　nulla tamen Minos Cretas ad arma vocat. 350
terror in his ipso maior solet esse periclo,
　　quaque timere libet, pertimuisse pudet.
Finge tamen, si vis, ingens consurgere bellum—
　　et mihi sunt vires, et mea tela nocent.
nec minor est Asiae quam vestrae copia terrae; 355
　　illa viris dives, dives abundat equis.
nec plus Atrides animi Menelaus habebit
　　quam Paris aut armis anteferendus erit.
paene puer caesis abducta armenta recepi,
　　hostibus et causam nominis inde tuli; 360
paene puer iuvenes vario certamine vici,
　　in quibus Ilioneus Deiphobusque fuit;
neve putes, non me nisi comminus esse timendum,
　　figitur in iusso nostra sagitta loco.
num potes haec illi primae dare facta iuventae? 365
　　instruere Atriden num potes arte mea?
omnia si dederis, numquid dabis Hectora fratrem?
　　unus is innumeri militis instar erit!
quid valeam nescis, et te mea robora fallunt;
　　ignoras, cui sis nupta futura viro. 370

---

a Alexandros, protector of men (the shepherds).

222

taken away before, tell me, has any one ever been sought back by arms? Believe me, that fear of yours is vain. In the name of Aquilo the Thracians took captive Erechtheus' child, and the Bistonian shore was safe from war; Pegasaean Jason in his new craft carried away the Phasian maid, and the land of Thessaly was never harmed by Colchian band. Theseus, too, he who stole you, stole Minos' daughter; yet Minos called the Cretans ne'er to arms. The terror in things like these is wont to be greater than the danger itself, and where 'tis our humour to fear, we shame to have feared too much.

³⁵³ Imagine none the less, if you wish, that a great war is set on foot—I, too, have power, and my weapons, too, are deadly. Nor is the resource of Asia less than that of your land; in men is that country rich, and richly abounds in horses. Nor will Menelaus, Atreus' son, have spirit more than Paris, or be esteemed before him in arms. While yet almost a child, I slew the enemy and got back our herds, and from the exploit received the name I bear ª; while yet almost a child, I overcame young men in varied contest, and among them Ilioneus and Deiphobus; and, lest you think me not to be feared but in the thick of the fight, my arrow is fixed in any spot you choose. Can you bespeak for him such deeds of first young manhood? can you claim for the son of Atreus skill like mine? If you should claim for him everything, could you give him Hector for a brother? He alone will have the might of un-numbered warriors! My powers you do not know, and my prowess you have never seen. You do not know the man whose bride you are to be.

Aut igitur nullo belli repetere tumultu,
    aut cedent Marti Dorica castra meo.
nec tamen indigner pro tanta sumere ferrum
    coniuge.   certamen praemia magna movent.
tu quoque, si de te totus contenderit orbis,   375
    nomen ab aeterna posteritate feres
spe modo non timida dis hinc egressa secundis ;
    exige cum plena munera pacta fide.

XVII

HELENE PARIDI

NUNC oculos tua cum violarit epistula nostros,
    non rescribendi gloria visa levis.
ausus es hospitii temerati, advena, sacris
    legitimam nuptae sollicitare fidem !
scilicet idcirco ventosa per aequora vectum   5
    excepit portu Taenaris ora suo,
nec tibi, diversa quamvis e gente venires,
    oppositas habuit regia nostra fores,
esset ut officii merces iniuria tanti !
    qui sic intrabas, hospes an hostis eras ?   10
Nec dubito, quin haec, cum sit tam iusta, vocetur
    rustica iudicio nostra querela tuo.
rustica sim sane, dum non oblita pudoris,
    dumque tenor vitae sit sine labe meae.
si non est ficto tristis mihi vultus in ore,   15
    nec sedeo duris torva superciliis,
fama tamen clara est, et adhuc sine crimine vixi,[1]
    et laudem de me nullus adulter habet.

           [1] vixi *P G ω* : lusi *many MSS.*

371 Either, then, you will be demanded back with no tumult of war, or the Doric camp will yield to my soldiery. Nor yet would I disdain to take up arms for such a bride. Great prizes stir great strife. And you, besides, if the whole world shall contend for you, will attain to fame among men forever more ! Only, take hope, cast off your fears, and leave this place, for the gods are with us; exact with full confidence the promised boon.

XVII

HELEN TO PARIS

Now that your letter has profaned my eyes, the glory of writing no reply has seemed to me but slight. You have dared, stranger, to violate the sacred pledge of hospitality, and to tamper with the faith of a lawful wife ! Of course it was for this that the Taenarian shore received you into its haven when tossed on the windy tides, and that, come though you were from another race, our royal home did not present closed doors to you—for this, that wrong should be the return for kindness so great ! You who so entered in, were you guest, or were you enemy ?

11 I doubt not that, just though it is, this complaint of mine is called rustic in your judgment. Let me by all means be rustic, only so I forget not my honour, and the course of my life be free from fault. If I do not feign a gloomy countenance, nor sit with stern brows grimly bent, my good name is nevertheless clear, and thus far I have lived without reproach, and no false lover makes his boast of me.

quo magis admiror, quae sit fiducia coepti,
    spemque tori dederit quae tibi causa mei.   20
an, quia vim nobis Neptunius attulit heros,
    rapta semel videor bis quoque digna rapi?
crimen erat nostrum, si delinita fuissem;
    cum sim rapta, meum quid nisi nolle fuit?
non tamen e facto fructum tulit ille petitum;   25
    excepto redii passa timore nihil.
oscula luctanti tantummodo pauca protervus
    abstulit; ulterius nil habet ille mei.
quae tua nequitia est, non his contenta fuisset—
    di melius! similis non fuit ille tui.   30
reddidit intactam, minuitque modestia crimen,
    et iuvenem facti paenituisse patet;
Thesea paenituit, Paris ut succederet illi,
    ne quando nomen non sit in ore meum?
nec tamen irascor—quis enim succenset amanti?—35
    si modo, quem praefers, non simulatur amor.
hoc quoque enim dubito—non quod fiducia desit,
    aut mea sit facies non bene nota mihi;
sed quia credulitas damno solet esse puellis,
    verbaque dicuntur vestra carere fide.   40
At peccant aliae, matronaque rara pudica est.
    quis prohibet raris nomen inesse meum?
nam mea quod visa est tibi mater idonea, cuius
    exemplo flecti me quoque posse putes,
matris in admisso falsa sub imagine lusae   45
    error inest; pluma tectus adulter erat.
nil ego, si peccem, possum nescisse, nec ullus
    error qui facti crimen obumbret erit.

---

       [a] Theseus.   [b] Leda and the swan.

For this I wonder the more what confidence inspires
your enterprise, and what cause has given you hope
to share my couch. Because the Neptunian hero[a]
employed violence with me, can it be that, stolen
once, I seem fit to be stolen, too, a second time?
The blame were mine, had I been lured away; but
seized, as I was, what could I do, more than refuse
my will? Yet he did not reap from his deed the
fruitage he desired; except my fright, I returned
with no harm. Kisses only, and few, the wanton
took, and those despite my struggles; farther than
that, he possesses naught of mine. Such villainy as
yours would not have been content with this—ye
gods do better by me! he was not a man like you.
He gave me back untouched, and moderation
lessened his blame; the youth repented of his
deed, 'tis plain. Did Theseus repent but for Paris
to follow in his steps, lest my name should sometime
cease from the lips of men? Yet I am not angered
—for who grows offended with a lover?—if only
what you profess is not pretended love. For I
doubt of this too—not that I lack ground for con-
fidence, or that my beauty is not well known to me;
but that quick belief is wont to bring harm upon a
woman, and your words are said to lack in faith.

[41] You say that others yield to sin, and the matron
is rare that is chaste. Who is to keep my name
from being among the rare? For, as to my mother's
seeming to you a fit example, and your thinking you
can turn me, too, by citing it, you are mistaken
there, since she fell through being deceived by a
false outside; her lover was disguised by plumage.[b]
For me, if I should sin I can plead ignorance of
nothing; there will be no error to obscure the crime

illa bene erravit vitiumque auctore redemit.
    felix in culpa quo Iove dicar ego ?   50
Sed [1] genus et proavos et regia nomina iactas.
    clara satis domus haec nobilitate sua est.
Iuppiter ut soceri proavus taceatur et omne
    Tantalidae Pelopis Tyndareique decus,[2]
dat mihi Leda Iovem cygno decepta parentem,   55
    quae falsam gremio credula fovit avem.
i nunc et Phrygiae late primordia gentis
    cumque suo Priamum Laumedonte refer !
quos ego suspicio ; sed qui tibi gloria magna est
    quintus, is a nostro nomine primus erit.   60
sceptra tuae quamvis rear esse potentia terrae,
    non tamen haec illis esse minora puto.
si iam divitiis locus hic numeroque virorum
    vincitur, at certe barbara terra tua est.
Munera tanta quidem promittit epistula dives   65
    ut possint ipsas illa movere deas;
sed si iam vellem fines transire pudoris,
    tu melior culpae causa futurus eras.
aut ego perpetuo famam sine labe tenebo,
    aut ego te potius quam tua dona sequar ;   70
utque ea non sperno, sic acceptissima semper
    munera sunt, auctor quae pretiosa facit.
plus multo est, quod amas, quod sum tibi causa laboris,
    quod tam per longas spes tua venit aquas.

[1] sed *Hous.*: quod *s* : ea *P* : et *many MSS.*
[2] decus *P* : genus *G V ω.*

of what I do. Her error was well made, and her sin redeemed by its author. With what Jove shall I be called happy in my fault?

⁵¹ But you boast your birth, your ancestry, and your royal name. This house of mine is glorious enough with its own nobility. To say naught of Jove, forefather of my husband's sire, and all the glory of Pelops, Tantalus' son, and of Tyndareus, Leda makes Jove my father, deceived by the swan, false bird she cherished in her trusting bosom. Go now, and loudly tell of remote beginnings of the Phrygian stock, and of Priam with his Laomedon! Them I esteem; but he who is your great glory and fifth from you, you will find is first from our name.ᵃ Although I believe the sceptres of your Troy are powerful, yet I think these of ours not less than they. If indeed this place is surpassed in riches and number of men, yours at any rate is a barbarous land.

⁶⁵ Your letter, to be sure, promises gifts so great they could move the goddesses themselves; but, were I willing to overstep the limit of my honour, yourself would have been a better cause of fault. Either I shall hold forever to my stainless name, or I shall follow you rather than your gifts; and if I do not scorn them, it is because those gifts are ever most welcome whose giver makes them precious. It is much more that you love me, that I am the cause of your toils, that your hope of me has led you over waters so wide.

ᵃ Helen, Jove; Paris, Priam, Laomedon, Ilus, Tros, Erichthonius, Dardanus, Jove. The usual pedigree makes Jove seventh from Paris.

Illa quoque, adposita quae nunc facis, inprobe,
     mensa,   75
  quamvis experiar dissimulare, noto—
cum modo me spectas oculis, lascive, protervis,
  quos vix instantes lumina nostra ferunt,
et modo suspiras, modo pocula proxima nobis
  sumis, quaque bibi, tu quoque parte bibis.   80
a, quotiens digitis, quotiens ego tecta notavi
  signa supercilio paene loquente dari !
et saepe extimui ne vir meus illa videret,
  non satis occultis erubuique notis !
saepe vel exiguo vel nullo murmure dixi :   85
  " nil pudet hunc . " nec vox haec mea falsa fuit.
orbe quoque in mensae legi sub nomine nostro,
  quod deducta mero littera fecit, AMO.
credere me tamen hoc oculo renuente negavi—
  ei mihi, iam didici sic ego posse loqui !   90
his ego blanditiis, si peccatura fuissem,
  flecterer ; his poterant pectora nostra capi.
est quoque, confiteor, facies tibi rara, potestque
  velle sub amplexus ire puella tuos ;
altera vel potius felix sine crimine fiat,   95
  quam cadat externo noster amore pudor.
disce meo exemplo formosis posse carere ;
  est virtus placitis abstinuisse bonis.
quam multos credis iuvenes optare quod optas,
  qui sapiant ? oculos an Paris unus habes ?   100
non tu plus cernis, sed plus temerarius audes ;
  nec tibi plus cordis, sed mïnus [1] oris, adest.

             [1] minus *PGω* : magis *s.*

⁷⁵ What you do now when our board has been spread, oh, shameless one! I also note, though I try to feign—when now you look on me, wanton, with those bold eyes which my own can scarcely meet when they assail me, and now sigh, and now again take up the goblet nearest me, and yourself, too, drink from the part where I have drunk. Oh, how often have I noted the covert signals you made with your fingers, how often those from your almost speaking brows! And oft I have been in terror lest my husband see it, and have reddened at the signs you did not well conceal. Oft in lowest murmur, or, rather, with no sound at all, I have said: "He has no shame for anything!" and this word of mine was not false. On the round surface of the table, too, I have read beneath my name, which had been writ with the tracing of wine: I LOVE. I could not believe you, none the less, and signified it with my eyes —ah me, already I have learned that thus one may speak! These are the blandishments, had I been disposed to sin, by which I could be bent; by these my heart could be taken prisoner. Your beauty, too, I confess, is rare, and a woman might well wish to submit to your embrace; but let another be happy without reproach rather than my honour fall before a stranger's love. Learn from my example how to live without the fair; there is virtue in abstinence from what delights. How many youths, think you, desire what you desire, and yet are wise? Or are you, Paris, the only one with eyes? You see no more clearly: your daring is only more rash; nor have you more spirit, but less of modesty.

Tunc ego te vellem celeri venisse carina,
   cum mea virginitas mille petita procis ;
si te vidissem, primus de mille fuisses.   105
   iudicio veniam vir dabit ipse meo.
ad possessa venis praeceptaque gaudia, serus ;
   spes tua lenta fuit ; quod petis, alter habet.
ut tamen optarem fieri tua Troica coniunx,
   invitam sic me nec Menelaus habet.   110
desine molle, precor, verbis convellere pectus,
   neve mihi, quam te dicis amare, noce ;
sed sine quam tribuit sortem fortuna tueri,
   nec spolium nostri turpe pudoris ave ! [1]
At Venus hoc pacta est, et in altae vallibus Idae 115
   tres tibi se nudas exhibuere deae,
unaque cum regnum, belli daret altera laudem,
   "Tyndaridis coniunx," tertia dixit, " eris ! "
credere vix equidem caelestia corpora possum
   arbitrio formam supposuisse tuo,   120
utque sit hoc verum, certe pars altera ficta est,
   iudicii pretium qua data dicor ego.
non est tanta mihi fiducia corporis, ut me
   maxima teste dea dona fuisse putem.
contenta est oculis hominum mea forma probari ; 125
   laudatrix Venus est invidiosa mihi.
sed nihil infirmo ; faveo quoque laudibus istis—
   nam mea vox quare, quod cupit, esse neget ?
nec tu succense, nimium mihi creditus aegre ;
   tarda solet magnis rebus inesse fides.   130

          [1] ave *Pa*.: habe *MSS*.

[103] I would the time of your swift keel's coming had been when my maiden hand was sought by a thousand suitors; had I seen you, of the thousand you would have been the first. My husband himself will pardon this judgment of mine. You come late—to joys already seized on and possessed; your hope has been tardy; what you seek, another has. Grant, none the less, that I longed to become your bride at Troy, even so think not Menelaus holds me against my will. Cease, I pray, to pluck with your words at my faltering heart, and do not give pain to her you say you love; but allow me to keep the lot that fortune has given, and do not covet to my shame the spoil of my honour.

[115] You say Venus gave her word for this; and that in the vales of Ida three goddesses presented themselves unclad before you; and that when one of them would give you a throne, and the second glory in war, the third said: "The daughter of Tyndareus shall be your bride!" I can scarce believe that heavenly beings submitted their beauty to you as arbiter: and, grant that this is true, surely the other part of your tale is fiction, in which I am said to have been given you as reward for your verdict. I am not so assured of my charms as to think myself the greatest gift in the divine esteem. My beauty is content to be approved in the eyes of men; the praise of Venus would bring envy on me. Yet I attempt no denial; I am even pleased with the praises you report—for why should my words deny what I much desire? Nor be offended that I am over slow to believe in you; faith is wont to be slow in matters of great moment.

OVID

Prima mea est igitur Veneri placuisse voluptas ;
  proxima, me visam praemia summa tibi,
nec te Palladios nec te Iunonis honores
  auditis Helenae praeposuisse bonis.
ergo ego sum virtus, ego sum tibi nobile regnum! 135
  ferrea sim, si non hoc ego pectus amem.
ferrea, crede mihi, non sum ; sed amare repugno
  illum, quem fieri vix puto posse meum.
quid bibulum curvo proscindere litus aratro,
  spemque sequi coner quam locus ipse negat ?   140
sum rudis ad Veneris furtum, nullaque fidelem—
  di mihi sunt testes—lusimus arte virum.
nunc quoque, quod tacito mando mea verba libello,
  fungitur officio littera nostra novo.
felices, quibus usus adest ! ego nescia rerum   145
  difficilem culpae suspicor esse viam.
Ipse malo metus est ; iam nunc confundor, et omnes
  in nostris oculos vultibus esse reor.
nec reor hoc falso ; sensi mala murmura vulgi,
  et quasdam voces rettulit Aethra mihi.   150
at tu dissimula, nisi si desistere mavis !
  sed cur desistas ? dissimulare potes.
lude, sed occulte ! maior, non maxima, nobis
  est data libertas, quod Menelaus abest.
ille quidem procul est, ita re cogente, profectus ; 155
  magna fuit subitae iustaque causa viae—
aut mihi sic visum est. ego, cum dubitaret an iret,
  "quam primum," dixi, "fac rediturus eas ! "
omine laetatus dedit oscula, "res" que "domusque
  et tibi sit curae Troicus hospes," ait.   160

234.

[131] My first pleasure, then, is to have found favour in the eyes of Venus; the next, that I seemed the greatest prize to you, and that you placed first the honours neither of Pallas nor of Juno when you had heard of Helen's parts. So, then, I mean valour to you, I mean a far-famed throne! I should be of iron, did I not love such a heart. Of iron, believe me, I am not; but I fight against my love for one who I think can hardly become my own. Why should I essay with curvèd plough to furrow the watery shore, and to follow a hope which the place itself denies? I am not practised in the theft of love, and never yet—the gods are my witnesses—have I artfully made sport of my lord. Even now, as I entrust my words to the voiceless page, my letter performs an office all unwonted. Happy they who are no novices! I, ignorant of the world, dream that the path of guilt is hard.

[147] My very fear is a burden, I am in confusion even now, and think that the eyes of all are on my face. Nor do I think so groundlessly; I have caught the evil murmurs of the crowd, and Aethra has brought back certain words to me. But you—do you feign, unless you choose rather to desist! Yet why should you desist?—you have the power to feign. Keep on with your play, yet secretly! Greater, yet not the greatest, freedom is given me by Menelaus' absence. He is away, to be sure, on a far journey, for so his affairs compelled; he had great and just cause for his sudden setting forth—or so it seemed to me. 'Twas I, when he was doubting whether to go, that said: "Go, but see that you return as soon as may be!" Glad at the omen, he kissed me, and, "Look you to my affairs, and to the household, and to our

vix tenui risum, quem dum conpescere luctor,
    nil illi potui dicere praeter " erit."
Vela quidem Creten ventis dedit ille secundis ;
    sed tu non ideo cuncta licere puta !
sic meus hinc vir abest ut me custodiat absens— 165
    an nescis longas regibus esse manus ?
fama quoque est oneri ; nam quo constantius ore
    laudamur vestro, iustius ille timet.
quae iuvat, ut nunc est, eadem mihi gloria damno est,
    et melius famae verba dedisse fuit.   170
nec quod abest hic me tecum mirare relictam ;
    moribus et vitae credidit ille meae.
de facie metuit, vitae confidit, et illum
    securum probitas, forma timere facit.
Tempora ne pereant ultro data praecipis, utque   175
    simplicis utamur commoditate viri.
et libet et timeo, nec adhuc exacta voluntas
    est satis ; in dubio pectora nostra labant.
et vir abest nobis, et tu sine coniuge dormis,
    inque vicem tua me, te mea forma capit ;   180
et longae noctes, et iam sermone coimus,
    et tu, me miseram ! blandus, et una domus.
et peream, si non invitant omnia culpam ;
    nescio quo tardor sed tamen ipsa metu !
quod male persuades, utinam bene cogere posses! 185
    vi mea rusticitas excutienda fuit.

guest from Troy," he says. I scarce could hold my laughter ; and, while I struggled to keep it back, could say to him nothing except " I will."

163 Yes, he has spread sail for Crete with favouring winds ; but think not for this that everything may be as you choose ! My lord is away, but in such wise that he guards me, even though away—or know you not that monarchs have far-reaching hands ? My fame, too, is a burden to me ; for, the more you men persist in your praise of me, the more justly does he fear. The glory that is my delight, just now is a bane as well, and it were better I had cheated fame. Nor let his absence cause you to wonder that I have been left here with you ; my character and way of life have taught him trust. My face makes him fearful, my life makes him sure ; he feels secure in my virtue, my charms rouse his fear.

175 You urge on me that opportunity freely offered should not be wasted, and that we should profit by the obliging ways of a simple husband. I both desire it and I am afraid. So far my will is not determined ; my heart is wavering in doubt. Both my lord is away from me, and you are without companion for your sleep, and your beauty takes me, and mine in turn you ; the nights, too, are long, and we already come together in speech, and you—wretched me !—are persuasive, and the same roof covers us. May I perish if all things do not invite me to my fall ; and yet some fear still holds me back ! What you basely urge on me, would that you could in honour compel me to ! You should have cast out by force the scruples of my rustic

utilis interdum est ipsis iniuria passis.
   sic certe felix esse coacta forem.
Dum novus est, potius coepto pugnemus amori !
   flamma recens parva sparsa resedit aqua.   190
certus in hospitibus non est amor ; errat, ut ipsi,
   cumque nihil speres firmius esse, fuit.
Hypsipyle testis, testis Minoia virgo est,
   in non exhibitis utraque lusa [1] toris.
tu quoque dilectam multos, infide, per annos   195
   diceris Oenonen destituisse tuam.
nec tamen ipse negas ; et nobis omnia de te
   quaerere, si nescis, maxima cura fuit.
adde, quod, ut cupias constans in amore manere,
   non potes.   expediunt iam tua vela Phryges ;   200
dum loqueris mecum, dum nox sperata paratur,
   qui ferat in patriam, iam tibi ventus erit.
cursibus in mediis novitatis plena relinques
   gaudia ; cum ventis noster abibit amor.
An sequar, ut suades, laudataque Pergama visam   205
   pronurus et magni Laumedontis ero ?
non ita contemno volucris praeconia famae,
   ut probris terras inpleat illa meis.
quid de me poterit Sparte, quid Achaia tota,
   quid gentes aliae,[2] quid tua Troia loqui ?   210
quid Priamus de me, Priami quid sentiet uxor,
   totque tui fratres Dardanidesque nurus ?
tu quoque, qui poteris fore me sperare fidelem,
   et non exemplis anxius esse tuis ?

   [1] lusa *s* : insta *P V G* : questa *Hein.*
   [2] aliae *P s* : Asiae *many MSS.*

heart. Wrong sometimes brings gain even to those themselves who suffer it. In this way, surely I could have been compelled to happiness.

189 While it is new, let us rather fight against the love we have begun to feel. A new-kindled flame dies down when sprinkled with but little water. Uncertain is the love of strangers; it wanders, like themselves, and when you expect nothing to be more sure, 'tis gone. Hypsipyle is witness, witness is the Minoan maid, both mocked in their unacknowledged marriage-beds. You, too, faithless one, they say have abandoned your Oenone, beloved for many years. Nor yet do you yourself deny it; and, if you do not know, to inquire into all concerning you has been my greatest care. Besides, though you should long to remain constant in love, you have not the power. The Phrygians are even now unfurling your sails; while you are speaking with me, while you are making ready for the hoped-for night, already the wind to bear you homeward will be here. In their mid course you will abandon joys yet full of freshness; away with the winds will go your love of me.

205 Or shall I follow as you urge, and look upon the Pergamum you praise, and be a bride of the grandchild of great Laomedon? I do not so despise the heraldings of the winged talk of men that I would let it fill the earth with my reproach. What will Sparta find to say of me, what all Achaia, what other peoples, what your Troy? What will Priam think of me, what Priam's wife, and all your many brothers and their Dardanian wives? You, too, how will you be able to hope that I shall keep faith and not be troubled by your own example? Whatever

quicumque Iliacos intraverit advena portus,   215
  is tibi solliciti causa timoris erit.
ipse mihi quotiens iratus "adultera!" dices,
  oblitus nostro crimen inesse tuum!
delicti fies idem reprehensor et auctor.
  terra, precor, vultus obruat ante meos!   220
At fruar Iliacis opibus cultuque beato,
  donaque promissis uberiora feram;
purpura nempe mihi pretiosaque texta dabuntur,
  congestoque auri pondere dives ero!
da veniam fassae—non sunt tua munera tanti;   225
  nescio quo tellus me tenet ipsa modo.
quis mihi, si laedar, Phrygiis succurret in oris?
  unde petam fratres, unde parentis opem?
omnia Medeae fallax promisit Iason—
  pulsa est Aesonia num minus illa domo?   230
non erat Aeetes, ad quem despecta rediret,
  non Idyia parens Chalciopeque soror.
tale nihil timeo—sed nec Medea timebat!
  fallitur augurio spes bona saepe suo.
omnibus invenies, quae nunc iactantur in alto,   235
  navibus a portu lene fuisse fretum.
Fax quoque me terret, quam se peperisse cruentam
  ante diem partus est tua visa parens;
et vatum timeo monitus, quos igne Pelasgo
  Ilion arsurum praemonuisse ferunt.   240
utque favet Cytherea tibi, quia vicit habetque
  parta per arbitrium bina tropaea tuum,
sic illas vereor, quae, si tua gloria vera est,
  iudice te causam non tenuere duae;

stranger shall have entered the harbours of Ilion
will be the cause of anxious fears for you. You
yourself, how often in anger will you say to me:
" Adulteress!" forgetful that your own reproach is
linked with mine! You will be at the same time
the censor and the author of my fault. Ere that, I
pray, may earth lie heavy o'er my face!

²²¹ But you say I shall enjoy the wealth of Ilion
and a life of all things rich, and shall have gifts more
splendid even than your promise; yes, purple and
precious webs will be given me, and I shall be rich
with heaped-up weight of gold! Forgive me if I say
it—your gifts are not worth so much; I know not
how, my land itself still holds me back. Who will
succour me on Phrygian shores if I meet with harm?
Where shall I look for brothers, where for a father's
aid? All things false Jason promised to Medea
—was she the less thrust forth from the house
of Aeson? There was no Aeëtes to receive the
scorned maid home, no mother Idyia, no sister
Chalciope. Naught like this do I fear—but neither
did Medea fear! Fair hope is often deceived in its
own augury. For every ship tossed now upon the
deep, you will find that the sea was gentle as it left
the harbour.

²³⁷ The torch, too, starts my fears—the bloody
torch your mother brought forth in vision before
the day of her travail; and I shrink at the words of
the seers who they say forewarned that Ilion would
burn with Pelasgian fire. And, just as Cytherea
favours you, because she was victorious and has a
twofold trophy won from the verdict you gave,
so I fear those two that—if your boast be true—lost
their causes by your judging; and I do not doubt

nec dubito, quin, te si prosequar, arma parentur. 245
    ibit per gladios, ei mihi! noster amor.
an fera Centauris indicere bella coegit
    Atracis Haemonios Hippodamia viros—
tu fore tam iusta lentum Menelaon in ira
    et geminos fratres Tyndareumque putas? 250
Quod bene te iactes et fortia facta loquaris,
    a verbis facies dissidet ista tuis.
apta magis Veneri, quam sunt tua corpora Marti.
    bella gerant fortes, tu, Pari, semper ama!
Hectora, quem laudas, pro te pugnare iubeto; 255
    militia est operis altera digna tuis.
his ego, si saperem pauloque audacior essem,
    uterer; utetur, siqua puella sapit—
aut ego deposito sapiam fortasse pudore
    et dabo cunctatas tempore victa manus. 260
Quod petis, ut furtim praesentes ista loquamur,
    scimus, quid captes conloquiumque voces;
sed nimium properas, et adhuc tua messis in herba est.
    haec mora sit voto forsan amica tuo.
Hactenus; arcanum furtivae conscia mentis 265
    littera iam lasso pollice sistat opus.
cetera per socias Clymenen Aethramque loquamur,
    quae mihi sunt comites consiliumque duae.

that, should I follow you, war would be set on foot.
Through swords, ah me ! our love will have to make
its way. Or did Hippodamia of Atrax compel
Haemonia's men to declare fierce war on the Cen-
taurs—and do you think that Menelaus and my
twin brethren and Tyndareus will be slow to act in
such righteous wrath ?

251 As for your loud vaunting and talk of brave
deeds, that face belies your words. Your parts are
better suited for Venus than for Mars. Be the
waging of wars for the valiant; for you, Paris, ever
to love ! Bid Hector, whom you praise, go warring
in your stead; 'tis the other campaigning befits your
prowess. That prowess, were I wise or something
bolder, I would employ; employed it will be by
whatever maid is wise—or I perchance, forgetting
modesty, shall learn wisdom and, overcome by time,
yield in tardy surrender.

261 You ask that we speak of these things in
secret, face to face. I know what it is you court,
and what you mean by speech with me ; but you
are over hasty, and your harvest is still in the
green. This delay perhaps may be friendly to
your wish.

265 Thus far now ; let the writing that shares the
secret of my heart now stay its furtive task, for my
hand is wearied. The rest let us say through my
companions Clymene and Aethra, the two who attend
and counsel me.

OVID

XVIII.

Leander Heroni

Mittit Abydenus, quam mallet ferre, salutem,
    si cadat unda maris, Sesta puella, tibi.
si mihi di faciles, si[1] sunt in amore secundi,
    invitis oculis haec mea verba leges.
sed non sunt faciles ; nam cur mea vota morantur   5
    currere me nota nec patiuntur aqua ?
ipsa vides caelum pice nigrius et freta ventis
    turbida perque cavas vix adeunda rates.
unus, et hic audax, a quo tibi littera nostra
    redditur, e portu navita movit iter ;   10
adscensurus eram, nisi quod, cum vincula prorae
    solveret, in speculis omnis Abydos erat.
non poteram celare meos, velut ante, parentes,
    quemque tegi volumus, non latuisset amor.
Protinus haec scribens, "felix, i, littera !" dixi,   15
    " iam tibi formosam porriget illa manum.
forsitan admotis etiam tangere labellis,
    rumpere dum niveo vincula dente volet."
talibus exiguo dictis mihi murmure verbis,
    cetera cum charta dextra locuta mea est.   20
at quanto mallem, quam scriberet, illa nataret,
    meque per adsuetas sedula ferret aquas !
aptior illa quidem placido dare verbera ponto ;
    est tamen et sensus apta ministra mei.

[1] si *Pa*.: et *P* : tibi *G V* : vel *s* : ut *s* : qui *s*.

---

[a] The story of Hero and Leander was very popular from
the time of Augustus on, but is not found in Greek
classical literature. Besides Ovid, Musaeus, a late Greek
(at least 500 A.D.), is the only prominent poet of antiquity to

XVIII

LEANDER TO HERO

HE of Abydos sends to you, Maid of Sestos, the greetings he would rather bring, if the waves of the sea should fall.[a] If the gods are kindly toward me, if they favour me in my love, you will read with unwilling eye these words of mine. But they are not kindly; for why do they delay my vows, nor suffer me to haste through the well-known waters? You yourself see how the heavens are blacker than pitch, and the straits turbid with winds, and how the hollowed ships can scarce set sail upon them. One seaman only, and he a bold one—he by whom this letter is brought to you—has put out from the harbour; I had embarked with him, but that, as he loosed the cables from the prow, Abydos all was looking down on him. I could not evade my parents, as before, and the love we wish to keep hid would have come to light.

15 Forthwith writing these words, " Go, happy letter!" I said; "soon she will reach forth for thee her beautiful hand. Perchance thou wilt even be touched by her approaching lips as she seeks to break thy bands with her snowy tooth." Speaking such words as these in lowest murmur, the rest I let my right hand say upon the sheet. But ah! how much rather would I have it swim than write, and eagerly bear me through the accustomed waves! It is more fit, I grant, for plying the stroke upon the tranquil deep; yet also apt minister of what I feel.

use it. Compare Byron's *Bride of Abydos*, and Marlowe's *Hero and Leander*.

Septima nox agitur, spatium mihi longius anno,   25
    sollicitum raucis ut mare fervet aquis.
his ego si vidi mulcentem pectora somnum
    noctibus, insani sit mora longa freti !
rupe sedens aliqua specto tua litora tristis
    et, quo non possum corpore, mente feror.   30
lumina quin etiam summa vigilantia turre
    aut videt aut acies nostra videre putat.
ter mihi deposita est in sicca vestis harena ;
    ter grave temptavi carpere nudus iter—
obstitit inceptis tumidum iuvenalibus aequor,   35
    mersit et inversis [1] ora natantis aquis.
At tu, de rapidis inmansuetissime ventis,
    quid mecum certa proelia mente geris ?
in me, si nescis, Borea, non aequora, saevis !
    quid faceres, esset ni tibi notus amor ?   40
tam gelidus quod sis, num te tamen, inprobe,
      quondam
    ignibus Actaeis incaluisse negas ?
gaudia rapturo siquis tibi claudere vellet
    aerios aditus, quo paterere modo ?
parce, precor, facilemque move moderatius auram—   45
    imperet Hippotades sic tibi triste nihil !
Vana peto ; precibusque meis obmurmurat ipse
    quasque quatit, nulla parte coercet aquas.
nunc daret audaces utinam mihi Daedalus alas—
    Icarium quamvis hinc prope litus abest !   50
quidquid erit, patiar, liceat modo corpus in auras
    tollere, quod dubia saepe pependit aqua.

    [1] et inversis *Pa.*: et ad inversis *P* : et adversis ω.

---

    [a] Orithyia of Athens.   [b] Aeolus.

²⁵ It is now the seventh night, space longer than a year to me, that the troubled sea has been boiling with hoarse-voiced waters. If in all these nights I have had sleep soothe my breast, may I be long kept from you by the raging deep! Sitting upon some rock, I look sadly on your shores, carried in my thoughts to where in body I cannot go. Nay, my vision even sees—or thinks it sees—lights waking in the topmost of your tower. Thrice have I laid down my garments upon the dry sand; thrice, naked, have I tried to enter on the heavy way—the swollen billows opposed the bold attempts of youth, and their waters, surging upon me as I swam, rolled over my head.

³⁷ But thou, most ungentle of the sweeping winds, why art thou bent on waging war with me? It is I, O Boreas, if thou dost not know, and not the waves, against whom thou ragest! What wouldst thou do, were it not that love is known to thee? Cold as thou art, canst thou yet deny, base wind, that of yore thou wert aflame with Actaean fires?ᵃ If, when eager to seek thy joys, someone were to close to thee the paths of air, in what wise wouldst thou endure it? Have mercy on me, I pray; be mild, and stir a more gentle breeze—so may the child of Hippotesᵇ lay upon thee no harsh command!

⁴⁷ Vain is my petition; my prayers are met by his murmurings, and the waves tossed up by him he nowhere curbs. Now would that Daedalus could give me his daring wings—though the Icarian strand is not far hence! Whatever might be I would endure, so I could only raise into air the body that oft has hung upon the dubious wave.

Interea, dum cuncta negant ventique fretumque,
  mente agito furti tempora prima mei.
nox erat incipiens—namque est meminisse
  voluptas—   55
  cum foribus patriis egrediebar amans.
nec mora, deposito pariter cum veste timore
  iactabam liquido bracchia lenta mari.
luna fere tremulum praebebat lumen eunti
  ut comes in nostras officiosa vias.   60
hanc ego suspiciens, "faveas, dea candida," dixi,
  "et subeant animo Latmia saxa tuo!
non sinit Endymion te pectoris esse severi.
  flecte, precor, vultus ad mea furta tuos!
tu dea mortalem caelo delapsa petebas;   65
  vera loqui liceat!—quam sequor ipsa[1] dea est.
neu referam mores caelesti pectore dignos,
  forma nisi in veras non cadit illa deas.
a Veneris facie non est prior ulla tuaque;
  neve meis credas vocibus, ipsa vide!   70
quantum, cum fulges radiis argentea puris,
  concedunt flammis sidera cuncta tuis,
tanto formosis formosior omnibus illa est.
  si dubitas, caecum, Cynthia, lumen habes."
Haec ego, vel certe non his diversa, locutus   75
  per mihi cedentes nocte ferebar aquas.
unda repercussae radiabat imagine lunae,
  et nitor in tacita nocte diurnus erat;
nullaque vox usquam, nullum veniebat ad aures
  praeter dimotae corpore murmur aquae.   80
Alcyones solae, memores Ceycis amati,
  nescio quid visae sunt mihi dulce queri.

  [1] ipse P_1.

⁵³ Meantime, while wind and wave deny me everything, I ponder in my heart the first times I stole to you. Night was but just beginning—for the memory has charm for me—when I left my father's doors on the errand of love. Nor did I wait, but, flinging away my garments, and with them my fears, I struck out with pliant arm upon the liquid deep. The moon for the most shed me a tremulous light as I swam, like a duteous attendant watchful over my path. Lifting to her my eyes, "Be gracious to me, shining deity," I said, "and let the rocks of Latmos rise in thy mind! Endymion will not have thee austere of heart. Bend, O I pray, thy face to aid my secret loves. Thou, a goddess, didst glide from the skies and seek a mortal love; ah, may it be allowed me to say the truth!—she I seek is a goddess too. To say naught of virtues worthy of heavenly breasts, beauty like hers falls to none but the true divine. After the beautiful face of Venus, and thine own, there is none before hers; and, that thou mayst not need to trust my words, look thou thyself! As much as all the stars are less than thy bright fires when thy silvery gleam goes forth with pure rays, so much more fair is she than all the fair. If thou dost doubt it, Cynthia, thy light is blind."

⁷⁵ These words I spake, or words at least not differing much from these, and was borne along in the night through waters that made way before my stroke. The wave was radiant with the image of the reflected moon, and there was a splendour as of day in the silent night; no note came anywhere to my ears, no sound but the murmur of the waters my body thrust aside. The Halcyons only, their hearts still true to beloved Ceyx, I heard in what seemed to me some sweet lament.

Iamque fatigatis umero sub utroque lacertis
    fortiter in summas erigor altus aquas.
ut procul aspexi lumen, "meus ignis in illo est :   85
    illa meum," dixi, " litora lumen [1] habent ! "
et subito lassis vires rediere lacertis,
    visaque, quam fuerat, mollior unda mihi.
frigora ne possim gelidi sentire profundi,
    qui calet in cupido pectore, praestat amor.   90
quo magis accedo propioraque litora fiunt,
    quoque minus restat, plus libet ire mihi.
cum vero possum cerni quoque, protinus addis
    spectatrix animos, ut valeamque facis.
nunc etiam nando dominae placuisse laboro,   95
    atque oculis iacto bracchia nostra tuis.
te tua vix prohibet nutrix descendere in altum—
    hoc quoque enim vidi, nec mihi verba dabas.
nec tamen effecit, quamvis retinebat euntem,
    ne fieret prima pes tuus udus aqua.   100
excipis amplexu feliciaque oscula iungis—
    oscula, di magni, trans mare digna peti !—
eque tuis demptos umeris mihi tradis amictus,
    et madidam siccas aequoris imbre comam.
Cetera nox et nos et turris conscia novit,   105
    quodque mihi lumen per vada monstrat iter.
non magis illius numerari gaudia noctis
    Hellespontiaci quam maris alga potest ;
quo brevius spatium nobis ad furta dabatur,
    hoc magis est cautum, ne foret illud iners.   110
Iamque fugatura Tithoni coniuge noctem
    praevius Aurorae Lucifer ortus erat ;

---

[1] lument *P* : numen *s.*

[83] And now my arms grow tired below the shoulder-joint, and with all my strength I raise myself aloft on the summit of the waters. Beholding, far off, a light, "It is my love shines in yonder flame," I cried; "it is my light yon shores contain!" And straight the strength came back to my wearied arms, and the wave seemed easier to me than before. To keep me from the chill of the cold deep, love lends his aid, hot in my eager breast. The nearer I approach, and the nearer draw the shores, and the less of the way remains, the greater my joy to hasten on. When in truth I can be seen as well as see, by your glance you straightway give me heart, and make me strong. Now, too, I strain in my course to pleasure my lady, and toss my arms in the stroke for you to see. Your nurse can scarce stay you from rushing down into the tide—for I saw this, too, and you did not cheat my eye. Yet, though she held you as you went, she could not keep you from wetting your foot at the water's edge. You welcome me with your embrace, share happy kisses with me—kisses, O ye great gods, worth seeking across the deep!—and from your own shoulders you strip the robes to give them over to me, and dry my hair all dripping with the rain of the sea.

[105] For the rest—night knows of that, and our-selves, and the tower that shares our secret, and the light that guides me on my passage through the floods. The joys of that dear night may no more be numbered than the weeds of the Hellespontic sea; the briefer the space that was ours for the theft of love, the more we made sure it should not idly pass.

[111] And now Aurora, the bride of Tithonus, was making ready to chase the night away, and Lucifer

oscula congerimus properata sine ordine raptim
  et querimur parvas noctibus esse moras.
atque ita cunctatus monitu nutricis amaro   115
  frigida deserta litora turre peto.
digredimur flentes, repetoque ego virginis aequor
  respiciens dominam, dum licet, usque meam.
siqua fides vero est, veniens hinc [1] esse natator,
  cum redeo, videor naufragus esse mihi.   120
hoc quoque, si credes : [2] ad te via prona videtur ;
  a te cum redeo, clivus inertis aquae.
invitus repeto patriam—quis credere possit ?
  invitus certe nunc moror urbe mea.
Ei mihi ! cur animis iuncti secernimur undis,   125
  unaque mens, tellus non habet una duos ?
vel tua me Sestus, vel te mea sumat Abydos ;
  tam tua terra mihi, quam tibi nostra placet.
cur ego confundor, quotiens confunditur aequor ?
  cur mihi causa levis, ventus, obesse potest ?   130
iam nostros curvi norunt delphines amores,
  ignotum nec me piscibus esse reor.
iam patet attritus solitarum limes aquarum,
  non aliter multa quam via pressa rota.
quod mihi non esset nisi sic iter, ante querebar ; 135
  at nunc per ventos hoc quoque deesse queror.
fluctibus inmodicis Athamantidos aequora canent,
  vixque manet portu tuta carina suo ;
hoc mare, cum primum de virgine nomina mersa,
  quae tenet, est nanctum, tale fuisse puto.   140
et satis amissa locus hic infamis ab Helle [a] est,
  utque mihi parcat, nomine crimen habet.

---

[1] hinc *Ehw.*: huc *MSS.*
[2] credes *Pa.*: credis *P ω Plan.*: credas *s.*

---

[a] Helle.

had risen, forerunner of the dawn; in haste we ply
our kisses, all disorderly, complaining that the night
allows brief lingering. So, tarrying till the nurse's
bitter warnings bid me go, I leave the tower and
make for the chilly shore. We part in tears, and I
return to the Maiden's sea,^a looking ever back to my
lady while I can. Believe me, it is true : going
hence, I seem a swimmer, but, when I return, a
shipwrecked man. This too, is true, will you but
believe : toward you, my way seems ever inclined ;
away from you, when I return, it seems a steep
of lifeless water. Against the wish of my heart
I regain my own land—who could believe ? Against
the wish of my heart I tarry now in my own town.

¹²⁵ Ah me! why are we joined in soul and
parted by the wave ; two beings of one mind, but
not of one land ? Either let your Sestos take me, or
my Abydos you ; your land is as dear to me as mine
is dear to you. Why must my heart be troubled as
oft as the sea is troubled ? Why must the wind,
slight cause, have power to hinder me ? Already the
curving dolphins have learned our loves, and I think
the very fishes know me. Already my accustomed
path through the waters is well trod, like to the road
pressed on by many a wheel. That there was no
other way open than this was my complaint before ;
but now, because of the winds, I complain that this
way, too, has failed. The sea of Athamas' child is
foaming white with immense billows, and scarcely
safe is the keel that remains in its own harbour;
such were these waters, I judge, when first they got
from the drownèd maid the name they bear. This
place is of evil fame enough for the loss of Helle,
and, though it spare me, its name reproaches it.

Invideo Phrixo, quem per freta tristia tutum
    aurea lanigero vellere vexit ovis ;
nec tamen officium pecoris navisve requiro,   145
    dummodo, quas findam corpore, dentur aquae.
arte egeo nulla ; fiat modo copia nandi,
    idem navigium, navita, vector ero !
nec sequor aut Helicen, aut, qua Tyros utitur,
    Arcton ;
    publica non curat sidera noster amor.   150
Andromedan alius spectet claramque Coronam,
    quaeque micat gelido Parrhasis Ursa polo ;
at mihi, quod Perseus et cum Iove Liber amarunt,
    indicium dubiae non placet esse viae.
est aliud lumen, multo mihi certius istis,   155
    non errat tenebris quo duce noster amor ;
hoc ego dum spectem, Colchos et in ultima Ponti,
    quaque viam fecit Thessala pinus, eam,
et iuvenem possim superare Palaemona nando
    miraque quem subito reddidit herba deum.   160
Saepe per adsiduos languent mea bracchia motus,
    vixque per inmensas fessa trahuntur aquas.
his ego cum dixi : "pretium non vile laboris,
    iam dominae vobis colla tenenda dabo,"
protinus illa valent, atque ad sua praemia ten-
      dunt,   165
    ut celer Eleo carcere missus equus.
ipse meos igitur servo, quibus uror, amores
    teque, magis caelo digna puella, sequor.
digna quidem caelo es—sed adhuc tellure morare,
    aut dic, ad superos et mihi qua sit iter !   170

---

    [a] Glaucus, the fisherman who ate of a curious grass in
which fish were swimming as if in water : Met. xiii. 905 ff.
    [b] At Olympia.

[143] I envy Phrixus, whom the ram with gold in its woolly fleece bore safely over the stormy seas; yet I ask not the office of ram or ship, if only I may have the waters to cleave with my body. I need no art; so only I am allowed to swim, I will be at once ship, seaman, passenger! I guide myself neither by Helice, nor by Arctos, the leading-star of Tyre; my love will none of the stars in common use. Let another fix his eyes on Andromeda and the bright Crown, and upon the Parrhasian Bear that gleams in the frozen pole; but for me, I care not for the loves of Perseus, and of Liber and Jove, to point me on my dubious way. There is another light, far surer for me than those, and when it leads me through the dark my love leaves not its course; while my eyes are fixed on this, I could go to Colchis or the farthest bounds of Pontus, and where the ship of Thessalian pine held on its course; and I could surpass the young Palaemon in my swimming, and him whom the wondrous herb made suddenly a god.[a]

[161] Often my arms grow heavy from the unceasing stroke, and scarce can drag their weary way through the endless floods. When I say to them: "No slight reward for toil shall be yours, for soon you shall have my lady's neck to hang about," forthwith they take on strength, and stretch forward to the winning of their prize, like the swift steed let go from the Elean starting-chamber.[b] And so I myself keep eyes on the love that burns me, and guide myself by you, maid worthy rather of the skies. For worthy of the skies you are—yet tarry still on earth, or tell me where I also may find a way to the gods above! You are here, yet your

hic es, et exigue misero contingis amanti,
    cumque mea fiunt turbida mente freta.
quid mihi, quod lato non separor aequore, prodest?
    num minus haec nobis tam brevis obstat aqua?
an [1] malim, dubito, toto procul orbe remotus   175
    cum domina longe spem quoque habere meam.
quo propius nunc es, flamma propiore calesco,
    et res non semper, spes mihi semper adest.
paene manu quod amo, tanta est vicinia, tango;
    saepe sed, heu, lacrimas hoc mihi "paene"
        movet!   180
velle quid est aliud fugientia prendere poma
    spemque suo refugi fluminis ore sequi?
Ergo ego te numquam, nisi cum volet unda, tenebo,
    et me felicem nulla videbit hiemps,
cumque minus firmum nil sit quam ventus et unda, 185
    in ventis et aqua spes mea semper erit?
aestus adhuc tamen est. quid, cum mihi laeserit
      aequor
    Plias et Arctophylax Oleniumque pecus?
aut ego non novi, quam sim temerarius, aut me
    in freta non cautus tum quoque mittet amor;   190
neve putes id [2] me, quod abest, promittere, tempus,
    pignora polliciti non tibi tarda dabo.
sit tumidum paucis etiamnunc noctibus aequor,
    ire per invitas experiemur aquas;
aut mihi continget felix audacia salvo,   195
    aut mors solliciti finis amoris erit!
optabo tamen ut partis expellar in illas,
    et teneant portus naufraga membra tuos;
flebis enim tactuque meum dignabere corpus
    et "mortis," dices, "huic ego causa fui!"   200

      [1] an *s* : num *P G ω*.   [2] in *Dilthey Ehw.*

---

       [a] Tantalus.

wretched lover has but small part in you, and when the sea grows turbid my heart is turbid, too. Of what avail to me that the billows are not broad that sunder us? Is this brief span of waters less an obstacle to me? I almost would that I were distant from you the whole world, so that my hopes were far removed, together with my lady. Now, the nearer you are, the nearer is the flame that kindles me, and hope is always with me, not always she I hope for. I can almost touch her with my hand, so near is she I love; but oft, alas! this "almost" starts my tears. What else than this was the catching at elusive fruits, and pursuing with the lips the hope of a retreating stream? [a]

[183] Am I, then, never to embrace you except when the wave so wills, and shall no tempest see me happy? and, though nothing is less certain than the wind and wave, must winds and water ever be my hope? And yet it still is summer. What when the seas have been assailed by the Pleiad, and the guardian of the Bear, and the Goat of Olenos? Either I know not how rash I am, or even then a love not cautious will send me forth on the deep. And, lest you deem I promise this because the time is not yet come, I will give you no tardy pledge of what I promise. Let the sea be swollen still for these few nights, and I shall essay to cross despite the waves; either happy daring shall leave me safe, or death shall be the end of my anxious love! Yet I shall pray to be cast up on yonder shores, and that my shipwrecked limbs may come into your haven; for you will weep over me, and not disdain to touch my body, and you will say: "Of the death he met, I was the cause!"

OVID

Scilicet interitus offenderis omine nostri,
    litteraque invisa est hac mea parte tibi.
desino—parce queri ! sed ut et mare finiat iram,
    accedant, quaeso, fac tua vota meis.
pace brevi nobis opus est, dum transferor isto ;   205
    cum tua contigero litora, perstet hiemps !
istic est aptum nostrae navale carinae,
    et melius nulla stat mea puppis aqua.
illic me claudat Boreas, ubi dulce morari est !
    tunc piger ad nandum, tunc ego cautus ero,   210
nec faciam surdis convicia fluctibus ulla
    triste nataturo nec querar esse fretum.
me pariter venti teneant tenerique lacerti,
    per causas istic inpediarque duas !
Cum patietur hiemps, remis ego corporis utar ;   215
    lumen in adspectu tu modo semper habe !
interea pro me pernoctet epistula tecum,
    quam precor ut minima prosequar ipse mora !

XIX

Hero Leandro

Quam mihi misisti verbis, Leandre, salutem
    ut possim missam rebus habere, veni !
longa mora est nobis omnis, quae gaudia differt.
    da veniam fassae ; non patienter amo !
urimur igne pari, sed sum tibi viribus inpar :   5
    fortius ingenium suspicor esse viris.
ut corpus, teneris ita mens infirma puellis—
    deficiam, parvi temporis adde moram !

201 You are hurt, no doubt, by this omen of my death, and my letter in this part stirs your displeasure. I cease—no more complain; but, that the sea, too, may end its anger, add, I beseech, your prayers to mine. I need a brief space of calm until I cross to you; when I shall have touched your shore, let the storm rage on! Yonder with you is an apt ship-yard for my keel, and in no waters rests my bark more safe. There let Boreas shut me in, where tarrying is sweet! Then will I be slow to swim, then will I be ware, nor cast revilement on the unhearing floods again, nor complain that the sea is rough when I fain would swim. Let me be stayed alike by the winds and your tender arms, and let there be double cause to keep me there!

215 When the storm permits, I shall make use of the oarage of my arms; do you only keep ever the beacon-light where I shall see! Meanwhile, my letter in my stead be with you throughout the night. I pray to follow it myself with least delay!

XIX

Hero to Leander

THAT I may enjoy in very truth the greeting you have sent in words, Leander, O come! Long to me is all delay that defers our joys. Forgive me what I say—I cannot be patient for love! We burn with equal fires, but I am not equal to you in strength; men, methinks, must have stronger natures. As the body, so is the soul of tender women frail— delay but a little longer, and I shall die!

Vos modo venando, modo rus geniale colendo
  ponitis in varia tempora longa mora.   10
aut fora vos retinent aut unctae dona [1] palaestrae,
  flectitis aut freno colla sequacis equi ;
nunc volucrem laqueo, nunc piscem ducitis hamo ;
  diluitur posito serior hora mero.
his mihi summotae, vel si minus acriter urar,   15
  quod faciam, superest praeter amare nihil.
quod superest facio, teque, o mea sola voluptas,
  plus quoque, quam reddi quod mihi possit, amo !
aut ego cum cara de te nutrice susurro,
  quaeque tuum, miror, causa moretur iter ;   20
aut mare prospiciens odioso concita vento
  corripio verbis aequora paene tuis ;
aut, ubi saevitiae paulum gravis unda remisit,
  posse quidem, sed te nolle venire, queror ;
dumque queror lacrimae per amantia lumina
      manant,   25
  pollice quas tremulo conscia siccat anus.
saepe tui specto si sint in litore passus,
  inpositas tamquam servet harena notas ;
utque rogem de te et scribam tibi, siquis Abydo
  venerit, aut, quaero, siquis Abydon eat.   30
quid referam, quotiens dem vestibus oscula, quas tu
  Hellespontiaca ponis iturus aqua ?
Sic ubi lux acta est et noctis amicior hora
  exhibuit pulso sidera clara die,
protinus in summo vigilantia lumina tecto   35
  ponimus, adsuetae signa notamque viae,

---

[1] mane *Bent.*

[9] You men, now in the chase, and now husband-
ing the genial acres of the country, consume long
hours in the varied tasks that keep you. Either
the market-place holds you, or the sports of the
supple wrestling-ground, or you turn with bit the
neck of the responsive steed ; now you take the bird
with the snare, now the fish with the hook ; and the
later hours you while away with the wine before you.
For me who am denied these things, even were I less
fiercely aflame, there is nothing left to do but love.
What there is left, I do ; and you, O sole delight of
mine, I love with even greater love than could be
returned to me! Either with my dear nurse I
whisper of you, and marvel what can keep you from
your way ; or, looking forth upon the sea, I chide
the billows stirred by the hateful wind, in words
almost your own ; or, when the heavy wave has a
little laid aside its fierce mood, I complain that you
indeed could come, but will not; and while I com-
plain tears course from the eyes that love you, and
the ancient dame who shares my secret dries them
with tremulous hand. Often I look to see whether
your footprints are on the shore, as if the sand would
keep the marks impressed on it; and, that I may
inquire about you, and write to you, I still am
asking if anyone has come from Abydos, or if anyone
is going to Abydos. Why tell how many times I
kiss the garments you lay aside when making ready
to stem the waters of the Hellespont?

[33] Thus, when the light is done and night's
more friendly hour has driven out day and set forth
the gleaming stars, straightway I place in the
highest of our abode my watchful lamps, the signals
to guide you on the accustomed way. Then, draw-

tortaque versato ducentes stamina fuso
　feminea tardas fallimus arte moras.
Quid loquar interea tam longo tempore, quaeris?
　nil nisi Leandri nomen in ore meo est.　　　　40
"iamne putas exisse domo mea gaudia, nutrix,
　an vigilant omnes, et timet ille suos?
iamne suas umeris illum deponere vestes,
　pallade iam pingui tinguere membra putas?"
adnuit illa fere;[1] non nostra quod oscula curet,　45
　sed movet obrepens somnus anile caput.
postque morae minimum "iam certe navigat,"
　　inquam,
　"lentaque dimotis bracchia iactat aquis."
paucaque cum tacta perfeci stamina terra,
　an medio possis, quaerimus, esse freto.　　　　50
et modo prospicimus, timida modo voce precamur,
　ut tibi det faciles utilis aura vias;
auribus incertas voces captamus, et omnem
　adventus strepitum credimus esse tui.
Sic ubi deceptae pars est mihi maxima noctis　　55
　acta, subit furtim lumina fessa sopor.
forsitan invitus mecum tamen, inprobe, dormis,
　et, quamquam non vis ipse venire, venis.
nam modo te videor prope iam spectare natantem,
　bracchia nunc umeris umida ferre meis,　　　　60
nunc dare, quae soleo, madidis velamina membris,
　pectora nunc iuncto nostra fovere sinu
multaque praeterea linguae reticenda modestae,
　quae fecisse iuvat, facta referre pudet.
me miseram! brevis est haec et non vera
　　voluptas;　　　　　　　　　　　　　　　65
　nam tu cum somno semper abire soles.

[1] fore *P V ω*.

ing with whirling spindle the twisted thread, with woman's art we beguile the slow hours of waiting.

[39] What, meanwhile, I say through so long a time, you ask? Naught but Leander's name is on my lips. "Do you think my joy has already come forth from his home, my nurse? or are all waking, and does he fear his kin? Now do you think he is putting off the robe from his shoulders, and now rubbing the rich oil into his limbs?" She signs assent, most likely; not that she cares for my kisses, but slumber creeps upon her and lets nod her ancient head. Then, after slightest pause, "Now surely he is setting forth on his voyage," I say, "and is parting the waters with the stroke of his pliant arms." And when I have finished a few strands and the spindle has touched the ground, I ask whether you can be mid way of the strait. And now I look forth, and now in timid tones I pray that a favouring breeze will give you an easy course; my ears catch at uncertain notes, and at every sound I am sure that you have come.

[55] When the greatest part of the night has gone by for me in such delusions, sleep steals upon my wearied eyes. Perhaps, false one, you yet pass the night with me, though against your will; perhaps you come, though yourself you do not wish to come. For now I seem to see you already swimming near, and now to feel your wet arms about my neck, and now to throw about your dripping limbs the accustomed coverings, and now to warm our bosoms in the close embrace—and many things else a modest tongue should say naught of, whose memory delights, but whose telling brings a blush. Ah me! brief pleasures these, and not the truth; for you are

firmius, o, cupidi tandem coeamus amantes,
　　nec careant vera gaudia nostra fide !
cur ego tot viduas exegi frigida noctes?
　　cur totiens a me, lente morator,[1] abes?　　　70
est mare, confiteor, nondum tractabile nanti ;
　　nocte sed hesterna lenior aura fuit.
cur ea praeterita est? cur non ventura timebas?
　　tam bona cur periit, nec tibi rapta via est?
protinus ut similis detur tibi copia cursus,　　　75
　　hoc melior certe, quo prior, illa fuit.
At cito mutata est iactati forma profundi.
　　tempore, cum properas, saepe minore venis.
hic, puto, deprensus nil, quod querereris, haberes,
　　meque tibi amplexo nulla noceret hiemps.　　　80
certe ego tum ventos audirem laeta sonantis,
　　et numquam placidas esse precarer aquas.
quid tamen evenit, cur sis metuentior undae
　　contemptumque prius nunc vereare fretum ?
nam memini, cum te saevum veniente minaxque　　85
　　non minus, aut multo non minus, aequor erat ;
cum tibi clamabam : " sic tu temerarius esto,
　　ne miserae virtus sit tua flenda mihi !"
unde novus timor hic, quoque illa audacia fugit ?
　　magnus ubi est spretis ille natator aquis?　　　90
Sis tamen hoc potius, quam quod prius esse solebas,
　　et facias placidum per mare tutus iter—
dummodo sis idem, dum sic, ut scribis, amemur,
　　flammaque non fiat frigidus illa cinis.

　　　　　　[1] morator $V P_1$ s : natator ωP_2.

ever wont to go when slumber goes. O more firmly let our eager loves be knit, and our joys be faithful and true! Why have I passed so many cold and lonely nights? Why, O tardy loiterer, are you so often away from me? The sea, I grant, is not yet fit for the swimmer; but yesternight the gale was gentler. Why did you let it pass? Why did you fear what was not to come? Why did so fair a night go by for naught, and you not seize upon the way? Grant that like chance for coming be given you soon; this chance was the better, surely, since 'twas the earlier.

77 But swiftly, you may say, the face of the storm-tossed deep was changed. Yet you often come in less time, when you are in haste. Overtaken here, you would have, methinks, no reason to complain, and while you held me close no storm would harm you. I surely should hear the sounding winds with joy, and should pray for the waters never to be calm. But what has come to pass, that you are grown more fearful of the wave, and dread the sea you before despised? For I call to mind your coming once when the flood was not less fierce and threatening—or not much less; when I cried to you: "Be ever rash with such good fortune, lest wretched I may have to weep for your courage!" Whence this new fear, and whither has that boldness fled? Where is that mighty swimmer who scorned the waters?

91 But no, be rather as you are than as you were wont to be before; make your way when the sea is placid, and be safe—so you are only the same, so we only love each other, as you write, and that flame of ours turn not to chill ashes. I do not fear so much

non ego tam ventos timeo mea vota morantes,   95
   quam similis vento ne tuus erret amor,
ne non sim tanti, superentque pericula causam,
   et videar merces esse labore minor.
Interdum metuo, patria ne laedar et inpar
   dicar Abydeno Thressa puella toro.   100
ferre tamen possum patientius omnia, quam si
   otia nescio qua paelice captus agis,
in tua si veniunt alieni colla lacerti,
   fitque novus nostri finis amoris amor.
a, potius peream, quam crimine vulnerer isto,   105
   fataque sint culpa nostra priora tua!
nec, quia venturi dederis mihi signa doloris,
   haec loquor aut fama sollicitata nova.
omnia sed vereor—quis enim securus amavit?
   cogit et absentes plura timere locus.   110
felices illas, sua quas praesentia nosse
   crimina vera iubet, falsa timere vetat!
nos tam vana movet, quam facta iniuria fallit,
   incitat et morsus error uterque pares.
o utinam venias, aut ut ventusve paterve   115
   causaque sit certe femina nulla morae!
quodsi quam sciero, moriar, mihi crede, dolendo;
   iamdudum pecca, si mea fata petis!
Sed neque peccabis, frustraque ego terreor istis,
   quoque minus venias, invida pugnat hiemps.   120
me miseram! quanto planguntur litora fluctu,
   et latet obscura condita nube dies!

the winds that hinder my vows as I fear that like the wind your love may wander—that I may not be worth it all, that your perils may outweigh their cause, and I seem a reward too slight for your toils.

⁹⁹ Sometimes I fear my birthplace may injure me, and I be called no match, a Thracian maid, for a husband from Abydos. Yet could I bear with greater patience all things else than have you linger in the bonds of some mistress's charms, see other arms clasped round your neck, and a new love end the love we bear. Ah, may I rather perish than be wounded by such a crime, may fate overtake me ere you incur that guilt ! I do not say these words because you have given sign that such grief will come to me, or because some recent tale has made me anxious, but because I fear everything— for who that loved was ever free from care ? The fears of the absent, too, are multiplied by distance. Happy they whom their own presence bids know the true charge, and forbids to fear the false ! Me wrongs imaginary fret, while the real I cannot know, and either error stirs equal gnawings in my heart. O, would you only come ! or did I only know that the wind, or your father—at least, no woman—kept you back ! Were it a woman, and I should know, I should die of grieving, believe me ; sin against me at once, if you desire my death !

¹¹⁹ But you will not sin against me, and my fears of such troubles are vain. The reason you do not come is the jealous storm that beats you back. Ah, wretched me ! with what great waves the shores are beaten, and what dark clouds envelop and hide the day ! It may be the loving mother of

forsitan ad pontum mater pia venerit Helles,
  mersaque roratis nata fleatur aquis—
an mare ab inviso privignae nomine dictum   125
  vexat in aequoream versa noverca deam?
non favet, ut nunc est,[1] teneris locus iste puellis;
  hac Helle periit, hac ego laedor aqua.
at tibi flammarum memori, Neptune, tuarum
  nullus erat ventis inpediendus amor—   130
si neque Amymone nec, laudatissima forma,
  criminis est Tyro fabula vana tui,
lucidaque Alcyone Calyceque Hecataeone nata,[2]
  et nondum nexis angue Medusa comis,
flavaque Laudice caeloque recepta Celaeno,   135
  et quarum memini nomina lecta mihi.
has certe pluresque canunt, Neptune, poetae
  molle latus lateri conposuisse tuo.
cur igitur, totiens vires expertus amoris,
  adsuetum nobis turbine claudis iter?   140
parce, ferox, latoque mari tua proelia misce!
  seducit terras haec brevis unda duas.
te decet aut magnas magnum iactare carinas,
  aut etiam totis classibus esse trucem;
turpe deo pelagi iuvenem terrere natantem,   145
  gloriaque est stagno quolibet ista minor.
nobilis ille quidem est et clarus origine, sed non
  a tibi suspecto ducit Ulixe genus.
da veniam servaque duos! natat ille, sed isdem
  corpus Leandri, spes mea pendet aquis.   150

[1] utcumque est *Dilthey Ehw.*
[2] ceuceque et aveone *P* : celiceque et aveone *G* : ceyce et
aveone *V* : Calyceque Ecatheone (Hecataeone) *Hein.*

---

[a] Nephele, mother of Phrixus and Helle.
[b] Ino, second wife of Helle's father Athamas.
[c] "Such learned enumerations of the love adventures of

THE HEROIDES XIX

Helle has come to the sea, and is lamenting in down-pouring tears the drowning of her child[a]—or is the step-dame, turned to a goddess of the waters, vexing the sea that is called by her step-child's hated name?[b] This place, such as 'tis now, is aught but friendly to tender maids; by these waters Helle perished, by them my own affliction comes. Yet, Neptune, wert thou mindful of thine own heart's flames, thou oughtst let no love be hindered by the winds—if neither Amymone, nor Tyro much bepraised for beauty, are stories idly charged to thee, nor shining Alcyone, and Calyce, child of Hecataeon, nor Medusa when her locks were not yet twined with snakes, nor golden-haired Laodice and Celaeno taken to the skies, nor those whose names I mind me of having read.[c] These, surely, Neptune, and many more, the poets say in their songs have mingled their soft embraces with thine own. Why, then, dost thou, who hast felt so many times the power of love, close up with whirling storm the way we have learned to know? Spare us, impetuous one, and mingle thy battles out upon the open deep! These waters, that separate two lands, are scant. It befits thee, who art mighty, either to toss about the mighty keel, or to be fierce even with entire fleets; 'tis shame for the god of the great sea to terrify a swimming youth— that glory is less than should come from troubling any pond. Noble he is, to be sure, and of a famous stock, but he does not trace his line from the Ulysses thou dost not trust. Have mercy on him, and save us both! It is he who swims, but the limbs of Leander and all my hopes hang on the selfsame wave.

gods appear to have been a form of poetry cultivated by the Alexandrines." Purser, in Palmer p. 475.

OVID

Sternuit en [1] lumen !—posito nam scribimus illo—
    sternuit et nobis prospera signa dedit.
ecce, merum nutrix faustos instillat in ignes,
    "cras" que "erimus plures," inquit, et ipsa bibit.
effice nos plures, evicta per aequora lapsus,   155
    o penitus toto corde recepte mihi !
in tua castra redi, socii desertor amoris ;
    ponuntur medio cur mea membra toro ?
quod timeas, non est ! auso Venus ipsa favebit,
    sternet et aequoreas aequore nata vias.   160
ire libet medias ipsi mihi saepe per undas,
    sed solet hoc maribus tutius esse fretum.
nam cur hac vectis Phrixo Phrixique sorore
    sola dedit vastis femina nomen aquis ?
Forsitan ad reditum metuas ne tempora desint,   165
    aut gemini nequeas ferre laboris onus.
at nos diversi medium coeamus in aequor
    obviaque in summis oscula demus aquis,
atque ita quisque suas iterum redeamus ad urbes ;
    exiguum, sed plus quam nihil illud erit !   170
vel pudor hic utinam, qui nos clam cogit amare,
    vel timidus famae cedere vellet amor !
nunc male res iunctae, calor et reverentia, pugnant.
    quid sequar, in dubio est ; haec decet, ille iuvat.
ut semel intravit Colchos Pagasaeus Iason,   175
    inpositam celeri Phasida puppe tulit ;
ut semel Idaeus Lacedaemona venit adulter,
    cum praeda rediit protinus ille sua.

[1] et *MSS.*: en *Bent. Hein.*

---

[a] She drops water into the flame of the lamp, either to clear the wick or to honour the omen.

[151] My lamp has sputtered, see !—for I am writing with it near—it has sputtered and given us favouring sign. Look, nurse is pouring drops into auspicious fires.[a] "To-morrow," she says, "we shall be more," and herself drinks of the wine. Ah, do make us more, glide over the conquered wave, O you whom I have welcomed to all my inmost heart! Come back to camp, deserter of your ally love ; why must I lay my limbs in the mid space of my couch ? There is naught for you to fear! Venus' self will smile upon your venture ; child of the sea, the paths of the sea she will make smooth. Oft am I prompted myself to go through the midst of the waves, but 'tis the wont of this strait to be safer for men. For why, though Phrixus and Phrixus' sister both rode this way, did the maiden alone give name to these wide waters ?

[165] Perhaps you fear the time may fail you for return, or you may not endure the effort of the twofold toil. Then let us both from diverse ways come together in mid sea, and give each other kisses on the waters' crest, and so return again each to his own town ; 'twill be little, but more than naught! Would that either this shame that compels us to secret loving would cease, or else the love that fears men's speech. Now, two things that ill go together, passion and regard for men, are at strife. Which I shall follow is in doubt ; the one becomes, the other delights. Once had Jason of Pagasae entered Colchis, and he set the maid of the Phasis in his swift ship and bore her off ; once had the lover from Ida come to Lacedaemon, and he straight returned together with his prize. But you, as oft

tu quam saepe petis, quod amas, tam saepe relinquis,
    et quotiens grave sit [1] puppibus ire, natas.   180
Sic tamen, o iuvenis tumidarum victor aquarum,
    sic facito spernas, ut vereare, fretum !
arte laboratae merguntur ab aequore naves ;
    tu tua plus remis bracchia posse putas ?
quod cupis, hoc nautae metuunt, Leandre, natare ; 185
    exitus hic fractis puppibus esse solet.
me miseram ! cupio non persuadere, quod hortor,
    sisque, precor, monitis fortior ipse meis—
dummodo pervenias excussaque saepe per undas
    inicias umeris bracchia lassa meis !   190
Sed mihi, caeruleas quotiens obvertor ad undas,
    nescio quae pavidum frigora [2] pectus habet.
nec minus hesternae confundor imagine noctis,
    quamvis est sacris illa piata meis.
namque sub aurora, iam dormitante lucerna,   195
    somnia quo cerni tempore vera solent,
stamina ·de digitis cecidere sopore remissis,
    collaque pulvino nostra ferenda dedi.
hic ego ventosas nantem delphina per undas
    cernere non dubia sum mihi visa fide,   200
quem postquam bibulis inlisit fluctus harenis,
    unda simul miserum vitaque deseruit.
quidquid id est, timeo ; nec tu mea somnia ride
    nec nisi tranquillo bracchia crede mari !
si tibi non parcis, dilectae parce puellae,   205
    quae numquam nisi te sospite sospes ero !

---

[1] sit *V*s *Bent. Hous.*: fit *P G*.
[2] *So Burm.*: quod *P*: quae *V G*: quid *G*₂: frigora *V*:
frigore *P G*: habent *s*: ha/// *V*: habet *P G*.

as you seek your love, so oft you leave her, and whene'er 'tis peril for boats to go, you swim.

181 Yet, O my young lover, though victor over the swollen waters, so spurn the sea as still to be in fear of it! Ships wrought with skill are overwhelmed by the wave; do you think your arms more powerful than oars? What you are eager for, Leander—to swim—is the sailor's fear; 'tis that follows ever on the wreck of ships. Ah, wretched me! I am eager not to persuade you to what I urge; may you be too strong, I pray, to yield to my admonition—only so you come to me, and cast about my neck the wearied arms oft beaten by the wave!

191 But, as often as I turn my face toward the dark blue wave, my fearful breast is seized by some hidden chill. Nor am I the less perturbed by a dream I had yesternight, though I have cleared myself of its threat by sacrifice. For, just before dawn, when my lamp was already dying down, at the time when dreams are wont to be true, my fingers were relaxed by sleep, the threads fell from them, and I laid my head down upon the pillow to rest. There in vision clear I seemed to see a dolphin swimming through the wind-tossed waters; and after the flood had cast it forth upon the thirsty sands, the wave, and at the same time life, abandoned the unhappy thing. Whatever it may mean, I fear; and you—nor smile at my dreams, nor trust your arms except to a tranquil sea! If you spare not yourself, spare the maid beloved by you, who never will be safe unless you are so! I have hope none the less that the waves

OVID

spes tamen est fractis vicinae pacis in undis;
  tu[1] placidas toto[2] pectore finde vias!
interea nanti,[3] quoniam freta pervia non sunt,
  leniat invisas littera missa moras.   210

XX

ACONTIUS CYDIPPAE

PONE metum! nihil hic iterum iurabis amanti;
  promissam satis est te semel esse mihi.
perlege! discedat sic corpore languor ab isto,
  quod meus est ulla parte dolere dolor!
Quid pudor ante subit? nam, sicut in aede Dianae, 5
  suspicor ingenuas erubuisse genas.
coniugium pactamque fidem, non crimina posco;
  debitus ut coniunx, non ut adulter amo.
verba licet repetas, quae demptus ab arbore fetus
  pertulit ad castas me iaciente manus;   10
invenies illic, id te spondere, quod opto
  te potius, virgo, quam meminisse deam.
nunc quoque idem timeo, sed idem tamen acrius
    illud;
  adsumpsit vires auctaque flamma mora est,
quique fuit numquam parvus, nunc tempore longo 15
  et spe, quam dederas tu mihi, crevit amor.

---

¹ tu $PG\omega$: tum Pa.   ² toto $PV\omega$: tuto $G_1 s$.
         ³ nanti s: nandi PG_1.

ᵃ In the temple of Diana at Delos, Acontius threw before
Cydippe an apple inscribed: "I swear by the sanctuary
274

are broken and peace is near; do you cleave their paths while placid with all your might! Meanwhile, since the billows will not let the swimmer come, let the letter that I send you soften the hated hours of delay.

XX

ACONTIUS TO CYDIPPE

LAY aside your fears! here you will give no second oath to your lover; that you have pledged yourself to me once is enough.[a] Read to the end, and so may the languor leave that body of yours; that it feel pain in any part is pain to me!

5 Why do your blushes rise before you read?—for I suspect that, just as in the temple of Diana, your modest cheeks have reddened. It is wedlock with you that I ask, and the faith you pledged me, not a crime; as your destined husband, not as a deceiver, do I love. You may recall the words which the fruit I plucked from the tree and threw to you brought to your chaste hands; you will find that in them you promise me what I pray that you, maiden, rather than the goddess, will remember. I am still as fearful as ever, but my fear has grown keener than it was; for the flame of my love has waxed with being delayed, and taken on strength, and the passion that was never slight has now grown great, fed by long time and the hope that you had given. Hope you had given; my ardent

of Diana that I will wed Acontius," which she read aloud, thus inadvertently pledging herself.

spem mihi tu dederas, meus hic tibi credidit ardor.
  non potes hoc factum teste negare dea.
adfuit et, praesens ut erat, tua verba notavit
  et visa est mota dicta tulisse [1] coma.   20
Deceptam dicas nostra te fraude licebit,
  dum fraudis nostrae causa feratur amor.
fraus mea quid petiit, nisi uti tibi iungerer, unum?
  id te, quod quereris, conciliare potest.
non ego natura nec sum tam callidus usu;   25
  sollertem tu me, crede, puella, facis.
te mihi conpositis—siquid tamen egimus—a me
  adstrinxit verbis ingeniosus Amor.
dictatis ab eo feci sponsalia verbis,
  consultoque fui iuris Amore vafer.   30
sit fraus huic facto nomen, dicarque dolosus,
  si tamen est, quod ames, velle tenere dolus!
En, iterum scribo mittoque rogantia verba!
  altera fraus haec est, quodque quereris habes.
si noceo, quod amo, fateor, sine fine nocebo   35
  teque petam; caveas tu licet, usque [2] petam.
per gladios alii placitas rapuere puellas;
  scripta mihi caute [3] littera crimen erit?
di faciant, possim plures inponere nodos,
  ut tua sit nulla libera parte fides!   40
mille doli restant—clivo sudamus in imo;
  ardor inexpertum nil sinet esse meus.
sit dubium, possisne capi; captabere certe.
  exitus in dis est, sed capiere tamen.

[1] tulisse *P G ω Plan.*(?) : probasse ω.
[2] usque *s* : ipse *P ω* : ipsa *G V s*.   [3] astute *Bent.*

heart put trust in you. You cannot deny that this was so—the goddess is my witness. She was there, and, present as she was, marked your words, and seemed, by the shaking of her locks, to have accepted them.

[21] I will give you leave to say you were deceived, and by wiles of mine, if only of those wiles my love be counted cause. What was the object of my wiles but the one thing—to be united with you? The thing you complain of has power to join you to me. Neither by nature nor by practice am I so cunning; believe me, maid, it is you who make me skilful. It was ingenious Love who bound you to me, with words—if I, indeed, have gained aught—that I myself drew up. In words dictated by him I made our betrothal bond; Love was the lawyer that taught me knavery. Let wiles be the name you give my deed, and let me be called crafty—if only the wish to possess what one loves be craft!

[33] Look, a second time I write, inditing words of entreaty! A second stratagem is this, and you have good ground for complaint. If I wrong you by loving, I confess I shall wrong you for ever, and strive to win you; though you shun my suit, I shall ever strive. With the sword have others stolen away the maids they loved; shall this letter, discreetly written, be called a crime? May the gods give me power to lay more bonds on you, so that your pledge may nowhere leave you free! A thousand wiles remain—I am only perspiring at the foot of the steep; my ardour will leave nothing unessayed. Grant 'tis doubtful whether you can be taken; the taking shall at least be tried. The issue rests with the gods, but you will be

ut partem effugias, non omnia retia falles,   45
   quae tibi, quam credis, plura tetendit Amor.
si non proficient artes, veniemus ad arma,
   inque [1] tui cupido rapta ferere sinu.
non sum, qui soleam Paridis reprehendere factum,
   nec quemquam, qui vir, posset ut esse, fuit.   50
nos quoque—sed taceo! mors huius poena rapinae
   ut sit, erit, quam te non habuisse, minor.
aut esses formosa minus, peterere modeste;
   audaces facie cogimur esse tua.
tu facis hoc oculique tui, quibus ignea cedunt   55
   sidera, qui flammae causa fuere meae;
hoc faciunt flavi crines et eburnea cervix,
   quaeque, precor, veniant in mea colla manus,
et decor et vultus [2] sine rusticitate pudentes,
   et, Thetidis qualis vix rear esse, pedes.   60
cetera si possem laudare, beatior essem,
   nec dubito, totum quin sibi par sit opus.
hac ego conpulsus, non est mirabile, forma
   si pignus volui vocis habere tuae.
Denique, dum captam tu te cogare fateri,   65
   insidiis esto capta puella meis.
invidiam patiar; passo sua praemia dentur.
   cur suus a tanto crimine fructus abest?
Hesionen Telamon, Briseida cepit Achilles;
   utraque victorem nempe secuta virum.   70
quamlibet accuses et sis irata licebit,
   irata liceat dum mihi posse frui.

        [1] inque *MSS.*: vique *Pa.*   [2] motus *Dilthey.*

taken none the less. You may evade a part, but you
will not escape all the nets which Love, in greater
number than you think, has stretched for you. If
art will not serve, I shall resort to arms, and you
will be seized and borne away in the embrace that
longs for you. I am not the one to chide Paris for
what he did, nor any one who, to become a husband,
has been a man.[a] I, too—but I say nothing! Allow
that death is fit punishment for this theft of you,
it will be less than not to have possessed you.
Or you should have been less beautiful, would you
be wooed by modest means; 'tis by your charms I am
driven to be bold. This is your work—your work,
and that of your eyes, brighter than the fiery stars,
and the cause of my burning love; this is the work
of your golden tresses and that ivory throat, and the
hands which I pray to have clasp my neck, and your
comely features, modest yet not rustic, and feet
which Thetis' own methinks could scarcely equal.
If I could praise the rest of your charms, I should be
happier; yet I doubt not that the work is like in all
its parts. Compelled by beauty such as this, it is no
cause for marvel if I wished the pledge of your word.

65 In fine, so only you are forced to confess your-
self caught, be, if you will, a maid caught by my
treachery. The reproach I will endure—only let
him who endures have his just reward. Why should
so great a charge lack its due profit? Telamon
won Hesione, Briseis was taken by Achilles; each of
a surety followed the victor as her lord. You may
chide and be angry as much as you will, if only you
let me enjoy you while you are angry. I who cause

[a] " Vir " is used in two senses—"husband" and "man of
courage."

idem, qui facimus, factam tenuabimus iram,
  copia placandi sit modo parva tui.
ante tuos liceat flentem [1] consistere vultus   75
  et liceat lacrimis addere verba sua,[2]
utque solent famuli, cum verbera saeva verentur,
  tendere submissas ad tua crura manus!
ignoras tua iura; voca! cur arguor absens?
  iamdudum dominae more venire iube.   80
ipsa meos scindas licet imperiosa capillos,
  oraque sint digitis livida nostra tuis.
omnia perpetiar; tantum fortasse timebo,
  corpore laedatur ne manus ista meo.
Sed neque conpedibus nec me conpesce catenis— 85
  servabor firmo vinctus amore tui!
cum bene se quantumque volet satiaverit ira,
  ipsa tibi dices: "quam patienter amat!"
ipsa tibi dices, ubi videris omnia ferre:
  "tam bene qui servit, serviat iste mihi!"   90
nunc reus infelix absens agor, et mea, cum sit
  optima, non ullo causa tuente perit.
Hoc quoque—quantumvis [3] sit scriptum iniuria
    nostrum,
  quod de me solo, nempe quereris habes.
non meruit falli mecum quoque Delia; si non   95
  vis mihi promissum reddere, redde deae.
adfuit et vidit, cum tu decepta rubebas,
  et vocem memori condidit aure tuam.
omina re careant! nihil est violentius illa,
  cum sua, quod nolim, numina laesa videt.   100

  [1] flentem *G V s Plan.*: flentes P_1: flentem liceat *ω*.
  [2] sua *Pa.*: sui *P*: suis *G*: meis *ω*: tuis *s*.
  [3] quantumvis *Pa. at first*: quod tu via *G Pa.*

it will likewise assuage the wrath I stirred, let me but have a slight chance of appeasing you. Let me have leave to stand weeping before your face, and my tears have leave to add their own speech; and let me, like a slave in fear of bitter stripes, stretch out submissive hands to touch your feet! You know not your own right; call me! Why am I accused in absence? Bid me come, forthwith, after the manner of a mistress. With your own imperious hand you may tear my hair, and make my face livid with your fingers. I will endure all; my only fear perhaps will be lest that hand of yours be bruised on me.

85 But bind me not with shackles nor with chains—I shall be kept in bonds by unyielding love for you. When your anger shall have had full course, and is sated well, you will say to yourself: "How enduring is his love!" You will say to yourself, when you have seen me bearing all: "He who is a slave so well, let him be slave to me!" Now, unhappy, I am arraigned in my absence, and my cause, though excellent, is lost because no one appears for me.

93 This further—however much that writing of mine was a wrong to you, it is not I alone, you must know, of whom you have cause to complain. She of Delos was not deserving of betrayal with me; if faith with me you cannot keep, keep faith with the goddess. She was present and saw when you blushed at being ensnared, and stored away your word in a remembering ear. May your omens be groundless! Nothing is more violent than she when she sees—what I hope will not be!—her godhead wronged. The boar of Calydon

OVID

testis erit Calydonis aper, sic saevus, ut illo
    sit magis in natum saeva reperta parens.
testis et Actaeon, quondam fera creditus illis,
    ipse dedit leto cum quibus ante feras ;
quaeque superba parens saxo per corpus oborto   105
    nunc quoque Mygdonia flebilis adstat humo.
Ei mihi ! Cydippe, timeo tibi dicere verum,
    ne videar causa falsa monere mea ;
dicendum tamen est.   hoc est,[1] mihi crede, quod aegra
    ipso nubendi tempore saepe iaces.   110
consulit ipsa tibi, neu sis periura, laborat,
    et salvam salva te cupit esse fide.
inde fit ut, quotiens existere perfida temptas,
    peccatum totiens corrigat illa tuum.
parce movere feros animosae virginis arcus ;   115
    mitis adhuc fieri, si patiare, potest.
parce, precor, teneros corrumpere febribus artus ;
    servetur facies ista fruenda mihi.
serventur vultus ad nostra incendia nati,
    quique subest niveo lenis[2] in ore rubor.   120
hostibus et siquis, ne fias nostra, repugnat,
    sic sit ut invalida te solet esse mihi !
torqueor ex aequo vel te nubente vel aegra
    dicere nec possum, quid minus ipse velim ;
maceror interdum, quod sim tibi causa dolendi   125
    teque mea laedi calliditate puto.
in caput ut nostrum dominae periuria quaeso
    eveniant ; poena tuta sit illa mea !

---

[1] tu *Ehw.*   [2] lenis *P ş* : levis *ω* : laetus *s.*

---

   a Meleager, whose mother Althaea's anger was inspired by Diana.
   b Niobe, with the children of whom she boasted, was slain

will be my witness—fierce, yet so that a mother[a] was found to be fiercer than he against her own son. Actaeon, too, will witness, once on a time thought a wild beast by those with whom himself had given wild beasts to death; and the arrogant mother, her body turned to rock, who still sits weeping on Mygdonian soil.[b]

[107] Alas me! Cydippe, I fear to tell you the truth, lest I seem to warn you falsely, for the sake of my plea; yet tell it I must. This is the reason, believe me, why you oft lie ill on the eve of marriage.[c] It is the goddess herself, looking to your good, and striving to keep you from a false oath; she wishes you kept whole by the keeping whole of your faith. This is the reason why, as oft as you attempt to break your oath, she corrects your sin. Cease to invite forth the cruel bow of the spirited virgin; she still may be appeased, if only you allow. Cease, I entreat, to waste with fevers your tender limbs; preserve those charms of yours for me to enjoy. Preserve those features that were born to kindle my love, and the gentle blush that rises to grace your snowy cheek. May my enemies, and any who would keep you from my arms, so fare as I when you are ill! I am alike in torment whether you wed, or whether you are ill, nor can I say which I should wish the less; at times I waste with grief at thought that I may be cause of pain to you, and my wiles the cause of your wounds. May the false swearing of my lady come upon my head, I pray; mine be the penalty, and she thus be safe!

by Diana and Apollo. A "weeping Niobe" rock was pointed out in Mygdonia, a province of Phrygia.
[c] The day was often postponed.

Ne tamen ignorem, quid agas, ad limina crebro
    anxius huc illuc dissimulanter eo ;   130
subsequor ancillam furtim famulumque requirens,
    profuerint somni quid tibi quidve cibi.
me miserum, quod non medicorum iussa ministro,
    effingoque manus, insideoque toro !
et rursus miserum, quod me procul inde remoto, 135
    quem minime vellem, forsitan alter adest !
ille manus istas effingit, et adsidet aegrae
    invisus superis cum superisque mihi,
dumque suo temptat salientem pollice venam,
    candida per causam bracchia saepe tenet,   140
contrectatque sinus, et forsitan oscula iungit.
    officio merces plenior ista suo est !
Quis tibi permisit nostras praecerpere messes ?
    ad spes alterius quis tibi fecit iter ?
iste sinus meus est ! mea turpiter oscula sumis ! 145
    a mihi promisso corpore tolle manus !
inprobe, tolle manus ! quam tangis, nostra futura
       est ;
    postmodo si facies istud, adulter eris.
elige de vacuis quam non sibi vindicet alter ;
    si nescis, dominum res habet ista suum.   150
nec mihi credideris—recitetur formula pacti ;
    neu falsam dicas esse, fac ipsa legat !
alterius thalamo, tibi nos, tibi dicimus, exi !
    quid facis hic ? exi ! non vacat iste torus !

^{129} Nevertheless, that I may not be ignorant of how you fare, now here, now there, I oft walk anxiously in secret before your door; I follow stealthily the maid-slave and the lackey, asking what change for good your sleep has brought, or what your food. Ah me, wretched, that I may not be the one to carry out the bidding of your doctors,^{a} and may not stroke your hands and sit at the side of your bed! and again wretched, because when I am far removed from you, perhaps that other, he whom I least could wish, is with you! He is the one to stroke those dear hands, and to sit by you while ill, hated by me and by the gods above—and while he feels with his thumb your throbbing artery, he oft makes this the excuse for holding your fair, white arm, and touches your bosom, and, it may be, kisses you. A hire like this is too great for the service given!

^{143} Who gave you leave to reap my harvests before me? Who laid open the road for you to enter upon another's hopes? That bosom is mine! mine are the kisses you take! Away with your hands from the body pledged to me! Scoundrel, away with your hands! She whom you touch is to be mine; henceforth, if you do that, you will be adulterous. Choose from those who are free one whom another does not claim; if you do not know, those goods have a master of their own. Nor need you take my word—let the formula of our pact be recited; and, lest you say 'tis false, have her read it herself! Out with you from another's chamber, out with you, I say! What are you doing there? Out! That couch is not free! Because you, too,

^{a} Administer the prescriptions.

OVID

nam quod habes et tu gemini verba altera pacti, 155
    non erit idcirco par tua causa meae.
haec mihi se pepigit, pater hanc tibi, primus
        ab illa ;
    sed propior certe quam pater ipsa sibi est.
promisit pater hanc, haec et iuravit amanti ;
    ille homines, haec est testificata deam.   160
hic metuit mendax,[1] haec et periura vocari ;
    an dubitas, hic sit maior an ille metus ?
denique, ut amborum conferre pericula possis,
    respice ad eventus—haec cubat, ille valet.
nos quoque dissimili certamina mente subimus ;   165
    nec spes par nobis nec timor aequus adest.
tu petis ex tuto ; gravior mihi morte repulsa est,
    idque ego iam, quod tu forsan amabis, amo.
si tibi iustitiae, si recti cura fuisset,
    cedere debueras ignibus ipse meis.   170
Nunc, quoniam ferus hic pro causa pugnat iniqua,
    ad quid, Cydippe, littera nostra redit ?
hic facit ut iaceas et sis suspecta Dianae ;
    hunc tu, si sapias, limen adire vetes.
hoc faciente subis tam saeva pericula vitae—   175
    atque utinam pro te, qui movet illa, cadat !
quem si reppuleris, nec, quem dea damnat, amaris,
    tu tunc continuo, certe ego salvus ero.
siste metum, virgo ! stabili potiere salute,
    fac modo polliciti conscia templa colas ;   180
non bove mactato caelestia numina gaudent,
    sed, quae praestanda est et sine teste, fide.

    [1] So $P_2 G V \omega$: ille timet mendax *Dilthey* P_1 *in erasure.*

have the words of a second pact, the twin of mine,
your case will not on that account be equal with
mine. She promised herself to me, her father her
to you; he is first after her, but surely she is
nearer to herself than her father is. Her father
but gave promise of her, while she, too, made
oath—to her lover; he called men to witness, she
a goddess. He fears to be called false, she to be
called forsworn also; do you doubt which—this or
that—is the greater fear? In a word, even grant
you could compare their hazards, regard the issue—
for she lies ill, and he is strong. You and I, too, are
entering upon a contest with different minds; our
hopes are not equal, nor are our fears the same.
Your suit is without risk; for me, repulse is heavier
than death, and I already love her whom you,
perhaps, will come to love. If you had cared for
justice, or cared for what was right, you yourself
should have given my passion the way.

171 Now, since his hard heart persists in its unjust
course, Cydippe, to what conclusion does my letter
come? It is he who is the cause of your lying
ill and under suspicion of Diana; he is the one
you would forbid your doors, if you were wise.
It is his doing that you are facing such dire
hazards of life—and would that he who causes them
might perish in your place! If you shall have
repulsed him and refused to love one the goddess
damns, then straightway you—and I assuredly—
will be whole. Stay your fears, maiden! You will
possess abiding health, if only you honour the
shrine that is witness of your pledge; not by slain
oxen are the spirits of heaven made glad, but
by good faith, which should be kept even though

ut valeant aliae, ferrum patiuntur et ignes,
    fert aliis tristem sucus amarus opem.
nil opus est istis ; tantum periuria vita   185
    teque simul serva meque datamque fidem !
praeteritae veniam dabit ignorantia culpae—
    exciderant animo foedera lecta tuo.
admonita es modo voce mea cum [1] casibus istis,
    quos, quotiens temptas fallere, ferre soles.   190
his quoque vitatis in partu nempe rogabis,
    ut tibi luciferas adferat illa manus ?
audiet haec—repetens quae sunt audita, requiret,
    iste tibi de quo coniuge partus eat.
promittes votum—scit te promittere falso ;   195
    iurabis—scit te fallere posse deos !
Non agitur de me ; cura maiore laboro.
    anxia sunt vitae pectora nostra tuae.
cur modo te dubiam pavidi flevere parentes,
    ignaros culpae quos facis esse tuae ?   200
et cur ignorent ? matri licet omnia narres.
    nil tua, Cydippe, facta ruboris [2] habent.
ordine fac referas ut sis mihi cognita primum
    sacra pharetratae dum facit ipsa deae ;
ut te conspecta subito, si forte notasti,   205
    restiterim fixis in tua membra genis ;
et, te dum nimium miror, nota certa furoris,
    deciderint umero pallia lapsa meo [3] ;
postmodo nescio qua venisse volubile malum,
    verba ferens doctis insidiosa notis,   210

---

[1] cum *Hous.*: modo *MSS.*   [2] pudoris *s.*
[3] humeris . . . meis *Plan.*(?) *Merk. Sedl. Ehw.*

---

    [a] A frequent epithet of Diana.

without witness. To win their health, some maids
submit to steel and fire; to others, bitter juices
bring their gloomy aid. There is no need of these;
only shun false oaths, preserve the pledge you have
given—and so yourself, and me! Excuse for past
offence your ignorance will supply—the agreement
you read had fallen from your mind. You have
but now been admonished not only by word of
mine, but as well by those mishaps of health you
are wont to suffer as oft as you try to evade your
promise. Even if you escape these ills, in child-birth
will you dare pray for aid from her light-bringing[a]
hands? She will hear these words—and then,
recalling what she has heard, will ask of you from
what husband come those pangs. You will promise
a votive gift—she knows your promises are false;
you will make oath—she knows you can deceive
the gods!

[197] 'Tis not a matter of myself; the care I labour
with is greater. It is concern for your life that
fills my heart. Why, but now when your life was
in doubt, did your frightened parents weep with
fear, whom you keep ignorant of your crime? And
why should they be ignorant?—you could tell your
mother all. What you have done, Cydippe, needs
no blush. See you relate in order how you first
became known to me, while she was herself making
sacrifice to the goddess of the quiver; how at sight
of you, if perchance you noticed, I straight stood
still with eyes fixed on your charms; and how,
while I gazed on you too eagerly—sure mark of
love's madness—my cloak slipped from my shoulder
and fell; how, after that, in some way came the
rolling apple, with its treacherous words in clever

quod quia sit lectum sancta praesente Diana,
   esse tuam vinctam numine teste fidem
ne tamen ignoret, scripti sententia quae sit,
   lecta tibi quondam nunc quoque verba refer.
"nube, precor," dicet, "cui te bona numina
   iungunt;   215
   quem fore iurasti, sit gener ille mihi.
quisquis is est, placeat, quoniam placet ante Dianae!"
   talis erit mater, si modo mater erit.
Sed tamen ut quaerat [1] quis sim qualisque, videto.
   inveniet vobis consuluisse deam.   220
insula, Coryciis quondam celeberrima nymphis,
   cingitur Aegaeo, nomine Cea, mari.
illa mihi patria est; nec, si generosa probatis
   nomina, despectis arguor ortus avis.
sunt et opes nobis, sunt et sine crimine mores; 225
   amplius utque nihil, me tibi iungit Amor.
appeteres talem vel non iurata maritum;
   iuratae vel non talis habendus erat.
Haec tibi me in somnis iaculatrix scribere Phoebe;
   haec tibi me vigilem scribere iussit Amor; 230
e quibus alterius mihi iam nocuere sagittae,
   alterius noceant ne tibi tela, cave!
iuncta salus nostra est—miserere meique tuique;
   quid dubitas unam ferre duobus opem?
quod si contigerit, cum iam data signa sonabunt, 235
   tinctaque votivo sanguine Delos erit,

---

[1] ut quaerat *s* : et quaerat *ω*.

---

[a] For the beginning of the ceremony.
[b] The sacrifices attendant upon Acontius' marriage to
Cydippe.

character; and how, because they were read in holy Diana's presence, you were bound by a pledge with deity to witness. For fear that after all she may not know the import of the writing, repeat now again to her the words once read by you. "Wed, I pray," she will say, "him to whom the good gods join you; the one you swore should be, let be my son-in-law. Whoever he is, let him be our choice, since he was Diana's choice before!" Such will be your mother's word, if only she is a mother.

219 And yet, see that she seeks out who I am, and of what ways. She will find that the goddess had you and yours at heart. An isle once thronged by the Corycian nymphs is girdled by the Aegean sea; its name is Cea. That is the land of my fathers; nor, if you look with favour on high-born names, am I to be charged with birth from grandsires of no repute. We have wealth, too, and we have a name above reproach; and, though there were nothing else, I am bound to you by Love. You would aspire to such a husband even though you had not sworn; now that you have sworn, even though he were not such, you should accept him.

229 These words Phoebe, she of the darts, bade me in my dreams to write you; these words in my waking hours Love bade me write. The arrows of the one of them have already wounded me; that the darts of the other wound not you, take heed! Your safety is joined with mine — have compassion on me and on yourself; why hesitate to aid us both at once? If you shall do this, in the day when the sounding signals*a* will be given and Delos be stained with votive blood,*b* a golden image

aurea ponetur mali felicis imago,
   causaque versiculis scripta duobus erit :

EFFIGIE POMI TESTATUR ACONTIUS HUIUS
   QUAE FUERINT IN EO SCRIPTA FUISSE RATA.   240

Longior infirmum ne lasset epistula corpus
   clausaque consueto sit sibi fine : vale !

XXI

CYDIPPE ACONTIO

PERTIMUI, scriptumque tuum sine murmure legi,
   iuraret ne quos inscia lingua deos.
et puto captasses iterum, nisi, ut ipse fateris,
   promissam scires me satis esse semel.
nec lectura fui, sed, si tibi dura fuissem,   5
   aucta foret saevae forsitan ira deae.
omnia cum faciam, cum dem pia tura Dianae,
   illa tamen iusta plus tibi parte favet,
utque cupis credi, memori te vindicat ira ;
   talis in Hippolyto vix fuit illa suo.[a]   10
at melius virgo favisset virginis annis,
   quos vereor paucos ne velit esse mihi.[1]
Languor enim causis non apparentibus haeret ;
   adiuvor et nulla fessa medentis ope.
quam tibi nunc gracilem vix haec rescribere quamque   15
   pallida vix cubito membra levare putas ?

     [1] *Good MSS. and Plan. do not contain 13—end.*

     [a] The chaste favourite of the goddess, courted by Phaedra,
who compassed his death because of his refusal. See iv.

of the blessed apple shall be offered up, and the cause
of its offering shall be set forth in verses twain :

BY THIS IMAGE OF THE APPLE DOTH ACONTIUS DECLARE
THAT WHAT ONCE WAS WRITTEN ON IT NOW HATH
HAD FULFILMENT FAIR.

That too long a letter may not weary your
weakened frame, and that it may close with the
accustomed end : fare well !

XXI

CYDIPPE TO ACONTIUS

ALL fearful, I read what you wrote without so
much as a murmur, lest my tongue unwittingly
might swear by some divinity. And I believe you
would have tried to snare me a second time, did
you not know, as you yourself confess, that one
pledge from me was enough. I should not have
read at all ; but had I been hard with you, the
anger of the cruel goddess might have grown.
Though I do everything, though I offer duteous
incense to Diana, she none the less favours you
more than your due, and, as you are eager for me
to believe, avenges you with unforgetting anger ;
scarce was she such toward her own Hippolytus.[a]
Yet the maiden goddess had done better to favour
the years of a maiden like me —years which I fear
she wishes few for me.

13 For the languor clings to me, for causes that do
not appear ; worn out, I find no help in the
physician's art. How thin and wasted am I now,
think you, scarce able to write this answer to you?

OVID

nunc timor accedit, ne quis nisi conscia nutrix
  colloquii nobis sentiat esse vices.
ante fores sedet haec quid agamque rogantibus intus,
  ut possim tuto scribere, "dormit," ait.   20
mox, ubi, secreti longi causa optima, somnus
  credibilis tarda desinit esse mora,
iamque venire videt quos non admittere durum est,
  excreat et ficta dat mihi signa nota.
sicut erant, properans verba inperfecta relinquo,   25
  et tegitur trepido littera coepta[1] sinu.
inde meos digitos iterum repetita fatigat;
  quantus sit nobis adspicis ipse labor.
quo peream si dignus eras, ut vera loquamur;
  sed melior iusto quamque mereris ego.   30
Ergo te propter totiens incerta salutis
  commentis poenas doque dedique tuis?
haec nobis formae te laudatore superbae
  contingit merces? et placuisse nocet?
si tibi deformis, quod mallem, visa fuissem,   35
  culpatum nulla corpus egeret ope;
nunc laudata gemo, nunc me certamine vestro
  perditis, et proprio vulneror ipsa bono.
dum neque tu cedis, nec se putat ille secundum,
  tu votis obstas illius, ille tuis.   40
ipsa velut navis iactor quam certus in altum
  propellit Boreas, aestus et unda refert,

------

[1] cauta *MSS.*: coepta *Dilthey.*

294

and how pale the body I scarce can raise upon my arm? And now I feel an added fear, lest someone besides the nurse who shares my secret may see that we are interchanging words. She sits before the door, and when they ask how I do within, answers, "She sleeps," that I may write in safety. Presently, when sleep, the excellent excuse for my long retreat, no longer wins belief because I tarry so, and now she sees those coming whom not to admit is hard, she clears her throat and thus gives me the sign agreed upon. Just as they are, in haste I leave my words unfinished, and the letter I have begun is hid in my trembling bosom. Taken thence, a second time it fatigues my fingers; how great the toil to me, yourself can see. May I perish if, to speak truth, you were worthy of it; but I am kinder than is just or you deserve.

[31] So, then, 'tis on your account that I am so many times uncertain of health, and 'tis for your lying tricks that I am and have been punished? Is this the reward that falls to my beauty, proud in your praise? Must I suffer for having pleased? If I had seemed misshapen to you—and would I had!—you would have thought ill of my body, and now it would need no help; but I met with praise, and now I groan; now you two with your strife are my despair, and my own beauty itself wounds me. While neither you yield to him nor he deems him second to you, you hinder his prayers, he hinders yours. I myself am tossed like a ship which steadfast Boreas drives out into the deep, and tide and wave bring back, and when the

cumque dies caris optata parentibus instat,
  inmodicus pariter corporis ardor adest—
ei mihi, coniugii tempus crudelis ad ipsum   45
  Persephone nostras pulsat acerba fores!
iam pudet, et timeo, quamvis mihi conscia non sim,
  offensos videar ne meruisse deos.
accidere haec aliquis casu contendit, at alter
  acceptum superis hunc negat esse virum;   50
neve nihil credas in te quoque dicere famam,
  facta veneficiis pars putat ista tuis.
causa latet, mala nostra patent; vos pace movetis
  aspera submota proelia, plector ego!
Dic mihi [1] nunc, solitoque tibi ne decipe more: 55
  quid facies odio, sic ubi amore noces?
si laedis, quod amas, hostem sapienter amabis—
  me, precor, ut serves, perdere velle velis!
aut tibi iam nulla est speratae cura puellae,
  quam ferus indigna tabe perire sinis,   60
aut, dea si frustra pro me tibi saeva rogatur,
  quid mihi te iactas? gratia nulla tua est!
elige, quid fingas: non vis placare Dianam—
  inmemor es nostri; non potes—illa tui est!
Vel numquam mallem vel non mihi tempore in
    illo   65
  esset in Aegaeis cognita Delos aquis!
tunc mea difficili deducta est aequore navis,
  et fuit ad coeptas hora sinistra vias.
quo pede processi! quo me pede limine movi!
  picta citae tetigi quo pede texta ratis!   70

_____

[1] dicam *MSS.*: dic a! *Pa.*: dic mihi *Bent.*

_____

[a] Eager and spirited.

day longed for by my parents dear draws nigh, at the same time unmeasured burning seizes on my frame—ah me, at the very time of marriage cruel Persephone knocks at my door before her day! I already am shamed, and in fear, though I feel no guilt within, lest I appear to have merited the displeasure of the gods. One contends that my affliction is the work of chance; another says that my destined husband finds not favour with the gods; and, lest you think yourself untouched by what men say, there are also some who think you the cause, by poisonous arts. Their source is hidden, but my ills are clear to see; you two stir up fierce strife and banish peace, and the blows are mine!

⁵⁵ Tell me now, and deceive me not in your wonted way: what will you do from hatred, when you harm me so from love? If you injure one you love, 'twill be reason to love your foe—to save me, I pray you, will to wish my doom! Either you care no longer for the hoped-for maid, whom with hard heart you are letting waste away to an unworthy death, or if in vain you beseech for me the cruel goddess, why boast yourself to me?—you have no favour with her! Choose which case you will: you do not wish to placate Diana—you have forgotten me; you have no power with her—'tis she has forgotten you!

⁶⁵ I would I had either never—or not at that time—known Delos in the Aegean waters! That was the time my ship set forth on a difficult sea, and I entered on a voyage in ill-omened hour. With what step ᵃ I came forth! With what step I started from my threshold! The painted deck of the swift ship—with what step I trod it! Twice,

bis tamen adverso redierunt carbasa vento—
    mentior, a demens! ille secundus erat!
ille secundus erat qui me referebat euntem,
    quique parum felix inpediebat iter.
atque utinam constans contra mea vela fuisset—   75
    sed stultum est venti de levitate queri.
Mota loci fama properabam visere Delon
    et facere ignava puppe videbar iter.
quam saepe ut tardis feci convicia remis,
    questaque sum vento lintea parca dari!   80
et iam transieram Myconon, iam Tenon et Andron,
    inque meis oculis candida Delos erat;
quam procul ut vidi, "quid me fugis, insula," dixi,
    "laberis in magno numquid, ut ante, mari?"
Institeram terrae, cum iam prope luce peracta   85
    demere purpureis sol iuga vellet equis.
quos idem solitos postquam revocavit ad ortus,
    comuntur nostrae matre iubente comae.
ipsa dedit gemmas digitis et crinibus aurum,
    et vestes umeris induit ipsa meis.   90
protinus egressae superis, quibus insula sacra est,[1]
    flava salutatis tura merumque damus;
dumque parens aras votivo sanguine tingit,
    festaque fumosis ingerit exta focis,
sedula me nutrix alias quoque ducit in aedes,   95
    erramusque vago per loca sacra pede.
et modo porticibus spatior modo munera regum
    miror et in cunctis stantia signa locis;

[1] grata est *P s Bent.*

none the less, my canvas put about before an adverse wind—ah, senseless that I am, I lie!—a favouring wind was that! A favouring wind it was that brought me back from my going, and hindered the way that had little happiness for me. Ah, would it had been constant against my sails—but it is foolish to complain of fickle winds.

[77] Moved by the fame of the place, I was in eager haste to visit Delos, and the craft in which I sailed seemed spiritless. How oft did I chide the oars for being slow, and complain that sparing canvas was given to the wind! And now I had passed Myconos, now Tenos and Andros, and Delos gleamed [a] before my eyes. When I beheld it from afar, "Why dost thou fly from me, O isle?" I cried; "art thou afloat in the great sea, as in days of yore?"

[85] I had set foot upon land; the light was almost gone, and the sun was making ready to take their yokes from his shining steeds. When he has likewise called them once more to their accustomed rising, my hair is dressed at the bidding of my mother. With her own hand she sets gems upon my fingers and gold in my tresses, and with her own hand places the robes about my shoulders. Straightway setting forth, we greet the deities to whom the isle is consecrate, and offer up the golden incense and the wine; and while my mother stains the altars with votive blood, and piles the solemn entrails on the smoking altar-flames, my busy nurse conducts me to other temples also, and we stray with wandering step about the holy precincts. And now I walk in the porticoes, now look with wonder on the gifts of kings, and the statues standing everywhere; I

---

[a] The Greek islands are masses of limestone.

miror et innumeris structam de cornibus aram,
    et de qua pariens arbore nixa dea est,   100
et quae praeterea—neque enim meminive libetve
    quidquid ibi vidi dicere—Delos habet.
Forsitan haec spectans a te spectabar, Aconti,
    visaque simplicitas est mea posse capi.
in templum redeo gradibus sublime Dianae—   105
    tutior hoc ecquis debuit esse locus?
mittitur ante pedes malum cum carmine tali—
    ei mihi, iuravi nunc quoque paene tibi!
sustulit hoc nutrix mirataque "perlege!" dixit.
    insidias legi, magne poeta, tuas!   110
nomine coniugii dicto confusa pudore,
    sensi me totis erubuisse genis,
luminaque in gremio veluti defixa tenebam—
    lumina propositi facta ministra tui.
inprobe, quid gaudes? aut quae tibi gloria parta
    est?   115
    quidve vir elusa virgine laudis habes?
non ego constiteram sumpta peltata securi,
    qualis in Iliaco Penthesilea solo;
nullus Amazonio caelatus balteus auro,
    sicut ab Hippolyte, praeda relata tibi est.   120
verba quid exultas tua si mihi verba dederunt,
    sumque parum prudens capta puella dolis?
Cydippen pomum, pomum Schoeneida cepit;
    tu nunc Hippomenes scilicet alter eris!

---

[a] A great wonder in its time; built by Apollo of the horns
of his sister's sacrificial victims.
   [b] Latona, mother of Apollo and Diana.
   [c] Penthesilea and Hippolyte were queens of the Amazons;

look with wonder, too, on the altar built of countless horns,[a] and the tree that stayed the goddess in her throes,[b] and all things else that Delos holds—for memory would not serve, nor mood allow, to tell of all I looked on there.

[103] Perhaps, thus gazing, I was gazed upon by you, Acontius, and my simple nature seemed an easy prey. I return to Diana's temple, with its lofty approach of steps—ought any place to be safer than this?—when there is thrown before my feet an apple with this verse that follows—ah me, now again I almost made oath to you! Nurse took it up, looked in amaze, and "Read it through!" she said. I read your treacherous verse, O mighty poet! At mention of the name of wedlock I was confused and shamed, and felt the blushes cover all my face, and my eyes I kept upon my bosom as if fastened there—those eyes that were made ministers to your intent. Wretch, why rejoice? or what glory have you gained? or what praise have you won, a man, by playing on a maid? I did not present myself before you with buckler and axe in hand, like a Penthesilea on the soil of Ilion; no sword-girdle, chased with Amazonian gold, was offered you for spoil by me, as by some Hippolyte.[c] Why exult if your words deceived me, and I, a girl of little wisdom, was taken by your wiles? Cydippe was snared by the apple, an apple snared Schoeneus' child;[d] you now of a truth will be a second Hippomenes! Yet had it been

the former was slain by Achilles at Troy, the latter's sword-belt was won by Hercules as his sixth labour, and she was given by him in marriage to Theseus for his aid.

[d] Atalanta, who lost the race by stopping for the golden apples dropped by Hippomenes.

at fuerat melius, si te puer iste tenebat,   125
  quem tu nescio quas dicis habere faces,[1]
more bonis solito spem non corrumpere fraude ;
  exoranda tibi, non capienda fui !
Cur, me cum peteres, ea non profitenda putabas,
  propter quae nobis ipse petendus eras?   130
cogere cur potius quam persuadere volebas,
  si poteram audita condicione capi?
quid tibi nunc prodest iurandi formula iuris
  linguaque praesentem testificata deam?
quae iurat, mens est.   nil coniuravimus illa ;   135
  illa fidem dictis addere sola potest.
consilium prudensque animi sententia iurat,
  et nisi iudicii vincula nulla valent.
si tibi coniugium volui promittere nostrum,
  exige polliciti debita iura tori ;   140
sed si nil dedimus praeter sine pectore vocem,
  verba suis frustra viribus orba tenes.
non ego iuravi—legi iurantia verba ;
  vir mihi non isto more legendus eras.
decipe sic alias—succedat epistula pomo !   145
  si valet hoc, magnas ditibus[2] aufer opes ;
fac iurent reges sua se tibi regna daturos,
  sitque tuum toto quidquid in orbe placet !
maior es hoc ipsa multo, mihi crede, Diana,
  si tua tam praesens littera numen habet.   150
Cum tamen haec dixi, cum me tibi firma negavi,
  cum bene promissi causa peracta mei est,
confiteor, timeo saevae Latoidos iram
  et corpus laedi suspicor inde meum.

---

[1] vices *Dilthey Ehw.*   [2] ditibus *Hein.*: divitis *MSS.*

better for you—if that boy really held you captive who you say has certain torches—to do as good men are wont, and not cheat your hope by dealing falsely ; you should have won me by persuasion, not taken me whether or no!

129 Why, when you sought my hand, did you not think worth declaring those things that made your own hand worth my seeking? Why did you wish to compel me rather than persuade, if I could be won by listening to your suit? Of what avail to you now the formal words of an oath, and the tongue that called on present deity to witness? It is the mind that swears, and I have taken no oath with that; it alone can lend good faith to words. It is counsel and the prudent reasoning of the soul that swear, and, except the bonds of the judgment, none avail. If I have willed to pledge my hand to you, exact the due rights of the promised marriage-bed ; but if I have given you naught but my voice, without my heart, you possess in vain but words without a force of their own. I took no oath—I read words that formed an oath ; that was no way for you to be chosen to husband by me. Deceive thus other maids —let a letter follow an apple! If this plan holds, win away their great wealth from the rich; make kings take oath to give their thrones to you, and let whatsoever pleases you in all the world be yours! You are much greater in this, believe me, than Diana's self, if your written word has in it such present deity.

151 Nevertheless, after saying this, after firmly refusing myself to you, after having finished pleading the cause of my promise to you, I confess I fear the anger of Leto's cruel daughter and suspect that from

nam quare, quotiens socialia sacra parantur,   155
    nupturae totiens languida membra cadunt ?
ter mihi iam veniens positas Hymenaeus ad aras
    fugit, et a thalami limine terga dedit,
vixque manu pigra totiens infusa resurgunt
    lumina, vix moto corripit igne faces.   160
saepe coronatis stillant unguenta capillis
    et trahitur multo splendida palla croco.
cum tetigit limen, lacrimas mortisque timorem
    cernit et a cultu multa remota suo,
proicit ipse sua deductas fronte coronas,   165
    spissaque de nitidis tergit amoma comis ;
et pudet in tristi laetum consurgere turba,
    quique erat in palla, transit in ora rubor.[1]
At mihi, vae miserae ! torrentur febribus artus
    et gravius iusto pallia pondus habent,   170
nostraque plorantes video super ora parentes,
    et face pro thalami fax mihi mortis adest.
parce laboranti, picta dea laeta pharetra,
    daque salutiferam iam mihi fratris opem.
turpe tibi est, illum causas depellere leti,   175
    te contra titulum mortis habere meae.
numquid, in umbroso cum velles fonte lavari,
    inprudens vultus ad tua labra tuli ?
praeteriine tuas de tot caelestibus aras,
    aque tua est nostra spreta parente parens ?   180

---

[1] 167, 168 *before* 165 *Merk.*

---

[a] A reference to Oeneus, whose neglect of Diana caused the coming of the Calydonian boar.

her comes my body's ill. For why is it that, as oft
as the sacraments for marriage are made ready, so
oft the limbs of the bride-to-be sink down in
languor? Thrice now has Hymenaeus come to
the altars reared for me and fled, turning his
back upon the threshold of my wedding-chamber;
the lights so oft replenished by his lazy hand
scarce rise again, scarce does he keep the torch
alight by waving it. Oft does the perfume distil
from his wreathèd locks, and the mantle he
sweeps along is splendid with much saffron.
When he has touched the threshold, and sees
tears and dread of death, and much that is far
removed from the ways he keeps, with his own
hand he tears the garlands from his brow and
casts them forth, and dries the dense balsam from
his glistening locks; he shames to stand forth
glad in a gloomy throng, and the blush that was
in his mantle passes to his cheeks.

[169] But for me—ah, wretched!—my limbs are
parchèd with fever, and the stuffs that cover me are
heavier than their wont; I see my parents weeping
over me, and instead of the wedding-torch the torch
of death is at hand. Spare a maid in distress, O
goddess whose joy is the painted quiver, and grant
me the health-bringing aid of thy brother! It is
shame to thee that he drive away the causes of
doom, and that thou, in contrast, have credit for my
death. Can it be that, when thou didst wish to bathe
in shady pool, I without witting cast eyes upon thee
at thy bath? Have I passed thy altars by, among
those of so many deities of heaven?[a] Has thy mother
been scorned by mine?[b] I have sinned in naught

[b] Niobe's boast of her children to Leto.

nil ego peccavi, nisi quod periuria legi
    inque parum fausto carmine docta fui.
Tu quoque pro nobis, si non mentiris amorem,
    tura feras ; prosint, quae nocuere, manus !
cur, quae succenset quod adhuc tibi pacta puella   185
    non tua sit, fieri ne tua possit, agit ?
omnia de viva tibi sunt speranda ; quid aufert
    saeva mihi vitam, spem tibi diva mei ?
Nec tu credideris illum, cui destinor uxor,
    aegra superposita membra fovere manu.   190
adsidet ille quidem, quantum permittitur, ipse
    sed meminit nostrum virginis esse torum.
iam quoque nescio quid de me sensisse videtur ;
    nam lacrimae causa saepe latente cadunt,
et minus audacter blanditur et oscula rara   195
    appetit [1] et timido me vocat ore suam.
nec miror sensisse, notis cum prodar apertis ;
    in dextrum versor, cum venit ille, latus,
nec loquor, et tecto simulatur lumine somnus,
    captantem tactus reicioque manum.   200
ingemit et tacito suspirat pectore, me quod
    offensam, quamvis non mereatur, habet.
ei mihi, quod gaudes, et te iuvat ista voluntas ! [2]
    ei mihi, quod sensus sum tibi fassa meos !
si mihi lingua foret,[3] tu nostra iustius ira,   205
    qui mihi tendebas retia, dignus eras.
Scribis, ut invalidum liceat tibi visere corpus.
    es procul a nobis, et tamen inde noces.
mirabar quare tibi nomen Acontius esset ;
    quod faciat longe vulnus, acumen habes.   210

   [1] appetit *Pa.*: accipit *MSS.*: admovet *Dilthey Ehw.*:
applicat *Hous.*
   [2] voluntas *J. F. Heusinger* : ista voluntas *P* : ipsa voluptas
Dilthey.   [3] So *Lv* : ei mihi lingua labat *Ehw.*: etc.

except that I have read a false oath, and been clever with unpropitious verse.

¹⁸³ Do you, too, if your love is not a lie, offer up incense for me; let the hands help which harmed me! Why does the hand which is angered because the maiden pledged you is not yet yours so act that yours she cannot become? While still I live you have everything to hope; why does the cruel goddess take from me my life, your hope of me from you?

¹⁸⁹ Do not believe that he whose destined wife I am lays his hand on me to fondle my sick limbs. He sits by me, indeed, as much as he may, but does not forget that mine is a virgin bed. He seems already, too, to feel in some way suspicion of me; for his tears oft fall for some hidden cause, his flatteries are less bold, he asks for few kisses, and calls me his own in tones that are but timid. Nor do I wonder he suspects, for I betray myself by open signs; I turn upon my right side when he comes, and do not speak, and close my eyes in simulated sleep, and when he tries to touch me I throw off his hand. He groans and sighs in his silent breast, for he suffers my displeasure without deserving it. Ah me, that you rejoice and are pleased by that state of my will! Ah me, that I have confessed my feelings to you! If my tongue should speak my mind, 'twere you more justly deserved my anger—you, for having spread the net for me.

²⁰⁷ You write for leave to come and see me in my illness. You are far from me, and yet you wrong me even from there. I marvelled why your name was Acontius; it is because you have the keen point

certe ego convalui nondum de vulnere tali,
    ut iaculo scriptis eminus icta tuis.
quid tamen huc venias? sane miserabile corpus,
    ingenii videas magna [1] tropaea tui!
concidimus macie; color est sine sanguine, qua-
       lem   215
    in pomo refero mente fuisse tuo,
candida nec mixto sublucent ora rubore.
    forma novi talis marmoris esse solet;
argenti color est inter convivia talis,
    quod tactum gelidae frigore pallet aquae.   220
si me nunc videas, visam prius esse negabis,
    "arte nec est," dices, "ista petita mea,"
promissique fidem, ne sim tibi iuncta, remittes,
    et cupies illud non meminisse deam.
forsitan et facies iurem ut contraria rursus,   225
    quaeque legam mittes altera verba mihi.
Sed tamen adspiceres vellem, quod et ipse roga-
       bas—
    adspiceres sponsae languida membra tuae!
durius et ferro cum sit tibi pectus, Aconti,
    tu veniam nostris vocibus ipse petas.   230
ne tamen ignores ope qua revalescere possim,
    quaeritur a Delphis fata canente deo.
is quoque nescio quam, nunc ut vaga fama susurrat,
    neclectam queritur testis habere fidem.
hoc deus, hoc vates, hoc et mea carmina dicunt— 235
    at desunt voto carmina nulla tuo!
unde tibi favor hic? nisi si [2] nova forte reperta est
    quae capiat magnos littera lecta deos.

    [1] magna *Dilthey*: bina *L*: digna *van Lennep*.
    [2] si *Pa.*: quod *L*: forte nova πυ.

---

    [a] Ἀκόντιον, a javelin, *iaculum*.
    [b] *I.e.* pray for the remission of my oath.

that deals a wound from afar.[a] At any rate, I am
not yet well of just such a wound, for I was pierced
by your letter, a far-thrown dart. Yet why should
you come to me? Surely but a wretched body you
would see—the mighty trophy of your skill. I have
wasted and fallen away; my colour is bloodless, such
as I recall to mind was the hue of that apple of
yours, and my face is white, with no rising gleam
of mingled red. Such is wont to be the fairness of
fresh marble; such is the colour of silver at the
banquet table, pale with the chill touch of icy water.
Should you see me now, you will declare you have
never seen me before, and say : " No arts of mine
e'er sought to win a maid like that." You will remit
me the keeping of my promise, in fear lest I become
yours, and will long for the goddess to forget it all.
Perhaps you will even a second time make me
swear, but in contrary wise, and will send me words
a second time to read.

[227] But none the less I could wish you to look
upon me, as you yourself entreated—to look upon
the languid limbs of your promised bride ! Though
your heart were harder than steel, Acontius, you
yourself would ask pardon for my uttered words.[b]
Yet, that you be not unaware, the god who sings
the fates at Delphi is being asked by what means
I may grow strong again. He, too, as vague rumour
whispers now, complains of the neglect of some
pledge he was witness to. This is what the god
says, this his prophet, and this the verses I read
—surely, the wish of your heart lacks no support in
prophetic verse ! Whence this favour to you ?—
unless perhaps you have found some new writing
the reading whereof ensnares even the mighty gods.

teque tenente deos numen sequor ipsa deorum,
    doque libens victas in tua vota manus ;   240
fassaque sum matri deceptae foedera linguae
    lumina fixa tenens plena pudoris humo.
cetera cura tua est ; plus hoc quoque virgine factum,
    non timuit tecum quod mea charta loqui.
iam satis invalidos calamo lassavimus artus,   245
    et manus officium longius aegra negat.
quid, nisi quod cupio me iam coniungere tecum,
    restat ? ut adscribat littera nostra : VALE.

And since you hold bound the gods, I myself follow their will, and gladly yield my vanquished hands in fulfilment of your prayers; with eyes full of shame held fast on the ground, I have confessed to my mother the pledge my tongue was trapped to give. The rest must be your care; even this, that my letter has not feared to speak with you, is more than a maid should do. Already have I wearied enough with the pen my weakened members, and my sick hand refuses longer its office. What remains for my letter, if I say that I long to be united with you soon? nothing but to add: FARE WELL!

II

THE AMORES

MANUSCRIPTS AND EDITIONS
OF THE AMORES

1. Codex Parisinus 8242, formerly called Puteanus, of the eleventh century, the best manuscript. It contains I. ii. 51—III. xii. 26; xiv. 3—xv. 8.

2. Codex Parisinus 7311 Regius, of the tenth century. It contains I. i. 3—ii. 49.

3. Codex Sangallensis 864, of the eleventh century. It contains I.—III. ix. 10, with omission of I. vi. 46—viii. 74.

The *Amores* were printed first in the two editiones principes of Ovid in 1471—one at Rome, and the other at Bologna, with independent texts. A Venetian edition appeared in 1491. They appeared in Heinsius in 1661.

The principal modern editions of the *Amores* are those of Heinsius-Burmann, Amsterdam, 1727; Lemaire, Paris, 1820; Merkel-Ehwald, Leipzig, 1888; Riese, 1889; Postgate's *Corpus Poetarum Latinorum*, 1894; Némethy, Budapest, 1907; Brandt, Leipzig, 1911.

SIGNS AND ABBREVIATIONS

P. = Parisinus.	Burm. = Burmann.
S. = Sangallensis.	Post. = Postgate.
Hein. = Heinsius.	Nem. = Némethy.
Merk. = Merkel.	Pa. = Palmer.
Ehw. = Ehwald.	Br. = Brandt.

IN APPRECIATION OF THE AMORES

THE reader will not look to the *Amores* for profundity of any sort, whether of thought or emotion. Except in a general way, they are not even the expression of personal experience, to say nothing of depth of passion. Corinna is only one of several loves to whom the poet pays literary court, and it is more than doubtful whether even she is real.

It is exactly this absence of the serious that gives the *Amores* their peculiar charm—a charm different from that of either Catullus, whose passion is real, or Tibullus and Propertius, who also sing in somewhat serious strain. For all of his much loving, the poet of the *Amores* is philosophic in love, and his light-hearted freedom from its pains finds light and airy expression. No small number of them, indeed, are but slightly connected with love, and only a very few, as I. vii. and III. xi., seem prompted by anything that approaches genuine feeling. The *Amores* are above all the product of poetic fancy; the poet's experience with love of course contributes, and contributes abundantly—but it only contributes; it is the element that serves for the fusing of his artist's instinct with the literature of love with which his mind is saturated—the poetry of his Greek and Roman predecessors.

The heart that indites the matter of the *Amores* is no less free from suspicion of heaviness than the hand that obeys the heart; their language is limpid, smooth, and flowing, fit medium of their fluent and limpid thought. For handling of themes of the literary sort, what could be more gracious and elegant than I. i., xv., II. i., xii., xviii., and III. i., ix., xv. ; or what more exquisitely light and playful, to mention a few of the many on amatory themes, than I. ii., ix., II. iv., ix., x., xii., xv., and III. iii. ; or what more pleasing than II. xvi. and III. ii., iii. as little pictures of ancient life ? for it must not be forgotten that the *Amores* afford us many a reflection of the Rome and Italy of their time.

The *Amores* are no exception in the literature of love, and here and there display offences against even a liberal taste. The translator has felt obliged to omit one poem entire, and to omit or disguise a few verses in other poems where, in spite of the poet's exquisite art, a faithful rendering might offend the sensibilities of the reader, if not the literary taste. Such omissions and disguises are, however, few ; if they are even too few, it is because the scholar shrinks from tampering with the integrity of the poet's work. To any who may resent either what has been omitted or what has been retained, the translator addresses the words of Howells, substituting the name of Ovid for that of Chaucer :

"I am not going to pretend that there are not things in Ovid which one would be the better for not reading ; and so far as these words of mine shall be taken for counsel, I am not willing that they should unqualifiedly praise him. The matter is by no means simple ; it is not easy to conceive of a means of purifying the literature of the past without weakening it, and even falsifying it ; but it is best to own that it is in all respects just what it is, and not to feign it otherwise."

P. OVIDI NASONIS AMORES

LIBER PRIMUS

EPIGRAMMA IPSIUS

Qui modo Nasonis fueramus quinque libelli,
   tres sumus ; hoc illi praetulit auctor opus.
ut iam nulla tibi nos sit legisse voluptas,
   at levior demptis poena duobus erit.

I

Arma gravi numero violentaque bella parabam
   edere, materia conveniente modis.
par erat inferior versus—risisse Cupido
   dicitur atque unum surripuisse pedem.
" Quis tibi, saeve puer, dedit hoc in carmina iuris ? 5
   Pieridum vates, non tua turba sumus.
quid, si praeripiat flavae Venus arma Minervae,
   ventilet accensas flava Minerva faces ?
quis probet in silvis Cererem regnare iugosis,
   lege pharetratae Virginis arva coli ?   10

THE
AMORES OF P. OVIDIUS NASO

BOOK THE FIRST

EPIGRAM OF THE POET HIMSELF

We who erewhile were five booklets of Naso now
are three; the poet has preferred to have his work
thus rather than as before. Though even now you
may take no joy of reading us, yet with two books
taken away your pains will be lighter.[a]

I

Arms, and the violent deeds of war, I was making
ready to sound forth—in weighty numbers, with
matter suited to the measure. The second verse
was equal to the first—but Cupid, they say, with a
laugh stole away one foot.
⁵ "Who gave thee, cruel boy, this right over
poesy? We bards belong to the Pierides; we are no
company of thine. What if Venus should seize away
the arms of golden-haired Minerva, if golden-haired
Minerva should fan into flame the kindled torch
of love? Who would approve of Ceres reigning on
the woodland ridges, and of fields tilled under the
law of the quiver-bearing Maid? Who would furnish

[a] The Amores as we have them are a second edition.

crinibus insignem quis acuta cuspide Phoebum
    instruat, Aoniam Marte movente lyram?
sunt tibi magna, puer, nimiumque potentia regna;
    cur opus adfectas, ambitiose, novum?
an, quod ubique, tuum est? tua sunt Heliconia
    tempe?   15
    vix etiam Phoebo iam lyra tuta sua est?
cum bene surrexit versu nova pagina primo,
    attenuat nervos proximus ille meos;
nec mihi materia est numeris levioribus apta,
    aut puer aut longas compta puella comas."   20
Questus eram, pharetra cum protinus ille soluta
    legit in exitium spicula facta meum,
lunavitque genu sinuosum fortiter arcum,
    "quod" que "canas, vates, accipe" dixit "opus!"
Me miserum! certas habuit puer ille sagittas.   25
    uror, et in vacuo pectore regnat Amor.
Sex mihi surgat opus numeris, in quinque residat:
    ferrea cum vestris bella valete modis!
cingere litorea flaventia tempora myrto,
    Musa, per undenos emodulanda pedes!   30

II

Esse quid hoc dicam, quod tam mihi dura videntur
    strata, neque in lecto pallia nostra sedent,
et vacuus somno noctem, quam longa, peregi,
    lassaque versati corporis ossa dolent?

forth Phoebus of the beautiful locks with sharp-pointed spear, and let Mars stir the Aonian lyre? Thou hast an empire of thine own—great, yea, all too potent; why dost lay claim to new powers, ambitious boy? Or is everything, wheresoever, thine? Thine are the vales of Helicon? Is even the lyre of Phoebus scarce longer safely his own? My new page of song rose well with first verse in lofty strain, when that next one—of thy making—changes to slightness the vigour of my work; and yet I have no matter suited to lighter numbers—neither a boy, nor a maiden with long and well-kept locks."

21 Such was my complaint—when forthwith he loosed his quiver, and chose from it shafts that were made for my undoing. Against his knee he stoutly bent moonshape the sinuous bow, and "Singer," he said, "here, take that will be matter for thy song!"

25 Ah, wretched me! Sure were the arrows that yon boy had. I am on fire, and in my but now vacant heart Love sits his throne.

27 In six numbers let my work rise, and sink again in five. Ye iron wars, with your measures, fare ye well! Gird with the myrtle that loves the shore the golden locks on thy temples, O Muse to be sung to the lyre in elevens! [a]

II

WHAT shall I say this means, that my couch seems so hard, and the coverlets will not stay in place, and I pass the long, long night untouched by sleep, and the weary bones of my tossing body are filled with

[a] In elegiac measure, with alternation of six-foot and five-foot verses.

nam, puto, sentirem, siquo temptarer amore.   5
   an subit et tecta callidus arte nocet?
sic erit; haeserunt tenues in corde sagittae,
   et possessa ferus pectora versat Amor.
Cedimus, an subitum luctando accendimus ignem?
   cedamus! leve fit, quod bene fertur, onus.   10
vidi ego iactatas mota face crescere flammas
   et vidi nullo concutiente mori.
verbera plura ferunt, quam quos iuvat usus aratri,
   detractant pressi dum iuga prima boves.
asper equus duris contunditur ora lupatis,   15
   frena minus sentit, quisquis ad arma facit.
acrius invitos multoque ferocius urget
   quam qui servitium ferre fatentur Amor.
En ego confiteor! tua sum nova praeda, Cupido;
   porrigimus victas ad tua iura manus.   20
nil opus est bello—veniam pacemque rogamus;
   nec tibi laus armis victus inermis ero.
necte comam myrto, maternas iunge columbas;
   qui deceat, currum vitricus ipse dabit,
inque dato curru, populo clamante triumphum,   25
   stabis et adiunctas arte movebis aves.
ducentur capti iuvenes captaeque puellae;
   haec tibi magnificus pompa triumphus erit.
ipse ego, praeda recens, factum modo vulnus habebo
   et nova captiva vincula mente feram.   30

ache?—for I should know, I think, were I in any wise assailed by love. Or can it be that love is stolen into me, and cunningly works my harm with covered art? Thus it must be; the subtle darts are planted in my heart, and cruel Love torments the breast where he is lord.

⁹ Shall I yield? or by resisting kindle still more the inward-stealing flame that has me? Let me yield! light grows the burden that is well borne. I have seen flames wax when fanned by movement of the torch, and I have seen them die down when no one waved it more. Oxen at the plough refusing the pressure of the first yoke endure more blows than those that pleasure in their toil. The mouth of the restive horse is bruised by the hard curb, and he feels the bridle less that yields himself to harness. More bitterly far and fiercely are the unwilling assailed by Love than those who own their servitude.

¹⁹ Look, I confess! I am new prey of thine, O Cupid; I stretch forth my hands to be bound, submissive to thy laws. There is no need of war—pardon and peace is my prayer; nor will it be praise for thine arms to vanquish me unarmed. Bind thy locks with the myrtle, yoke thy mother's doves; thy stepsire ᵃ himself shall give thee fitting car, and in the car he gives shalt thou stand, while the people cry thy triumph, and shalt guide with skill the yoked birds. In thy train shall be captive youths and captive maids; such a pomp will be for thee a stately triumph. Myself, a recent spoil, shall be there with wound all freshly dealt, and bear my new bonds with unresisting heart. Conscience shall

ᵃ Mars.

Mens Bona ducetur manibus post terga retortis,
　et Pudor, et castris quidquid Amoris obest.
omnia te metuent ; ad te sua bracchia tendens
　vulgus " io " magna voce " triumphe ! " canet.
blanditiae comites tibi erunt Errorque Furorque,　35
　adsidue partes turba secuta tuas.
his tu militibus superas hominesque deosque ;
　haec tibi si demas commoda, nudus eris.
Laeta triumphanti de summo mater Olympo
　plaudet et adpositas sparget in ora rosas.　　40
tu pinnas gemma, gemma variante capillos
　ibis in auratis aureus ipse rotis.
tunc quoque non paucos, si te bene novimus, ures ;
　tunc quoque praeteriens vulnera multa dabis.
non possunt, licet ipse velis, cessare sagittae ;　45
　fervida vicino flamma vapore nocet.
talis erat domita Bacchus Gangetide terra ;
　tu gravis alitibus, tigribus ille fuit.
Ergo cum possim sacri pars esse triumphi,
　parce tuas in me perdere, victor, opes !　　50
adspice cognati felicia Caesaris arma—
　qua vicit, victos protegit ille manu.

III

Iusta precor : quae me nuper praedata puella est,
　aut amet aut faciat, cur ego semper amem !

be led along, with hands tied fast behind her back,
and Modesty, and all who are foes to the camp of
Love. Before thee all shall tremble; the crowd,
stretching forth their hands to thee, shall chant with
loud voice: "Ho Triumph!" Caresses shall be
at thy side, and Error, and Madness—a rout that
ever follows in thy train. With soldiers like these
dost thou vanquish men and gods; strip from thee
aids like these, thou wilt be weaponless.

[39] All joyously as thou dost pass in triumph, thy
mother shall applaud from Olympus' heights and
scatter upon thy head the roses offered at her
altars. With gems to deck thy wings, with gems
to adorn thy hair, thyself golden, on golden wheels
thou shalt ride along. Then, too, shalt thou touch
with thy flame no few, if I know thee well; then,
too, as thou passest by, shalt thou deal full many
a wound. Thine arrows could not cease, even
shouldst thou so wish thyself; thy fervid flame
brings dole with its heat as thou comest near.
Such was Bacchus, the land of the Ganges overcome.
Thou wilt be dread with thy span of birds; with
tigers dread was he.

[49] Since, then, I am thine to be part of thy sacred
triumph, spare to waste upon me, O victor, thy
power! Look but on the fortunate arms of thy
kinsman Caesar—the hand that has made him victor,
he uses to shield the vanquished.

III

JUST is my prayer: let the maid who has lately
made me her prey either give me love, or give me

a, nimium volui—tantum patiatur amari;
  audierit nostras tot Cytherea preces!
Accipe, per longos tibi qui deserviat annos;   5
  accipe, qui pura norit amare fide!
si me non veterum commendant magna parentum
  nomina, si nostri sanguinis auctor eques,
nec meus innumeris renovatur campus aratris,
  temperat et sumptus parcus uterque parens—   10
at Phoebus comitesque novem vitisque repertor
  hac[1] faciunt, et[2] me qui tibi donat, Amor,
et[3] nulli cessura fides, sine crimine mores
  nudaque simplicitas purpureusque pudor.
non mihi mille placent, non sum desultor amoris: 15
  tu mihi, siqua fides, cura perennis eris.
tecum, quos dederint annos mihi fila sororum,
  vivere contingat teque dolente mori!
te mihi materiem felicem in carmina praebe—
  provenient causa carmina digna sua.   20
carmina nomen habent exterrita cornibus Io,
  et quam fluminea lusit adulter ave,
quaeque super pontum simulato vecta iuvenco
  virginea tenuit cornua vara manu.
nos quoque per totum pariter cantabimur orbem, 25
  iunctaque semper erunt nomina nostra tuis.

[1] hac *Pa.*: haec *Ps* : hinc *Merk. Nem. Br.*
[2] et me *s*: ut me *P*: at me *Merk. Nem. Br.*
[3] et *MSS. Nem.*: at *Ehw. Br.*

reason for ever to love! Ah, I have asked too
much—let her but suffer herself to be loved; may
Cytherea hear my many prayers!

⁵ Take one who would be your slave through
long years; take one who knows how to love with
pure faith! If I have not ancient ancestry and great
name to commend me, if the author of my line
was but a knight, and my fields are not renewed
with ploughshares numberless, if both my parents
guard frugally their spending—yet Phoebus and his
nine companions and the finder of the vine are on my
side, and so is Love, who makes me his gift to you,
and I have good faith that will yield to none,
and ways without reproach, and unadorned sim-
plicity, and blushing modesty. I am not smitten
with a thousand—I am no flit-about in love; you,
if there be any truth, shall be my everlasting care.
With you may it be my lot to live the years which
the Sisters' threads have spun for me, and to be
sorrowed over by you when I die! Give me yourself
as happy matter for my songs—and my songs will
come forth worthy of their cause. Through song
came fame to Io frightened by her horns, and
to her a lover beguiled in guise of the river-bird,
and to her who was carried over the deep on the
pretended bull while she grasped with virgin hand
his bended horns.ᵃ You and I, too, shall be sung
in like manner through all the earth, and my name
shall be ever joined with yours.

ᵃ Io was transformed to a heifer, Leda was loved by
Jove as a swan, and Europa was carried away by Jove in
the form of a bull.

OVID

IV

Vir tuus est epulas nobis aditurus easdem—
  ultima coena tuo sit, precor, illa viro!
ergo ego dilectam tantum conviva puellam
  adspiciam? tangi quem iuvet, alter erit,
alteriusque sinus apte subiecta fovebis?   5
  iniciet collo, cum volet, ille manum?
desine mirari, posito quod candida vino
  Atracis ambiguos traxit in arma viros!
nec mihi silva domus, nec equo mea membra co-
      haerent—
  vix a te videor posse tenere manus!   10
Quae tibi sint facienda tamen cognosce, nec Euris
  da mea nec tepidis verba ferenda Notis!
ante veni, quam vir—nec quid, si veneris ante,
  possit agi video; sed tamen ante veni.
cum premet ille torum, vultu comes ipsa modesto 15
  ibis, ut accumbas—clam mihi tange pedem!
me specta nutusque meos vultumque loquacem;
  excipe furtivas et refer ipsa notas.
verba superciliis sine voce loquentia dicam;
  verba leges digitis, verba notata mero.   20
cum tibi succurret Veneris lascivia nostrae,
  purpureas tenero pollice tange genas.
siquid erit, de me tacita quod mente queraris,
  pendeat extrema mollis ab aure manus.

ᵃ The story of the fight of Centaurs and Lapiths at the
wedding-feast of Pirithous and Hippodamia. The charms of
Hippodamia were such that the Centaurs tried to carry
her off.

IV

THAT husband of yours will attend the same banquet with us — may that dinner, I pray, be your husband's last! Must I then merely look upon the girl I love, be merely a fellow-guest? Is the delight of feeling your touch to be another's, and must it be another's breast you warm, reclining close to him? Shall he throw his arm about your neck whenever he wills? No longer marvel that when the wine had been set the fair daughter of Atrax drove to combat the men of ambiguous form![a] My dwelling-place is not the forest, nor are my members partly man and partly horse—yet I seem scarce able to keep my hands from you!

[11] Yet learn what your task must be, nor give my words to the East-wind to be borne away, nor to the tepid South! Arrive before your husband—and yet I do not see what can be done if you do arrive before; and yet, arrive before him. When he shall press the couch, you will come yourself with modest mien to recline beside him—in secret give my foot a touch! Keep your eyes on me, to get my nods and the language of my eyes; and catch my stealthy signs, and yourself return them. With my brows I shall say to you words that speak without sound; you will read words from my fingers, you will read words traced in wine. When you think of the wanton delights of our love, touch your rosy cheeks with tender finger. If you have in mind some silent grievance against me, let your hand gently hold to the lowest part of your ear. When what I do

cum tibi, quae faciam, mea lux, dicamve, placebunt, 25
    versetur digitis anulus usque tuis.
tange manu mensam, tangunt quo more precantes,
    optabis merito cum mala multa viro.
Quod tibi miscuerit, sapias, bibat ipse, iubeto ;
    tu puerum leviter posce, quod ipsa voles.   30
quae tu reddideris ego primus pocula sumam,
    et, qua tu biberis, hac ego parte bibam.
si tibi forte dabit, quod praegustaverit ipse,
    reice libatos illius ore cibos.
nec premat inpositis sinito tua colla lacertis,   35
    mite nec in rigido pectore pone caput ;
nec sinus admittat digitos habilesve papillae ;
    oscula praecipue nulla dedisse velis !
oscula si dederis, fiam manifestus amator
    et dicam " mea sunt !" iniciamque manum.   40
Haec tamen adspiciam, sed quae bene pallia celant,
    illa mihi caeci causa timoris erunt.
nec femori committe femur nec crure cohaere
    nec tenerum duro cum pede iunge pedem.
multa miser timeo, quia feci multa proterve,   45
    exemplique metu torqueor, ecce, mei.
saepe mihi dominaeque meae properata voluptas
    veste sub iniecta dulce peregit opus.
hoc tu non facies ; sed, ne fecisse puteris,
    conscia de tergo pallia deme tuo.   50
vir bibat usque roga—precibus tamen oscula desint!—
    dumque bibit, furtim si potes, adde merum.

or what I say shall please you, light of mine, keep turning your ring about your finger. Lay your hand upon the table as those who place their hands in prayer, when you wish your husband the many ills he deserves.

²⁹ The wine he mingles for you, be wise and bid him drink himself; quietly ask the slave for the kind you yourself desire. The cup that you give to him to fill, I will be first to take, and I'll drink from the part where you have drunk. If he chance to give you food that he has tasted first, refuse what his lips have touched. And don't allow him to place his arms about your neck, don't let your yielding head lie on his rigid breast; and don't let your hidden charms submit to his touch; and, more than all, don't let him kiss you—not once! If you let him kiss you, I'll declare myself your lover before his eyes, and say, "Those kisses are mine!" and lay hand to my claim.

⁴¹ Yet these offences I shall see, but those that the robe well hides will rouse in me blind fears. Bring not thigh near thigh, nor press with the limb, nor touch rough feet with tender ones. There are many things I wretchedly fear, because there are many I have wantonly wrought, and I am in torment, see! from fear of my own example. Oft have my lady-love and I stolen in haste our sweet delights with her robe to cover us. This you will not do; but lest you be thought to have done it, remove from your shoulders the conspiring mantle. Keep pressing your husband to drink—only add no kisses to your prayers!—and while he drinks, in secret if you can, keep pouring him pure wine. If once we

si bene conpositus somno vinoque iacebit,
    consilium nobis resque locusque dabunt.
cum surges abitura domum, surgemus et omnes,   55
    in medium turbae fac memor agmen eas.
agmine me invenies aut invenieris in illo :
    quidquid ibi poteris tangere, tange mei.
Me miserum! monui, paucas quod prosit in horas ;
    separor a domina nocte iubente mea.   60
nocte vir includet, lacrimis ego maestus obortis,
    qua licet, ad saevas prosequar usque fores.
oscula iam sumet, iam non tantum oscula sumet :
    quod mihi das furtim, iure coacta dabis.
verum invita dato—potes hoc—similisque coactae ; 65
    blanditiae taceant, sitque maligna Venus.
si mea vota valent, illum quoque ne iuvet, opto ;
    si minus, at certe te iuvet inde nihil.
sed quaecumque tamen noctem fortuna sequetur,
    cras mihi constanti voce dedisse nega !   70

V

Aestus erat, mediamque dies exegerat horam ;
    adposui medio membra levanda toro.
pars adaperta fuit, pars altera clausa fenestrae ;
    quale fere silvae lumen habere solent,
qualia sublucent fugiente crepuscula Phoebo,   5
    aut ubi nox abiit, nec tamen orta dies.

have him laid to rest in sleep and wine, our counsel we can take from place and circumstance. When you rise to go home, and all the rest of us rise, remember to lose yourself in the midst of the crowd. You will find me there in that crowd, or will be found by me. Wherever you can touch me there, lay hand on me.

[59] Miserable that I am, I have urged you to what will help for only a few scant hours; I must be separated from my lady-love—night will command it. At night your husband will shut you in, and I all gloomy and pouring forth my tears, shall follow you—as far as I may—up to the cruel doors. Then he will take kisses from you, yes, then he will take not only kisses; what you give me in secret, you will give him as a right, because you must. But give against your will—this much you can do—and like one made to yield; let your favours be without word, and let him find Venus ill-disposed. If my vows have any weight, I pray she grant him no delight; if not, may you at least have no delight from him. But whatsoever, none the less, shall be the fortune of the night, to-morrow with steadfast voice tell me you were not kind!

V

'Twas sultry, and the day had passed its mid hour; I laid my members to rest them on the middle of my couch. One shutter of my window was open, the other shutter was closed; the light was such as oft in a woodland, or as the faint glow of the twilight when Phoebus just is taking leave, or when night has gone and still the day is not

illa verecundis lux est praebenda puellis,
   qua timidus latebras speret habere pudor.
ecce, Corinna venit, tunica velata recincta,
   candida dividua colla tegente coma—   10
qualiter in thalamos famosa Semiramis isse
   dicitur, et multis Lais amata viris.
Deripui tunicam—nec multum rara nocebat;
   pugnabat tunica sed tamen illa tegi.
quae cum ita pugnaret, tamquam quae vincere
      nollet,   15
   victa est non aegre proditione sua.
ut stetit ante oculos posito velamine nostros,
   in toto nusquam corpore menda fuit.
quos umeros, quales vidi tetigique lacertos !
   forma papillarum quam fuit apta premi !   20
quam castigato planus sub pectore venter !
   quantum et quale latus ! quam iuvenale femur !
Singula quid referam ? nil non laudabile vidi
   et nudam pressi corpus ad usque meum.
Cetera quis nescit ? lassi requievimus ambo.   25
   proveniant medii sic mihi saepe dies !

VI

Ianitor—indignum !—dura religate catena,
   difficilem moto cardine pande forem !
quod precor, exiguum est—aditu fac ianua parvo
   obliquum capiat semiadaperta latus.

sprung. It was such a light as shrinking maids should have whose timid modesty hopes to hide away—when lo! Corinna comes, draped in tunic girded round, with divided hair falling over fair, white neck—such as 'tis said was famed Semiramis when passing to her bridal chamber, and Lais loved of many men.

[13] I tore away the tunic—and yet 'twas fine, and scarcely marred her charms; but still she struggled to have the tunic shelter her. Even while thus she struggled, as one who would not overcome, was she overcome—and 'twas not hard—by her own betrayal. As she stood before my eyes with drapery laid all aside, nowhere on all her body was sign of fault. What shoulders, what arms did I see—and touch! How suited for caress the form of her breasts! How smooth her body beneath the faultless bosom! What a long and beautiful side! How youthfully fair the thigh!

[23] Why recount each charm? Naught did I see not worthy of praise, and I clasped her undraped form to mine.

[25] The rest, who does not know? Outwearied, we both lay quiet in repose.

May my lot bring many a midday like to this!

VI

JANITOR—unworthy fate!—bound with the hard chain, move on its hinge the surly portal, and open it! What I entreat is slight—see that the door stand but half ajar, enough to receive me sidewise through the small approach. Long loving has

longus amor tales corpus tenuavit in usus   5
  aptaque subducto corpore membra dedit.
ille per excubias custodum leniter ire
  monstrat ; inoffensos dirigit ille pedes.
At quondam noctem simulacraque vana timebam ;
  mirabar, tenebris quisquis iturus erat.   10
risit, ut audirem, tenera cum matre Cupido
  et leviter "fies tu quoque fortis" ait.
nec mora, venit amor—non umbras nocte volantis,
  non timeo strictas in mea fata manus.
te nimium lentum timeo, tibi blandior uni ;   15
  tu, me quo possis perdere, fulmen habes.
Adspice—et ut videas,[1] inmitia claustra relaxa—
  uda sit ut lacrimis ianua facta meis !
certe ego, cum posita stares ad verbera veste,
  ad dominam pro te verba tremente tuli.   20
ergo quae valuit pro te quoque gratia quondam—
  heu facinus !—pro me nunc valet illa parum ?
redde vicem meritis ! grato licet esse ; quid opstas ?[2]
  tempora noctis eunt ; excute poste seram !
Excute ! sic umquam longa relevere catena,   25
  nec tibi perpetuo serva bibatur aqua !
ferreus orantem nequiquam, ianitor, audis,
  roboribus duris ianua fulta riget.
urbibus obsessis clausae munimina portae
  prosunt ; in media pace quid arma times ?   30

---

[1] et ut videas *Gronovius, from MSS.*: uti videas *Ehw. Nem. Br.*: et *omitted* P s : invideas s.
[2] quid opstas *Hein.*: quod optas *MSS. Br.*: quis obstat *Nem.*

thinned my frame for practices like this, and has made my body apt thereto by wasting away my flesh. Love it is that teaches me how to walk softly past the watchful guard; love is the guide that keeps my steps from stumbling.

⁹ Yet once I was ever in fear of the night and its empty phantoms; I marvelled at whosoever would venture abroad in darkness. Cupid laughed in my ear, with his tender mother, too, and lightly said: "You, too, shall become valiant!" And without delay came love—no shades that flit by night, no arms raised up to deal my doom, do I fear now. You alone I fear, too unyielding to my wish; on you alone I fawn; it is you who hold the thunderbolt can ruin me.

¹⁷ Look!—and that you may see, unloose the pitiless barriers—how the door has been made wet with my tears! Surely, when you stood stripped and ready for the scourge, and trembling, it was I that went to your mistress in your behalf. So, then, the act of grace which once availed even for you— ah, the outrage!—is the same act now to avail so little for me? Render the return I merit! 'Tis in your power to be grateful; why do you hinder me? The hours of the night are going; away with the bar from the door!

²⁵ Away with it!—and so may you be forever lightened of your long chain, nor have to drink for all time the waters of slavery! With heart of iron you listen as I vainly entreat, O janitor, and the door stands rigid with the unyielding oaken brace. It is towns beleaguered that look for protection to the closing of their gates; you are in the midst of peace, and why fear arms? What will you do to an

337

OVID

quid facies hosti, qui sic excludis amantem?
    tempora noctis eunt; excute poste seram!
Non ego militibus venio comitatus et armis;
    solus eram, si non saevus adesset Amor.
hunc ego, si cupiam, nusquam dimittere possum; 35
    ante vel a membris dividar ipse meis.
ergo Amor et modicum circa mea tempora vinum
    mecum est et madidis lapsa corona comis.
arma quis haec timeat? quis non eat obvius illis?
    tempora noctis eunt; excute poste seram! 40
Lentus es: an somnus, qui te male perdat,
    amantis [1]
    verba dat in ventos aure repulsa tua?
at, memini, primo, cum te celare volebam,
    pervigil in mediae sidera noctis eras.
forsitan et tecum tua nunc requiescit amica— 45
    heu, melior quanto sors tua sorte mea!
dummodo sic, in me durae transite catenae!
    tempora noctis eunt; excute poste seram!
Fallimur, an verso sonuerunt cardine postes,
    raucaque concussae signa dedere fores? 50
fallimur—inpulsa est animoso ianua vento.
    ei mihi, quam longe spem tulit aura meam!
si satis es raptae, Borea, memor Orithyiae,
    huc ades 'et surdas flamine tunde foris!
urbe silent tota, vitreoque madentia rore 55
    tempora noctis eunt; excute poste seram!

---

[1] *So Ehw. Nem. Br.*: te *Ps*: prodit *MSS.*: perdat *P*:
amantis *Hein.*: amanti *P*: se praebet amanti *vulg.*: qui te
male prodit *Post.*

---

[a] The repetition of a line as a refrain occurs also in
Heroides ix. In employing this device, Ovid is following
Virgil, Ecl. viii., and Theocritus ii. One of many modern
examples is Spenser's *Epithalamium*.

enemy, who thus exclude a lover? The hours of the night are going; away with the bar from the door![a]

[33] I come with no following of soldiers, and under arms; I were alone, were cruel Love not at my side. Him, even should I wish, I can nowhere dismiss; ere that, I shall be divided from my very self. And so, you see, it is Love, and moderate wine coursing through my temples, and a chaplet falling from my perfume-laden hair, that are my escort. Who would tremble before arms like these? Who would not go to face them? The hours of night are going; away with the bar from the door!

[41] You are unyielding; or does sleep—and may it be the ruin of you!—give to the winds the lover's words your ears repulse? Yet at first, I remember, when I wished to escape your eye, you were wakeful up to the midnight stars. It may be that you, too, have a love, who is resting even now at your side— alas, how much better your lot than mine! Could I be only in such case, come hither, hard chains, to me! The hours of the night are going; away with the bar from the door!

[49] Am I deceived, or did the post sound with the turning of the hinge, and was that the hoarse signal given by a shaken door? I am deceived—it was only the beating of a gusty wind upon the portal. Ah me, how far has that breeze borne away my hope! If thou rememberest well thy stolen Orithyia, Boreas, come hither, and beat down with thy blast these deaf doors! Through all the city there is silence, and, wet with the crystal dew, the hours of the night are passing; away with the bar from the door!

Aut ego iam ferroque ignique paratior ipse,[1]
    quem face sustineo, tecta superba petam.
nox et Amor vinumque nihil moderabile suadent;
    illa pudore vacat, Liber Amorque metu.   60
omnia consumpsi, nec te precibusque minisque
    movimus, o foribus durior ipse tuis.
non te formosae decuit servare puellae
    limina, sollicito carcere dignus eras.
Iamque pruinosus molitur Lucifer axes,   65
    inque suum miseros excitat ales opus.
at tu, non laetis detracta corona capillis,
    dura super tota limina nocte iace !
tu dominae, cum te proiectam mane videbit,
    temporis absumpti tam male testis eris.   70
Qualiscumque vale sentique abeuntis honorem ;
    lente nec admisso turpis amante, vale !
vos quoque, crudeles rigido cum limine postes
    duraque conservae ligna, valete, fores !

VII

ADDE manus in vincla meas—meruere catenas—
    dum furor omnis abit, siquis amicus ades !

[1] O ianitor ipso *Hein. Nem.*

[57] Else I myself, better armed, with iron, and with the fire I carry in my torch, will soon assail your haughty dwelling! Night, and Love, and wine are no counsellors of self-restraint; the first knows naught of shame, and Liber and Love know naught of fear. All things have I tried, and have moved you neither by entreaty nor by threat, O harder yourself than your own doors! Not you were the one to be given ward of my beautiful lady-love's threshold; you were fit only to guard a gloomy dungeon.

[65] Already rimy Lucifer is setting in motion his axles, and the bird of dawn is rousing wretched mortals to their tasks. But thou, O chaplet torn from my unhappy locks, lie thou there upon the unfeeling threshold the whole night through. Thou, when she sees thee cast down there in the early morn, shalt be a witness to my mistress of the time I passed so wretchedly.

[71] And you, despite what you are, farewell, and receive the honour of my parting word; O unyielding, undisgraced by the admission of the lover, fare you well! You, too, cruel posts with your rigid threshold, and you doors with your unfeeling beams, you fellow-slaves of him who guards you, fare you well!

VII

O FRIEND, if any friend be here, put the shackle upon my hands—they have deserved the chain—till my madness all is past! For madness it was that

nam furor in dominam temeraria bracchia movit;
    flet mea vaesana laesa puella manu.
tunc ego vel caros potui violare parentes   5
    saeva vel in sanctos verbera ferre deos!
Quid? non et clipei dominus septemplicis Aiax
    stravit deprensos lata per arva greges,
et, vindex in matre patris, malus ultor, Orestes
    ausus in arcanas poscere tela deas?   10
ergo ego digestos potui laniare capillos?
    nec dominam motae dedecuere comae.
sic formosa fuit. talem Schoeneida[a] dicam
    Maenalias arcu sollicitasse feras;
talis periuri promissaque velaque Thesei   15
    flevit praecipites Cressa tulisse Notos;
sic, nisi vittatis quod erat Cassandra capillis,
    procubuit templo, casta Minerva, tuo.
Quis mihi non "demens!" quis non mihi
    "barbare!" dixit?
    ipsa nihil; pavido est lingua retenta metu.   20
sed taciti fecere tamen convicia vultus;
    egit me lacrimis ore silente reum.
ante meos umeris vellem cecidisse lacertos;
    utiliter potui parte carere mei.
in mea vaesanas habui dispendia vires   25
    et valui poenam fortis in ipse meam.
quid mihi vobiscum, caedis scelerumque ministrae?
    debita sacrilegae vincla subite manus!
an, si pulsassem minimum de plebe Quiritem,
    plecterer—in dominam ius mihi maius erit?   30

---

[a] Atalanta.

moved me to raise reckless hands against my lady-love; my sweetheart is in tears from the hurt of my raging blows. 'Twas in me then to lay hands on even the parents I love, or to deal out cruel strokes even to the holy gods!

⁷ Well? did not Ajax, too, lord of the seven-fold shield, seize and lay low the flocks over the broad fields? and did not Orestes, ill avenger exacting from his mother ill vengeance for his sire, dare ask for weapons against the mystic goddesses? What! Had I on that account the right to rend the well-wrought hair of my lady-love? And yet her disordered locks did not become her ill. She was beautiful so. Such, I should say, was Schoeneus' daughter[a] when she harried the Maenalian wild; such the Cretan maid as she wept that the headlong winds of the south had borne away both sails and promises of perjured Theseus; thus was Cassandra—except that fillets bound her hair—when down she sank at thy shrine, O chaste Minerva.

¹⁹ Who did not say to me: "Madman!" who did not say: "Barbarian!" Herself said naught; her tongue was kept from it by trembling fear. But her face, for all her silence, uttered reproaches none the less; tears charged me with my crime, though her lips were dumb. I would that my arms had sooner dropped from their shoulders; I could better have done without a part of myself. I have used my maddened strength to my own cost, and myself have been strong to my own hurt. What have I with you, ye ministers of blood and crime! Unholy hands, submit to the shackles you deserve! What! if I had struck the least of the Quirites among the crowd, should I be punished—and shall

343

pessima Tydides scelerum monimenta reliquit.
    ille deam primus perculit—alter ego !
et minus ille nocens.   mihi, quam profitebar amare
    laesa est ; Tydides saevus in hoste fuit.
I nunc, magnificos victor molire triumphos,   35
    cinge comam lauro votaque redde Iovi,
quaeque tuos currus comitatus turba sequetur,
    clamet " io ! forti victa puella viro est ! "
ante eat effuso tristis captiva capillo,
    si sinerent laesae, candida tota, genae.   40
aptius impressis fuerat livere labellis
    et collo blandi dentis habere notam.
denique, si tumidi ritu torrentis agebar,
    caecaque me praedam fecerat ira suam,
nonne satis fuerat timidae inclamasse puellae,   45
    nec nimium rigidas intonuisse minas,
aut tunicam summa deducere turpiter ora
    ad mediam ?—mediae zona tulisset opem.
At nunc sustinui raptis a fronte capillis
    ferreus ingenuas ungue notare genas.   50
adstitit illa amens albo et sine sanguine vultu,
    caeduntur Pariis qualia saxa iugis.
exanimisartus et membra trementia vidi—
    ut cum populeas ventilat aura comas,
ut leni Zephyro gracilis vibratur harundo,   55
    summave cum tepido stringitur unda Noto ;
suspensaeque diu lacrimae fluxere per ora,
    qualiter abiecta de nive manat aqua.

---

^a Venus, in battle before Troy.

my right o'er my lady-love be greater ? The son of
Tydeus left most vile example of offence. He was
the first to smite a goddess ^a—I am the second ! And
he was less guilty than I. I injured her I professed
to love ; Tydeus' son was cruel with a foe.

³⁵ Go now, victor, make ready mighty triumphs,
circle your hair with laurel and pay your vows to
Jove, and let the thronging retinue that follow
your car cry out: " Ho ! our valiant hero has been
victorious over a girl ! " Let her walk before, a
downcast captive with hair let loose—from head to
foot pure white, did her wounded cheeks allow !
More fit had it been for her to be marked with the
pressure of my lips, and to bear on her neck the
print of caressing tooth. Finally, if I must needs
be swept along like a swollen torrent, and blind
anger must needs make me its prey, were it not
enough to have cried out at the frightened girl,
without the too hard threats I thundered ? or to
have shamed her by tearing apart her gown from
top to middle ?—her girdle would have come to the
rescue there.

⁴⁹ But, as it was, I could endure to rend cruelly
the hair from her brow and mark with my nail
her free-born cheeks. She stood there bereft of
sense, with face bloodless and white as blocks of
marble hewn from Parian cliffs. I saw her limbs all
nerveless and her frame a-tremble—like the leaves
of the poplar shaken by the breeze, like the slender
reed set quivering by gentle Zephyr, or the surface
of the wave when ruffled by the warm South-wind ;
and the tears, long hanging in her eyes, came
flowing o'er her cheeks even as water distils from
snow that is cast aside. 'Twas then that first I

tunc ego me primum coepi sentire nocentem—
    sanguis erant lacrimae, quas dabat illa, meus.   60
ter tamen ante pedes volui procumbere supplex ;
    ter formidatas reppulit [1] illa manus.
At tu ne dubita—minuet vindicta dolorem—
    protinus in vultus unguibus ire meos.
nec nostris oculis nec nostris parce capillis :   65
    quamlibet infirmas adiuvat ira manus ;
neve mei sceleris tam tristia signa supersint,
    pone recompositas in statione comas !

VIII

Est quaedam—quicumque volet cognoscere lenam,
    audiat !—est quaedam nomine Dipsas anus.
ex re nomen habet—nigri non illa parentem
    Memnonis in roseis sobria vidit equis.
illa magas artes Aeaeaque carmina novit   5
    inque caput liquidas arte recurvat aquas ;
scit bene, quid gramen, quid torto concita rhombo
    licia, quid valeat virus amantis equae.
cum voluit, toto glomerantur nubila caelo ;
    cum voluit, puro fulget in orbe dies.   10
sanguine, siqua fides, stillantia [2] sidera vidi ;
    purpureus Lunae sanguine vultus erat.
hanc ego nocturnas versam volitare per umbras
    suspicor et pluma corpus anile tegi.

---

[1] retulit *P* : reppulit *usual reading* : rettudit *Ehw. Br.*
[2] stillantia *usual reading* : stellantia *P Nem.*

---

[a] Meaning " thirsty."   [b] Aurora, the dawn.

began to feel my guilt—my blood it was that flowed when she shed those tears. Thrice, none the less, I would have cast myself before her feet a suppliant; though thrice thrust she back my dreadful hands.

[63] But you, stay not—for your vengeance will lessen my grief—from straight assailing my features with your nails. Spare neither my eyes nor yet my hair: however weak the hand, ire gives it strength; or at least, that the sad signs of my misdeed may not survive, once more range in due rank your ordered locks.

VIII

THERE is a certain—whoso wishes to know of a bawd, let him hear !—a certain old dame there is by the name of Dipsas. Her name [a] accords with fact— she has never looked with sober eye upon black Memnon's mother, her of the rosy steeds.[b] She knows the ways of magic, and Aeaean incantations, and by her art turns back the liquid waters upon their source; she knows well what the herb can do, what the thread set in motion by the whirling magic wheel, what the poison of the mare in heat. Whenever she has willed, the clouds are rolled together over all the sky; whenever she has willed, the day shines forth in a clear heaven. I have seen, if you can believe me, the stars letting drop down blood; crimson with blood was the face of Luna. I suspect she changes form and flits about in the shadows of night, her aged body covered with plumage. I suspect, and rumour bears me out.

suspicor, et fama est. oculis quoque pupula duplex 15
    fulminat, et gemino lumen ab orbe venit.[1]
evocat antiquis proavos atavosque sepulcris
    et solidam longo carmine findit humum.
Haec sibi proposuit thalamos temerare pudicos ;
    nec tamen eloquio lingua nocente caret.   20
fors me sermoni testem dedit ; illa monebat
    talia—me duplices occuluere fores :
" scis here te, mea lux, iuveni placuisse beato ?
    haesit et in vultu constitit usque tuo.
et cur non placeas ? nulli tua forma secunda est ; 25
    me miseram, dignus corpore cultus abest !
tam felix esses quam formosissima, vellem—
    non ego, te facta divite, pauper ero.
stella tibi oppositi nocuit contraria Martis.
    Mars abiit ; signo nunc Venus apta suo.   30
prosit ut adveniens, en adspice ! dives amator
    te cupiit ; curae, quid tibi desit, habet.
est etiam facies, quae se tibi conparet, illi ;
    si te non emptam vellet, emendus erat."
Erubuit. " decet alba quidem pudor ora, sed iste, 35
    si simules, prodest ; verus obesse solet.
cum bene deiectis gremium spectabis ocellis,
    quantum quisque ferat, respiciendus erit.
forsitan inmundae Tatio regnante Sabinae
    noluerint habiles pluribus esse viris ;   40
nunc Mars externis animos exercet in armis,
    at Venus Aeneae regnat in urbe sui.

[1] venit *P*: micat *P₁ Nem. Br.*

---

[a] Pliny, *N.H.* vii. 16, 17, 18, speaks of women with double
pupils.

From her eyes, too, double pupils dart their light-
nings, with rays that issue from twin orbs.[a] She
summons forth from ancient sepulchres the dead of
generations far remote, and with long incantations
lays open the solid earth.

[19] This old dame has set herself to profane a
modest union; her tongue is none the less with-
out a baneful eloquence. Chance made me witness
to what she said; she was giving these words of
counsel—the double doors concealed me : "Know
you, my light, that yesterday you won the favour of
a wealthy youth ? Caught fast, he could not keep
his eyes from your face. And why should you not
win favour ? Second to none is your beauty. Ah
me, apparel worthy of your person is your lack ! I
could wish you as fortunate as you are most fair—
for with you become rich, I shall not be poor. Mars
with contrary star is what has hindered you. Mars
is gone ; now favouring Venus' star is here. How her
rising brings you fortune, lo, behold ! A rich lover
has desired you; he has interest in your needs.
He has a face, too, that may match itself with
yours; were he unwilling to buy, he were worthy
to be bought.

[35] My lady blushed.

"Blushes, to be sure, become a pale face, but
the blush one feigns is the one that profits; real
blushing is wont to be loss. With eyes becomingly
cast down you will look into your lap, and regard
each lover according to what he brings. It may be
that in Tatius' reign the unadornèd Sabine fair
would not be had to wife by more than one ; but
now in wars far off Mars tries the souls of men, and
'tis Venus reigns in the city of her Aeneas. The

349

OVID

ludunt formosae; casta est, quam nemo rogavit—
    aut, si rusticitas non vetat, ipsa rogat.
has quoque, quas frontis rugas in vertice portas,[1]   45
    excute; de rugis crimina multa cadent.
Penelope iuvenum vires temptabat in arcu;
    qui latus argueret, corneus arcus erat.
labitur occulte fallitque volubilis aetas,
    et celer admissis labitur annus equis.[2]   50
aera nitent usu, vestis bona quaerit haberi,
    canescunt turpi tecta relicta situ—
forma, nisi admittas, nullo exercente senescit.
    nec satis effectus unus et alter habent;
certior e multis nec iam invidiosa rapina est.   55
    plena venit canis de grege praeda lupis.
Ecce, quid iste tuus praeter nova carmina vates
    donat? amatoris milia multa leges.[3]
ipse deus vatum palla spectabilis aurea
    tractat inauratae consona fila lyrae.   60
qui dabit, ille tibi magno sit maior Homero;
    crede mihi, res est ingeniosa dare.
nec tu, siquis erit capitis mercede redemptus,
    despice; gypsati crimen inane pedis.
nec te decipiant veteres circum atria cerae.   65
    tolle tuos tecum, pauper amator, avos!
quin, quia pulcher erit, poscet sine munere noctem!
    quod det, amatorem flagitet ante suum!
Parcius exigito pretium, dum retia tendis,
    ne fugiant; captos legibus ure tuis!   70

[1] *So the MSS.*: quae . . . portant *Burm. Ehw. Nem. Br.*
[2] ut . . . amnis aquis *N. Hein. Nem.*   [3] feres *Nem.*

---

[a] The wrinkles are those of feigned austerity, the mask of
a wanton life.
   [b] Apollo.   [c] Slaves offered for sale were thus marked.

350

beautiful keep holiday ; chaste is she whom no one
has asked—or, be she not too countrified, she
herself asks first. Those wrinkles, too, which you
carry high on your brow, shake off; from the
wrinkles many a naughtiness will fall.[a] Penelope,
when she used the bow, was making trial of
the young men's powers; of horn was the bow
that proved their strength. The stream of a lifetime
glides smoothly on and is past before we know, and
swift the year glides by with horses at full speed.
Bronze grows bright with use ; a fair garment asks
for the wearing ; the abandoned dwelling moulders
with age and corrupting neglect—and beauty, so
you open not your doors, takes age from lack of use.
Nor, do one or two lovers avail enough ; more sure
your spoil, and less invidious, if from many. 'Tis
from the flock a full prey comes to hoary wolves.

[57] "Think, what does your fine poet give you
besides fresh verses ? You will get many thousands
of lover's lines to read. The god of poets himself [b]
attracts the gaze by his golden robe, and sweeps
the harmonious chords of a lyre dressed in gold.
Let him who will give be greater for you than great
Homer ; believe me, giving calls for genius. And
do not look down on him if he be one redeemed
with the price of freedom ; the chalk-marked
foot [c] is an empty reproach. Nor let yourself be
deluded by ancient masks about the hall. Take thy
grandfathers and go, thou lover who art poor ! Nay,
should he ask your favours without paying because
he is fair, let him first demand what he may give
from a lover of his own.

[69] "Exact more cautiously the price while you
spread the net, lest they take flight; once taken,

OVID

nec nocuit simulatus amor ; sine, credat amari,
    et [1] cave ne gratis hic tibi constet amor !
saepe nega noctes.   capitis modo finge dolorem,
    et modo, quae causas praebeat, Isis erit.
mox recipe, ut nullum patiendi colligat usum,   75
    neve relentescat saepe repulsus amor.
surda sit oranti tua ianua, laxa ferenti ;
    audiat exclusi verba receptus amans ;
et, quasi laesa prior, nonnumquam irascere laeso—
    vanescit culpa culpa repensa tua.   80
sed numquam dederis spatiosum tempus in iram ;
    saepe simultates ira morata facit.
quin etiam discant oculi lacrimare coacti,
    et faciant udas ille vel ille genas ;
nec, siquem falles, tu periurare timeto—   85
    commodat in lusus numina surda Venus.
servus et ad partes sollers ancilla parentur,
    qui doceant, apte quid tibi possit emi ;
et sibi pauca rogent—multos si pauca rogabunt,
    postmodo de stipula grandis acervus erit.   90
et soror et mater, nutrix quoque carpat amantem ;
    fit cito per multas praeda petita manus.
cum te deficient poscendi munera causae,
    natalem libo testificare tuum !
Ne securus amet nullo rivale, caveto ;   95
    non bene, si tollas proelia, durat amor.
ille viri videat toto vestigia lecto
    factaque lascivis livida colla notis.
munera praecipue videat, quae miserit alter.
    si dederit nemo, Sacra roganda Via est.   100

[1] et *P*: at *vulg.*: sed *ed. prin.*

---

a Where there were many shops.

prey upon them on terms of your own. Nor is there harm in pretended love; allow him to think he is loved, and take care lest this love bring you nothing in! Often deny your favours. Feign headache now, and now let Isis be what affords you pretext. After a time, receive him, lest he grow used to suffering, and his love grow slack through being oft repulsed. Let your portal be deaf to prayers, but wide to the giver; let the lover you welcome overhear the words of the one you have sped; sometimes, too, when you have injured him, be angry, as if injured first— charge met by counter-charge will vanish. But never give to anger long range of time; anger that lingers long oft causes breach. Nay, even let your eyes learn to drop tears at command, and the one or the other bedew at will your cheeks; nor fear to swear falsely if deceiving anyone—Venus lends deaf ears to love's deceits. Have slave and handmaid skilled to act their parts, to point out the apt gift to buy for you; and have them ask little gifts for themselves—if they ask little gifts from many persons, there will by-and-bye grow from straws a mighty heap. And have your sister and your mother, and your nurse, too, keep plucking at your lover; quickly comes the spoil that is sought by many hands. When pretext fails for asking gifts, have a cake to be sign to him your birthday is come.

⁹⁵ "Take care lest he love without a rival, and feel secure; love lasts not well if you give it naught to fight. Let him see the traces of a lover o'er all your couch, and note about your neck the livid marks of passion. Above all else, have him see the presents another has sent. If no one has sent, you must ask of the Sacred Way.ᵃ When you have taken from

OVID

cum multa abstuleris, ut non tamen omnia donet,
    quod numquam reddas, commodet, ipsa roga!
lingua iuvet mentemque tegat—blandire noceque;
    inpia sub dulci melle venena latent.
Haec si praestiteris usu mihi cognita longo,   105
    nec tulerint voces ventus et aura meas,
saepe mihi dices vivae bene, saepe rogabis,
    ut mea defunctae molliter ossa cubent."
Vox erat in cursu, cum me mea prodidit umbra,
    at nostrae vix se continuere manus,   110
quin albam raramque comam lacrimosaque vino
    lumina rugosas distraherentque genas.
di tibi dent nullosque Lares inopemque senectam,
    et longas hiemes perpetuamque sitim!

IX

MILITAT omnis amans, et habet sua castra Cupido;
    Attice, crede mihi, militat omnis amans.
quae bello est habilis, Veneri quoque convenit aetas.
    turpe senex miles, turpe senilis amor.
quos petiere duces animos[1] in milite forti,   5
    hos petit in socio bella puella viro.[2]
pervigilant ambo; terra requiescit uterque—
    ille fores dominae servat, at ille ducis.
militis officium longa est via; mitte puellam,
    strenuus exempto fine sequetur amans.   10

[1] *Rautenberg*   [2] toro *Hein. Merk.*

him many gifts, in case he still give up not all
he has, yourself ask him to lend—what you never
will restore! Let your tongue aid you, and
cover up your thoughts—wheedle while you despoil;
wicked poisons have for hiding-place sweet honey.

105 "If you fulfil these precepts, learned by me
from long experience, and wind and breeze carry
not my words away, you will often speak me well as
long as I live, and often pray my bones lie softly
when I am dead."

109 Her words were still running, when my
shadow betrayed me. But my hands could scarce
restrain themselves from tearing her sparse white
hair, and her eyes, all lachrymose from wine, and her
wrinkled cheeks. May the gods give you no abode
and helpless age, and long winters and everlasting
thirst!

IX

EVERY lover is a soldier, and Cupid has a camp of
his own; Atticus, believe me, every lover is a soldier.
The age that is meet for the wars is also suited to
Venus. 'Tis unseemly for the old man to soldier,
unseemly for the old man to love. The spirit that
captains seek in the valiant soldier is the same the
fair maid seeks in the man who mates with her.
Both wake through the night; on the ground each
takes his rest—the one guards his mistress's door,
the other his captain's. The soldier's duty takes
him a long road; send but his love before, and the
strenuous lover, too, will follow without end. He

ibit in adversos montes duplicataque nimbo
    flumina, congestas exteret ille nives,
nec freta pressurus tumidos causabitur Euros
    aptaque verrendis sidera quaeret aquis.
quis nisi vel miles vel amans et frigora noctis   15
    et denso mixtas perferet imbre nives ?
mittitur infestos alter speculator in hostes ;
    in rivale oculos alter, ut hoste, tenet.
ille graves urbes, hic durae limen amicae
    obsidet ; hic portas frangit, at ille fores.   20
Saepe soporatos invadere profuit hostes
    caedere et armata vulgus inerme manu.
sic fera Threicii ceciderunt agmina Rhesi,
    et dominum capti deseruistis equi.
saepe maritorum somnis utuntur amantes,   25
    et sua sopitis hostibus arma movent.
custodum transire manus vigilumque catervas
    militis et miseri semper amantis opus.
Mars dubius nec certa Venus ; victique resurgunt,
    quosque neges umquam posse iacere, cadunt.   30
Ergo desidiam quicumque vocabat amorem,
    desinat.   ingenii est experientis amor.
ardet in abducta Briseide magnus Achilles—
    dum licet, Argivas frangite, Troes, opes !
Hector ab Andromaches conplexibus ibat ad arma, 35
    et, galeam capiti quae daret, uxor erat.
summa ducum, Atrides, visa Priameide fertur
    Maenadis effusis obstipuisse comis.

---

^a Under the arms of Ulysses and Diomedes.

will climb opposing mountains and cross rivers doubled by pouring rain, he will tread the high-piled snows, and when about to ride the seas he will not prate of swollen East-winds and look for fit stars ere sweeping the waters with his oar. Who but either soldier or lover will bear alike the cold of night and the snows mingled with dense rain? The one is sent to scout the dangerous foe; the other keeps eyes upon his rival as on a foeman. The one besieges mighty towns, the other the threshold of an unyielding mistress; the other breaks in doors, the one, gates. /

²¹ Oft hath it proven well to rush on the enemy sunk in sleep, and to slay with armèd hand the unarmed rout. Thus fell the lines of Thracian Rhesus,[a] and you, O captured steeds, left your lord behind. Oft lovers, too, take vantage of the husband's slumber, and bestir their own weapons while the enemy lies asleep. To pass through companies of guards and bands of sentinels is ever the task both of soldier and wretched lover. Mars is doubtful, and Venus, too, not sure; the vanquished rise again, and they fall you would say could never be brought low.

³¹ Then whoso hath called love spiritless, let him cease. Love is for the soul ready for any proof. Aflame is great Achilles for Briseis taken away—men of Troy, crush while ye may, the Argive strength! Hector from Andromache's embrace went forth to arms, and 'twas his wife that set the helmet on his head. The greatest of captains, Atreus' son, they say, stood rapt at sight of Priam's daughter,[b] Maenad-like with her streaming hair.

[b] Cassandra and Agamemnon.

Mars quoque deprensus fabrilia vincula sensit;
   notior in caelo fabula nulla fuit.   40
ipse ego segnis eram discinctaque in otia natus;
   mollierant animos lectus et umbra meos.
inpulit ignavum formosae cura puellae
   iussit et in castris aera merere suis.
inde vides agilem nocturnaque bella gerentem.   45
   qui nolet fieri desidiosus, amet!

X

Qualis ab Eurota Phrygiis avecta carinis
   coniugibus belli causa duobus erat,
qualis erat Lede, quam plumis abditus albis
   callidus in falsa lusit adulter ave,
qualis Amymone siccis erravit in agris,[1]   5
   cum premeret summi verticis urna comas—
talis eras; aquilamque in te taurumque timebam,
   et quidquid magno de Iove fecit amor.
Nunc timor omnis abest, animique resanuit error,
   nec facies oculos iam capit ista meos.   10
cur sim mutatus, quaeris? quia munera poscis.
   haec te non patitur causa placere mihi.
donec eras simplex, animum cum corpore amavi;
   nunc mentis vitio laesa figura tua est.
et puer est et nudus Amor; sine sordibus annos   15
   et nullas vestes, ut sit apertus, habet.

[1] Argis *Burm.*

---

[a] The tale of Mars and Venus and Vulcan, told in Odyssey
viii. 266–369.
   [b] *I.e.* The couch on which he wrote his verses lying in the
shade.

Mars, too, was caught, and felt the bonds of the smith; no tale was better known in heaven.[a] For myself, my bent was all to dally in ungirt idleness; my couch and the shade[b] had made my temper mild. Love for a beautiful girl has started me from craven ways and bidden me take service in her camp. For this you see me full of action, and waging the wars of night. Whoso would not lose all his spirit, let him love!

X

Such as was she who was carried from the Eurotas in Phrygian keel to be cause of war to her two lords; such as was Leda, whom the cunning lover deceived in guise of the bird with gleaming plumage; such as was Amymone,[c] going through thirsty fields with full urn pressing the locks on her head—such were you; and in my love for you I feared the eagle and the bull, and what other form soever love has caused great Jove to take.

[9] Now my fear is all away, and my heart is healed of straying; those charms of yours no longer take my eyes. Why am I changed, you ask? Because you demand a price. This is the cause that will not let you please me. As long as you were simple, I loved you soul and body; now your beauty is marred by the fault of your heart. Love is both a child and naked: his guileless years and lack of raiment are sign that he is free. Why bid the child

[c] Sent by her father Danaus for water, she attracted Neptune.

quid puerum Veneris pretio prostare iubetis?
  quo pretium condat,[1] non habet ille sinum!
nec Venus apta feris Veneris nec filius armis—
  non decet inbelles aera merere deos.   20
Stat meretrix certo cuivis mercabilis aere,
  et miseras iusso corpore quaerit opes;
devovet imperium tamen haec lenonis avari
  et, quod vos facitis sponte, coacta facit.
Sumite in exemplum pecudes ratione carentes;   25
  turpe erit, ingenium mitius esse feris.
non equa munus equum, non taurum vacca poposcit;
  non aries placitam munere captat ovem.
sola viro mulier spoliis exultat ademptis,
  sola locat noctes, sola locanda venit,   30
et vendit quod utrumque iuvat quod uterque petebat,
  et pretium, quanti gaudeat ipsa, facit.
quae Venus ex aequo ventura est grata duobus,
  altera cur illam vendit et alter emit?
cur mihi sit damno, tibi sit lucrosa voluptas,   35
  quam socio motu femina virque ferunt?
Non bene conducti vendunt periuria testes,
  non bene selecti iudicis arca patet.
turpe reos empta miseros defendere lingua;
  quod faciat magnas, turpe tribunal, opes;   40
turpe tori reditu census augere paternos,
  et faciem lucro prostituisse suam.
gratia pro rebus merito debetur inemptis;
  pro male conducto gratia nulla toro.

[1] condas P.

---

  [a] *Sinus*, a pocket-like fold in the ancient garment.
  [b] One of the praetor's panel.

of Venus offer himself for gain? He has no pocket
where to put away his gain! [a] Neither Venus nor
her son is apt at service of cruel arms—it is not
meet that unwarlike gods should draw the soldier's
pay.

[21] 'Tis the harlot stands for sale at the fixed price
to anyone soe'er, and wins her wretched gains with
body at the call; yet even she calls curses on the
power of the greedy pander, and does because
compelled what you perform of your own will.

[25] Look for pattern to the beasts of the field, un-
reasoning though they are; 'twill shame you to find
the wild things gentler than yourself. Mare never
claimed gift from stallion, nor cow from bull; the
ram courts not the favoured ewe with gift. 'Tis only
woman glories in the spoil she takes from man, she
only hires out her favours, she only comes to be
hired, and makes a sale of what is delight to both
and what both wished, and sets the price by the
measure of her own delight. The love that is to
be of equal joy to both—why should the one make
sale of it, and the other purchase? Why should
my pleasure cause me loss, and yours to you bring
gain—the pleasure that man and woman both
contribute to?

[37] It is not honour for witnesses to make false
oaths for gain, nor for the chosen juror's [b] purse to lie
open for the bribe. 'Tis base to defend the wretched
culprit with purchased eloquence; the court that
makes great gains is base; 'tis base to swell a
patrimony with a revenue from love, and to offer
one's own beauty for a price. Thanks are due and
deserved for boons unbought; no thanks are felt
for love that is meanly hired. He who has made

OVID

omnia conductor solvit ; mercede soluta   45
  non manet officio debitor ille tuo.
parcite, formosae, pretium pro nocte pacisci ;
  non habet eventus sordida praeda bonos.
non fuit armillas tanti pepigisse [1] Sabinas,
  ut premerent sacrae virginis arma caput ;   50
e quibus exierat, traiecit viscera ferro
  filius, et poenae causa monile fuit.
Nec tamen indignum est a divite praemia posci ;
  munera poscenti quod dare possit, habet.
carpite de plenis pendentes vitibus uvas ;   55
  praebeat Alcinoi poma benignus ager !
officium pauper numerat studiumque fidemque ;
  quod quis habet, dominae conferat omne suae.
est quoque carminibus meritas celebrare puellas
  dos mea ; quam volui, nota fit arte mea.   60
scindentur vestes, gemmae frangentur et aurum ;
  carmina quam tribuent, fama perennis erit.
nec dare, sed pretium posci dedignor et odi ;
  quod nego poscenti, desine velle, dabo !

XI

COLLIGERE incertos et in ordine ponere crines
  docta neque ancillas inter habenda Nape,

[1] eligisse *P*: tetigisse *s*: pepigisse sinistras *ed. prin.*

[a] The Vestal Tarpeia asked as the price of her treason what the Sabines had on their left arms, meaning their armlets of gold, but was crushed beneath the shields they carried there.

the hire pays all; when the price is paid he remains no more a debtor for your favour. Spare, fair ones, to ask a price for your love; a sordid gain can bring no good in the end. 'Twas not worth while for the holy maid to bargain for the Sabine armlets, only that arms should crush her down;[a] a son once pierced with the sword the bosom whence he came, and a necklace was the cause of the mother's pain.[b]

53 And yet it is no shame to ask for presents from the rich; they have wherefrom to give you when you ask. Pluck from full vines the hanging clusters; let the genial field of Alcinous yield its fruits! He who is poor counts out to you as pay his service, zeal, and faithfulness; the kind of wealth each has, let him bring it all to the mistress of his heart. My dower, too, it is to glorify the deserving fair in song; whoever I have willed is made famous by my art. Gowns will be rent to rags, and gems and gold be broke to fragments; the glory my songs shall give will last for ever. 'Tis not the giving but the asking of a price, that I despise and hate. What I refuse at your demand, cease only to wish, and I will give!

XI

NAPE, O adept in gathering and setting in order scattered locks, and not to be numbered among handmaids, O Nape known for useful ministry in

---

[b] Knowing that the Fates had decreed his death in case he went, Eriphyle, for a necklace, caused her husband Amphiaraus to be one of the seven against Thebes, and was slain by Alcmaeon, her son.

inque ministeriis furtivae cognita noctis
    utilis et dandis ingeniosa notis
saepe venire ad me dubitantem hortata Corinnam,   5
    saepe laboranti fida reperta mihi—
accipe et ad dominam peraratas mane tabellas
    perfer et obstantes sedula pelle moras !
nec silicum venae nec durum in pectore ferrum,
    nec tibi simplicitas ordine maior adest.   10
credibile est et te sensisse Cupidinis arcus—
    in me militiae signa tuere tuae !
si quaeret quid agam, spe noctis vivere dices ;
    cetera fert blanda cera notata manu.
Dum loquor, hora fugit. vacuae bene redde
      tabellas,   15
    verum continuo fac tamen illa legat.
adspicias oculos mando frontemque legentis ;
    e tacito vultu scire futura licet.
nec mora, perlectis rescribat multa, iubeto ;
    odi, cum late splendida cera vacat.   20
conprimat ordinibus versus, oculosque moretur
    margine in extremo littera rasa meos.
Quid digitos opus est graphio lassare tenendo ?
    hoc habeat scriptum tota tabella "veni !"
non ego victrices lauro redimire tabellas   25
    nec Veneris media ponere in aede morer.
subscribam : " VENERI FIDAS SIBI NASO MINISTRAS
    DEDICAT, AT NUPER VILE FUISTIS ACER."

the stealthy night and skilled in the giving of the
signal, oft urging Corinna when in doubt to come
to me, often found tried and true to me in times
of trouble—receive and take early to your mistress
these tablets I have inscribed, and care that
nothing hinder or delay! Your breast has in it
no vein of flint or unyielding iron, nor are you
simpler than befits your station. One could believe
you, too, had felt the darts of Cupid—in aiding
me defend the standards of your own campaigns!
Should she ask how I fare, you will say 'tis my
hope of her favour that lets me live; as for the rest,
'tis charactered in the wax by my fond hand.

¹⁵ While I speak, the hour is flying. Give her the
tablets while she is happily free, but none the less
see that she reads them straight. Regard her eyes
and brow, I enjoin you, as she reads; though
she speak not, you may know from her face
what is to come. And do not wait, but bid her
write much in answer when she has read; I hate
when a fine, fair page is widely blank. See she
pack the lines together, and long detain my eyes
with letters traced on the outermost marge.

²³ What need to tire her fingers by holding of the
pen? Let the whole tablet have writ on it only
this: "Come!" Then straight would I take the
conquering tablets, and bind them round with laurel,
and hang them in the mid of Venus' shrine. I
would write beneath: "TO VENUS NASO DEDICATES HIS
FAITHFUL AIDS; YET BUT NOW YOU WERE ONLY MEAN
MAPLE."

XII

FLETE meos casus—tristes rediere tabellae
    infelix hodie littera posse negat.
omina sunt aliquid ; modo cum discedere vellet,
    ad limen digitos restitit icta Nape.
missa foras iterum limen transire memento   5
    cautius atque alte sobria ferre pedem !
Ite hinc, difficiles, funebria ligna, tabellae,
    tuque, negaturis cera referta notis !—
quam, puto, de longae collectam flore cicutae
    melle sub infami Corsica misit apis.   10
at tamquam minio penitus medicata rubebas—
    ille color vere sanguinolentus erat.
proiectae triviis iaceatis, inutile lignum,
    vosque rotae frangat praetereuntis onus !
illum etiam, qui vos ex arbore vertit in usum,   15
    convincam puras non habuisse manus.
praebuit illa arbor misero suspendia collo,
    carnifici diras praebuit illa cruces ;
illa dedit turpes ravis [1] bubonibus umbras,
    vulturis in ramis et strigis ova tulit.   20
his ego commisi nostros insanus amores
    molliaque ad dominam verba ferenda dedi ?
aptius hae capiant vadimonia garrula cerae,
    quas aliquis duro cognitor ore legat ;
inter ephemeridas melius tabulasque iacerent,   25
    in quibus absumptas fleret avarus opes.

---

[1] ravis *N. Hein.*: rasis *P*: raris *Arund.*: raucis *many*.

XII

WEEP for my misfortune—my tablets have returned with gloomy news! The unhappy missive says: "Not possible to-day." There is something in omens; just now as Nape would leave, she tripped her toe upon the threshold and stopped. When next you are sent abroad, remember to take more care as you cross, and soberly to lift your foot full clear!

[7] Away from me, ill-natured tablets, funereal pieces of wood, and you, wax close writ with characters that will say me nay!—wax which I think was gathered from the flower of the long hemlock by the bee of Corsica and sent us under its ill-famed honey. Yet you had a blushing hue, as if tinctured deep with minium—but that colour was really a colour from blood. Lie there at the crossing of the ways, where I throw you, useless sticks, and may the passing wheel with its heavy load crush you! Yea, and the man who converted you from a tree to an object for use, I will assure you, did not have pure hands. That tree, too, lent itself to the hanging of some wretched neck, and furnished the cruel cross to the executioner; it gave its foul shade to hoarse horned owls, and its branches bore up the eggs of the screech-owl and the vulture. To tablets like these did I insanely commit my loves and give my tender words to be carried to my lady? More fitly would such tablets receive the wordy bond, for some judge to read in dour tones; 'twere better they should lie among day-ledgers, and accounts in which some miser weeps o'er money spent.

OVID

Ergo ego vos rebus duplices pro nomine sensi.
 auspicii numerus non erat ipse boni.
quid precer iratus, nisi vos cariosa senectus
 rodat, et inmundo cera sit alba situ?   30

XIII

IAM super oceanum venit a seniore marito
 flava pruinoso quae vehit axe diem.
" Quo properas, Aurora? mane!—sic Memnonis
  umbris
 annua sollemni caede parentet avis !
nunc iuvat in teneris dominae iacuisse lacertis;   5
 si quando, lateri nunc bene iuncta meo est.
nunc etiam somni pingues et frigidus aer,
 et liquidum tenui gutture cantat avis.
quo properas, ingrata viris, ingrata puellis ?
 roscida purpurea supprime lora manu !   10
Ante tuos ortus melius sua sidera servat
 navita nec media nescius errat aqua ;
te surgit quamvis lassus veniente viator,
 et miles saevas aptat ad arma manus.
prima bidente vides oneratos arva colentes;   15
 prima vocas tardos sub iuga panda boves.
tu pueros somno fraudas tradisque magistris,
 ut subeant tenerae verbera saeva manus ;[1]

  [1] 15-18 *omitted by P s : elsewhere after* 10.

---

  [a] They were *tabellae duplices*, double tablets.
  [b] Tithonus was immortal, but not immortally young.
  [c] From the ashes of Memnon, Aurora's son, king of

368

[27] Yes, I have found you double in your dealings, to accord with your name.[a] Your very number was an augury not good. What prayer should I make in my anger, unless that rotten old age eat you away, and your wax grow colourless from foul neglect?

XIII

She is coming already over the ocean from her too-ancient husband [b]—she of the golden hair who with rimy axle brings the day.

[3] " Whither art thou hasting, Aurora? Stay!—so may his birds each year make sacrifice to the shades of Memnon their sire in the solemn combat![c] 'Tis now I delight to lie in the tender arms of my love; if ever, 'tis now I am happy to have her close by my side. Now, too, slumber is deep and the air is cool, and birds chant liquid song from their slender throats. Whither art thou hasting, O unwelcome to men, unwelcome to maids? Check with rosy hand the dewy rein!

[11] " Before thy rising the seaman better observes his stars, and does not wander blindly in mid water; at thy coming rises the wayfarer, however wearied, and the soldier fits his savage hands to arms. Thou art the first to look on men tilling the field with the heavy mattock; thou art the first to summon the slow-moving steer beneath the curvèd yoke. Thou cheatest boys of their slumbers and givest them over to the master, that their tender hands may yield to the cruel stroke; and likewise many dost thou send

Ethiopia, sprang the Memnonides, birds which honoured him in the manner described.

atque eadem sponsum multos [1] ante atria mittis,
    unius ut verbi grandia damna ferant.   20
nec tu consulto, nec tu iucunda diserto ;
    cogitur ad lites surgere uterque novas.
tu, cum feminei possint cessare labores,
    lanificam revocas ad sua pensa manum.
Omnia perpeterer—sed surgere mane puellas,   25
    quis nisi cui non est ulla puella ferat ?
optavi quotiens, ne nox tibi cedere vellet,
    ne fugerent vultus sidera mota tuos !
optavi quotiens, aut ventus frangeret axem,
    aut caderet spissa nube retentus equus ! [2]   30
invida, quo properas ? quod erat tibi filius ater,   33
    materni fuerat pectoris ille color.
Tithono vellem de te narrare liceret ;   35
    femina non caelo turpior ulla foret.
illum dum refugis, longo quia grandior aevo,
    surgis ad invisas a sene mane rotas.
at si, quem mavis,[3] Cephalum conplexa teneres,
    clamares: " lente currite, noctis equi !"   40
Cur ego plectar amans, si vir tibi marcet ab annis ?
    num me nupsisti conciliante seni ?
adspice, quot somnos iuveni donarit amato
    Luna !—neque illius forma secunda tuae.
ipse deum genitor, ne te tam saepe videret,   45
    commisit noctes in sua vota duas."

[1] *So Withof*: sponsum cultos *P*: sponsum consulti *s*:
sponsum cives *Pa.*: atque vades sponsum stultos *Ehw.*
[2] 31, 32 *omitted by P s* :
      quid, si Cephalio numquam flagraret amore ?
        an putat ignotam nequitiam esse suam ?
[3] mavis *Riese* : malis *Merk.*: magis *P* : manibus *s.*

as sponsors before the court, to undergo great losses through a single word. Thou bringest joy neither to lawyer nor to pleader; each is ever compelled to rise for cases new. 'Tis thou, when women might cease from toil, who callest back to its task the hand that works the wool.

²⁵ " I could endure all else—but who, unless he were one without a maid, could bear that maids should rise betimes? How often have I longed that night should not give place to thee, that the stars should not be moved to fly before thy face! How often have I longed that either the wind should break thine axle, or thy steed be tripped by dense cloud, and fall! O envious, whither dost thou haste? The son born to thee was black, and that colour was the hue of his mother's heart.

³⁵ " I would Tithonus were free to tell of thee; no woman in heaven would be known for greater shame. Flying from him because long ages older, thou risest early from the ancient man to go to the chariot-wheels he hates. Yet, hadst thou thy favoured Cephalus in thy embrace, thou wouldst cry : ' Run softly, steeds of night!'

⁴¹ " Why should I be harried in love because thy mate is wasting with years? Didst thou wed an ancient man because I made the match? Look, how many hours of slumber has Luna bestowed upon the youth she loves! ᵃ—and her beauty is not second to thine. The very father of the gods, that he need not see thee so oft, made two nights into one to favour his desires." ᵇ

ᵃ Endymion.
ᵇ Jove and Alcmene, mother of Hercules.

Iurgia finieram. scires audisse : rubebat—
  nec tamen adsueto tardius orta dies !

XIV

DICEBAM " medicare tuos desiste capillos ! "
  tingere quam possis, iam tibi nulla coma est.
at si passa fores, quid erat spatiosius illis ?
  contigerant imum, qua patet usque, latus.
quid, quod erant tenues, et quos ornare timeres ?   5
  vela colorati qualia Seres habent,
vel pede quod gracili deducit aranea filum,
  cum leve deserta sub trabe nectit opus.
nec tamen ater erat nec erat tamen aureus ille,
  sed, quamvis neuter, mixtus uterque color—   10
qualem clivosae madidis in vallibus Idae
  ardua derepto cortice cedrus habet.
Adde, quod et dociles et centum flexibus apti
  et tibi nullius causa doloris erant.
non acus abrupit, non vallum pectinis illos.   15
  ornatrix tuto corpore semper erat ;
ante meos saepe est oculos ornata nec umquam
  bracchia derepta saucia fecit acu.
saepe etiam nondum digestis mane capillis
  purpureo iacuit semisupina toro.   20
tum quoque erat neclecta decens, ut Threcia Bacche,
  cum temere in viridi gramine lassa iacet.
Cum graciles essent tamen et lanuginis instar,
  heu, male [1] vexatae quanta tulere comae !

---

[1] male *P s* : mala *vulg.*

[47] I had brought my chiding to an end. You might know she had heard : she blushed—and yet the day arose no later than its wont !

XIV

I used to say: "Stop drugging that hair of yours !" Now you have no locks to dye ! Yet, had you suffered it, what were more abundant than they ? They had come to touch your side even to its lowest part. Yes, and they were fine in texture, so fine that you feared to dress them ; they were like the gauzy coverings the dark-skinned Seres wear, or the thread drawn out by the slender foot of the spider when he weaves his delicate work beneath the deserted beam. And yet their colour was not black, nor yet was it golden, but, although neither, a mingling of both hues—such as in the dewy vales of precipitous Ida belongs to the lofty cedar stripped of its bark.

[13] Add that they were both docile and suited to a hundred ways of winding, and never caused you whit of pain. The needle did not tear them, nor the palisade of the comb. The hair-dresser's person was ever safe ; oft has my love's toilet been made before my eyes, and she never snatched up hairpin to wound her servant's arms. Often, too, in early morning when her hair was not yet dressed, she has lain half supine on her purple couch. Even then, in her neglect, she was comely, like a Thracian Bacchante lying careless and wearied on the green turf.

[23] And yet, seeing they were delicate and like to down, alas, what woes were theirs, and what tortures they endured ! With what patience did

quam se praebuerunt ferro patienter et igni,   25
  ut fieret torto nexilis [1] orbe sinus!
clamabam: "scelus est istos, scelus urere crines!
  sponte decent; capiti, ferrea, parce tuo!
vim procul hinc remove! non est, qui debeat uri;
  erudit [2] admotas ipse capillus acus."   30
Formosae periere comae—quas vellet Apollo,
  quas vellet capiti Bacchus inesse suo!
illis contulerim, quas quondam nuda Dione
  pingitur umenti sustinuisse manu.
quid male dispositos quereris periisse capillos?   35
  quid speculum maesta ponis, inepta, manu?
non bene consuetis a te spectaris ocellis;
  ut placeas, debes inmemor esse tui.
non te cantatae laeserunt paelicis herbae,
  non anus Haemonia perfida lavit aqua;   40
nec tibi vis morbi nocuit—procul omen abesto!—
  nec minuit densas invida lingua comas.
facta manu culpaque tua dispendia sentis;
  ipsa dabas capiti mixta venena tuo.
Nunc tibi captivos mittet Germania crines;   45
  culta triumphatae munere gentis eris.
o quam saepe comas aliquo mirante rubebis,
  et dices: "empta nunc ego merce probor,
nescio quam pro me laudat nunc iste Sygambram.
  fama tamen memini cum fuit ista mea."   50

[1] nexilis *vulg.*: rexilis *P*: textilis *s*: flexilis *Burm. Ném.*
[2] circuit *Martinon.*

---

[a] Pliny mentions a picture of Venus rising from the sea, by Apelles.

they yield themselves to iron and fire to form the close-curling ringlet with its winding orb ! I kept crying out : " 'T is crime, 't is crime to burn those tresses ! They are beautiful of themselves ; spare your own head, O iron-hearted girl ! Away from there with force ! That is no hair should feel the fire ; your curls themselves can school the irons you apply ! "

[31] The beautiful tresses are no more—such as Apollo could desire, such as Bacchus could desire, for their own heads ! I could compare with them the tresses which nude Dione is painted holding up of yore with dripping fingers.[a] Why do you lament the ruin of your ill-ordered hair ? why lay aside your mirror with sorrowing hand, silly girl ? You are gazed upon by yourself with eyes not well accustomed to the sight ; to find pleasure there, you must forget your old-time self. No rival's enchanted herbs have wrought you ill, no treacherous grandam has laved your hair with water from Haemonian land ;[b] nor has violent illness harmed—far from us be the omen ! —nor envious tongue diminished your dense locks. The loss you feel was wrought you by your own hand and fault ; yourself applied the mingled poison to your head.

[45] Now Germany will send you tresses from captive women ; you will be adorned by the bounty of the race we lead in triumph. O how oft, when someone looks at your hair, will you redden, and say : " The ware I have bought is what brings me favour now. 'T is some Sygambrian woman that yonder one is praising now, instead of me. Yet I remember when that glory was my own."

[b] Thessaly was famed as the home of sorcery.

OVID

Me miserum! lacrimas male continet oraque
    dextra
  protegit ingenuas picta rubore genas.
sustinet antiquos gremio spectatque capillos,
  ei mihi, non illo munera digna loco!
Collige cum vultu mentem! reparabile damnum
    est.   55
  postmodo nativa conspiciere coma.

XV

Quid mihi, Livor edax, ignavos obicis annos,
  ingeniique vocas carmen inertis opus;
non me more patrum, dum strenua sustinet aetas,
  praemia militiae pulverulenta sequi,
nec me verbosas leges ediscere nec me   5
  ingrato vocem prostituisse foro?
Mortale est, quod quaeris, opus. mihi fama
    perennis
  quaeritur, in toto semper ut orbe canar.
vivet Maeonides, Tenedos dum stabit et Ide,
  dum rapidas Simois in mare volvet aquas;   10
vivet et Ascraeus, dum mustis uva tumebit,
  dum cadet incurva falce resecta Ceres.
Battiades semper toto cantabitur orbe;
  quamvis ingenio non valet, arte valet.
nulla Sophocleo veniet iactura cothurno;   15
  cum sole et luna semper Aratus erit;
dum fallax servus, durus pater, inproba lena
  vivent et meretrix blanda, Menandros erit;

---

[a] Homer, Hesiod, and Callimachus are the first three poets
referred to.

[51] Ah, wretched me! Scarce keeping back her tears, with her right hand she covers her face, her generous cheeks o'er painted with blushing. The hair of yore she holds in her lap and gazes upon— alas, me! a gift unworthy of that place.

[55] Calm your heart, and stop your tears! Your loss is one may be repaired. Not long, and you will be admired for locks your very own.

XV

Why, biting Envy, dost thou charge me with slothful years, and call my song the work of an idle wit, complaining that, while vigorous age gives strength, I neither, after the fashion of our fathers, pursue the dusty prizes of a soldier's life, nor learn garrulous legal lore, nor set my voice for common case in the ungrateful forum?

[7] It is but mortal, the work you ask of me; but my quest is glory through all the years, to be ever known in song throughout the earth. Maeonia's son[a] will live as long as Tenedos shall stand, and Ida, as long as Simois shall roll his waters rushing to the sea; the poet of Ascra, too, will live as long as the grape shall swell for the vintage, as long as Ceres shall fall beneath the stroke of the curving sickle. The son of Battus shall aye be sung through all the earth; though he sway not through genius, he sways through art. No loss shall ever come to the buskin of Sophocles; as long as the sun and moon Aratus shall live on; as long as tricky slave, hard father, treacherous bawd, and wheedling harlot shall be found, Menander will endure; Ennius the

Ennius arte carens animosique Accius oris
    casurum nullo tempore nomen habent.   20
Varronem primamque ratem quae nesciet aetas,
    aureaque Aesonio terga petita duci ?
carmina sublimis tunc sunt peritura Lucreti,
    exitio terras cum dabit una dies ;
Tityrus et segetes Aeneiaque arma legentur,   25
    Roma triumphati dum caput orbis erit ;
donec erunt ignes arcusque Cupidinis arma,
    discentur numeri, culte Tibulle, tui ;
Gallus et Hesperiis et Gallus notus Eois,
    et sua cum Gallo nota Lycoris erit.   30
Ergo, cum silices, cum dens patientis aratri
    depereant aevo, carmina morte carent.
cedant carminibus reges regumque triumphi,
    cedat et auriferi ripa benigna Tagi !
vilia miretur vulgus ; mihi flavus Apollo   35
    pocula Castalia plena ministret aqua,
sustineamque coma metuentem frigora myrtum,
    atque ita sollicito multus amante legar !
pascitur in vivis Livor ; post fata quiescit,
    cum suus ex merito quemque tuetur honos.   40
ergo etiam cum me supremus adederit ignis,
    vivam, parsque mei multa superstes erit.

rugged in art, and Accius of the spirited tongue, possess names that will never fade. Varro and the first of ships—what generation will fail to know of them, and of the golden fleece, the Aesonian chieftain's quest? The verses of sublime Lucretius will perish only then when a single day shall give the earth to doom. Tityrus and the harvest, and the arms of Aeneas, will be read as long as Rome shall be capital of the world she triumphs o'er; as long as flames and bow are the arms of Cupid, thy numbers shall be conned, O elegant Tibullus; Gallus shall be known to Hesperia's sons, and Gallus to the sons of Eos, and known with Gallus shall his own Lycoris be.

[31] Yea, though hard rocks and though the tooth of the enduring ploughshare perish with passing time, song is untouched by death. Before song let monarchs and monarchs' triumphs yield—yield, too, the bounteous banks of Tagus bearing gold! Let what is cheap excite the marvel of the crowd; for me may golden Apollo minister full cups from the Castalian fount, and may I on my locks sustain the myrtle that fears the cold; and so be ever conned by anxious lovers! It is the living that Envy feeds upon; after doom it stirs no more, when each man's fame guards him as he deserves. I, too, when the final fires have eaten up my frame, shall still live on, and the great part of me survive my death.[a]

---

[a] This charming poem is a literary convention: compare Horace's *exegi monumentum* (iii. 30), and Shakespeare's "Not marble nor the gilded monuments" (Sonnet lv).

LIBER SECUNDUS

I

Hoc quoque conposui Paelignis natus aquosis,
    ille ego nequitiae Naso poeta meae.
hoc quoque iussit Amor—procul hinc, procul este,
    severae !
    non estis teneris apta theatra modis.
me legat in sponsi facie non frigida virgo,   5
    et rudis ignoto tactus amore puer ;
atque aliquis iuvenum quo nunc ego saucius arcu
    agnoscat flammae conscia signa suae,
miratusque diu " quo " dicat " ab indice doctus
    conposuit casus iste poeta meos ? "   10
Ausus eram, memini, caelestia dicere bella
    centimanumque Gyen [1]—et satis oris erat—
cum male se Tellus ulta est, ingestaque Olympo
    ardua devexum Pelion Ossa tulit.
in manibus nimbos et cum Iove fulmen habebam, 15
    quod bene pro caelo mitteret ille suo—
Clausit amica fores ! ego cum Iove fulmen omisi ;
    excidit ingenio Iuppiter ipse meo.
Iuppiter, ignoscas ! nil me tua tela iuvabant ;
    clausa tuo maius ianua fulmen habet.   20

---

[1] Gyan *several MSS.*: gygen *P s.*

---

[a] Sulmo was in a valley with plenteous rains and streams.

BOOK THE SECOND

I

THIS, too, is the work of my pen—mine, Naso's, born among the humid Paeligni,^{a} the well-known singer of my own worthless ways. This, too, have I wrought at the bidding of Love—away from me, far away, ye austere fair! Ye are no fit audience for my tender strains. For my readers I want the maid not cold at the sight of her promised lover's face, and the untaught boy touched by passion till now unknown; and let some youth who is wounded by the same bow as I am now, know in my lines the record of his own heart's flame, and, long wondering, say: "From what tatler has this poet learned, that hehas put in verse my own mishaps?"

^{11} I had dared, I remember, to sing—nor was my utterance too weak—of the wars of Heaven, and Gyas of the hundred hands, when Earth made her ill attempt at vengeance, and steep Ossa, with shelving Pelion on its back, was piled upon Olympus. I had in hand the thunder-clouds, and Jove with the lightning he was to hurl to save his own heaven.

^{17} My beloved closed her door! I—let fall Jove with his lightning; Jove's very self dropped from my thoughts. Jove, pardon me! Thy bolts could not serve me; that door she closed was a thunderbolt greater than thine. I have taken again to my proper

blanditias elegosque levis, mea tela, resumpsi ;
   mollierunt duras lenia verba fores.
carmina sanguineae deducunt cornua lunae,
   et revocant niveos solis euntis equos ;
carmine dissiliunt abruptis faucibus angues,   25
   inque suos fontes versa recurrit aqua.
carminibus cessere fores, insertaque posti,
   quamvis robur erat, carmine victa sera est.
Quid mihi profuerit velox cantatus Achilles?
   quid pro me Atrides alter et alter agent,   30
quique tot errando, quot bello, perdidit annos,
   raptus et Haemoniis flebilis Hector equis ?
at facie tenerae laudata [1] saepe puellae,
   ad vatem, pretium carminis, ipsa venit.
magna datur merces ! heroum clara valete   35
   nomina ; non apta est gratia vestra mihi !
ad mea formosos vultus adhibete, puellae,
   carmina, purpureus quae mihi dictat Amor !

II

Quem penes est dominam servandi cura, Bagoe,
   dum perago tecum pauca, sed apta, vaca.
hesterna vidi spatiantem luce puellam
   illa, quae Danai porticus agmen habet.
protinus, ut placuit, misi scriptoque rogavi.   5
   rescripsit trepida " non licet ! " illa manu ;

---

[1] *So Merk. Post. Ném.*: at facies tenerae laudata *P s*: ut
facies tenerae laudatast *Ehw. Br.*: facie *Hein.*

arms—the light and bantering elegy; its gentle words have softened the hard-hearted door. Song brings down the horns of the blood-red moon, and calls back the snowy steeds of the departing sun; song bursts the serpent's jaws apart and robs him of his fangs, and sends the waters rushing back upon their source. Song has made doors give way, and the bolt inserted in the post, although of oak, has been made to yield by song.

29 Of what avail will it be to me to have sung of swift Achilles? What will the sons of Atreus, the one or the other, do for me, and he who in wandering lost as many years as in war, and Hector the lamented, dragged by Haemonian steeds? But a tender belovèd, at my oft praising of her beauty has come of herself to the poet as the reward for his song. Great is my recompense! Renownèd names of heroes, fare ye well; your favours are not the kind for me! And fair ones, turn hither your beauteous faces as I sing the songs which rosy Love dictates to me!

II

You whose trust is the guarding of your mistress, attend, Bagoas, while I say a few words, but apt. Yesterday I saw the fair one walking in the portico—the one that has the train of Danaus.*a* Forthwith—for I was smitten—I sent and asked her favours in a note. She wrote back with trembling hand: "It is not possible!" and when I asked why "it was not

---

a The portico of Augustus' temple of Apollo on the Palatine, with the fifty daughters of Danaus in marble. Propertius saw its dedication, ii. 31.

et, cur non liceat, quaerenti reddita causa est,
    quod nimium dominae cura molesta tua est.
Si sapis, o custos, odium, mihi crede, mereri
    desine ; quem metuit quisque, perisse cupit.   10
vir quoque non sapiens ; quid enim servare laboret,
    unde nihil, quamvis non tueare, perit ?
sed gerat ille suo morem furiosus amori
    et castum, multis quod placet, esse putet ;
huic furtiva tuo libertas munere detur,   15
    quam dederis illi, reddat ut illa tibi.
conscius esse velis—domina est obnoxia servo ;
    conscius esse times—dissimulare licet.
scripta leget secum—matrem misisse putato !
    venerit ignotus—postmodo notus erit.   20
ibit ad adfectam, quae non languebit, amicam :
    visat ! iudiciis aegra sit illa tuis.
si faciet tarde, ne te mora longa fatiget,
    inposita gremio stertere fronte potes.
nec tu, linigeram fieri quid possit ad Isim,   25
    quaesieris nec tu curva theatra time !
conscius adsiduos commissi tollet honores—
    quis minor est autem quam tacuisse labor ?
ille placet versatque domum neque verbera sentit ;
    ille potens—alii, sordida turba, iacent.   30
huic, verae ut lateant causae, finguntur inanes ;
    atque ambo domini, quod probat una, probant.
cum bene vir traxit vultum rugasque coegit,
    quod voluit fieri blanda puella, facit.

possible," gave this reason, that your guard of your mistress was too strict.

⁹ If you are wise, good guardian, cease, believe me, to merit hate; whom each man fears, he longs to see destroyed. Her husband, too, is anything but wise; for why take pains to watch over that from which, even did you not guard, nothing would be lost? But let him, mad fool, do as his passion prompts him, and let him think she can be chaste who takes the eye of many; be you the means of giving her stolen liberty, that she may render back to you the freedom you gave to her. Be willing to conspire with her—the mistress is bound to the slave; fear you to conspire—you can pretend. She will read a missive by herself —think that her mother sent it! One comes not known to you—in a moment you will know him well! She will go to a sick friend, who will not be ill—let her go to see her; let the friend be ill in your judgment! Is she late in coming back, you need not let long waiting tire you out, but may lay your head in your lap and snore. And make it not your business to ask into what happens at linen-clad Isis' temple, nor concern yourself about the curving theatre! The accomplice in a secret will reap continual reward—and what is less labour, too, than keeping silence? He is one favoured, and rules in the house, and feels no blows; he is one with power —the rest, a mean crowd, are at his feet. For the husband empty reasons are fashioned to keep the true ones hid; and both master and mistress approve what the mistress alone approves. After her lord has put on a scowling face and bent his brows, he does what the wheedling wife has willed shall be done.

Sed tamen interdum tecum quoque iurgia nectat, 35
    et simulet lacrimas carnificemque vocet.
tu contra obicies, quae tuto diluat illa ;
    in verum [1] falso crimine deme fidem.
sic tibi semper honos, sic alta peculia crescent.
    haec fac, in exiguo tempore liber eris. 40
Adspicis indicibus nexas per colla catenas ?
    squalidus orba fide pectora carcer habet.
quaerit aquas in aquis et poma fugacia captat
    Tantalus—hoc illi garrula lingua dedit.
dum nimium servat custos Iunonius Ion, 45
    ante suos annos occidit ; illa dea est !
vidi ego conpedibus liventia crura gerentem,
    unde vir incestum scire coactus erat.
poena minor merito. nocuit mala lingua duobus ;
    vir doluit, famae damna puella tulit. 50
crede mihi, nulli sunt crimina grata marito,
    nec quemquam, quamvis audiat, illa iuvant.
seu tepet, indicium securas prodis [2] ad aures ;
    sive amat, officio fit miser ille tuo.
Culpa nec ex facili quamvis manifesta probatur ; 55
    iudicis illa sui tuta favore venit.
viderit ipse licet, credet tamen ille neganti
    damnabitque oculos et sibi verba dabit.
adspiciat dominae lacrimas, plorabit et ipse,
    et dicet : " poenas garrulus iste dabit ! " 60
quid dispar certamen inis ? tibi verbera victo
    adsunt, in gremio iudicis illa sedet.

---

[1] in verum *P s* : in vero *P₂ s₂*.
[2] prodis *P* : perdis *vulg.*

[35] But let her sometimes none the less cross words with you, too, and feign to weep, and call you executioner. You, in turn, will charge her with what she can safely explain away; by false accusation take away faith in the true. In this way will your honour ever increase, in this way your pile of savings grow high. Do this, in short time you will be free.

[41] Do you note that tellers of tales wear chains tied round their necks? The squalid dungeon is the home of hearts barren of faith. Tantalus seeks for water in the midst of waters and catches at ever escaping fruits—that was the fate he got for his garrulous tongue. Juno's watchman, guarding Io too intently, falls before his time; she—becomes a goddess! I have seen in shackles the livid legs of a man who had forced a husband to know himself a cuckold. The punishment was less than he deserved. His evil tongue brought harm to two; the husband suffered grief, the wife the loss of her good name. Believe me, accusations are welcome to no husband, nor do they please him, even though he hear. If he is cool, you bring your traitorous tales to careless ears; if he loves, your service only makes him wretched.

[55] Nor is a fault, however manifest, an easy thing to prove; the wife comes off unharmed, safe in the favour of her judge. Though he himself have seen, he will yet believe when she denies, accuse his own eyes, and give himself the lie. Let him but look on his lady's tears, and he himself, too, will begin to wail, and say: "The gabbler that slandered you shall pay for it!" Why enter on a contest with odds against you? You will lose and get a flogging in the end, while she will look on from the lap of her judge

Non scelus adgredimur, non ad miscenda coimus
    toxica, non stricto fulminat ense manus.
quaerimus, ut tuto per te possimus amare.   65
    quid precibus nostris mollius esse potest?

III

Ei mihi, quod dominam nec vir nec femina servas
    mutua nec Veneris gaudia nosse potes!
qui primus pueris genitalia membra recidit,
    vulnera quae fecit, debuit ipse pati.
mollis in obsequium facilisque rogantibus esses,   5
    si tuus in quavis praetepuisset amor.
non tu natus equo, non fortibus utilis armis;
    bellica non dextrae convenit hasta tuae.
ista mares tractent; tu spes depone viriles.
    sunt tibi cum domina signa ferenda tua.   10
hanc inple meritis, huius tibi gratia prosit;
    si careas illa, quis tuus usus erit?
Est etiam facies, sunt apti lusibus anni;
    indigna est pigro forma perire situ.
fallere te potuit, quamvis habeare molestus;   15
    non caret effectu, quod voluere duo.
aptius ut[1] fuerit precibus temptasse, rogamus,
    dum bene ponendi munera tempus habes.

              [1] at *Ném.*

[63] 'Tis no crime we are entering on; we are not coming together to mingle poisons; no drawn sword flashes in our hands. What we ask is that you will give us the means to love in safety. What can be more modest than our prayers?

III

MISERABLE me, that you who guard your mistress are neither man nor woman, and cannot know the joys of mutual love! He who first robbed boys of their nature should himself have suffered the wounds he made. Readily would you be compliant and yielding to lovers' prayers, if you had ever grown warm with love for any woman. You were not born for a horse, nor for the strenuous service of arms; the warlike spear fits not your right hand. Let men engage in those ways of life; do you lay aside all manly hopes. The standards you bear must be of your mistress's service. She is the one for you to ply with deserving deeds; hers is the favour to bring you gain; should you lack her, what then will be your use?

[13] Then, too, she has charms, and her years are apt for love's delights; 'tis a shame for her beauty to perish by dull neglect. She could have eluded you, strict guardian though you are called; what two have willed lacks not accomplishment. Yet since 'twill be better to have tried entreaty, we ask your aid, while you still have power to place your favours well.

OVID

IV

Non ego mendosos ausim defendere mores
   falsaque pro vitiis arma movere meis.
confiteor—siquid prodest delicta fateri;
   in mea nunc demens crimina fassus eo.
odi, nec possum, cupiens, non esse quod odi;   5
   heu, quam quae studeas ponere ferre grave est!
Nam desunt vires ad me mihi iusque regendum;
   auferor ut rapida concita puppis aqua.
non est certa meos quae forma invitet amores—
   centum sunt causae, cur ego semper amem.   10
sive aliqua est oculos in se deiecta modestos,
   uror, et insidiae sunt pudor ille meae;
sive procax aliqua est, capior, quia rustica non est,
   spemque dat in molli mobilis esse toro.
aspera si visa est rigidasque imitata Sabinas,   15
   velle, sed ex alto dissimulare puto.
sive es docta, places raras dotata per artes;
   sive rudis, placita es simplicitate tua.
est, quae Callimachi prae nostris rustica dicat
   carmina—cui placeo, protinus ipsa placet.   20
est etiam, quae me vatem et mea carmina culpet—
   culpantis cupiam sustinuisse femur.
molliter incedit—motu capit; altera dura est—
   at poterit tacto mollior esse viro.
haec quia dulce canit flectitque facillima vocem,   25
   oscula cantanti rapta dedisse velim;

IV

I WOULD not venture to defend my faulty morals or to take up the armour of lies to shield my failings. I confess—if owning my short-comings aught avails; and now, having owned them, I madly assail my sins. I hate what I am, and yet, for all my desiring, I cannot but be what I hate; ah, how hard to bear the burden you long to lay aside!

[7] For I lack the strength and will to rule myself; I am swept along like a ship tossed on the rushing flood. 'Tis no fixed beauty that calls my passion forth—there are a hundred causes to keep me always in love. Whether 'tis some fair one with modest eyes downcast upon her lap, I am aflame, and that innocence is my ensnaring; whether 'tis some saucy jade, I am smitten because she is not rustic simple, and gives me hope of enjoying her supple embrace on the soft couch. If she seem austere, and affects the rigid Sabine dame, I judge she would yield, but is deep in her deceit. If you are taught in books, you win me by your dower of rare accomplishments; if crude, you win me by your simple ways. Some fair one tells me Callimachus' songs are rustic beside mine—one who likes me I straightway like myself. Another calls me no poet, and chides my verses—and I fain would clasp the fault-finder to my arms. One treads softly—and I fall in love with her step; another is hard—but can be made softer by the touch of love. Because this one sings sweetly, with easiest modulation of the voice, I would snatch kisses as she sings; this other runs with nimble finger over

OVID

haec querulas habili percurrit pollice chordas—
  tam doctas quis non possit amare manus?
illa placet gestu numerosaque bracchia ducit
  et tenerum molli torquet ab arte latus—   30
ut taceam de me, qui causa tangor ab omni,
  illic Hippolytum pone, Priapus erit!
tu, quia tam longa es, veteres heroidas aequas
  et potes in toto multa iacere toro.
haec habilis brevitate sua est. corrumpor utraque; 35
  conveniunt voto longa brevisque meo.
non est culta—subit, quid cultae accedere possit;
  ornata est—dotes exhibet ipsa suas.
candida me capiet, capiet me flava puella,
  est etiam in fusco grata colore Venus.   40
seu pendent nivea pulli cervice capilli,
  Leda fuit nigra conspicienda coma;
seu flavent, placuit croceis Aurora capillis.
  omnibus historiis se meus aptat amor.
me nova sollicitat, me tangit serior aetas;   45
  haec melior, specie corporis illa placet.[1]
Denique quas tota quisquam probet urbe puellas,
  noster in has omnis ambitiosus amor.

V

NULLUS amor tanti est—abeas, pharetrate Cupido!—
  ut mihi sint totiens maxima vota mori.

[1] placet *Ps et al.*: sapit *Hein. from MSS.*

---

[a] Examples of chastity and lust.

the querulous string—who could but fall in love
with such cunning hands? Another takes me by
her movement, swaying her arms in rhythm and
curving her tender side with supple art—to say
naught of myself, who take fire from every cause,
put Hippolytus in my place, and he will be
Priapus![a] You, because you are so tall, are not
second to the ancient daughters of heroes, and can
lie the whole couch's length. Another I find apt be-
cause she is short. I am undone by both; tall and
short are after the wish of my heart. She is not well
dressed—I dream what dress would add; she is well
arrayed—she herself shows off her dower of charms.
A fair white skin will make prey of me, I am prey
to the golden-haired, and even a love of dusky
hue will please. Do dark locks hang on a neck
of snow—Leda was fair to look upon for her black
locks; are they of golden hue—Aurora pleased
with saffron locks. To all the old tales my
love can fit itself. Fresh youth steals away my
heart, I am smitten with later years; the one has
more worth, the other wins me with charm of
person.

[47] In fine, whatever fair ones anyone could praise
in all the city—my love is candidate for the favours
of them all.[b]

V

No love is worth so much—away, Cupid with the
quiver!—that so often my most earnest prayer should
be for death. For death my prayers are, whenever

[b] For spirit, compare Thomas Moore's "The time I've
lost in wooing."

vota mori mea sunt, cum te peccare[1] recordor,
    ei mihi, perpetuum nata puella malum !
Non mihi deceptae[2] nudant tua facta tabellae,   5
    nec data furtive munera crimen habent.
o utinam arguerem sic, ut non vincere possem !
    me miserum ! quare tam bona causa mea est ?
felix, qui quod amat defendere fortiter audet,
    cui sua " non feci ! " dicere amica potest.   10
ferreus est nimiumque suo favet ille dolori,
    cui petitur victa palma cruenta rea.
Ipse miser vidi, cum me dormire putares,
    sobrius adposito crimina vestra mero.
multa supercilio vidi vibrante loquentes ;   15
    nutibus in vestris pars bona vocis erat.
non oculi tacuere tui, conscriptaque vino
    mensa, nec in digitis littera nulla fuit.
sermonem agnovi, quod non videatur, agentem
    verbaque pro certis iussa valere notis.   20
iamque frequens ierat mensa conviva relicta ;
    conpositi iuvenes unus et alter erant.
inproba tum vero iungentes oscula vidi—
    illa mihi lingua nexa fuisse liquet—
qualia non fratri tulerit germana severo,   25
    sed tulerit cupido mollis amica viro ;
qualia credibile est non Phoebo ferre Dianam,[3]
    sed Venerem Marti saepe tulisse suo.
"Quid facis?" exclamo, "quo nunc mea gaudia differs?
    iniciam dominas in mea iura manus !   30

[1] peccare *Mueller from P* : peccasse *vulg.*
[2] deprensae *Ehw.*
[3] *So Bent.* : Phoebum . . . Dianae *MSS.*

I think you false to me—ah, girl born for my everlasting ill!

[5] No intercepted note it is that lays bare to me your deeds, nor the secret giving of gifts that accuses you. Oh, would that my charge were such that I could not win! Wretched me! why is my cause so strong? Happy he who dares boldly defend his beloved, to whom his mistress can say, "I did not do it!" Iron of heart is he, and too much favours his own pain, who would win a bloodstained triumph by the downfall of the guilty.

[13] I saw your guilty acts my wretched self with sober eye, when the wine had been placed and you thought I slept. I saw you both say many things with quiverings of the brow; in your nods was much of speech. Your eyes, too, girl, were not dumb, and the table was written o'er with wine, nor did any letter fail your fingers. Your speech, too, I recognized was busied with hidden message, and your words charged to stand for certain meanings. And now the throng of guests had already left the board and gone; there were left a youth or two, asleep in wine. 'Twas then indeed I saw you sharing shameful kisses—it is clear to me they were kisses of the tongue—not such as sister bestows on austere brother, but such as yielding sweetheart gives her eager lover; not such as one could think Diana grants to Phoebus, but such as Venus oft bestowed on Mars.

[29] "What are you doing?" I cry out. "Where now are you scattering joys that are mine? I will lay my sovereign hands upon my rights. Those kisses are common to you with me, and common

haec tibi sunt mecum, mihi sunt communia tecum—
    in bona cur quisquam tertius ista venit?"
Haec ego, quaeque dolor linguae dictavit; at illi
    conscia purpureus venit in ora pudor,
quale coloratum Tithoni coniuge caelum   35
    subrubet, aut sponso visa puella novo;
quale rosae fulgent inter sua lilia mixtae,
    aut ubi cantatis Luna laborat equis,
aut quod, ne longis flavescere possit ab annis,
    Maeonis Assyrium femina tinxit ebur.   40
hic erat aut alicui color ille simillimus horum,
    et numquam visu[1] pulchrior illa fuit.
spectabat terram—terram spectare decebat;
    maesta erat in vultu—maesta decenter erat.
sicut erant, et erant culti, laniare capillos   45
    et fuit in teneras impetus ire genas—
Ut faciem vidi, fortes cecidere lacerti;
    defensa est armis nostra puella suis.
qui modo saevus eram, supplex ultroque rogavi,
    oscula ne nobis deteriora daret.   50
risit et ex animo dedit optima—qualia possent
    excutere irato tela trisulca Iovi;
torqueor infelix, ne tam bona senserit alter,
    et volo non ex hac illa fuisse nota.
haec quoque, quam docui, multo meliora fuerunt, 55
    et quiddam visa est addidicisse novi.
quod nimium placuere, malum est, quod tota labellis
    lingua tua est nostris, nostra recepta tuis.
nec tamen hoc unum doleo—non oscula tantum
    iuncta queror, quamvis haec quoque iuncta
        queror;   60
illa nisi in lecto nusquam potuere doceri.
    nescio quis pretium grande magister habet.

[1] visu *Hous.*: casu *MSS.*

to me with you—why does any third attempt to share those goods?"

[33] These were my words, and whatever passion dictated to my tongue; but she—her conscious face mantled with ruddy shame, like the sky grown red with the tint of Tithonus' bride, or maid gazed on by her newly betrothed; like roses gleaming among the lilies where they mingle, or the moon in labour with enchanted steeds, or Assyrian ivory Maeonia's daughter tinctures to keep long years from yellowing it. Like one of these, or very like, was the colour she displayed, and never was she fairer to look upon. She kept her eyes on the ground—to keep them on the ground was becoming; there was grief in her face—grief made her comely. Just as it was, and it was neatly dressed, I was moved to tear her hair and to fly at her tender cheeks—

[47] When I looked on her face, my brave arms dropped; my love was protected by armour of her own. But a moment before in a cruel rage, I was humble now, and e'en entreated her to give me kisses not less sweet than those. She smiled, and gave me her best with all her heart—kisses that could make irate Jove let drop from his hand the three-forked bolt; I am in wretched torment for fear my rival has tasted them as sweet, and I would not have his kisses of the same seal. Much better, too, were these than I had taught, and something new she seemed to have learned. Their too much pleasing was an ill sign, for her kiss was voluptuous. Yet this one thing is not all my grief—I complain not merely that her kisses are close, and yet that they are close I do complain; those kisses could have been no wise but lewdly taught. Some master has had a great reward for his teaching.

OVID

VI

Psittacus, Eois imitatrix ales ab Indis,
    occidit—exequias ite frequenter, aves!
ite, piae volucres, et plangite pectora pinnis
    et rigido teneras ungue notate genas;
horrida pro maestis lanieter pluma capillis,   5
    pro longa resonent carmina vestra tuba!
quod scelus Ismarii quereris, Philomela, tyranni,
    expleta est annis ista querela suis;
alitis in rarae miserum devertere funus—
    magna, sed antiqua est causa doloris Itys.   10
Omnes, quae liquido libratis in aere cursus,
    tu tamen ante alios, turtur amice, dole!
plena fuit vobis omni concordia vita,
    et stetit ad finem longa tenaxque fides.
quod fuit Argolico iuvenis Phoceus Orestae,   15
    hoc tibi, dum licuit, psittace, turtur erat.
Quid tamen ista fides, quid rari forma coloris,
    quid vox mutandis ingeniosa sonis,
quid iuvat, ut datus es, nostrae placuisse puellae?—
    infelix, avium gloria, nempe iaces!   20
tu poteras fragiles pinnis hebetare zmaragdos
    tincta gerens rubro Punica rostra croco.
non fuit in terris vocum simulantior ales—
    reddebas blaeso tam bene verba sono!
Raptus es invidia—non tu fera bella movebas;   25
    garrulus et placidae pacis amator eras.

ª Ismarus wronged Philomela, sister of Procne, his wife,
and the two slew Itys, his son, in revenge.

VI

OUR parrot, wingèd mimic from Indian land of dawn, is no more—come flocking, ye birds, to his obsequies! Come, all ye feathered faithful, come beat your breasts with the wing, and mark your tender cheeks with the rigid claw; let your ruffled plumage be rent in place of mourning hair, and in place of the long trumpet let your songs sound out! If you, Philomela, are lamenting the deed of the tyrant of Ismarus,*a* that lament has been fulfilled by its term of years; turn aside to the hapless funeral of no common bird—great cause for grief is Itys, but belongs to the ancient past.

[11] All ye who poise your flight in liquid air, O grieve—yet thou before all others, friendly turtle-dove! The life that you two shared was filled with all harmony; your loyalty was long and firm, and stood fast to the end. What the youth of Phocis was to Argive Orestes, this was the turtle-dove to you, O parrot, so long as fate allowed.

[17] And yet, of what avail that loyalty, of what your rare and beauteous colour, of what that voice adept in mimicry of sounds, of what my darling's favour as soon as you were hers?—ah, hapless one, glory of birds, you surely are no more! You could dim with your wings the fragile jasper, and your beak was Punic-red with ruddy saffron tinge. On earth there was no bird could better imitate speech —you rendered words so well in your throaty tone!

[25] 'Twas envious fate swept you away—you were no mover of battles fierce; you were a prattling lover of placid peace. Look! quails are ever battling

OVID

ecce, coturnices inter sua proelia vivunt ;
    forsitan et fiant[1] inde frequenter anus.
plenus eras minimo, nec prae sermonis amore
    in multos poteras ora vacare cibos.   30
nux erat esca tibi, causaeque papavera somni,
    pellebatque sitim simplicis umor aquae.
vivit edax vultur ducensque per aera gyros
    miluus et pluviae graculus auctor aquae ;
vivit et armiferae cornix invisa Minervae—   35
    illa quidem saeclis vix moritura novem ;
occidit illa loquax humanae vocis imago,
    psittacus, extremo munus ab orbe datum !
optima prima fere manibus rapiuntur avaris ;
    inplentur numeris deteriora suis.   40
tristia Phylacidae Thersites funera vidit,
    iamque cinis vivis fratribus Hector erat.
Quid referam timidae pro te pia vota puellae—
    vota procelloso per mare rapta Noto ?
septima lux venit non exhibitura sequentem,   45
    et stabat vacuo iam tibi Parca colo.
nec tamen ignavo stupuerunt verba palato ;
    clamavit moriens lingua : " Corinna, vale !"
Colle sub Elysio nigra nemus ilice frondet,
    udaque perpetuo gramine terra viret.   50
siqua fides dubiis, volucrum locus ille piarum
    dicitur, obscenae quo prohibentur aves.
illic innocui late pascuntur olores
    et vivax phoenix, unica semper avis ;
explicat ipsa suas ales Iunonia pinnas,   55
    oscula dat cupido blanda columba mari.

---

[1] fiunt *Ném.*

[a] Protesilaus, the first of the Greeks to die at Troy ;
addressed in *Heroid.* xiii.

with their kind ; and perhaps 'tis the cause of their often living to old-wives' age. You were sated with very little ; speech you loved so well that your beak had no time for many foods. A nut was your fare, and poppy-seeds brought you sleep, and drops of unmixed water drove away your thirst. The greedy vulture lives on, and the kite that traces circles through the air, and the daw, the harbinger of rain ; the raven, too, hated by armour-bearing Minerva, lives on—it, at least, will hardly die after nine generations ; the parrot, that loquacious image of the human voice, gift brought from the limit of the world, is no more ! Best things are all too oft first swept away by the greedy hands of fate ; the worse are suffered to fill out their tale of years. Thersites looked upon the sad funeral of him of Phylace,[a] and Hector was ashes while yet his brothers lived.

[43] Why call to mind the pious vows of my love in her fear for you—vows swept to sea by the gusty South ? The seventh dawn came, that was not to bring another in its train, and Fate stood over you with distaff empty now. Yet the words were not silenced on your nerveless palate ; your dying tongue cried out : " Corinna, fare you well ! "

[49] At the foot of a hill in Elysium is a leafy grove of dark ilex, and the moist earth is green with never-fading grass. If we may have faith in doubtful things, that place, we are told, is the abode of the pious wingèd kind, and from it impure fowl are kept away. There far and wide feed the harmless swans and the long-lived phoenix, bird ever alone of its kind ; there the bird of Juno spreads for her own eye her plumage, and the winsome dove gives kisses to her eager mate. Our parrot, welcomed among

psittacus has inter nemorali séde receptus
    convertit volucres in sua verba pias.
Ossa tegit tumulus—tumulus pro corpore magnus—
    quo lapis exiguus par sibi carmen habet :   60

COLLIGOR EX IPSO DOMINAE PLACUISSE SEPULCRO.
    ORA FUERE MIHI PLUS AVE DOCTA LOQUI.

VII

ERGO sufficiam reus in nova crimina semper ?
    ut vincam, totiens dimicuisse piget.
sive ego marmorei respexi summa theatri,
    eligis e multis, unde dolere velis ;
candida seu tacito vidit me femina vultu,   5
    in vultu tacitas[1] arguis esse notas.
siquam laudavi, misero petis ungue capillos ;
    si culpo, crimen dissimulare putas.
sive bonus color est, in te quoque frigidus esse,
    seu malus, alterius dicor amore mori.   10
Atque ego peccati vellem mihi conscius essem !
    aequo animo poenam, qui meruere, ferunt ;
nunc temere insimulas credendoque omnia frustra
    ipsa vetas iram pondus habere tuam.
adspice, ut auritus miserandae sortis asellus   15
    adsiduo domitus verbere lentus eat !

[1] tectas *Pa.*

them to this woodland seat, attracts to himself by his words the feathered faithful.

[59] His bones are covered by a mound—mound such as fits his body's size—on which a scant stone bears a legend that just fits the space :—

> " YOU MAY JUDGE FROM MY VERY MONUMENT MY
>   MISTRESS LOVED ME WELL.
> I HAD A MOUTH WAS SKILLED IN SPEECH BEYOND A
>   BIRD."

VII

AM I then to stand trial on new complaints for ever? Grant that I win, I am wearied of fighting my case so many times. If I have looked back on the highest rows of the marble theatre, you pick out one of the many women there as a ground for grievance; or if a fair beauty has looked on me with unspeaking face, you charge that in her face were unspoken signals. If I have praised some girl, poor me! your fingers make for my hair; if I pick flaws in her, you think I am hiding a crime. If my colour is good, you charge me with coolness toward you also; if bad, with dying of love for another.

[11] I would I were even conscious of some wrong done! Those who have merited punishment bear it with even mind; but now you accuse me without reason, and by lending belief to every groundless notion yourself keep your ire from having weight. Look at the long-eared, pitiable ass, how slowly he moves, broken by never-ending blows!

OVID

Ecce novum crimen ! sollers ornare Cypassis
    obicitur dominae contemerasse torum.
di melius, quam me, si sit peccasse libido,
    sordida contemptae sortis amica iuvet !   20
quis Veneris famulae conubia liber inire
    tergaque conplecti verbere secta velit ?
adde, quod ornandis illa est operata capillis
    et tibi perdocta est grata ministra manu—
scilicet ancillam, quae tam tibi fida,[1] rogarem !   25
    quid, nisi ut indicio iuncta repulsa foret ?
per Venerem iuro puerique volatilis arcus,
    me non admissi criminis esse reum !

VIII

Ponendis in mille modos perfecta capillis,
    comere sed solas digna, Cypassi, deas,
et mihi iucundo non rustica cognita furto,
    apta quidem dominae, sed magis apta mihi—
quis fuit inter nos sociati corporis index ?   5
    sensit concubitus unde Corinna tuos ?
num tamen erubui ? num, verbo lapsus in ullo,
    furtivae Veneris conscia signa dedi ?
Quid, quod in ancilla siquis delinquere possit,
    illum ego contendi mente carere bona ?   10
Thessalus ancillae facie Briseidos arsit ;
    serva Mycenaeo Phoebas amata duci.
nec sum ego Tantalide maior, nec maior Achille ;
    quod decuit reges, cur mihi turpe putem ?

[1] *So Merk.*: qui erat *P* : quae sit *vulg.*: quia erat *Pa.*

404

[17] And look now, a fresh charge! Cypassis, the deft girl that tires your hair, is cast at me, accused of wronging her mistress' couch. Ye gods grant me better, if I have a mind to sin, than find my pleasure in a love of mean and despisèd lot! What man that is free would willingly mate with a slave, and clasp a waist that was cut with the lash? Add that her work is to dress your hair, and she pleases you with the ministry of her cunning hand; of course I would tamper with a servant so faithful to you! With what issue, except to be repulsed, and then betrayed? By Venus I swear, and by the bows of her wingèd boy, I am not guilty of the charge you bring!

VIII

PERFECT in setting hair aright in a thousand ways, but worthy to dress only that of goddesses, Cypassis, you whom I have found in our stolen delight not wholly simple, apt for your mistress' service, but more apt for mine—who is the tattler has told of our coming together? Where did Corinna get wind of your affair with me? Can I have blushed? Can I have let slip a single word that gave a tell-tale sign of our stolen love?

[9] Well, suppose I did contend that he who could lose his heart to a slave was out of his senses? The Thessalian took fire at the charms of the slave Briseis; a slave, Phoebas, was loved by the Mycenean chief. I am neither greater than Tantalus' son, nor greater than Achilles; why should I judge base for me what was fit for kings?

Ut tamen iratos in te defixit ocellos,   15
   vidi te totis erubuisse genis ;
at quanto, si forte refers, praesentior ipse
   per Veneris feci numina magna fidem !
tu, dea, tu iubeas animi periuria puri
   Carpathium tepidos per mare ferre Notos !   20
Pro quibus officiis pretium mihi dulce repende
   concubitus hodie, fusca Cypassi, tuos !
quid renuis fingisque novos, ingrata, timores ?
   unum est e dominis emeruisse satis.
quod si stulta negas, index anteacta fatebor,   25
   et veniam culpae proditor ipse meae,
quoque loco tecum fuerim, quotiensque, Cypassi,
   narrabo dominae, quotque quibusque modis !

IX

A

O NUMQUAM pro me satis indignate Cupido,
   o in corde meo desidiose puer—
quid me, qui miles numquam tua signa reliqui,
   laedis, et in castris vulneror ipse meis ?
cur tua fax urit, figit tuus arcus amicos ?   5
   gloria pugnantes vincere maior erat.
Quid ? non Haemonius, quem cuspide perculit, heros
   confossum medica postmodo iuvit ope ?

---

   a Telephus, incurably wounded, was told by the oracle
that he who had wounded would also heal him (ὁ τρώσας καὶ

¹⁵ Yet, when she fixed her angered eyes on you, I saw the blushes completely overspread your cheeks; but how much more contained was I, if you happen to remember, when I swore to my faithfulness in mighty Venus' name! Thou, goddess, mayst thou bid the warm South-wind sweep o'er the Carpathian deep the false oaths of a harmless heart!

²¹ In return for these offices to you, dusky Cypassis, pay me to-day the sweet price of your caress! Why do you shake your head and refuse, ungrateful girl, and feign fresh fears? 'Twill suffice to have earned the favour of only one of your masters. But if you stupidly say no, I shall turn informer and confess all we have done before; I shall stand forth the betrayer of my own guilt, and tell your mistress where I have met you, and how many times, Cypassis, and how many ways, and what they were!

IX

A

O Cupid, never enough roused in my behalf, O boy lodged in my heart and doing naught for me—why dost harm me, the soldier who have never left thy standards, and why am I wounded in my own camp? Why doth thy torch burn friends, and thy bow transfix them? 'Twere greater glory to vanquish them that oppose.

⁷ What? did not the hero of Haemonia afterward help with the healer's art him he had smit and pierced with the spear?^a The huntsman pursues

ἰάσεται), and went to Achilles, who applied to the wound the rust of his spear.

OVID

venator sequitur fugientia; capta relinquit
    semper et inventis ulteriora petit.   10
nos tua sentimus, populus tibi deditus, arma;
    pigra reluctanti cessat in hoste manus.
quid iuvat in nudis hamata retundere tela
    ossibus? ossa mihi nuda relinquit amor.
tot sine amore viri, tot sunt sine amore puellae!— 15
    hinc tibi cum magna laude triumphus eat.
Roma, nisi inmensum vires movisset in orbem,
    stramineis esset nunc quoque tecta casis.
Fessus in acceptos miles deducitur agros;
    mittitur in saltus carcere liber equus;   20
longaque subductam celant navalia pinum,
    tutaque deposito poscitur ense rudis.
me quoque, qui totiens merui sub amore puellae,
    defunctum placide vivere tempus erat.[1]

B

"Vive" deus "posito" siquis mihi dicat "amore!" 25
    deprecer—usque adeo dulce puella malum est.
cum bene pertaesum est, animoque relanguit ardor,
    nescio quo miserae turbine mentis agor.
ut rapit in praeceps dominum spumantia frustra
    frena retentantem durior oris equus;   30
ut subitus, prope iam prensa tellure, carinam
    tangentem portus ventus in alta rapit—
sic me saepe refert incerta Cupidinis aura,
    notaque purpureus tela resumit Amor.

            [1] *Mueller divides the poem.*

---

[a] The gladiator's discharge was marked by the gift of a
wooden foil.

the quarry that flies; what he has taken he leaves
behind, and ever strains to the prey ahead. We, a
people who have surrendered to thee, feel the weight
of thy weapons; with the foe that resists, thy hand
is slow to move. Of what avail to blunt thy barbèd
arrows on naked bones?—for love is leaving my
bones naked. So many men there are without love,
without love so many maids!—there is thy field for
great and glorious triumph. Rome, had she not
employed her powers against the boundless world,
would be filled even now with straw-thatched huts.

[19] The tired-out soldier is let retire to the acres he
received; the race-horse free from the course is sent
to the pastures; and the long docks receive to cover
the drawn-up ship of pine, and the harmless foil [a] is
claimed when the sword has been laid aside. I, too,
who have served so oft in the wars of woman's love
—'twere time, my labours o'er, I lived in peace.

B

"Lay aside thy loves," should some god say to me,
"and live without them," I would pray him not ask
it—even so sweet an evil are the fair. When I have
grown weary of love and the ardour of my heart has
cooled, my soul is somehow seized upon by a whirl-
wind of wretchedness. As a hard-mouthed horse
bears headlong in flight the master who strives in
vain to hold him back with foaming bit; as on a
sudden, when land is now all but gained and the
keel is touching the haven, the wind sweeps it out
to the deep—so am I oft carried away again by the
veering gale of Cupid, and bright Love takes up
again the weapons I know well.

Fige, puer! positis nudus tibi praebeor armis;   35
    hic tibi sunt vires, hic [1] tua dextra facit;
huc tamquam iussae veniunt iam sponte sagittae—
    vix illis prae me nota pharetra sua est!
infelix, tota quicumque quiescere nocte
    sustinet et somnos praemia magna vocat!   40
stulte, quid est somnus, gelidae nisi mortis imago!
    longa quiescendi tempora fata dabunt.
me modo decipiant voces fallacis amicae;
    sperando certe gaudia magna feram.
et modo blanditias dicat, modo iurgia nectat;   45
    saepe fruar domina, saepe repulsus eam.
Quod dubius Mars est, per te, privigne Cupido, est;
    et movet exemplo vitricus arma tuo.
tu levis es multoque tuis ventosior alis,
    gaudiaque ambigua dasque negasque fide.   50
si tamen exaudis, pulchra cum matre, Cupido,[2]
    indeserta meo pectore regna gere!
accedant regno, nimium vaga turba, puellae!
    ambobus populis sic venerandus eris.

X

Tu mihi, tu certe, memini, Graecine, negabas
    uno posse aliquem tempore amare duas.
per te ego decipior, per te deprensus inermis—
    ecce, duas uno tempore turpis amo!

        [1] huc N. *Hein.*   [2] rogantem P_2.

[35] Transfix me, child! I have laid aside my defences, and stand unarmed before thee; here is a place for thy powers, here thy right hand may strike; hither, as if bid, thine arrows come now of their own accord—they scarcely know their quiver because of me! Unhappy he who can rest the whole night through, and calls his slumbers a great boon! Fool! what else is sleep but the image of chill death? As for repose, the fates will give long time for that. For me—let only the words of a deceiving sweetheart lure me on; mere hoping will surely bring me great delight. And let her now speak winningly, and now still chide; let me oft enjoy my lady-love, oft go repulsed away.

[47] That Mars is inconstant, thou, his step-son Cupid, art the cause; thy step-sire wields doubtful arms, and after thy example. Thou art light, more quick to feel the wind than thine own wings, and dost grant and deny thy joys with a faith that is never sure. Yet, none the less, if thou and thy beautiful mother will heed my prayer, come, set up your thrones in my heart and reign there for evermore! Let the fair, too, be your subjects in that realm—a fickle, fickle throng! thus will you be adored by peoples twain.

X

'Twas you, Graecinus, 'twas surely you, I remember, who declared to me that for any man to love two maids at once was a thing impossible. To you I owe my fall; to you I owe being caught without my arms—lo! to my shame in love I am with two

411

utraque formosa est, operosae cultibus ambae ;   5
    artibus in dubio est haec sit an illa prior.
pulchrior hac illa est, haec est quoque pulchrior illa ;
    et magis haec nobis, et magis illa placet !
errant ut ventis discordibus acta phaselos
    dividuumque tenent alter et alter amor.   10
quid geminas, Erycina, meos sine fine dolores ?
    non erat in curas una puella satis ?
quid folia arboribus, quid pleno sidera caelo,
    in freta collectas alta quid addis aquas ?
Sed tamen hoc melius, quam si sine amore
    iacerem—   15
    hostibus eveniat vita severa meis !
hostibus eveniat viduo dormire cubili
    et medio laxe ponere membra toro !
at mihi saevus amor somnos abrumpat inertes,
    simque mei lécti non ego solus onus !   20
me mea disperdat nullo prohibente puella—
    si satis una potest, si minus una, duae !
sufficiam—graciles, non sunt sine viribus artus ;
    pondere, non nervis corpora nostra carent ;
et lateri dabit in vires alimenta voluptas.   25
    decepta est opera nulla puella mea ;
saepe ego lascive consumpsi tempora [1] noctis,
    utilis et forti corpore mane fui.
felix, quem Veneris certamina mutua perdunt !
    di faciant, leti causa sit ista mei !   30
Induat adversis contraria pectora telis
    miles et aeternum sanguine nomen emat.
quaerat avarus opes et, quae lassarit arando,
    aequora periuro naufragus ore bibat.

    [1] *So P s* : lascivae consumpto tempore *N. Hein.*

maids at once. Each one is beautiful, both taste-
ful in their dress; in accomplishment, 'tis doubtful
whether the one or the other is first. The one
is fairer than the other—and the other is also
fairer than she; one pleases me the more—and so
does the other, too! Like a yacht that is driven
by contrary winds, my love is now for the one and
now for the other; it veers about, and keeps me
torn in two. Why, O lady of Eryx, dost thou double
endlessly my woes? Was not one love enough to
keep me anxious? Why add leaves to the trees,
stars to a full sky, and heaped-up waters to the deep
seas?

[15] And yet 'tis better thus than if I were loveless
and alone—to my enemies fall the austere life! To
my enemies fall the lot of sleep in a lonely bed, and
the laying their limbs loosely in its midst. But for
me—let cruel love break off my lazy slumbers, and
may I not be the only burden of my bed! Let
my powers be waste by love, and no one say me
nay—if one suffices, well; if not, then two! I shall
meet the test—slender my limbs, but not without
strength; 'tis bulk, not sinew, my body lacks; and
delight will feed the vigour of my loins. No fair
one has ever been deceived in me; oft have I made
merry through all the hours of night, and reached
the morning fit and strong. Happy he whom the
mutual strife of Love lays low! Ye gods, let my
end come from such a cause!

[31] Let the soldier give his breast to cover with
hostile darts, and buy eternal glory with his blood.
Let the grasping trader's quest be wealth, and his
perjured mouth drink in when he is wrecked the
billow his ploughing keel has tired. But for me—

at mihi contingat Veneris languescere motu,   35
    cum moriar, medium solvar et inter opus ;
atque aliquis nostro lacrimans in funere dicat :
    " conveniens vitae mors fuit ista tuae ! "

XI

PRIMA malas docuit mirantibus aequoris undis
    Peliaco pinus vertice caesa vias,
quae concurrentis inter temeraria cautes
    conspicuam fulvo vellere vexit ovem.
o utinam, nequis remo freta longa moveret,   5
    Argo funestas pressa bibisset aquas !
Ecce, fugit notumque torum sociosque Penates
    fallacisque vias ire Corinna parat.
quid [1] tibi, me miserum ! Zephyros Eurosque timebo
    et gelidum Borean egelidumque Notum ?   10
non illic urbes, non tu mirabere silvas ;
    una est iniusti caerula forma maris.
nec medius tenuis conchas pictosque lapillos
    pontus habet ; bibuli litoris illa mora est.
litora marmoreis pedibus signate, puellae ;   15
    hactenus est tutum—cetera caeca via est.
et vobis alii ventorum proelia narrent ;
    quas Scylla infestet, quasve Charybdis aquas ;
et quibus emineant violenta Ceraunia saxis ;
    quo lateant Syrtes magna minorque sinu.   20
haec alii referant ad [2] vos ; quod quisque loquetur,
    credite ! credenti [3] nulla procella nocet.

---

[1] quam *Ném.*   [2] referant ; at vos *vulg. Post.*
[3] credenti *vulg.*: quaerenti *Ehw. from P.*

414

may it be my lot when I die to languish in Venus'
embrace, and be dissolved in the midst of its delight ;
and may one, dropping tears at my funeral, say :
" Thine was a death accorded with thy life ! "

XI

'Twas the pine felled on Pelion's top that first
taught men the evil paths of the sea, while the waves
looked on in wonder—the craft that rashly sailed
between the clashing rocks and bore away the wool
sightly with yellow flock. O that the Argo had
been o'erwhelmed and drunk the waters of doom,
so that no one should trouble with oar the far-
stretching seas !

[7] Lo ! Corinna flies from the couch that knows
her, and the Penates she has shared, and makes
ready to venture forth on treacherous paths. Why,
ah, wretched me !—must I fear for you the West-
wind and the East, and frozen Boreas, and the balmy
South ? Not yonder will you gaze on towns, not
upon groves ; there is only the deep-blue form of
the unjust sea. Nor do the waters in the mid of
the deep have delicate shells and painted pebbles ;
for those we linger on the thirsty strand. Print ye
the strand with marble-white feet, fair maids ; so far
is safe—the rest of the way is blind. And let others
tell you tales of battling winds ; of waters that Scylla
makes dread, or Charybdis ; of rocks where the
violent Ceraunians tower from the sea ; of the fold
in the shore where the Syrtes, great and lesser, lie
in wait. These things let others tell you ; whatever
each shall say, believe it ! Believing brings no harm
from any storm.

Sero respicitur tellus, ubi fune soluto
    currit in inmensum panda carina salum;
navita sollicitus cum ventos horret iniquos   25
    et prope tam letum, quam prope cernit aquam.
quod si concussas Triton exasperet undas,
    quam tibi sit toto nullus in ore color!
tum generosa voces fecundae sidera Ledae
    et "felix," dicas "quem sua terra tenet!"   30
Tutius est fovisse torum, legisse libellos,
    Threiciam digitis increpuisse lyram.
at, si vana ferunt volucres mea dicta procellae,
    aequa tamen puppi sit Galatea tuae!
vestrum crimen erit talis iactura puellae,   35
    Nereidesque deae Nereidumque pater.
vade memor nostri vento reditura secundo;
    inpleat illa tuos fortior aura sinus!
tum mare in haec magnus proclinet litora Nereus;
    huc venti spirent, huc agat aestus aquas!   40
ipsa roges, Zephyri veniant in lintea pleni,[1]
    ipsa tua moveas turgida vela manu!
primus ego adspiciam notam de litore puppim,
    et dicam: "nostros advehit illa deos!"
excipiamque umeris et multa sine ordine carpam   45
    oscula.   pro reditu victima vota cadet;
inque tori formam molles sternentur harenae,
    et tumulus mensae quilibet esse potest.[2]
Illic adposito narrabis multa Lyaeo—
    paene sit ut mediis obruta navis aquis;   50

[1] pleni *P s* : soli *vulg.*   [2] esse potest *P s* : instar erit *vulg.*

---

[a] Gemini, Castor and Pollux.

[23] Too late you look back upon the land, when the cable is loosed and the curving keel is rushing out to the measureless brine; when the anxious sailor shudders at unfavouring winds, and sees death near, as near as he sees the water. But should Triton smite and roughen the waves, how your whole face would show no trace of colour! Then would you call for aid on the high-born stars, the sons of fruitful Leda,[a] and say: "Happy she her own land retains!"

[31] The safer course was fondly to keep your couch, to read your books, to sound with your fingers the Thracian lyre. Yet, if the flying gale must bear away my empty words, may Galatea none the less be kindly to your craft! 'Twill be your crime if such a girl is lost, O daughters divine of Nereus—yours and your sire's. As you go, remember me, and return with favouring wind; may the breeze that then fills your sails be a stronger one! Then let mighty Nereus make slope the sea toward these our shores; hitherward let blow the winds, hitherward the tide roll the waters! You yourself, pray Zephyr strike full your sheets, you yourself stir with your hand the swelling sails! I shall be first to get sight of the well-known craft from the shore, and shall say: "That sail bears hither my gods!" And I will take you in my arms, and wildly snatch kiss on kiss. The victim vowed against your return shall fall; the yielding sands shall be levelled in form of a couch, and some mound be reared, of whatever sort, to serve for table.

[49] There, when the wine is set, you will tell me many a tale—how your ship was all but engulfed in the midst of the waters; and how, while hasting

dumque ad me properas, neque iniquae tempora noctis
    nec te praecipites extimuisse Notos.
omnia pro veris credam, sint ficta licebit—
    cur ego non votis blandiar ipse meis?
haec mihi quamprimum caelo nitidissimus alto   55
    Lucifer admisso tempora portet equo !

XII

ITE triumphales circum mea tempora laurus !
    vicimus : in nostro est, ecce, Corinna sinu,
quam vir, quam custos, quam ianua firma, tot hostes,
    servabant, nequa posset ab arte capi !
haec est praecipuo victoria digna triumpho,   5
    in qua, quaecumque est, sanguine praeda caret.
non humiles muri, non parvis oppida fossis
    cincta, sed est ductu capta puella meo !
Pergama cum caderent bello superata bilustri,
    ex tot in Atridis pars quota laudis erat ?   10
at mea seposita est et ab omni milite dissors
    gloria, nec titulum muneris alter habet.
me duce ad hanc voti finem, me milite veni ;
    ipse eques, ipse pedes, signifer ipse fui.
nec casum fortuna meis inmiscuit actis—   15
    huc ades, o cura parte Triumphe mea !
Nec belli est nova causa mei.   nisi rapta fuisset
    Tyndaris, Europae pax Asiaeque foret.

418

home to me, you feared neither hours of un-
friendly night nor headlong winds of the south.
All I shall take for truth, though you invent
it all—why should I not flatter my own heart's de-
sires? May Lucifer, most brilliant in the lofty
sky, with loose-reined steed full quickly bring that
hour!

XII

COME lie about my temples, ye laurels of the
triumph! Victory is mine; look, Corinna is in my
arms, whom her husband, whom her keeper, whom
the unyielding door—such a troop of enemies!—all
guarded in fear she be taken by some wile! Here
is a victory deserves a special triumph, for no
part of the spoil is stained by blood. It is no lowly
walls, no towns girt round by little moats, that I
have taken by my generalship—but a girl!

9 When Pergamum fell, o'ercome in a war two
lustrums long, from among so many men what part
of the praise fell to Atreus' son? But my glory is
a thing apart for me, unshared by any soldier; and
none other may pretend to my renown. I myself
have been captain in the march to my prayed-for
end, I myself the soldiery; 'tis I have been cavalry,
'tis I have been infantry, 'tis I have been standard-
bearer. Nor has fortune mingled chance with my
achievements—hither come, O Triumph won by care
alone!

17 Nor is the cause of my warfare new. Had
Tyndareus' daughter not been stolen, Europe and
Asia would have been at peace. 'Twas woman

femina silvestris Lapithas populumque biformem
  turpiter adposito vertit in arma mero;   20
femina Troianos iterum nova bella movere
  inpulit in regno, iuste Latine, tuo;
femina Romanis etiamnunc urbe recenti
  inmisit soceros armaque saeva dedit.
Vidi ego pro nivea pugnantes coniuge tauros;   25
  spectatrix animos ipsa iuvenca dabat.
me quoque, qui multos, sed me sine caede, Cupido
  iussit militiae signa movere suae.

XIII

Dum labefactat onus gravidi temeraria ventris,
  in dubio vitae lassa Corinna iacet.
illa quidem clam me tantum molita pericli
  ira digna mea; sed cadit ira metu.
sed tamen aut ex me conceperat—aut ego credo; 5
  est mihi pro facto saepe, quod esse potest.
Isi, Paraetonium genialiaque arva Canopi
  quae colis et Memphin palmiferamque Pharon,
quaque celer Nilus lato delapsus in alveo
  per septem portus in maris exit aquas,   10
per tua sistra precor, per Anubidis ora verendi—
  sic tua sacra pius semper Osiris amet,
pigraque labatur circa donaria serpens,
  et comes in pompa corniger Apis eat!

---

^a The Centaurs.   ^b The war of Aeneas and Turnus over
Lavinia, daughter of Latinus.

turned the sylvan Lapiths and the double-membered folk[a] to unseemly arms o'er wine; 'twas woman moved the Trojans a second time to set new wars afoot, in thy realms, O just Latinus[b]; 'twas woman, when the city still was young, that sent against the Romans their fathers-in-law, and put the cruel weapons in their hands.[c]

[25] I have seen bulls contending for the snowy mate; the heifer herself stood by to see, and spurred their hearts. Cupid, who orders many, has ordered me, too—but me without shedding of blood—to take up the standard for his campaigns.

XIII

CORINNA, rashly seeking to rid her heavy bosom of its load, lies languishing in peril of life. Surely for trying without my knowledge a course so filled with danger she merits my anger; but my anger falls before my fear. And yet, either 'twas I that caused her trouble—or so I believe; with me, what might be oft is held for truth.

[7] O Isis, thou that lovest Paraetonium and Canopus' genial fields, Memphis, and Pharos rich in palms, and where swift Nile glides down and from his broad bed comes forth to the waters of the sea through seven mouths, by thy sistrums I beseech, by the face of revered Anubis—so may loyal Osiris ever love thy rites,[d] and the sluggish serpent glide about thy altar-gifts, and hornèd Apis be thy comrade in the pomp!—turn hither thy counten-

[c] The rape of the Sabines.
[d] Osiris, husband of Isis, was worshipped with her.

421

huc adhibe vultus, et in una parce duobus !   15
    nam vitam dominae tu dabis, illa mihi.
saepe tibi sedit certis operata diebus,
    qua tangit[1] laurus Gallica turma tuas.
Tuque laborantes utero miserata puellas,
    quarum tarda latens corpora tendit onus,   20
lenis ades precibusque meis fave, Ilithyia !
    digna est, quam iubeas muneris esse tui.
ipse ego tura dabo fumosis candidus aris,
    ipse feram ante tuos munera vota pedes.
adiciam titulum : "servata Naso Corinna !"   25
    tu modo fac titulo muneribusque locum.
Si tamen in tanto fas est monuisse timore,
    hac tibi sit pugna dimicuisse satis !

XIV

Quid iuvat inmunes belli cessare puellas,
    nec fera peltatas agmina velle sequi,
si sine Marte suis patiuntur vulnera telis,
    et caecas armant in sua fata manus ?
Quae prima instituit teneros convellere fetus,   5
    militia fuerat digna perire sua.
scilicet, ut careat rugarum crimine venter,
    sternetur pugnae tristis harena tuae ?

            [1] *Ném.*: tingit *MSS.*

---

[a] There was a temple to Isis in the Campus Martius. About it were laurels, and the Gallic squadron may refer to

ance, and in one spare us both! For thou wilt
give life to my lady, and she to me. Oft has
she sat in ministration to thee on the days fixed for
thy service, where the Gallic squadron rides near thy
laurel-trees.[a]

[19] And thou who hast compassion for women in
their pangs, when their heavy bodies are tense with
the hidden load, do thou attend in mercy and give
ear to my prayers, O Ilithyia![b] She is worthy of
aid from thee—do thou bid her live! Myself
in shining robes will offer incense on thy smoking
altars, myself bring votive gifts and lay them at
thy feet. I will add the legend: "NASO, FOR
CORINNA SAVED!" Do thou but give occasion for
the legend and the gifts.

[27] And you—if it be right amid such fear still
to utter warning—see that this battle be the end
of such strife for you!

XIV

OF what avail to fair woman to rest free from
the burdens of war, nor choose with shield in arm
to march in the fierce array, if, free from peril of
battle, she suffer wounds from weapons of her own,
and arm her unforeseeing hands to her own undoing?

[5] She who first plucked forth the tender life
deserved to die in the warfare she began. Can it be
that, to spare your bosom the reproach of lines, you
would scatter the tragic sands of deadly combat?[c]

---

[a] Roman riders on Gallic horses in the neighbouring exercise-
grounds: Horace *Od.* i. 8.
[b] Goddess of birth.   [c] A reference to the arena.

si mos antiquis placuisset matribus idem,
    gens hominum vitio deperitura fuit,   10
quique iterum iaceret generis primordia nostri
    in vacuo lapides orbe, parandus erat.
quis Priami fregisset opes, si numen aquarum
    iusta recusasset pondera ferre Thetis?
Ilia si tumido geminos in ventre necasset,   15
    casurus dominae conditor Urbis erat;
si Venus Aenean gravida temerasset in alvo,
    Caesaribus tellus orba futura fuit.
tu quoque, cum posses nasci formosa, perisses,
    temptasset, quod tu, si tua mater opus;   20
ipse ego, cum fuerim melius periturus amando,
    vidissem nullos matre necante dies.
Quid plenam fraudas vitem crescentibus uvis,
    pomaque crudeli vellis acerba manu?
sponte fluant matura sua—sine crescere nata;   25
    est pretium parvae non leve vita morae.
vestra quid effoditis subiectis viscera telis,
    et nondum natis dira venena datis?
Colchida respersam puerorum sanguine culpant
    atque sua caesum matre queruntur Ityn;   30
utraque saeva parens, sed tristibus utraque causis
    iactura socii sanguinis ulta virum.
dicite, quis Tereus, quis vos inritet Iaso
    figere sollicita corpora vestra manu?
hoc neque in Armeniis tigres fecere latebris,   35
    perdere nec fetus ausa leaena suos.

---

   a Deucalion, who survived the flood, and with Pyrrha
renewed the race by casting stones backward over their
heads.

If vicious ways like this had found favour with mothers of olden time, the race of mortal men would have perished from the earth, and someone must have been found to cast abroad a second time in the vacant world the stones that were the first beginnings of our kind.[a] Who would have crushed the might of Priam if divine Thetis of the waves had refused to bear the burden hers by due? Had Ilia slain the twins in her swelling bosom, 'twould have been doom to the founder of the City that rules the earth; had Venus laid rash hand to Aeneas in her heavy womb, the world to come would have been orphaned of its Caesars. You, too, though you were to be born fair, would have perished had your mother tried what you have tried; and I myself, though a death through love was to be my better fate, would never have seen the day had my mother slain me.

23 Why cheat the full vine of the growing cluster, and pluck with ruthless hand the fruit yet in the green? What is ripe will fall of its self—let grow what has once become quick; a life is no slight reward for a short delay. Ah, women, why will you thrust and pierce with the instrument, and give dire poisons to your children yet unborn? The maid of Colchis stained with the blood of her children, we condemn, and lament the murder of Itys by the mother who brought him forth; but each was a cruel parent, each had tragic reasons for avenging herself on the husband by shedding blood that she shared with him. Tell me, what Tereus provokes you on, what Jason, to pierce your bodies with aggrievèd hand? This neither the tigress has done in jungles of Armenia, nor has lioness had the heart

425

OVID

at tenerae faciunt, sed non inpune, puellae;
    saepe, suos utero quae necat, ipsa perit.
ipsa perit, ferturque rogo resoluta capillos,
    et clamant "merito!" qui modo cumque vident. 40
Ista sed aetherias vanescant dicta per auras,
    et sint ominibus pondera nulla meis!
di faciles, peccasse semel concedite tuto,
    et satis est; poenam culpa secunda ferat!

XV

ANULE, formosae digitum vincture puellae,
    in quo censendum nil nisi dantis amor,
munus eas gratum! te laeta mente receptum
    protinus articulis induat illa suis;
tam bene convenias, quam mecum convenit illi,   5
    et digitum iusto commodus orbe teras!
Felix, a domina tractaberis, anule, nostra;
    invideo donis iam miser ipse meis.
o utinam fieri subito mea munera possem[1]
    artibus Aeaeae Carpathiive senis!   10
tunc ego te cupiam, domina, et tetigisse papillas,
    et laevam tunicis inseruisse manum—
elabar digito quamvis angustus et haerens,
    inque sinum mira laxus ab arte cadam.
idem ego, ut arcanas possim signare tabellas,   15
    neve tenax ceram siccaque gemma trahat,

---

[1] possim *vulg.*

to destroy her unborn young; yet tender woman does it—but not unpunished; oft she who slays her own in her bosom dies herself. She dies herself, and is borne to the pyre with hair unloosed, and all who behold cry out: "'Tis her desert!"

[41] But may the words I am saying to you be carried away on the winds of heaven, and may my ominous speech have no ill end! Ye gods of mercy, grant she has sinned this once in safety, 'tis all I ask; for a second fault, let her bear her punishment!

XV

O RING, that art to circle the finger of my fair lady, in which naught is of value but the giver's love, mayst thou go to her a welcome gift! May she receive thee with glad heart and straightway slip thee on her finger; mayst thou fit her as well as she fits me, and press her finger with aptly adjusted circle!

[7] Happy ring, thou wilt be touched by the hands of my lady-love; already, ah me, I envy my own gift. Ah, might I suddenly become that gift, by the arts of her of Aeaea, or of the ancient one of Carpathus![a] Then would I wish you, my lady, both to touch your breasts, and lay your left hand within your tunic—I would slip from your finger, however tight and close; I would grow loose with wondrous art and fall into your bosom. Likewise, to help her seal her secret missives, and to keep the dry, clinging gem from drawing away the wax, I should first touch

[a] Circe and Proteus, both adepts in the art of transformation.

427

umida formosae tangam prius ora puellae—
    tantum ne signem scripta dolenda mihi.
si dabor[1] ut condar loculis, exire negabo,
    adstringens digitos orbe minore tuos.   20
non ego dedecori tibi sim, mea vita, futurus,
    quodve tener digitus ferre recuset, onus.
me gere, cum calidis perfundes[2] imbribus artus,
    damnaque sub gemma perfer euntis[3] aquae—
sed, puto, te nuda mea membra libidine surgent,   25
    et peragam partes anulus ille viri.
Inrita quid voveo? parvum proficiscere munus;
    illa datam tecum sentiat esse fidem!

XVI

PARS me Sulmo tenet Paeligni tertia ruris—
    parva, sed inriguis ora salubris aquis.
sol licet admoto tellurem sidere findat,
    et micet Icarii stella proterva canis,
arva pererrantur Paeligna liquentibus undis,   5
    et viret in tenero fertilis herba solo.
terra ferax Cereris multoque feracior uvis;
    dat quoque baciferam Pallada rarus ager;
perque resurgentes rivis labentibus herbas
    gramineus madidam caespes obumbrat humum.   10
At meus ignis abest. verbo peccavimus uno!—
    quae movet ardores est procul; ardor adest.

---

[1] sit labor *Ehw. Br.*: si trahar *Ném.*
[2] perfundis *Ps*: perfunderis *Hein. Ném. Br.*
[3] perfer euntis *MSS.*: fer pereuntis *Dousa Ehw. Br.*

the moist lips of my beautiful love—only so that I sealed no missive that would bring me pain. If you wish me given over to the casket's keeping, I will refuse to leave your finger, and lessen my circle to keep firm hold. I would not ill become you, my life, nor be a burden your tender finger would refuse to bear. Wear me when you spray yourself with the warm rain of the bath, nor shrink at the harm from water creeping beneath the gem—but methinks my passions would rise at sight of your fairness, and I, though naught but that ring, would play the human part.

[27] Why pray for what cannot be? Little gift, go on thy way; let my lady feel that with thee my true love comes!

XVI

Sulmo holds me now, third part of the Paelignian fields—a land that is small, but wholesome with channelled streams. Though the sun draw nigh and crack the earth with heat, and the wanton star of the Icarian dog blaze forth, the acres of the Paeligni are wandered through by the liquid wave, and green in the tender soil rises the fruitful plant. 'Tis a land rich in corn, and richer still in the grape; here and there its fields bring forth, too, the berry-bearing tree of Pallas; and over the mead whose herbage ever springs again along the gliding streams, the grassy turf hides thickly the moistened ground.

[11] But my heart's flame is not here. I was wrong in one word!—she who fires my heart is afar; the fire is here. No, could I be set between Pollux

OVID

non ego, si medius Polluce et Castore ponar,
    in caeli sine te parte fuisse velim.
solliciti iaceant terraque premantur iniqua,   15
    in longas orbem qui secuere vias !—
aut iuvenum comites iussissent ire puellas,
    si fuit in longas terra secanda vias !
tum mihi, si premerem ventosas horridus Alpes,
    dummodo cum domina, molle fuisset iter.   20
cum domina Libycas ausim perrumpere Syrtes
    et dare non aequis vela ferenda Notis.
non quae virgineo portenta sub inguine latrant,
    nec timeam vestros, curva Malea, sinus ;
non quae ¹ submersis ratibus saturata Charybdis   25
    fundit et effusas ore receptat aquas.
Quod si Neptuni ventosa potentia vincit,
    et subventuros auferet unda deos,
tu nostris niveos umeris inpone lacertos ;
    corpore nos facili dulce feremus onus.   30
saepe petens Heron iuvenis transnaverat undas ;
    tum quoque transnasset, sed via caeca fuit.
At sine te, quamvis operosi vitibus agri
    me teneant, quamvis amnibus arva natent,
et vocet in rivos currentem rusticus undam,   35
    frigidaque arboreas mulceat aura comas,
non ego Paelignos videor celebrare salubres,
    non ego natalem, rura paterna, locum—
sed Scythiam Cilicasque feros viridesque ² Britannos,
    quaeque Prometheo saxa cruore rubent.   40

¹ quae *s* : qua *P* : quas *old editions*.   ² vitreosque *Ném.*

ᵃ The images of the gods placed at the stern. Such images
were on the "ship of Alexandria whose sign was Castor and
Pollux," of Acts xxviii. 12.   ᵇ *Heroides* xviii., xix.
    ᶜ Where Prometheus was chained while preyed upon by
the vulture sent by Zeus.

and Castor, with you not by, I would not wish a share in heaven. May they lie restless, weighed down by ungracious clay, who have cut long roads upon the earth!—else they should have ordered maids to go as comrades to young men, if long roads must needs be cut upon the earth! Then if, shivering, I were setting foot on the windy Alps, so only my lady-love were with me, my journey were made with ease. Were my lady-love with me, I should dare to steer my ship through the Libyan Syrtes, and spread my sails to be driven by the unpropitious South. I should feel no fear of the monsters that bay from the maiden's groin, nor shrink at thy winding gulfs, O curving Malea; nor the waters which Charybdis, sated with sunken ships, pours forth, and, poured forth, catches back in her jaws again.

[27] But if the windy power of Neptune holdeth sway, and the wave shall sweep away the gods that should aid us,[a] O place your snowy arms about my neck; I shall bear the sweet burden along with easy stroke. Full oft the young lover had swum across the waters to see his Hero; the last time, too, he would have swum across, but the way was blind.[b]

[33] But here without you, though round about me are fields of vines with their busy life, though the countryside is saturate with running streams, and the rustic summons to the rivulets the flowing wave, and the cool breeze caresses the branches of the trees, I seem to dwell not in the healthful Paelignian land, nor in my natal place, my father's acres—but in Scythia, and among the fierce Cilicians, and the woaded Britons, and the rocks ruddy with Promethean gore.[c]

Ulmus amat vitem, vitis non deserit ulmum ;
    separor a domina cur ego saepe mea ?
at mihi te comitem iuraras usque futuram—
    per me perque oculos, sidera nostra, tuos !
verba puellarum, foliis leviora caducis,   45
    inrita, qua visum est, ventus et unda ferunt.
Siqua mei tamen est in te pia cura relicti,
    incipe pollicitis addere facta tuis,
parvaque quamprimum rapientibus esseda mannis
    ipsa per admissas concute lora iubas !   50
at vos, qua veniet, tumidi, subsidite, montes,
    et faciles curvis vallibus este, viae !

XVII

Siquis erit, qui turpe putet servire puellae,
    illo convincar iudice turpis ego !
sim licet infamis, dum me moderatius urat,
    quae Paphon et fluctu pulsa Cythera tenet.
atque utinam dominae miti quoque praeda fuissem 5
    formosae quoniam praeda futurus eram !
dat facies animos.   facie violenta Corinna est—
    me miserum ! cur est tam bene nota sibi ?
scilicet a speculi sumuntur imagine fastus,
    nec nisi conpositam se prius illa videt !   10
Non, tibi si facies animum [1] dat et omina [2] regni—
    o facies oculos nata tenere meos !—
collatum idcirco tibi me contemnere debes ;
    aptari magnis inferiora licet.

[1] animum *P(?) s* : nimium *vulg.*
[2] So *Owen* : nomina *P s* : in omnia *vulg.*

[41] The elm loves the vine, the vine abandons not the elm; why am I oft separated from the mistress of my heart? Yet you had sworn that you would ever be comrade of mine—by me and by your eyes, those stars of mine! The words of women, lighter than falling leaves, go all for naught, swept away by the whim of wind and wave.

[47] Yet, if still in your heart is some feeling of faith toward me who am left alone, begin to make good your promises by deeds, and as soon as you may, with your own hand shake the rein above the flying manes of the ponies that whirl your light car along. And O, wherever she passes, sink down, ye hills, and be easy in the winding vales, ye ways!

XVII

If there be one who thinks it base to be a slave to woman, before his judgment seat shall I be proved guilty of being base! Yet let me lose my name, so she consume me with milder fires who is queen of Paphos and wave-beaten Cythera. Ah, would I had fallen prey to a merciful mistress, too, since I must fall prey to a beauteous one! Beauty breeds arrogance. 'Tis Corinna's fair face makes her hard with me—O wretched me! why does she know herself so well? Surely, 'tis from her image in the glass she gets her haughtiness—and she never sees her image before her toilet is made!

[11] Not even if your charms do give you pride and promise of empire—O charms born to captivate my eyes!—should you therefore scorn me when compared with yourself; lesser things may be fitted to

traditur et nymphe mortalis amore Calypso   15
    capta recusantem detinuisse virum.
creditur aequoream Phthio Nereida regi,
    Egeriam iusto concubuisse Numae,
Vulcano Venerem, quamvis incude relicta
    turpiter obliquo claudicet ille pede.   20
carminis hoc ipsum genus inpar ; sed tamen apte
    iungitur herous cum breviore modo.
tu quoque me, mea lux, in quaslibet accipe leges ;
    te deceat medio iura dedisse foro.[1]
Non tibi crimen ero, nec quo laetere remoto ;   25
    non erit hic nobis infitiandus amor.
sunt mihi pro magno felicia carmina censu,
    et multae per me nomen habere volunt ;
novi aliquam, quae se circumferat esse Corinnam.
    ut fiat, quid non illa dedisse velit ?   30
sed neque diversi ripa labuntur eadem
    frigidus Eurotas populiferque Padus,
nec nisi tu nostris cantabitur ulla libellis ;
    ingenio causas tu dabis una meo.

XVIII

CARMEN ad iratum dum tu perducis Achillen
    primaque iuratis induis arma viris,
nos, Macer, ignava Veneris cessamus in umbra,
    et tener ausuros grandia frangit Amor.
saepe meae " tandem " dixi " discede " puellae—   5
    in gremio sedit protinus illa meo.
saepe " pudet ! " dixi—lacrimis vix illa retentis
    " me miseram ! iam te " dixit " amare pudet ? "

---

[1] foro *P* : toro *vulg.*

---

[a] Ulysses.   [b] Thetis and Peleus, parents of Achilles.

the great. We are told that even the nymph Calypso
was smit with love for a mortal, and kept him for
her mate against his will.[a] 'Tis believed that Nereus'
sea-born daughter was wed to the Phthian king,[b] and
Egeria to Numa skilled in law; that Vulcan was wed
by Venus, though when he leaves the forge he limps
with wretched sidelong gait. This very kind of
verse is unequal; and yet the heroic line is fitly
joined to the shorter. Do you, too, O light of mine,
take me—on whatever terms you please; let it suit
you dictate law to me as if in the midst of the forum.

[25] I shall not cause you to complain, nor will you
be glad to see me go; this will be no love we shall
need to disavow. Felicitous song, instead of great
possession, is mine, and many a fair one wishes for
glory through me; I know one who bruits it about
she is Corinna. To have it so, what would she not
have given? But neither do the cold Eurotas and
poplar-fringed Po, far-separated, glide between the
same banks, nor shall any but you be sung in my little
books; the spur to my genius you alone shall be.

XVIII

While you, Macer, are bringing your poem to the
time of Achilles' wrath and clothing the conspiring
chiefs with the war's first arms, I dally in the
slothful shade of Venus, and tender Love is bringing
to naught the lofty ventures I would make. Oft
have I said to my love: "At last leave me to
myself!"—and she has come forthwith and sat upon
my lap. Oft have I said: "I am ashamed!"
—scarce keeping back her tears, she has answered:
"Poor me! are you so soon ashamed of love?"

inplicuitque suos circum mea colla lacertos
  et, quae me perdunt, oscula mille dedit.   10
vincor, et ingenium sumptis revocatur ab armis,
  resque domi gestas et mea bella cano.
Sceptra tamen sumpsi, curaque tragoedia nostra
  crevit, et huic operi quamlibet aptus eram.
risit Amor pallamque meam pictosque cothurnos 15
  sceptraque privata tam cito sumpta manu.
hinc quoque me dominae numen deduxit iniquae,
  deque cothurnato vate triumphat Amor.
Quod licet, aut artes teneri profitemur Amoris—
  ei mihi, praeceptis urgeor ipse meis!—   20
aut, quod Penelopes verbis reddatur Ulixi,
  scribimus et lacrimas, Phylli relicta, tuas,
quod Paris et Macareus et quod male gratus Iaso
  Hippolytique parens Hippolytusque legant,
quodque tenens strictum Dido miserabilis ensem 25
  dicat et Aoniae[1] Lesbis amata lyrae.
Quam cito de toto rediit meus orbe Sabinus
  scriptaque diversis rettulit ille locis!
candida Penelope signum cognovit Ulixis;
  legit ab Hippolyto scripta noverca suo.   30
iam pius Aeneas miserae rescripsit Elissae,
  quodque legat Phyllis, si modo vivit, adest.
tristis ad Hypsipylen ab Iasone littera venit;
  det votam Phoebo Lesbis amata lyram.

[1] Aoniae *P s*, *see* I, i, 12: Aeoliae *vulg.*

---

[a] He teaches the art in the *Ars Amatoria*.
[b] All these are references to the *Heroides*.
[c] Sabinus wrote replies to the letters of the *Heroides*.

and has wound her arms about my neck and given me a thousand kisses, to my undoing. I am vanquished, and summon back my genius from the taking up of arms to sing of exploits at home and of my own campaigns.

[13] None the less, I did begin to sing of sceptres, and through my effort tragedy grew in favour, and for that task no one more fit than I. But Love laughed at my pall and painted buskins, and at the sceptre I had so promptly grasped in my unkinglike hand. From this ambition, too, the worshipful will of my lady drew me away—for she liked it not—and Love triumphant drags in his train the buskined bard.

[19] What I may, I do. I either profess the art of tender love [a]—ah me, I am caught in the snares of my own teaching !—or I write the words Penelope sends her Ulysses, and thy tearful plaint, abandoned Phyllis ; what Paris and Marcareus are to read, and what ungrateful Jason, and Hippolytus, and Hippolytus' sire ; and what pitiable Dido, with drawn blade in her hand, indites, and the Lesbian, loved of the Aonian lyre.[b]

[27] How quickly has my Sabinus returned from the ends of the earth and brought back missives writ in far-distant places ! [c] Spotless Penelope has recognized the seal of Ulysses ; the stepdame has read what was penned by her Hippolytus. Already devout Aeneas has written back to wretched Elissa, and a letter is here for Phyllis to read, if only she live. A missive grievous for Hypsipyle has come from Jason ; the daughter of Lesbos, her love returned, may offer to Phoebus the lyre she vowed.

Nec tibi, qua tutum vati, Macer, arma canenti   35
   aureus in medio Marte tacetur Amor.
et Paris est illic et adultera, nobile crimen,
   et comes extincto Laudamia viro.
si bene te novi, non bella libentius istis
   dicis, et a vestris in mea castra venis.   40

XIX

Si tibi non opus est servata, stulte, puella,
   at mihi fac serves, quo magis ipse velim!
quod licet, ingratum est; qu d non licet acrius
   urit.
   ferreus est, siquis, quod sinit alter, amat.
speremus pariter, pariter metuamus amantes,   5
   et faciat voto rara repulsa locum.
quo mihi fortunam, quae numquam fallere curet?
   nil ego, quod nullo tempore laedat, amo!
Viderat hoc in me vitium versuta Corinna,
   quaque capi possem, callida norat opem.   10
a, quotiens sani capitis mentita dolores
   cunctantem tardo iussit abire pede!
a, quotiens finxit culpam, quantumque licebat
   insonti, speciem praebuit esse nocens!
sic ubi vexarat tepidosque refoverat ignis,   15
   rursus erat votis comis et apta meis.
quas mihi blanditias, quam dulcia verba parabat
   oscula, di magni, qualia quotque dabat!

[35] Nor do you, too, Macer, so far as the bard may who sings of arms, leave golden Love unsung amid your warlike strain. Both Paris and she who loved him, misdeed far-famed, are in your song, and Laodamia, comrade to her lord in death. If I know you well, not more gladly you sing of wars than of themes like these, and are passing from your camp to mine.

XIX

IF you feel no need of guarding your love for yourself, O fool, see that you guard her for me, that I may desire her the more! What one may do freely has no charm; what one may not do pricks more keenly on. He has a heart of iron who loves what another concedes. Let us hope while we fear and fear while we hope, we lovers, and let repulse sometimes be ours to make a place for vows. What care I for the fortune that never troubles to deceive? May nothing be mine that never wounds!

[9] Corinna the artful had marked this weakness in me, and shrewdly recognised the means by which to snare me. Ah, how often has she feigned an aching head when wholly well, and bid me go away when my tardy foot delayed! Ah, how oft has she feigned a charge, and put on the air—as far as she could with a guiltless man—of attacking me! Thus, when she had stirred me up, and fanned into flame again the cooling fires, she would be friendly once more, and compliant to my prayers. What winsome ways she would have, how sweet she would make her words! And kisses, O great gods, what kisses, and how many she would give!

Tu quoque, quae nostros rapuisti nuper ocellos,
  saepe time insidias, saepe rogata nega;   20
et sine me ante tuos proiectum in limine postis
  longa pruinosa frigora nocte pati.
sic mihi durat amor longosque adolescit in annos;
  hoc iuvat; haec animi sunt alimenta mei.
pinguis amor nimiumque patens in taedia nobis   25
  vertitur et, stomacho dulcis ut esca, nocet.
si numquam Danaen habuisset aenea turris,
  non esset Danae de Iove facta parens;
dum servat Iuno mutatam cornibus Ion,
  facta est, quam fuerat, gratior illa Iovi.   30
quod licet et facile est quisquis cupit, arbore
    frondis
  carpat et e magno flumine potet aquam.
siqua volet regnare diu, deludat amantem.
  ei mihi, ne monitis torquear ipse meis!
quidlibet eveniat, nocet indulgentia nobis—   35
  quod sequitur, fugio; quod fugit, ipse sequor.
At tu, formosae nimium secure puellae,
  incipe iam prima claudere nocte forem.
incipe, quis totiens furtim tua limina pulset,
  quaerere, quid latrent nocte silente canes,   40
quas ferat et referat sollers ancilla tabellas,
  cur totiens vacuo secubet ipsa toro.
mordeat ista tuas aliquando cura medullas,
  daque locum nostris materiamque dolis.
ille potest vacuo furari litore harenas,   45
  uxorem stulti siquis amare potest.
iamque ego praemoneo: nisi tu servare puellam
  incipis, incipiet desinere esse mea!

[19] You, too, who have lately stolen my eyes away, see that oft you be fearful of plots, and oft when entreated say me nay; and allow me to stretch myself on the threshold of your door and suffer long cold through the rimy night. 'Tis thus my love grows hardy, and keeps on waxing through long years; this is what helps it; 'tis this that nourishes my passion. A love fed fat and too compliant is turned to cloying, and harms us, like sweet fare that harms the stomach. Had Danae never been mewed in the brazen tower, Danae would never have been made mother by Jove; as long as Juno guarded Io, changed to a hornèd beast, she made her charm greater than before to Jove. Whoever desires the unforbidden and easy, let him pluck leaves from the tree, and drink water from the mighty stream. Would any fair one reign long, let her delude her lover. Ah me, may I not meet torment from my own advice! Yet, come what may, to be indulged is a bane to me—what follows, I fly; what flies, I follow in turn.

[37] But you, too careless of your pretty dear, begin already at nightfall to close your door. Begin to ask who it is that so often stealthily beats on your threshold,[a] why the dogs bay in the silence of the night, what tablets the cunning slave-girl brings and takes, why your lady rests so often apart from you. Let cares like that gnaw sometimes into your marrows, and give me place and matter for my wiles. Who would make love with the wife of a fool could steal the sands from a deserted shore. I give you warning now in time: unless you begin to watch your lady, she will begin to cease being mine! I have borne

[a] An ancient way of knocking at the door.

multa diuque tuli ; speravi saepe futurum,
    cum bene servasses, ut bene verba darem.   50
lentus es et pateris nulli patienda marito ;
    at mihi concessi[1] finis amoris erit !
Scilicet infelix numquam prohibebor adire ?
    nox mihi sub nullo vindice semper erit ?
nil metuam ? per nulla traham suspiria somnos ?   55
    nil facies, cur te iure perisse velim ?
quid mihi cum facili, quid cum lenone marito ?
    corrumpit[2] vitio gaudia nostra suo.
quin alium, quem tanta iuvat[3] patientia, quaeris ?
    me tibi rivalem si iuvat esse, veta !   60

---

[1] concessa *Merk*.   [2] corrumpis *Merk*.
[3] tanta iubat *P* : iubet *Post*.

much, and for long ; I have often hoped the time
would come when you would watch her well, that I
might trick you well. You are slow, and endure
things unendurable to any husband ; but ah ! for me,
your complaisance will be the end of love !

⁵³ Unhappy that I am, shall I really never be kept
from seeing her ?   Shall the night never threaten
me with someone's revenge ?   Am I to fear nothing ?
Shall I heave no sighs in the midst of my slumbers ?
Will you do nothing to give me reason to wish you
dead ?   What do I want with a facile husband—with
a husband who is a pander ?   With his failing he
ruins our joys.   Why not seek another, whom such
long-suffering pleases ?   If you please to have me
your rival, forbid it !

LIBER TERTIUS

I

Stat vetus et multos incaedua silva per annos ;
  credibile est illi numen inesse loco.
fons sacer in medio speluncaque pumice pendens,
  et latere ex omni dulce queruntur aves.
Hic ego dum spatior tectus nemoralibus umbris— 5
  quod mea, quaerebam, Musa moveret opus—
venit odoratos Elegeia nexa capillos,
  et, puto, pes illi longior alter erat.
forma decens, vestis tenuissima, vultus amantis,
  et pedibus vitium causa decoris erat.   10
venit et ingenti violenta Tragoedia passu :
  fronte comae torva, palla iacebat humi ;
laeva manus sceptrum late regale movebat,
  Lydius alta pedum vincla cothurnus erat.
Et prior " ecquis erit," dixit, " tibi finis amandi, 15
  O argumenti lente poeta tui ?
nequitiam vinosa tuam convivia narrant,
  narrant in multas conpita secta vias.
saepe aliquis digito vatem designat euntem,
  atque ait ' hic, hic est, quem ferus urit Amor ! ' 20
fabula, nec sentis, tota iactaris in urbe,
  dum tua praeterito facta pudore refers.

444

BOOK THE THIRD

I

ANCIENT, and spared by the axe through many years, there stands a grove ; you could believe a deity indwelt the place. A sacred spring is in its midst, and a cave with overhanging rock, and from every side comes the sweet complaint of birds.

⁵ Whilst I was strolling here enveloped in woodland shadows, asking myself what work my Muse should venture on—came Elegy with coil of odorous locks, and, I think, one foot longer than its mate. She had a comely form, her robe was gauzy light, her face suffused with love, and the fault in her carriage added to her grace. There came, too, raging Tragedy, with mighty stride : her locks o'erhung a darkling brow, her pall trailed on the ground ; her left hand swayed wide a kingly sceptre, and on her foot was the high-bound Lydian buskin.

¹⁵ And she was first to speak : " Will there ever be an end to thy making love," she said, " O poet ever clinging to thy theme ? Thy worthless ways are the talk at dinners over wine, the talk at the crossings cut by many roads. Oft someone points with finger to the bard as he passes, and says : ' He, he is the one fierce Love is burning up !' Thou art not ware, but thou art tossed on the tongues of all the city while, casting away all shame, thou bruitest abroad thy deeds. 'Tis time thou wert

tempus erat, thyrso pulsum graviore moveri ;
    cessatum satis est—incipe maius opus !
materia premis ingenium. cane facta virorum.   25
    ' haec animo,' dices, ' area facta meo est ! '
quod tenerae cantent, lusit tua Musa, puellae,
    primaque per numeros acta iuventa suos.
nunc habeam per te Romana Tragoedia nomen !
    inplebit leges spiritus iste meas.''   30
Hactenus, et movit pictis innixa cothurnis
    densum caesarie terque quaterque caput.
altera, si memini, limis subrisit ocellis—
    fallor, an in dextra myrtea virga fuit ?
" Quid gravibus verbis, animosa Tragoedia," dixit, 35
    " me premis ? an numquam non gravis esse potes ?
inparibus tamen es numeris dignata moveri ;
    in me pugnasti versibus usa meis.
non ego contulerim sublimia carmina nostris ;
    obruit exiguas regia vestra fores.   40
sum levis, et mecum levis est, mea cura, Cupido ;
    non sum materia fortior ipsa mea.
rustica sit sine me lascivi mater Amoris ;
    huic ego proveni lena comesque deae.
quam tu non poteris duro reserare cothurno,   45
    haec est blanditiis ianua laxa meis ;
et tamen emerui plus quam tu posse, ferendo
    multa supercilio non patienda tuo.
per me decepto didicit custode Corinna
    liminis adstricti sollicitare fidem,   50
delabique toro tunica velata soluta
    atque inpercussos nocte movere pedes.

---

    [a] The staff of Bacchus, patron-god of the drama.

stirred by the stroke of a greater thyrsus;[a] thou
hast dallied enough—enter on greater work! Thy
theme obscures thy genius. Sing deeds of heroes.
'This,' thou wilt say, 'is the race for my soul to
run!' Thy Muse has been but playing—with matter
for tender maiden's song—and thy first youth has
been given to numbers that belong to youth. Now,
let me, Roman Tragedy, win through thee renown!
Thou hast the inspiration will fulfill my needs."

[31] Thus far she spake, and, stately on her painted
buskins, shook thrice and four times her head with
its clustered hair. The other, if I remember, cast
sidelong eyes on me, and smiled—am I mistaken, or
was a branch of myrtle in her hand?

[35] "Why weary me with your heavy words, O
haughty Tragedy?" she said; "or can you never be
otherwise than heavy? Yet you have deigned to
suit yourself to unequal numbers; in assailing me
'twas my verse you used. I would not compare
your lofty strains with mine; your queenly hall o'er-
shadows my humble doors. I am but light, and
Cupid, my heart's fond care, is light as well;
myself am not stronger than the theme I sing. The
mother of sportive Love, without me, would be but a
rustic jade; to be go-between and comrade to this
goddess was I brought forth. The door which you
will never unbolt with your austere buskin—that
door lies freely open before my blandishments; and
yet I have earned this greater power than yours by
bearing much your haughty brow would not endure.
Through me Corinna has learned to elude her guard
and tamper with the faith of tight-closed door, to
slip away from her couch in tunic ungirdled and
move in the night with unstumbling foot. O how

vel quotiens foribus duris incisa [1] pependi,
    non verita a populo praetereunte legi !
quin ego me memini, dum custos saevus abiret,   55
    ancillae missam delituisse sinu.
quid, cum me munus natali mittis, at illa
    rumpit et adposita barbara mersat [2] aqua ?
prima tuae movi felicia semina mentis ;
    munus habes, quod te iam petit ista, meum."   60
Desierat.   coepi : "per vos utramque rogamus,
    in vacuas aures verba timentis eant.
altera me sceptro decoras altoque cothurno ;
    iam nunc contacto magnus in ore sonus.
altera das nostro victurum nomen amori—   65
    ergo ades et longis versibus adde brevis !
exiguum vati concede, Tragoedia, tempus !
    tu labor aeternus ; quod petit illa, breve est."
Mota dedit veniam—teneri properentur Amores,
    dum vacat ; a tergo grandius urguet opus !   70

II

"Non ego nobilium sedeo studiosus equorum ;
    cui tamen ipsa faves, vincat ut ille, precor.
ut loquerer tecum veni, tecumque sederem,
    ne tibi non notus, quem facis, esset amor.
tu cursus spectas, ego te ; spectemus uterque   5
    quod iuvat, atque oculos pascat uterque suos.
O, cuicumque faves, felix agitator equorum !
    ergo illi curae contigit esse tuae ?

---

[1] incisa *vulg.*: infixa *some MSS.*: inlisa *Ehw. from* s.
[2] mersat *Ehw.*: mersit *MSS.*

oft have I been graved on unyielding doors, not shaming there to be read by the passer by![a] Nay, once I mind I was sent in keeping of a slave, hid away in her bosom till the fierce guard went. How, when you send me as a birthday gift, and my dear barbarian rends me, and drowns me in the water standing near? 'Twas I who first made swell the fruitful seeds of your mind; to me you owe it that she who stands yonder claims you now."

[61] She had ceased. I began: "By both and each of you I pray, let my fearful words find your ears attentive. One honours me with sceptre and lofty buskin; my tongue already feels thy touch, and mighty speech is on my lips. The other gives everlasting glory to my love—come, then, and join short verses with the long! Indulge thy bard a short space, O Tragedy! A labour eternal art thou; what she asks is but brief."

[69] She was moved, and granted my prayer—let the tender Loves come hasting, while I am free; close after me presses a greater task!

II

"I sit not here because fond of high-bred horses; yet, the one you favour I pray may win.[b] To talk with you I came, and to sit with you, so that you might not miss knowing the love you stir. You gaze on the races, I on you; let us both gaze on what delights, both feast our own eyes.

[7] "O, happy driver, whoe'er he be, that wins your favour! Ah, so 'twas he had the fortune to enlist your concern? Be that fortune mine, and when my

---

[a] The lover carved verses (elegy) on his lady's door.
[b] The poet is relating what he said to a fair one at the races.

hoc mihi contingat, sacro de carcere missis
    insistam forti mente vehendus equis,   10
et modo lora dabo, modo verbere terga notabo,
    nunc stringam metas interiore rota.
si mihi currenti fueris conspecta, morabor,
    deque meis manibus lora remissa fluent.
at quam paene Pelops Pisaea concidit hasta,   15
    dum spectat vultus, Hippodamia, tuos !
nempe favore suae vicit tamen ille puellae.
    vincamus dominae quisque favore suae !
Quid frustra refugis ? cogit nos linea iungi.
    haec in lege loci commoda circus habet—   20
tu tamen a dextra, quicumque es, parce puellae ;
    contactu lateris laeditur ista tui.
tu quoque, qui spectas post nos, tua contrahe crura,
    si pudor est, rigido nec preme terga genu !
Sed nimium demissa iacent tibi pallia terra.   25
    collige—vel digitis en ego tollo meis !
invida vestis eras, quae tam bona crura tegebas ;
    quoque magis spectes—invida vestis eras !
talia Milanion Atalantes crura fugacis
    optavit manibus sustinuisse suis.   30
talia pinguntur succinctae crura Dianae
    cum sequitur fortes, fortior ipsa, feras.
his ego non visis arsi ; quid fiet ab ipsis ?[1]
    in flammam flammas, in mare fundis aquas.
suspicor ex istis et cetera posse placere,   35
    quae bene sub tenui condita veste latent.

---

[1] ipsis *Mueller* : istis *MSS.*

coursers dash from the starting-chamber, with fearless heart will I tread the car and urge them on, now giving the rein, now striping their backs with the lash, now grazing the turning-post with inner wheel. Have I caught sight of you as I career, I will stop, and the reins, let go from my hands, will drop. Yea, how near Pelops came to falling by Pisaean spear while looking on thy face, Hippodamia! Yet he won, of course through the favour of his lady. May we owe our victories, all of us, to the favour of our loves!

[19] "Why draw back from me?—'twill do no good; the line compels us to sit close.[a] This advantage the circus gives, with its rule of space—yet you there on the right, whoever you are, have a care; your pressing against my lady's side annoys. You, too, who are looking on from behind, draw up your legs, if you care for decency, and press not her back with your hard knee!

[25] "But your cloak is let fall too far, and is trailing on the ground. Gather it up—or look, with my own fingers I'll get it up. Envious wrap you were, to cover such pretty limbs! And the more one looks—ah, envious wrap you were! Such were the limbs of fleet Atalanta that Milanion burned to hold up with his hands. Such in pictures are the limbs of upgirt Diana pursuing the bold wild beasts, herself more bold than they. I burned before, when I had not seen; what will become of me now that I have? You add flames to flame, and waters to the sea. I suspect from them that all else, too, that lies well hidden under your delicate gown, might please.

[a] There were lines to separate the seats.

Vis tamen interea faciles arcessere ventos?
    quos faciet nostra mota tabella manu.
an magis hic meus est animi, non aeris aestus,
    captaque femineus pectora torret amor?   40
dum loquor, alba levi sparsa est tibi pulvere vestis.
    sordide de niveo corpore pulvis abi!
Sed iam pompa venit—linguis animisque favete!
    tempus adest plausus—aurea pompa venit.
prima loco fertur passis Victoria pinnis—   45
    huc ades et meus hic fac, dea, vincat amor!
plaudite Neptuno, nimium qui creditis undis!
    nil mihi cum pelago; me mea terra capit.
plaude tuo Marti, miles! nos odimus arma;
    pax iuvat et media pace repertus amor.   50
auguribus Phoebus, Phoebe venantibus adsit!
    artifices in te verte, Minerva, manus!
ruricolae Cereri teneroque adsurgite Baccho!
    Pollucem pugiles, Castora placet eques!
nos tibi, blanda Venus, puerisque potentibus arcu 55
    plaudimus; inceptis adnue, diva, meis
daque novae[1] mentem dominae! patiatur amari!
    Adnuit et motu signa secunda dedit.
quod dea promisit, promittas ipsa, rogamus;
    pace loquar Veneris, tu dea maior eris.   60
per tibi tot iuro testes pompamque deorum,
    te dominam nobis tempus in omne peti!

[1] novae *P s* : novam *many MSS.*

---

[a] Immediately before the races the gods were carried in procession about the course.

[37] " Would you like, while we wait, to bid soft breezes blow? I'll take the fan in my hand and start them. Or is this rather the heat of my heart and not of the air, and does love for a woman burn my ravished breast? While I am talking, a sprinkling of light dust has got on your white dress. Vile dust, away from this snowy body!

[43] " But now the procession is coming—keep silence all, and attend! The time for applause is here—the golden procession is coming.[a] First in the train is Victory, borne with wings outspread—come hither, goddess, and help my love to win! Applaud Neptune, ye who trust o'ermuch the wave! Naught will I with the sea; I choose that the land keep me. Applaud thy Mars, O soldier! Arms I detest; peace is my delight, and love that is found in the midst of peace. And Phoebus—let him be gracious to augurs, and Phoebe gracious to huntsmen! Minerva, turn in applause to thee the craftsman's hands! Ye country dwellers, rise to Ceres and tender Bacchus! Let the boxer court Pollux, the horseman Castor! We, winsome Venus, we applaud thee, and thy children potent with the bow; smile, O goddess, upon my undertakings, and put the right mind in my heart's new mistress! Let her endure to be loved!

[58] " She nodded, and by the movement gave favouring sign. What the goddess has promised, yourself promise, I ask; with Venus' permission let me say it, you will be the greater goddess. I swear to you by all these witnesses and by the train of the gods, I am asking you to be for all time to come my queen!

OVID

Sed pendent tibi crura.   potes, si forte iuvabit,
  cancellis primos inseruisse pedes.
maxima iam vacuo praetor spectacula circo   65
  quadriiugos aequo carcere misit equos.
cui studeas, video.   vincet, cuicumque favebis.
  quid cupias, ipsi scire videntur equi.
me miserum, metam spatioso circuit orbe !
  quid facis ? admoto proxumus axe subit.   70
quid facis, infelix ? perdis bona vota puellae.
  tende, precor, valida lora sinistra manu !
favimus ignavo—sed enim revocate, Quirites,
  et date iactatis undique signa togis !
en, revocant !—at, ne turbet toga mota capillos, 75
  in nostros abdas te licet usque sinus.
Iamque patent iterum reserato carcere postes ;
  evolat admissis discolor agmen equis.
nunc saltem supera spatioque insurge patenti !
  sint mea, sint dominae fac rata vota meae !   80
Sunt dominae rata vota meae, mea vota supersunt.
  ille tenet palmam ; palma petenda mea est."
Risit, et argutis quiddam promisit ocellis.
  "Hoc satis hic ; [1] alio cetera redde loco ! "

[1] *So Hein. from MSS.*: hoc satis est *P* : hic satis est *Ehw.*

[a] From the gates of the *carceres*, or starting-chambers, so
arranged that each driver was equally distant from the lines
where the race began.

[63] " But your feet are dangling. If you like, you you can stick your toes in the grating. The circus is clear now for the greatest part of the shows, and the praetor has started the four-horse cars from the equal barrier.[a] I see the one you are eager for. He will win if he has your favour, whoever he be. What you desire the very horses seem to know! Ah, miserable me, he has circled the post in a wide curve! What are you doing? The next hugs close with his axle, and gains on you. What are you doing, wretch? You will lose my love the prayer of her heart. Pull, I entreat, the left rein with all your might! We are favouring a good-for-naught— but call them back, Quirites, and toss your togas in signal from every side![b] See, they call them back!—but for fear a waving toga spoil your hair, come, you may hide your head in the folds of my cloak.

[77] " And now the starting-chambers are unbarred again, and the gates are open wide; the many-coloured rout comes flying forth with reins let loose to their steeds. This time, at least, get past them, and bend to your work on the open space! See that you fulfil my vows, and my lady-love's!

[81] " Fulfilled are my lady-love's vows, but my vows remain. Yon charioteer has received his palm; my palm is yet to be won."

[83] She smiled, and with speaking eyes promised— I know not what.

[84] " That is enough for here—in some other place render the rest!"

[b] The dissatisfied populace could thus demand a fresh start.

III

Esse deos, i, crede [1]—fidem iurata fefellit,
    et facies illi, quae fuit ante, manet!
quam longos habuit nondum peritura capillos,
    tam longos, postquam numina laesit, habet.
candida candorem roseo suffusa rubore   5
    ante fuit—niveo lucet in ore rubor.
pes erat exiguus—pedis est artissima forma.
    longa decensque fuit—longa decensque manet.
argutos habuit—radiant ut sidus ocelli,
    per quos mentita est perfida saepe mihi.   10
scilicet aeterno falsum iurare puellis
    di quoque concedunt, formaque numen habet.
perque suos illam nuper iurasse recordor
    perque meos oculos : et doluere mei!
Dicite, di, si vos inpune fefellerat illa,   15
    alterius meriti cur ego damna tuli?
an [2] non invidiae vobis Cepheia virgo est,
    pro male formosa iussa parente mori?
non satis est, quod vos habui sine pondere testis,
    et mecum lusos ridet inulta deos?   20
·ut sua per nostram redimat periuria poenam,
    victima deceptus decipientis ero?
aut sine re nomen deus est frustraque timetur
    et stulta populos credulitate movet ;
aut, siquis deus est, teneras amat ille puellas   25
    et nimium [3] solas omnia posse iubet.

[1] hic crede *Ps* : i, crede *Hein.*
[2] An *Riese* : ad *P* : at *vulg.*
[3] et nimium *MSS. Br.* : nimirum *Ném.* : et mirum *Post.*

III

Go, believe there are gods—she swore and has failed her oath, and still her face is fair, as 'twas before! She has hair as long since she insulted the gods, as she had still unforsworn. Before, she was dazzling fair, and her fairness was mingled with rosy red—the rosy red still glows in her snowy cheeks. Her foot was small—her foot is still of daintiest form. She was tall and handsome —tall and handsome she remains. She had sparkling eyes—like stars still beam the eyes by which she has often falsely lied to me. Surely, the gods, too, indulge the fair in eternal swearing false, and beauty has its privilege divine. By her own eyes not long ago she swore, I mind me, and by mine—and mine have been the ones to smart!

¹⁵ Say, O ye gods, if she deceived you and has gone unpunished, why have I borne the pains for another's desert? Or is Cepheus' daughter no reproach to you—she whom you bade to die for her mother's ill-starred beauty?[a] Is it not enough that I have found your witness without weight, and that unpunished she makes the gods her mirth as well as me? That she may redeem her perjuries, am I to suffer, and, though deceived, be victim to my deceiver? Either God is a name without substance and feared for naught, moving peoples through stupid trustfulness, or, if there is a god, he is in love with the tender fair, and too quick to ordain that they alone may do all things. 'Tis

[a] Andromache and Cassiopeia.

OVID

nobis fatifero Mavors accingitur ense ;
   nos petit invicta Palladis hasta manu.
nobis flexibiles curvantur Apollinis arcus ;
   in nos alta Iovis dextera fulmen habet.   30
formosas superi metuunt offendere laesi
   atque ultro, quae se non timuere, timent.
et quisquam pia tura focis inponere curat ?
   certe plus animi debet inesse viris !
Iuppiter igne suo[1] lucos iaculatur et arces   35
   missaque periuras tela ferire vetat.
tot meruere peti—Semele miserabilis arsit !
   officio est illi poena reperta suo ;
at si venturo se subduxisset amanti,
   non pater in Baccho matris haberet opus.   40
Quid queror et toto facio convicia caelo ?
   di quoque habent oculos, di quoque pectus habent !
si deus ipse forem, numen sine fraude liceret
   femina mendaci falleret ore meum ;
ipse ego iurarem verum iurare puellas   45
   et non de tetricis dicerer esse deus.
tu tamen illorum moderatius utere dono—
   aut oculis certe parce, puella, meis !

IV

Dure vir, inposito tenerae custode puellae
   nil agis ; ingenio est quaeque tuenda suo.

[1] suo *MSS.*: suos *Riese.*

[a] Bacchus was born from the thigh of Jove.

458

against us men that Mars girds on death-dealing
sword; 'tis we are the target for the spear from
unconquered Pallas' hand. For us are bent Apollo's
flexile bows; on us descends the bolt from Jove's
upraised right hand. Fair women the gods on high
fear to offend even when wronged, and stand in
awe themselves of those who have felt no awe of
them. And does anyone care to place pious incense
on their altars? Surely, there should be more
courage in men!

35 Jove hurls his own lightning on sacred groves
and citadels, and forbids his bolts to strike the fair
forsworn. So many have deserved his stroke—
hapless Semele alone has burned! Her own com-
plaisance brought the penalty upon her; yet, had
she shunned the coming lover, the father would not
have filled the mother's office in Bacchus' birth.[a]

41 Why complain I, and scold in the face of all
heaven? Gods, too, have eyes, gods, too, have
hearts! Were I myself divine, unharmed might
women cheat my godhead with lying lips. I myself
would swear that womankind swore true, nor let
myself be called a god of the austere sort. Yet
you, my lady, make more measured use of their gift
—or spare, at least, my eyes![b]

IV

HARD husband, by setting a keeper over your
tender wife you nothing gain; 'tis her own nature
must be each woman's guard. If she is pure when

[b] By not swearing by them; see v. 14.

siqua metu dempto casta est, ea denique casta est;
   quae, quia non liceat, non facit, illa facit!
ut iam servaris bene corpus, adultera mens est;   5
   nec custodiri, ne [1] velit, ulla [2] potest.
nec corpus servare potes, licet omnia claudas;
   omnibus exclusis intus adulter erit.
cui peccare licet, peccat minus; ipsa potestas
   semina nequitiae languidiora facit.   10
desine, crede mihi, vitia inritare vetando;
   obsequio vinces aptius illa tuo.
Vidi ego nuper equum contra sua vincla tenacem
   ore reluctanti fulminis ire modo;
constitit ut primum concessas sensit habenas   15
   frenaque in effusa laxa iacere iuba!
nitimur in vetitum semper cupimusque negata;
   sic interdictis imminet aeger aquis.
centum fronte oculos, centum cervice gerebat
   Argus—et hos unus saepe fefellit Amor;   20
in thalamum Danae ferro saxoque perennem
   quae fuerat virgo tradita, mater erat;
Penelope mansit, quamvis custode carebat,
   inter tot iuvenes intemerata procos.
Quidquid servatur cupimus magis, ipsaque furem   25
   cura vocat; pauci, quod sinit alter, amant.
nec facie placet illa sua, sed amore mariti;
   nescio quid, quod te ceperit, esse putant.
non proba fit, quam vir servat, sed adultera cara;
   ipse timor pretium corpore maius habet.   30
indignere licet, iuvat inconcessa voluptas;
   sola placet, "timeo!" dicere siqua potest.

---

[1] ne *P*: ni *vulg.*   [2] ulla *P s*: illa *vulg.*

freed from every fear, then first is she pure; she who sins not because she may not—she sins! Grant you have guarded well the body, the mind is untrue; and no watch can be set o'er a woman's will. Nor can you guard her body, though you shut every door; with all shut out, a traitor will be within. She to whom erring is free, errs less; very power makes less quick the seeds of sin. Ah, trust to me, and cease to spur on to fault by forbidding; indulgence will be the apter way to win.

[13] But recently I saw a horse rebellious against the curb take bit in his obstinate mouth and career like thunderbolt; he stopped the very moment he felt the rein was given, and the lines were lying loose on his flying mane! We ever strive for what is forbid, and ever covet what is denied; so the sick man longingly hangs over forbidden water. A hundred eyes before, a hundred behind, had Argus—and these Love alone did oft deceive; the chamber of Danae was eternally strong with iron and rock, yet she who had been given a maid to its keeping became a mother. Penelope, although without a guard, remained inviolate among so many youthful wooers.

[25] Whatever is guarded we desire the more, and care itself invites the thief; few love what another concedes. And that fair one of yours wins not because of her beauty, but because of her husband's love; something there is, they think, for you to be smitten with. She whom her husband guards is not made honest thereby, but a mistress much desired; fear itself gives her greater price than her charms. Be wrathful if you will, 'tis forbidden joys delight; she only charms whoe'er can say: " I fear!" And yet 'tis not right to watch a free-born

nec tamen ingenuam ius est servare puellam—
   hic metus externae corpora gentis agat !
scilicet ut possit custos "ego" dicere "feci,"   35
   in laudem servi casta sit illa tui ?
Rusticus est nimium, quem laedit adultera coniunx,
   et notos mores non satis urbis habet
in qua Martigenae non sunt sine crimine nati
   Romulus Iliades Iliadesque Remus.   40
quo tibi formosam, si non nisi casta placebat ?
   non possunt ullis ista coire modis.
Si sapis, indulge dominae vultusque severos
   exue, nec rigidi iura tuere viri,
et cole quos dederit—multos dabit—uxor amicos. 45
   gratia sic minimo magna labore venit ;
sic poteris iuvenum convivia semper inire
   et, quae non dederis, multa videre domi.

V [1]

" Nox erat, et somnus lassos submisit ocellos ;
   terruerunt animum talia visa meum :
Colle sub aprico creberrimus ilice lucus
   stabat, et in ramis multa latebat avis.
area gramineo suberat viridissima prato,   5
   umida de guttis lene sonantis aquae.
ipse sub arboreis vitabam frondibus aestum—
   fronde sub arborea sed tamen aestus erat—

    [1] *V is not Ovid's, Merk. L. Mueller : it is in Ps.*

wife—let this fear vex women of other blood than ours ! [a] Is your wife, forsooth, to be chaste merely that her keeper may say : " I am the cause "—merely for the glory of your slave ?

[37] He is too countrified who is hurt when his wife plays false, and is but slightly acquaint with the manners of the city in which the sons of Mars were born not without reproach—Romulus, child of Ilia, and Ilia's child Remus. Why did you marry a beauty if none but a chaste would suit ? Those two things can never in any wise combine.

[43] If you are wise, indulge your lady ; put off stern looks and do not insist on the rights of a rigid husband, and cherish the friends your wife will bring—and she will bring many ! You will be in great favour thus, and with very little effort ; thus will you find yourself ever going to dine with the young, and at home see many presents not of your giving.

V

" 'Twas night, and slumber weighed my weary eyelids down—when a vision terrified my soul. 'Twas on this wise :

[3] " At the foot of a sunny hill was a grove thick-standing with ilex, and in its branches was hidden many a bird. Near by was a plot of deepest green, a grassy mead, humid with the tricklings of gently sounding water. I was seeking refuge from the heat beneath the branches of the trees—though beneath the trees' branches came none the less

[a] Slaves and freedwomen.

ecce ! petens variis inmixtas floribus herbas
    constitit ante oculos candida vacca meos,   10
candidior nivibus, tunc cum cecidere recentes,
    in liquidas nondum quas mora vertit aquas ;
candidior, quod adhuc spumis stridentibus albet
    et modo siccatam, lacte, reliquit ovem.
taurus erat comes huic, feliciter ille maritus,   15
    cumque sua teneram coniuge pressit humum.
Dum iacet et lente revocatas ruminat herbas
    atque iterum pasto pascitur ante cibo,
visus erat, somno vires adimente ferendi,[1]
    cornigerum terra deposuisse caput.   20
huc levibus cornix pinnis delapsa per auras
    venit et in viridi garrula sedit humo,
terque bovis niveae petulanti pectora rostro
    fodit et albentis abstulit ore iubas.
illa locum taurumque diu cunctata relinquit—   25
    sed niger in vaccae pectore livor erat ;
utque procul vidit carpentes pabula tauros—
    carpebant tauri pabula laeta procul—
illuc se rapuit gregibusque inmiscuit illis
    et petiit herbae fertilioris humum.   30
Dic age, nocturnae, quicumque es, imaginis augur,
    siquid habent veri, visa quid ista ferant."
Sic ego ; nocturnae sic dixit imaginis augur,
    expendens animo singula dicta suo :
" Quem tu mobilibus foliis vitare volebas,   35
    sed male vitabas, aestus amoris erat.

       [1] ferendi *Bent.*: ferenti *P s* : feraci *L. Mueller.*

the heat—when lo! coming to crop the herbage
mingled with varied flowers there stood before my
eyes a shining white heifer, more shining white
than snows just freshly fallen and not yet turned
by time to flowing waters; more shining white
than the milk that gleams with still hissing foam,
and has just left the sheep drained dry. A bull was
companion to her, a happy consort he, and pressed
the tender ground beside his mate.

[17] "While he lay there, slowly chewing the grassy
cud that rose again, and feeding a second time on
what he had fed on before, in my vision I thought
that sleep took away his power of holding up his
head, and he laid its hornèd weight upon the earth.
Thither, gliding down through the air, on pinions
light, came a crow, and settled chattering on the
verdant ground, and, pecking thrice with wanton
beak at the breast of the snowy heifer, carried
away in his mouth white tufts of hair. The heifer,
lingering long, went away from the place and from
the bull—but a darkly livid mark was on her
breast; and, seeing bulls afar cropping the pastur-
age—there were bulls cropping the glad pasturage
afar—she ran quickly thither and mingled with
those herds, choosing the ground where the herbage
was more lush.

[31] "Come, tell me, augur of visions by night, who-
e'er thou art, what mean those things I saw, if
aught they hide of truth."

[33] Thus I ; and thus spake the augur of visions
by night, weighing in mind each single thing I
said :

[35] "The heat you wished to shun beneath the
fluttering leaves, and shunned but ill, was the heat

vacca puella tua est—aptus color ille puellae;
    tu vir et in vacca conpare taurus eras.
pectora quod rostro cornix fodiebat acuto,
    ingenium dominae lena movebat anus.   40
quod cunctata diu taurum sua vacca reliquit,
    frigidus in viduo destituere toro.
livor et adverso maculae sub pectore nigrae
    pectus adulterii labe carere negant."
Dixerat interpres.   gelido mihi sanguis ab ore   45
    fugit, et ante oculos nox stetit alta meos.

VI

AMNIS harundinibus limosas obsite ripas,
    ad dominam propero—siste parumper aquas!
nec tibi sunt pontes nec quae sine remigis ictu
    concava traiecto cumba rudente vehat.
parvus eras, memini, nec te transire refugi,   5
    summaque vix talos contigit unda meos.
nunc ruis adposito nivibus de monte solutis
    et turpi crassas gurgite volvis aquas.
quid properasse iuvat, quid parca dedisse quieti
    tempora, quid nocti conseruisse diem,   10
si tamen hic standum est, si non datur artibus ullis
    ulterior nostro ripa premenda pedi?
nunc ego, quas habuit pinnas Danaeius heros,
    terribili densum cum tulit angue caput,

of love. The heifer was your love—that colour matches your love. You, her beloved, were the bull with the heifer for mate. The pecking of her breast by the crow's sharp beak meant a pandering old dame was meddling with your mistress' heart. The lingering long e'er the heifer left her bull was sign that you will be left cold in a deserted bed. The dark colour and the black spots on her breast in front were signs that her heart is not without stain of unfaithfulness."

[45] The interpreter had said. I was cold; the blood fled from my face, and before my eyes stood deep night.

VI

O stream whose muddy banks are choked with reeds, I am in haste to see my lady-love—stay for a little time thy waters! Neither hast thou bridges, nor hollowed boat to carry me without stroke of oar by cable stretched across. Small wert thou, I remember, nor did I fear to cross, and thy highest water scarce touched my ankles. Now the snows have melted from the near-by mountain, and thou art rushing on, rolling gross waters in muddy, whirling floods. What boots it I have hastened, what that I gave scant hours to rest, what that I have linked day to night, if I yet must stand here, if by no art I may press with my foot the farther shore? 'Tis now I wish I had the pinions the hero son of Danae wore when he bare away the head thick-tressed with dreadful snakes; [a] now I wish

[a] Perseus, slayer of the Medusa, with winged sandals.

nunc opto currum, de quo Cerealia primum   15
   semina venerunt in rude missa solum.
prodigiosa loquor veterum mendacia vatum ;
   nec tulit haec umquam nec feret ulla dies.
Tu potius, ripis effuse capacibus amnis—
   sic aeternus eas—labere fine tuo !   20
non eris invidiae, torrens, mihi crede, ferendae,
   si dicar per te forte retentus amans.
flumina deberent iuvenes in amore iuvare ;
   flumina senserunt ipsa, quid esset amor.
Inachus in Melie Bithynide pallidus isse   25
   dicitur et gelidis incaluisse vadis.
nondum Troia fuit lustris obsessa duobus,
   cum rapuit vultus, Xanthe, Neaera tuos.
quid ?   non Alpheon diversis currere terris
   virginis Arcadiae certus adegit amor ?   30
te quoque promissam Xutho, Penee, Creusam
   Phthiotum terris occuluisse ferunt.
quid referam Asopon, quem cepit Martia Thebe,
   natarum Thebe quinque futura parens ?
cornua si tua nunc ubi sint, Acheloe, requiram,   35
   Herculis irata fracta querere manu ;
nec tanti Calydon nec tota Aetolia tanti,
   una tamen tanti Deianira fuit.
ille fluens dives septena per ostia Nilus,
   qui patriam tantae tam bene celat aquae,   40
fertur in Euanthe collectam Asopide flammam
   vincere gurgitibus non potuisse suis.
siccus ut amplecti Salmonida posset Enipeus,
   cedere iussit aquam ; iussa recessit aqua.

ª The car was drawn through the air by serpents.

that mine were the car from which first came the
seeds of Ceres when cast on the untilled ground.[a]
But the wonders whereof I speak are false tales of
olden bards ; no day e'er brought them forth, and
no day will.

[19] Do thou choose rather, O stream poured wide
beyond thy capacious banks—so mayst thou flow on
for ever—to glide within thy bounds ! Thine, O
torrent, will be hate unbearable, believe, if I per-
chance am said to have been kept by thee—I, a
lover ! Rivers ought to aid young men in love ; what
love is, rivers themselves have felt. The Inachus,
they say, went pale for Bithynian Melie, and his
chill waves felt love's warmth. Not yet had Troy
been under siege two lustrums when Neaera ravished
thine eyes, O Xanthus. What ? did not Alpheus
flow in far-separate lands, driven by faithful love
for Arcadian maid ?[b] Thou, too, Peneus, they say
didst hide away, in the land of the Phthiotes,
Creusa, promised bride to Xuthus. Why call to
mind Asopus, smitten with Thebe, child of Mars—
Thebe, destined mother of daughters five ? If I
ask of thee, Achelous, where are now thy horns,
thou wilt complain of their breaking by wrathful
Hercules' hand ; what neither Calydon could win
from him, nor all Aetolia, Deianira none the less
alone could win. Rich Nile yonder, who flows
through seven mouths and hides so well the home-
land of his mighty waters, 'tis said could not drown
out with his own floods the fires Asopus' child
Euanthe kindled in him. Enipeus, to dry himself
for the arms of Salmoneus' child, bade his waters
retire ; the waters, so bid, retired.

[b] Arethusa was pursued from Elis to Sicily, under the sea.

Nec te praetereo, qui per cava saxa volutans [1]   45
    Tiburis Argei pomifera [2] arva rigas,
Ilia cui placuit, quamvis erat horrida cultu,
    ungue notata comas, ungue notata genas.
illa gemens patruique nefas delictaque Martis
    errabat nudo per loca sola pede.   50
hanc Anien rapidis animosus vidit ab undis
    raucaque de mediis sustulit ora vadis
atque ita " quid nostras " dixit " teris anxia ripas,
    Ilia, ab Idaeo Laumedonte genus?
quo cultus abiere tui? quid sola vagaris,   55
    vitta nec evinctas inpedit alba comas?
quid fles et madidos lacrimis corrumpis ocellos
    pectoraque insana plangis aperta manu?
ille habet et silices et vivum in pectore ferrum,
    qui tenero lacrimas lentus in ore videt.   60
Ilia, pone metus! tibi regia nostra patebit,
    teque colent amnes.   Ilia, pone metus!
tu centum aut plures inter dominabere nymphas;
    nam centum aut plures flumina nostra tenent.
ne me sperne, precor, tantum, Troiana [3] propago; 65
    munera promissis uberiora feres."
Dixerat.   illa oculos in humum deiecta modestos
    spargebat teneros flebilis imbre sinus.
ter molita fugam ter ad altas restitit undas,
    currendi vires eripiente metu.   70
sera tamen scindens inimico pollice crinem
    edidit indignos ore tremente sonos :

[1] volutans *vulg.*: volutus *s*.
[2] pomifera *Bent.*: ponifer *P s* : spumifer *vulg.*
[3] Romana *P s*.

[a] Or Rhea Silvia, mother of Romulus and Remus.

[45] Nor do I pass thee by, stream tumbling over the hollowed rocks and moisting the fruit-bearing acres of Argive Tibur, thee whom Ilia [a] charmed, ill kept though she appeared, with hair that showed the nail, and cheeks that showed the nail. Bemoaning the crime of her uncle and the wrongs of Mars, with unshod feet she wandered through lone places. Her did eager Anio behold, looking forth from his sweeping floods, and reared from amid the wave his hoarse-toned mouth, and " Why dost thou anxiously," thus spake he, " tread my shores, O Ilia, blood of Idaean Laomedon ? Whither hath gone thy comely raiment ? Why art abroad alone, with no white fillet to keep thy hair bound up ? Why art thou weeping, and staining thine eyes with dropping tears ? and why dost lay open and beat thy breast with maddened hand ? He hath both flint and native iron in his breast who can look unmoved on the tears in thy tender eyes. Ilia, lay aside thy fears ! To thee my royal hall shall open, and thee my waves shall honour. Ilia, lay aside thy fears ! Thou shalt be mistress among a hundred nymphs, or more ; for a hundred, or more, are the nymphs that dwell in my stream. Only spurn me not, I entreat, thou sprung of the Trojan line ; thou shalt win gifts of greater richness than my promise."

[67] He had said. She stood with modest eyes downcast upon the ground, letting spray on her tender bosom a rain of tears. Thrice made she to flee, and thrice stopped she beside the deep flood, her power of flying swept away by fear. Yet, after long time, rending her hair with unfriendly finger, she sounded with trembling lips the words her

" o utinam mea lecta forent patrioque sepulcro
    condita, cum poterant virginis ossa legi !
cur, modo Vestalis, taedas invitor ad ullas   75
    turpis et Iliacis infitianda focis?
quid moror et digitis designor adulteıa vulgi?
    desint famosus quae notet ora pudor ! "
Hactenus, et vestem tumidis praetendit ocellis
    atque ita se in rapidas perdita misit aquas.   80
supposuisse manus ad pectora lubricus amnis
    dicitur et socii iura dedisse tori.
Te quoque credibile est aliqua caluisse puella ;
    sed nemora et silvae crimina vestra tegunt.
dum loquor, increvit[1] latis spatiosior[2] undis,   85
    nec capit admissas alveus altus aquas.
quid mecum, furiose, tibi ?   quid mutua differs
    gaudia ? quid coeptum, rustice, rumpis iter ?
quid ? si legitimum flueres, si nobile flumen,
    si tibi per terras maxima fama foret—   90
nomen habes nullum, rivis collecte caducis,
    nec tibi sunt fontes nec tibi certa domus !
fontis habes instar pluviamque nivesque solutas,
    quas tibi divitias pigra ministrat hiemps ;
aut lutulentus agis brumali tempore cursus,   95
    aut premis arentem pulverulentus humum.
quis te tum potuit sitiens haurire viator ?
    quis dixit grata voce " perennis eas " ?

[1] increscis *Ehw.*
[2] spatiosior *Bent.*: spatiosus in *P s*: spatiosius *Merk. from Mar. MS.*

---

[a] Vesta's fires, brought by Aeneas from Troy.

wrongs called forth : " Oh, would that my bones had
been gathered and laid away in the tomb of my
fathers when they yet could be gathered the bones
of a maid ! Why, but now a Vestal, am I bid to
any marriage-torch, disgraced and to be denied my
place at Ilion's altar-fires ? [a] Why tarry I alive to
be pointed out a jade by the finger of the crowd ?
Perish the face that bears the brand of shame and
disrespect ! "

[79] Thus far, and she held her cloak before her
tumid eyes, gave up all hope, and so threw herself
into the rushing waters. The smooth-gliding stream,
they say, laid his hands to her breast and bore her
up, and shared with her the rights of the wedded
couch.

[83] Thou, too, 'tis easy to believe, hast warmed
for some fair maid ; but grove and forest cover
up thy fault. Even while I speak, thy waters have
grown more deep and wide, and thy channel, though
deep, contains not the headlong waves. What have
I with thee, mad stream ? Why dost thou defer
the joys I am to share ? Why dost thou, churl,
break off the journey I have begun ? What ? wert
thou called rightly stream, wert thou a river of
name, were thine greatest fame o'er all the earth —
but thou hast no name, thou art but gathered
from failing rivulets, and hast neither fountain-source
nor fixed abode ! In place of source thou hast only
the rain and the melted snows, riches that sluggish
winter serves to thee ; either thou runnest a
muddy course in the brumal time, or hast a dried
and dusty bed. What thirsty farer has e'er been
able then to drink of thee ? Who in grateful tone
has said of thee : " Mayst thou flow on for ever ? "

damnosus pecori curris, damnosior agris.
  forsitan haec alios ; me mea damna movent.   100
Huic ego, vae ! demens narrabam fluminum amores !
  iactasse indigne nomina tanta pudet.
nescio quem hunc spectans Acheloon et Inachon
    amnem
  et potui nomen, Nile, referre tuum !
at tibi pro meritis, opto, non candide torrens,   105
  sint rapidi soles siccaque semper hiemps !

VIII [1]

Et quisquam ingenuas etiamnunc suspicit artes,
  aut tenerum dotes carmen habere putat ?
ingenium quondam fuerat pretiosius auro ;
  at nunc barbaria est grandis, habere nihil.
cum pulchrae dominae nostri placuere libelli,   5
  quo licuit libris, non licet ire mihi ;
cum bene laudavit, laudato ianua clausa est.
  turpiter huc illuc ingeniosus eo.
Ecce, recens dives parto per vulnera censu
  praefertur nobis sanguine pastus eques !   10
hunc potes amplecti formosis, vita, lacertis ?
  huius in amplexu, vita, iacere potes ?
si nescis, caput hoc galeam portare solebat ;
  ense latus cinctum, quod tibi servit, erat ;

[1] For VII see p. 506.

---

[a] The soldier had recently been enrolled an eques. Ovid's

Thou art a current harmful to the flocks, more harmful to the fields. These wrongs perhaps touch others; me my own wrongs touch.

[101] To a stream like this—out upon it!—I was fool enough to tell of the loves of rivers! I shame to have uttered unworthily names so great. To think that, looking on this nothing of a stream, I could mention your names, Achelous and Inachus, and thine, O Nile! Indeed, for thee, as thou deservest, O torrent aught but clear, I pray that suns be ever fierce and winter ever dry!

VIII

AND does anyone still respect the freeborn arts, or deem tender verse brings any dower? Time was when genius was more precious than gold; but now to have nothing is monstrous barbarism. When my little books have won my lady, where my books could go, I may not go myself; when she has praised me heartily, to him she has praised the door is closed. Disgracefully hither and thither I go, for all my poet's gift.

[9] Look you, a newly-rich, a knight[a] fed fat on blood, who won his rating by dealing wounds, is preferred to me! A being like that can you, my life, embrace with your beautiful arms? In such a one's embrace, my life, can you let yourself be clasped? If you do not know, that head used to wear a helmet; a sword was girt to the side that now serves you;

own family had the same rank, but it was of long standing. Birth or the possession of about £3,200 determined it.

laeva manus, cui nunc serum male convenit
    aurum,   15
  scuta tulit ; dextram tange—cruenta fuit !
qua periit aliquis, potes hanc contingere dextram ?
  heu, ubi mollities pectoris illa tui ?
cerne cicatrices, veteris vestigia pugnae—
  quaesitum est illi corpore, quidquid habet.   20
forsitan et, quotiens hominem iugulaverit, ille
  indicet ! hoc fassas tangis, avara, manus ?
ille ego Musarum purus Phoebique sacerdos
  ad rigidas canto carmen inane fores ?
discite, qui sapitis, non quae nos scimus inertes,   25
  sed trepidas acies et fera castra sequi
proque bono versu primum deducite pilum !
  hoc tibi, si velles, posset, Homere, dari.
Iuppiter, admonitus nihil esse potentius auro,
  corruptae pretium virginis ipse fuit.   30
dum merces aberat, durus pater, ipsa severa,
  aerati postes, ferrea turris erat ;
sed postquam sapiens in munera venit adulter,
  praebuit ipsa sinus et dare iussa dedit.
at cum regna senex caeli Saturnus haberet,   35
  omne lucrum tenebris alta premebat humus.
aeraque et argentum cumque auro pondera ferri
  manibus admorat, nullaque massa fuit.
at meliora dabat—curvo sine vomere fruges
  pomaque et in quercu mella reperta cava.   40

---

^a The badge of an eques.   ^b Danae.

that left hand, which now the late-gotten gold
ring so ill becomes,[a] has carried a shield; that
right hand—touch it!—has been stained with blood.
The hand by which someone has died—can you
touch that right hand? Alas! where is the ten-
derness of heart you had? Look at those scars,
marks of the bygone fight—that man has earned
with his body whatever he has. Perhaps he could
even tell you how many times he has plunged the
steel in a human throat. Do you touch, greedy
girl, hands that tell such tales? and do I, the
unstained priest of Phoebus and the Muses, sing
verses all in vain before your unyielding doors?
Ah, ye who are wise, learn not what we know, we
sluggards, but to follow battle's alarms and the
fierce tented field, and marshall, in place of good
verse, the foremost spears! This, Homer, had been
thy fortune, didst thou wish.

[29] Jove, knowing well that naught was more
potent than gold, himself became the price of a
maid's betrayal.[b] So long as there was no gain to
get, hard was the father, the maid herself severe,
brazen the door, and iron the tower; yet when
the astute lover had come in the form of a price,
the maid herself opened her arms and gave her
favours at command. But when ancient Saturn had
his kingdom in the sky, the deep earth held lucre
all in its dark embrace. Copper and silver and gold
and heavy iron he had hid away in the lower realms,
and there was no massy metal. Yet better were
his gifts—increase without the curved share, and
fruits and honeys brought to light from the hollow
oak. And no one broke the glebe with the strong
share, no measurer marked the limit of the soil,

477

nec valido quisquam terram scindebat [1] aratro,
  signabat nullo limite mensor humum,
non freta demisso verrebant eruta remo;
  ultima mortali tum via litus erat.
Contra te sollers, hominum natura, fuisti   45
  et nimium damnis ingeniosa tuis.
quo tibi, turritis incingere moenibus urbes?
  quo tibi, discordes addere in arma manus?
quid tibi cum pelago—terra contenta fuisses!
  cur non et caelum, tertia regna, petis?   50
qua licet, adfectas caelum quoque—templa
      Quirinus,
  Liber et Alcides et modo Caesar habent.
eruimus terra solidum pro frugibus aurum.
  possidet inventas sanguine miles opes.
curia pauperibus clausa est—dat census honores;   55
  inde gravis iudex, inde severus eques!
Omnia possideant; illis Campusque forumque
  serviat, hi pacem crudaque bella gerant—
tantum ne nostros avidi liceantur amores,
  et—satis est—aliquid pauperis esse sinant!   60
at nunc, exaequet tetricas licet illa Sabinas,
  imperat ut captae qui dare multa potest;
me prohibet custos, in me timet illa maritum.
  si dederim, tota cedet uterque domo!
o si neclecti quisquam deus ultor amantis   65
  tam male quaesitas pulvere mutet opes!

[1] findebat *vulg.*

they did not sweep the seas, stirring the waters with dipping oar ; the shore in those days was the utmost path for man.

⁴⁵ Thine own genius, O human kind, hath been thy foe, and thy wit o'er great to thine own undoing. What boots it thee to girdle cities with towered walls ? What boots it to place the weapon in hands at strife ? What was the sea to thee—with the land thou shouldst have been content ! Why dost not aspire to the skies, too, for a third dominion ? Where thou mayst, thou dost pretend to the skies as well—Quirinus has his temple, and Liber, and Alcides, and Caesar now. We draw from the earth, instead of increase, the massy gold. The soldier possesses wealth begotten of his blood. The senate is closed to the poor—'tis rating brings office ; 'tis that gives the juror weight, 'tis that makes a pattern of the knight !

⁵⁷ Let them have all ; let these have Campus and Forum slaves to them, and those rule the issues of peace and bloody war—only let them not in their greed buy away our loves, and let them leave something—'tis enough—for the poor to win ! But now, though she I love match the austere Sabine dames, he who has much to give commands her as if a captive ; while I—am denied by her guard ; when it comes to me, she fears her husband. If I chance to have given, both guard and husband will leave me the whole house free ! O were there only some god to avenge the neglected lover, and change to dust gains so ill-got.

IX

MEMNONA si mater, mater ploravit Achillem,
    et tangunt magnas tristia fata deas,
flebilis indignos, Elegeia, solve capillos!
    a, nimis ex vero nunc tibi nomen erit!—
ille tui vates operis, tua fama, Tibullus   5
    ardet in extructo, corpus inane, rogo.
ecce, puer Veneris fert eversamque pharetram
    et fractos arcus et sine luce facem;
adspice, demissis ut eat miserabilis alis
    pectoraque infesta tundat aperta manu!   10
excipiunt lacrimas sparsi per colla capilli,
    oraque singultu concutiente sonant.
fratris in Aeneae sic illum funere dicunt
    egressum tectis, pulcher Iule, tuis;
nec minus est confusa Venus moriente Tibullo,   15
    quam iuveni rupit cum ferus inguen aper.
at sacri vates et divum cura vocamur;
    sunt etiam qui nos numen habere putent.
Scilicet omne sacrum mors inportuna profanat,
    omnibus obscuras inicit illa manus!   20
quid pater Ismario, quid mater profuit Orpheo?
    carmine quid victas obstipuisse feras?
et Linon[1] in silvis idem pater "aelinon!" altis
    dicitur invita concinuisse lyra.
adice Maeoniden, a quo ceu fonte perenni   25
    vatum Pieriis ora rigantur aquis—

---

[1] *So Ehw.*: aelinon—aelinon *vulg.*

[a] Apollo and the Muse Calliope.
[b] "Woe, Linus," a dirge.　　[c] Homer.

IX

IF Memnon was bewailed by his mother, if a mother bewailed Achilles, and if sad fates are touching to great goddesses, be thou in tears, O Elegy, and loose thine undeserving hair! Ah, all too truthful now will be thy name!—he, that singer of thy strain, that glory of thine, Tibullus, lies burning on the high-reared pyre, an empty mortal frame. See, the child of Venus comes, with quiver reversed, with bows broken, and lightless torch; look, how pitiable he comes, with drooping wings, how he beats his barèd breast with hostile hand! His tears are caught by the locks hanging scattered about his neck, and from his lips comes the sound of shaking sobs. In such plight, they say, he was at Aeneas his brother's laying away, when he came forth of thy dwelling, fair Iulus; nor was Venus' heart less wrought when Tibullus died than when the fierce boar crushed the groin of the youth she loved. Yes, we bards are called sacred, and the care of the gods; there are those who even think we have the god within.

19 Too true it is, death rudely profaneth every sacred thing, and layeth darksome hands on all! Of what avail to Ismarian Orpheus was his sire, of what avail his mother?[a] Of what that the wild beast stopped in amaze, o'ermastered by his song? The same sire, 'tis said, mourned Linus, too, singing "aelinon!"[b] in the deep wood to unresponsive lyre. Add to these Maeonia's child,[c] from whom as from fount perennial the lips of bards are bedewed with Pierian waters—him, too, a final day submerged in

hunc quoque summa dies nigro submersit Averno.
  defugiunt [1] avidos carmina sola rogos ;
durat opus vatum, Troiani fama laboris
  tardaque nocturno tela retexta dolo.   30
sic Nemesis longum, sic Delia nomen habebunt,
  altera cura recens, altera primus amor.
Quid vos sacra iuvant ? quid nunc Aegyptia prosunt
  sistra ? quid in vacuo secubuisse toro ?
cum rapiunt mala fata bonos—ignoscite fasso !—   35
  sollicitor nullos esse putare deos.
vive pius—moriere ; pius cole sacra—colentem
  mors gravis a templis in cava busta trahet ;
carminibus confide bonis—iacet, ecce, Tibullus :
  vix manet e toto, parva quod urna capit !   40
tene, sacer vates, flammae rapuere rogales
  pectoribus pasci nec timuere tuis ?
aurea sanctorum potuissent templa deorum
  urere, quae tantum sustinuere nefas !
avertit vultus, Erycis quae possidet arces ;   45
  sunt quoque, qui lacrimas continuisse negant.
Sed tamen hoc melius, quam si Phaeacia tellus
  ignotum vili supposuisset humo.
hinc certe madidos fugientis pressit ocellos
  mater et in cineres ultima dona tulit ;   50
hinc soror in partem misera cum matre doloris
  venit inornatas dilaniata comas,

  [1] defugiunt *J. C. Jahn from two MSS.*: diffugiunt *vulg.*

---

  [a] Tibullus, in i. 3, 23–26, refers to Delia's devotion to Isis.
The sistrum was an Egyptian musical instrument used in her
worship.

black Avernus. 'Tis song alone escapes the greedy pyre. The work of bards—the renown of the toils of Troy, and the tardy web unwoven with nightly wile—endures for aye. So Nemesis, so Delia, will long be known to fame, the one a recent passion, the other his first love.

[33] What boot your sacrifices? What now avail the sistrums of Egypt?[a] What your repose apart in faithful beds? When evil fate sweeps away the good—forgive me who say it!—I am tempted to think there are no gods. Live the duteous life— you will die; be faithful in your worship—in the very act of worship heavy death will drag you from the temple to the hollow tomb; put your trust in beautiful song—behold, Tibullus lies dead: from his whole self there scarce remains what the slight urn receives! Is it really thee, thou consecrated bard, whom the flames of the pyre have seized, and is it thy breast they have not feared to feed upon? Flames that shrank not from such awful wrong could have burned the golden temples of the blessed gods! She turned her face away who holds the heights of Eryx; some, too, there are who say she kept not back the tear.

[47] And yet, 'tis better so than if Phaeacian land[b] had laid mean soil o'er thy nameless corse. To this 'tis due that at least thy mother closed thy swimming eyes as thou didst pass from life, and bestowed on thy ashes the final boon; to this 'tis due that thy sister came, with hair disordered and torn, to share the poor mother's grief, and Nemesis, and

[b] Corcyra, where Tibullus had once been dangerously ill. In i. 3, 3–10, composed at the time, he prays to be spared from death away from his mother, sister, and Delia.

483

cumque tuis sua iunxerunt Nemesisque priorque
  oscula nec solos destituere rogos.
Delia descendens "felicius" inquit "amata   55
  sum tibi; vixisti, dum tuus ignis eram."
cui Nemesis "quid" ait "tibi sunt mea damna
    dolori?
  me tenuit moriens deficiente manu."
Si tamen e nobis aliquid nisi nomen et umbra
  restat, in Elysia valle Tibullus erit.   60
obvius huic venias hedera iuvenalia cinctus
  tempora cum Calvo, docte Catulle, tuo;
tu quoque, si falsum est temerati crimen amici,
  sanguinis atque animae prodige Galle tuae.
his comes umbra tua est; siqua est modo corporis
    umbra,   65
  auxisti numeros, culte Tibulle, pios.
ossa quieta, precor, tuta requiescite in urna,
  et sit humus cineri non onerosa tuo!

X

ANNUA venerunt Cerealis tempora sacri;
  secubat in vacuo sola puella toro.
flava Ceres, tenues spicis redimita capillos,
  cur inhibes sacris commoda nostra tuis?
Te, dea, munificam gentes ubiquaque loquuntur,   5
  nec minus humanis invidet ulla bonis.
ante nec hirsuti torrebant farra coloni,
  nec notum terris area nomen erat,

her thou lovedst before, added their kisses to those from thine own kin, and left not desolate thy pyre. "More happily," spake Delia, descending from the pyre, "was I beloved by thee; thou wert living as long as I kindled thee." To whom Nemesis, "Why," said she, "do you mourn for a loss which is mine? 'Twas I to whom he clung when his hand failed in death."

⁵⁹ Yet, if aught survives from us beyond mere name and shade, in the vale of Elysium Tibullus will abide. Mayst thou come to meet him, thy youthful temples encircled with the ivy, and thy Calvus with thee, learned Catullus; thou too, if the charge be false thou didst wrong thy friend, O Gallus lavish of thy blood and of thy soul. To these is thy shade comrade; if shade there be that survives the body, thou hast increased the number of the blest, refined Tibullus. O bones, rest quiet in protecting urn, I pray, and may the earth weigh light upon thine ashes!

X

The time for Ceres' yearly festival is come; my love is in retreat, and rests alone.ᵃ O golden Ceres, thy delicate tresses crowned with ears of wheat, why dost thou with thy festival put ban upon our joys?

⁵ Thee, goddess, do people everywhere call giver of gifts, nor is there goddess less envies men their blessings. Before thee, neither did shaggy countryman parch the corn, nor known upon the earth was the name of threshing-floor, but the oak, first

---

ᵃ The festival was in August, and accompanied by fasting and other abstinence.

sed glandem quercus, oracula prima, ferebant ;
    haec erat et teneri caespitis herba cibus.   10
prima Ceres docuit turgescere semen in agris
    falce coloratas subsecuitque comas ;
prima iugis tauros supponere colla coegit,
    et veterem curvo dente revellit humum.
Hanc quisquam lacrimis laetari credit amantum   15
    et bene tormentis secubituque coli ?
nec tamen est, quamvis agros amet illa feraces,
    rustica nec viduum pectus amoris habet.
Cretes erunt testes—nec fingunt omnia Cretes.
    Crete nutrito terra superba Iove.   20
illic, sideream mundi qui temperat arcem,
    exiguus tenero lac bibit ore puer.
Magna fides testi : testis laudatur alumno.
    fassuram Cererem crimina nostra puto.
viderat Iasium Cretaea diva sub Ida   25
    figentem certa terga ferina manu.
vidit, et ut tenerae flammam rapuere medullae,
    hinc pudor, ex illa parte trahebat amor.
victus amore pudor ; sulcos arere videres
    et sata cum minima parte redire sui.   30
cum bene iactati pulsarant arva ligones,
    ruperat et duram vomer aduncus humum,
seminaque in latos ierant aequaliter agros,
    inrita decepti vota colentis erant.
diva potens frugum silvis cessabat in altis ;   35
    deciderant longae spicea serta comae.
sola fuit Crete fecundo fertilis anno ;
    omnia, qua tulerat se dea, messis erat ;

---

    a At the primeval shrine of Jove at Dodona were oaks whose
rustling was oracular.   *b* Cf. Titus, i. 12, Κρῆτες ἀεὶ ψευσταί.

of our oracles,*a* brought forth the acorn ; this, and the herb that sprang from the tender turf, were his food. 'Twas Ceres first taught the seed to swell in the fields, and cut with sickle the coloured locks of the corn ; 'twas she first made the steer bend neck to the yoke, and turned with the share's curved tooth the ancient mould.

¹⁵ Does any think this a goddess to joy in the tears of lovers, and to see fit worship in the torments of lying apart ? However much she loves her fruitful fields, she is yet no simple rustic, nor has heart void of love. The Cretans will be my witness—and the Cretans are not wholly false.*b* Crete is the land proud of the nurture of Jove. 'Twas there that he who sways the starry heights of the world drank in the milk with the tender mouth of a little child.

²³ We have great faith in their witness—witness approved by their foster-son. Ceres herself, I think, will own to my impeachment. Under Cretan Ida the goddess had seen Iasius with sure hand piercing the wild beast's side. She looked on him, and when her tender heart had caught the fire, she was victim now of shame, and now again of love. Her shame was overcome by love ; you might see the furrows of the field grown dry and the sown grain returning with scantest part of itself. When the well-wielded mattock had wrought upon the acre, and the hookèd share had broken the dour glebe, and the seed had gone forth equal over the broad plowed fields, the deluded husbandman had vowed in vain. The goddess potent over increase dallied in the deep woods ; fallen from her long tresses were the woven spikes of corn. Crete only was fruitful with fecund year ; wherever the goddess

ipse[1] locus nemorum, canebat frugibus Ide,[2]
    et ferus in silva farra metebat aper.   40
optavit Minos similes sibi legifer annos,
    optavit, Cereris longus ut esset amor.
Quod tibi secubitus tristes, dea flava, fuissent,
    hoc cogor sacris nunc ego ferre tuis?
cur ego sim tristis, cum sit tibi nata reperta   45
    regnaque quam Iuno sorte minore regat?
festa dies Veneremque vocat cantusque merumque;
    haec decet ad dominos munera ferre deos.

XI a

MULTA diuque tuli; vitiis patientia victa est;
    cede fatigato pectore, turpis amor!
scilicet adserui iam me fugique catenas,
    et quae non puduit ferre, tulisse pudet.
vicimus et domitum pedibus calcamus amorem;   5
    venerunt capiti cornua sera meo.
perfer et obdura![3] dolor hic tibi proderit olim;
    saepe tulit lassis sucus amarus opem.
Ergo ego sustinui, foribus tam saepe repulsus,
    ingenuum dura ponere corpus humo?   10
ergo ego nescio cui, quem tu conplexa tenebas,
    excubui clausam servus ut ante domum?

[1] ipsa *Ném.*   [2] Ide *vulg.*: Idae *P.*
[3] *So vulg.*: perferre obdura, *P*$_1$ *Merk.*

had bent her step, all was rich with the garner; Ida, the very home of forests, was white with harvest, and the wild boar reaped the grain in the woodland. Minos, giver of laws, wished for seasons ever like this, wished that Ceres' love might long endure.

[43] Because lying apart was sad for thee, O golden Goddess, must I now suffer thus on thy holy day? Why must I be sad, when for thee thy daughter is found,[a] and reigns o'er realms of lesser state than only Juno's? A festal day calls for love, and songs, and wine; these are the gifts that are fitly tendered the gods our masters.

XI a

MUCH have I endured, and for long time; my wrongs have overcome my patience; withdraw from my tired-out breast, base love! Surely, now I have claimed my freedom, and fled my fetters, ashamed of having borne what I felt no shame while bearing. Victory is mine, and I tread under foot my conquered love; courage has entered my heart, though late. Persist, and endure! this smart will some day bring thee good; oft has bitter potion brought help to the languishing.

[9] Can it be I have endured it—to be so oft repulsed from your doors, and to lay my body down, a free born man, on the hard ground? Can it be that, for some no one you held in your embrace, I have lain, like a slave keeping vigil, before your tight-closed home? I have seen when the lover

[a] Proserpina.

OVID

vidi, cum foribus lassus prodiret amator,
    invalidum referens emeritumque latus;
hoc tamen est levius, quam quod sum visus ab
    illo—   15
    eveniat nostris hostibus ille pudor!
Quando ego non fixus lateri patienter adhaesi,
    ipse tuus custos, ipse vir, ipse comes?
scilicet et populo per me comitata[1] placebas;
    causa fuit multis noster amoris amor.   20
turpia quid referam vanae mendacia linguae
    et periuratos in mea damna deos?
quid iuvenum tacitos inter convivia nutus
    verbaque conpositis dissimulata notis?
dicta erat aegra mihi—praeceps amensque cucurri; 25
    veni, et rivali non erat aegra meo!
His et quae taceo duravi saepe ferendis;
    quaere alium pro me, qui queat ista pati.
iam mea votiva puppis redimita corona
    lenta tumescentes aequoris audit aquas.   30
desine blanditias et verba, potentia quondam,
    perdere—non ego sum stultus, ut ante fui![2]

b

LUCTANTUR pectusque leve in contraria tendunt
    hac amor hac odium, sed, puto, vincit amor.
odero, si potero; si non, invitus amabo.   35
    nec iuga taurus amat; quae tamen odit, habet.
nequitiam fugio—fugientem forma reducit;
    aversor morum crimina—corpus amo.

[1] comitata P: cantata Burm. from Francf. MS.
[2] Mueller makes the division.

490

came forth from your doors fatigued, with frame exhausted and weak from love's campaign; yet this is a slighter thing than being seen by him—may shame like that befall my enemies!

[17] When have I not in patience clung close to your side, myself your guard, myself your lover, myself your companion? Be sure, too, that people liked you because you were at my side; my love for you has won you love from many. Why repeat the shameful lies of your empty tongue, and recall the perjured oaths to the gods you have sworn to my undoing? Why tell of the silent nods of young lovers at the banquet board, and of words concealed in the signal agreed upon? Say I had been told she was ill—headlong and madly I ran to her; I came, and she was not ill—to my rival!

[27] Oft bearing such-like things, and others I say naught of, I have hardened; seek another in my stead who can submit to them. Already my craft is decked with votive wreath, and listens undisturbed to the sea's swelling waters. Cease wasting your caresses, and the words that once had weight—I am not a fool, as once I was!

b

STRUGGLING over my fickle heart, love draws it now this way, and now hate that—but love, I think, is winning. I will hate, if I have strength; if not, I shall love unwilling. The ox, too, loves not the yoke; what he hates he none the less bears. I fly from your baseness—as I fly, your beauty draws me back; I shun the wickedness of your ways—your

sic ego nec sine te nec tecum vivere possum,
    et videor voti nescius esse mei.   40
aut formosa fores minus, aut minus inproba, vellem ;
    non facit ad mores tam bona forma malos.
facta merent odium, facies exorat amorem—
    me miserum, vitiis plus valet illa suis !
Parce, per o lecti socialia iura, per omnis   45
    qui dant fallendos se tibi saepe deos,
perque tuam faciem, magni mihi numinis instar,
    perque tuos oculos, qui rapuere meos !
quidquid eris, mea semper eris ; tu selige tantum,
    me quoque velle velis, anne coactus amem !   50
lintea dem potius ventisque ferentibus utar,
    ut,[1] quamvis nolim, cogar amare velim.

XII

Quis fuit ille dies, quo tristia semper amanti
    omina non albae concinuistis aves ?
quodve putem sidus nostris occurrere fatis,
    quosve deos in me bella movere querar ?
quae modo dicta mea est, quam coepi solus amare, 5
    cum multis vereor ne sit habenda mihi.
Fallimur, an nostris innotuit illa libellis ?
    sic erit—ingenio prostitit illa meo.
et merito ! quid enim formae praeconia feci ?
    vendibilis culpa facta puella mea est.   10

---

[1] ut *MSS.*: quam *Rautenberg.*

person I love. Thus I can live neither with you
nor without, and seem not to know my own heart's
prayer. I would you were either less beauteous or
less base ; beauty so fair mates not with evil ways.
Your actions merit hate, your face pleads winningly
for love—ah ! wretched me, it has more power than
its owner's misdeeds.

⁴⁵ Spare me, O by the laws of love's comradeship,
by all the gods who oft lend themselves for you to
deceive, and by that face of yours, to me the image
of high divinity, and by your eyes, that have taken
captive mine ! Whatever you be, mine ever will
you be ; choose you only whether you wish me also
willing, or to love because constrained ! Let me
rather spread my sails and use the favouring breeze,
that I may wish, though against my will, for love's
constraint.

XII

WHAT day was that, ye birds not white, on which
you chanted omens ill-boding to the poet ever in
love ? or what ill star shall I think is rising on my
fate, or what gods shall I complain are moving war
against me ? She who but now was called my own,
whom I began alone to love, must now, I fear, be
shared with many.

⁷ Am I mistaken, or is it my books of verse
have made her known ? So will it prove—'tis my
genius has made her common. And I deserve it !
for why was I the crier of her beauty ? Through
my fault she I love has become a thing of sale. I

493

me lenone placet, duce me perductus amator,
  ianua per nostras est adaperta manus.
An prosint, dubium, nocuerunt carmina semper;
  invidiae nostris illa fuere bonis.
cum Thebe, cum Troia foret, cum Caesaris acta,   15
  ingenium movit sola Corinna meum.
aversis utinam tetigissem carmina Musis,
  Phoebus et inceptum destituïsset opus!
Nec tamen ut testes mos est audire poetas;
  malueram verbis pondus abesse meis.   20
per nos Scylla patri caros furata capillos
  pube premit rapidos[1] inguinibusque canes;
nos pedibus pinnas dedimus, nos crinibus angues;
  victor Abantiades alite fertur equo.
idem per spatium Tityon porreximus ingens,   25
  et tria vipereo fecimus ora cani;
fecimus Enceladon iaculantem mille lacertis,
  ambiguae captos virginis ore viros.
Aeolios Ithacis inclusimus utribus Euros;
  proditor in medio Tantalus amne sitit.   30
de Niobe silicem, de virgine fecimus ursam.
  concinit Odrysium Cecropis ales Ityn;
Iuppiter aut in aves aut se transformat in aurum
  aut secat inposita virgine taurus aquas.
Protea quid referam Thebanaque semina, dentes;   35
  qui vomerent flammas ore, fuisse boves;

[1] rabidos *vulg.*: rapidos *P.*

[a] Scylla, daughter of Nisus, king of Megara, took from her father's head the purple lock on which his life depended, and was afterward changed to the monster.

[b] Perseus and Mercury; Medusa; Perseus, Pegasus, and Andromeda.

am the pander has helped her to please, I have been guide to lead the lover, by my hand has her door been opened.

13 Whether verses are good for aught, I doubt; they have always been my bane, and stood in the light of my good. Though there was Thebes, though Troy, though Caesar's deeds, Corinna only has stirred my genius. Would that the Muses had looked away when I first touched verse, and Phoebus refused me aid when my attempt was new!

19 And yet 'tis not the custom to heed the poet's witness; my verses, too, I had preferred should have no weight. 'Twas we poets made Scylla steal from her sire^a his treasured locks, and hide in her groin the devouring dogs; 'tis we have placed wings on feet, and mingled snakes with hair; our song made Abas' child a victor with the wingèd horse.^b We, too, stretched Tityos out through a mighty space, and gave to the viperous dog three mouths; we made Enceladus, hurling the spear with a thousand arms, and the heroes snared by the voice of the doubtful maid.^c We shut in the skins of the Ithacan the East-winds of Aeolus; made the traitor Tantalus thirst in the midst of the stream. Of Niobe we made a rock, and turned a maiden to a bear.^d 'Tis due to us that the bird of Cecrops^e sings Odrysian Itys; that Jove transforms himself now to a bird, and now to gold, or cleaves the waters a bull with a maiden on his back. Why tell of Proteus, and those Theban seeds, the dragon's teeth; that cattle once there were that spewed forth flames from their mouths;

^c The Sirens.
^d Callisto, transformed by Juno and placed in the sky by Jove as Ursa Major. ^e Philomela, the nightingale.

flere genis electra tuas, Auriga, sorores ;
　　quaeque rates fuerint, nunc maris esse deas ;
aversumque diem mensis furialibus Atrei,
　　duraque percussam saxa secuta lyram ?　　　40
Exit in inmensum fecunda licentia vatum,
　　obligat historica nec sua verba fide.
et mea debuerat falso laudata videri
　　femina ; credulitas nunc mihi vestra nocet.

XIII

Cum mihi pomiferis coniunx foret orta Faliscis,
　　moenia contigimus victa, Camille, tibi.
casta sacerdotes Iunoni festa parabant
　　per celebres ludos indigenamque bovem ;
grande morae pretium ritus cognoscere, quamvis　　5
　　difficilis clivis huc via praebet iter.
Stat vetus et densa praenubilus arbore lucus ;
　　adspice—concedas numen inesse loco.[1]
accipit ara preces votivaque tura piorum—
　　ara per antiquas facta sine arte manus.　　　10
hinc, ubi praesonuit sollemni tibia cantu,
　　it per velatas annua pompa vias ;
ducuntur niveae populo plaudente iuvencae,
　　quas aluit campis herba Falisca suis,
et vituli nondum metuenda fronte minaces,　　　15
　　et minor ex humili victima porcus hara,

---

[1] numinis esse locum *vulg.*

[a] The sisters of Phaethon, the charioteer, were changed to
trees, and their tears to amber.

of thy sisters, Auriga, weeping tears of amber o'er their cheeks [a]; of what were ships, but now are goddesses of the sea [b]; of the ill-starred day at Atreus' maddened tables, and the rocks that followed at stroke of the lyre?

[41] Measureless pours forth the creative wantonness of bards, nor trammels its utterance with history's truth. My praising of my lady, too, you should have taken for false; now your easy trust is my undoing.

XIII

SINCE she I wed was sprung from the fruit-bearing Faliscan town,[c] it chanced we came to the walls brought low, Camillus, by thee. The priestesses were making ready chaste festival to Juno, with solemn games and a cow of native stock; 'twas well worth while to tarry and learn the rites, though the way thither is a toilsome road with steep ascents.

[7] There stands an ancient sacred grove, all dark with shadows from dense trees; behold it—you would agree a deity indwelt the place. An altar receives the prayers and votive incense of the faithful—an artless altar, upbuilt by hands of old. From here, when the pipe has sounded forth in solemn strain, advances over carpeted ways the annual pomp; snowy heifers are led along mid the plaudits of the crowd, heifers reared in their native meadows of Faliscan grass, and calves that threaten with brow not yet to be feared, and, lesser victim, a pig from the lowly sty,

[b] Aeneas' ships, transformed that Turnus might not burn them.
[c] Usually called Falerii. Its site is occupied by Civitè Castellana.

duxque gregis cornu per tempora dura recurvo.
    invisa est dominae sola capella deae ;
illius indicio silvis inventa sub altis
    dicitur inceptam destituisse fugam.   20
nunc quoque per pueros iaculis incessitur index
    et pretium auctori vulneris ipsa datur.
Qua ventura dea est, iuvenes timidaeque puellae
    praeverrunt latas veste iacente vias.
virginei crines auro gemmaque premuntur,   25
    et tegit auratos palla superba pedes ;
more patrum Graio velatae vestibus albis
    tradita supposito vertice sacra ferunt.
ore favent populi tunc cum venit aurea pompa,
    ipsa sacerdotes subsequiturque suas.   30
Argiva est pompae facies ; Agamemnone caeso
    et scelus et patrias fugit Halaesus opes
iamque pererratis profugus terraque fretoque
    moenia felici condidit alta manu.
ille suos docuit Iunonia sacra Faliscos.   35
    sint mihi, sint populo semper amica suo !

XIV

Non ego, ne pecces, cum sis formosa, recuso,
    sed ne sit misero scire necesse mihi ;
nec te nostra iubet fieri censura pudicam,
    sed tamen, ut temptes dissimulare, rogat.

and the leader of the flock, with hard temples over-
hung by the curving horn. The she-goat only is hate-
ful to the mistress-deity ; through her tale-telling,
they say, the goddess was found in the deep forest
and made to cease the flight she had entered on.[a]
Now, even children assail the tattler with their darts,
and she herself is prize to whoever deals the wound.

[23] Wherever the goddess will pass, youths and
timid maidens go before, sweeping the broad ways
with trailing robe. The maidens' locks are pressed
by gold and gems, and the proud palla covers feet
that are bright with gold ; in the manner of their
Grecian sires of yore, veiled in white vestments they
bear on their heads the sacred offerings of old. The
crowd keep reverent silence as the golden pomp
comes on, with the goddess' self close in the wake
of her ministers.

[31] From Argos is the form of the pomp ; when
Agamemnon fell, Halaesus left behind both the crime
and the riches of his fatherland, and after wandering
an exile over land and sea founded with auspicious
hand these lofty walls. 'Twas he who taught his
Faliscans the holy rites of Juno. Ever friendly to
me, and ever to their folk, may those rites be.

XIV

THAT you should not err, since you are fair, is not
my plea, but that I be not compelled, poor wretch,
to know it ; no censor am I who demands that you
become chaste, but one who asks that you attempt

---

[a] A story not otherwise known.

non peccat, quaecumque potest peccasse negare,   5
   solaque famosam culpa professa facit.
quis furor est, quae nocte latent, in luce fateri,
   et quae clam facias facta referre palam?
ignoto meretrix corpus iunctura Quiriti
   opposita populum summovet ante sera;   10
tu tua prostitues famae peccata sinistrae
   commissi perages indiciumque tui?
sit tibi mens melior, saltemve imitare pudicas,
   teque probam, quamvis non eris, esse putem.
quae facis, haec facito; tantum fecisse negato,   15
   nec pudeat coram verba modesta loqui!
Est qui nequitiam locus exigat; omnibus illum
   deliciis inple, stet procul inde pudor!
hinc simul exieris, lascivia protinus omnis
   absit, et in lecto crimina pone tuo.   20
illic nec tunicam tibi sit posuisse pudori
   nec femori inpositum sustinuisse femur;
illic purpureis condatur lingua labellis,
   inque modos Venerem mille figuret amor;
illic nec voces nec verba iuvantia cessent,   25
   spondaque lasciva mobilitate tremat!
indue cum tunicis metuentem crimina vultum,
   et pudor obscenum diffiteatur opus;
da populo, da verba mihi; sine nescius errem,
   et liceat stulta credulitate frui!   30
Cur totiens video mitti recipique tabellas?
   cur pressus prior est interiorque torus?
cur plus quam somno turbatos esse capillos
   collaque conspicio dentis habere notam?
tantum non oculos crimen deducis ad ipsos;   35
   si dubitas famae parcere, parce mihi!
mens abit et morior quotiens peccasse fateris,
   perque meos artus frigida gutta fluit.

to feign. She does not sin who can deny her sin, and 'tis only the fault avowed that brings dishonour. What madness is this, to confess in the light of day the hidden things of night, and spread abroad your secret deeds? Even the jade that receives some unknown son of Quirinus is careful first to slip the bolt and exclude the crowd; and you—will you expose your faults to the mercy of evil tongues and be the informer to tell of your own misdeeds? Put on a better mind, and imitate, at least, the modest of your sex, and let me think you honest though you are not. What you are doing, continue to do; only deny that you have done, nor be ashamed to use modest speech in public.

¹⁷ There is a spot that calls for wantonness; fill that with all delights, and let blushing be far away. Once you are forth from there, straight lay all lewdness aside, and leave your faults in the couch . . . . Put on with your dress a face that shrinks from guilt, and let a modest aspect deny the harlot's trade. Cheat the people, cheat me; allow me to mistake through ignorance, to enjoy a fool's belief in you!

³¹ Why must I see so often the sending and getting of notes? Why that your couch has been pressed in every place? Why do I gaze on hair disordered by more than sleep, and see the mark of a tooth upon your neck? You all but bring your sin before my very eyes; if you hesitate to spare your name, at least spare me! My mind fails me and I suffer death each time you confess your sin, and through my frame the blood runs cold.

tunc amo, tunc odi frustra quod amare necesse est ;
    tunc ego, sed tecum, mortuus esse velim !   40
Nil equidem inquiram, nec quae celare parabis
    insequar, et falli muneris instar erit.
si tamen in media deprensa tenebere culpa,
    et fuerint oculis probra videnda meis,
quae bene visa mihi fuerint, bene visa negato—   45
    concedent verbis lumina nostra tuis.
prona tibi vinci cupientem vincere palma est,
    sit modo " non feci ! " dicere lingua memor.
cum tibi contingat verbis superare duobus,
    etsi non causa, iudice vince tuo !   50

XV

QUAERE novum vatem, tenerorum mater Amorum !
    raditur hic elegis ultima meta meis ;
quos ego conposui, Paeligni ruris alumnus—
    nec me deliciae dedecuere meae—
siquid id est, usque a proavis vetus ordinis heres,   5
    non modo militiae turbine factus eques.
Mantua Vergilio, gaudet Verona Catullo ;
    Paelignae dicar gloria gentis ego,
quam sua libertas ad honesta coegerat arma,
    cum timuit socias anxia Roma manus.   10

Then do I love you, then try in vain to hate what I love perforce; then would I gladly be dead—but dead with you!

⁴¹ I will make no inquiry, be assured, and will not follow out what you will make ready to hide; to be deceived shall be as a duty. If none the less I shall find you out in the midst of a fault, and my eyes perforce shall have looked upon your shame, see you deny that I clearly saw what was clearly seen—my eyes will yield to your words. 'Twill be an easy palm for you—to be victor over one who is eager to be vanquished; all that you need is a tongue that remembers "I did not do it!" When you may win the day by a mere two words, if you cannot through your cause, be victor through your judge!

XV

Seek a new bard, mother of tender Loves! I am come to the last turning-post my elegies will graze; the elegies whose poet am I—nor have these my delights dishonoured me—child reared on Paelignian acres, and heir, if that be aught, of a line of grandsires far removed, no knight created but now amid the whirlwind of war.

⁷ Mantua joys in Virgil, Verona in Catullus; 'tis I shall be called the glory of the Paelignians, race whom their love of freedom compelled to honourable arms when anxious Rome was in fear of the allied bands;ᵃ and some stranger, looking on

ᵃ The Social War, 90–89 B.C., by which Rome was compelled to grant citizenship to the Italians. The Paeligni were leaders.

atque aliquis spectans hospes Sulmonis aquosi
    moenia, quae campi iugera pauca tenent,
"Quae tantum" dicat "potuistis ferre poetam,
    quantulacumque estis, vos ego magna voco."
Culte puer puerique parens Amathusia culti,   15
    aurea de campo vellite signa meo!
corniger increpuit thyrso graviore Lyaeus:
    pulsanda est magnis area maior equis.
inbelles elegi, genialis Musa, valete,
    post mea mansurum fata superstes opus!   20

watery Sulmo's walls, that guard the scant acres of her plain, may say : " O thou who couldst beget so great a poet, however small thou art, I name thee mighty ! "

15 O worshipful child, and thou of Amathus, mother of the worshipful child, pluck ye up from my field your golden standards ! The hornèd Lyaean hath dealt me a sounding blow with weightier thyrsus ; I must smite the earth with mighty steeds on a mightier course. Unwarlike elegies, congenial Muse, O fare ye well, work to live on when I am no more !

VII

At non formosa est, at non bene culta puella,
    at, puto, non votis saepe petita meis !
hanc tamen in nullos tenui male languidus usus,
    sed iacui pigro crimen onusque toro ;
nec potui cupiens, pariter cupiente puella,   5
    inguinis effeti parte iuvante frui.
illa quidem nostro subiecit eburnea collo
    bracchia Sithonia candidiora nive,
osculaque inseruit cupide luctantia linguis
    lascivum femori supposuitque femur,   10
et mihi blanditias dixit dominumque vocavit,
    et quae praeterea publica verba iuvant.
tacta tamen veluti gelida mea membra cicuta
    segnia propositum destituere meum ;
truncus iners iacui, species et inutile pondus,   15
    et non exactum, corpus an umbra forem.
Quae mihi ventura est, siquidem ventura, senectus,
    cum desit numeris ipsa iuventa suis ?
a, pudet annorum cum[1] me iuvenemque virumque
    nec iuvenem nec me sensit amica virum !   20
sic flammas aditura pias aeterna sacerdos
    surgit et a caro fratre verenda soror.
at nuper bis flava Chlide, ter candida Pitho,
    ter Libas officio continuata meo est ;
exigere a nobis angusta nocte Corinnam   25
    me memini numeros sustinuisse novem.
Num mea Thessalico languent devota veneno
    corpora ? num misero carmen et herba nocent,

---

[1] cum (quom) *Pa.*: quo *P Br.*: quod *vulg.*: cur *Merk.*:
quare *Ném.*

sagave poenicea [1] defixit nomina cera
    et medium tenuis in iecur egit acus?   30
carmine laesa Ceres sterilem vanescit in herbam,
    deficiunt laesi carmine fontis aquae,
ilicibus glandes cantataque vitibus uva
    decidit, et nullo poma movente fluunt.
quid vetat et nervos magicas torpere per artes?   35
    forsitan inpatiens sit latus inde meum.
huc pudor accessit facti; pudor ipse nocebat;
    ille fuit vitii causa secunda mei.
At qualem vidi tantum tetigique puellam!
    sic etiam tunica tangitur illa sua.   40
illius ad tactum Pylius iuvenescere possit
    Tithonosque annis fortior esse suis.
haec mihi contigerat; sed vir non contigit illi.
    quas nunc concipiam per nova vota preces?
credo etiam magnos, quo sum tam turpiter usus,   45
    muneris oblati paenituisse deos.
optabam certe recipi—sum nempe receptus;
    oscula ferre—tuli; proximus esse—fui.
quo mihi fortunae tantum? quo regna sine usu?
    quid, nisi possedi dives avarus opes?   50
sic aret mediis taciti vulgator in undis
    pomaque, quae nullo tempore tangat, habet.
a tenera quisquam sic surgit mane puella,
    protinus ut sanctos possit adire deos?
Sed, puto, non blande, non optima perdidit in
    me   55
oscula; non omni sollicitavit ope!
illa graves potuit quercus adamantaque durum
    surdaque blanditiis saxa movere suis.
digna movere fuit certe vivosque virosque;
    sed neque tum vixi nec vir, ut ante, fui.   60

        [1] poenicea *vulg.*: sanguinea *P s.*

OVID

quid iuvet, ad surdas si cantet Phemius aures?
  quid miserum Thamyran picta tabella iuvat?
At quae non tacita formavi gaudia mente!
  quos ego non finxi disposuique modos!
nostra tamen iacuere velut praemortua membra   65
  turpiter hesterna languidiora rosa—
quae nunc, ecce, vigent intempestiva valentque,
  nunc opus exposcunt militiamque suam.
quin istic pudibunda iaces, pars pessima nostri?
  sic sum pollicitis captus et ante tuis.   70
tu dominum fallis; per te deprensus inermis
  tristia cum magno damna pudore tuli.
Hanc etiam non est mea dedignata puella
  molliter admota sollicitare manu;
sed postquam nullas consurgere posse per artes   75
  inmemoremque sui procubuisse videt,
"quid me ludis?" ait, "quis te, male sane, iubebat
  invitum nostro ponere membra toro?
aut te traiectis Aeaea venefica lanis
  devovet, aut alio lassus amore venis."   80
nec mora, desiluit tunica velata soluta—
  et decuit nudos proripuisse pedes!—
neve suae possent intactam scire ministrae,
  dedecus hoc sumpta dissimulavit aqua.

INDEX

I. HEROIDES

OVID.

INDEX

Amyntor, father of Phoenix, III. 27

Anactorie, a friend of Sappho : XV. 17

Anchises, father of Aeneas : VII. 162; XVI. 203

Androgeus, brother of Ariadne and son of Minos of Crete, who imposed on Athens the tribute of seven youths and seven maidens because of his son's death there : X. 99

Andromache : V. 107; VIII. 13

Andromede, Andromeda, daughter of Cepheus, rescued by Perseus : XV. 36; XVIII. 151

Andros, an island in the Aegean : XXI. 81

Anna : VII. 191

Antaeus, King of Libya, the famous wrestler throttled by Hercules : IX. 71

Antenor, a Trojan warrior, counsellor of Priam : V. 95

Antilochus, son of Nestor, slain by Memnon · I. 15

Antinous, suitor of Penelope : I. 92

Aonius, of the Aonian mountains, in Boeotia : IX. 133

Apollo : VIII. 83; XV. 23

Aquilo, the north-wind : XI. 13; XVI. 345

Arabs : XV. 76

Arctophylax, Bootes : XVIII. 188

Arctos, the Lesser Bear : XVIII, 149

Argo, the ship of the Argonauts : VI. 65; XII. 9

Argolicus : I. 25; VI. 80; VIII. 74; XIII. 71

Argolides : VI. 81

Argos : XIV. 34

Ariadne, daughter of Minos, king of Crete. Having aided Theseus of Athens to find his way in the Labyrinth and thus slay her own brother the Minotaur, she flies with him, but is abandoned by him on the isle of Naxos, whence her letter is written : X., title

Ascanius, son of Aeneas : VII. 77

Asia : XVI. 177, 355

Atalanta, daughter of Iasius of Arcadia, loved by Meleager : IV. 99

Athamas, son of Aeolus and father of Phrixus and Helle : XVIII. 137

Athenae : II. 83

Atlans, Atlas, who supported the world : IX. 18; XVI. 62

Atracis, of Atrax, a town in Thessaly : XVII. 248

Atreus, father of Agamemnon and Menelaus : VIII. 27

Atrides, Atreus' son, Agamemnon or Menelaus : III. 39, 148; V. 101; XVI. 357, 366

Atthis, a friend of Sappho : XV. 18

Auge, a princess of Arcadia, loved by Hercules : IX. 49

Aulis, the port from which the Greeks sailed for Troy : XIII. 3

Aurora, the dawn-goddess : IV. 95; XV. 87; XVI. 201; XVIII. 112

Baccha : X. 48

Bacchus : IV. 47; V. 115; XV. 24, 25

Belides, descendant of Belus, father of Danaus and Aegyptus : XIV. 73

Bicorniger, Bacchus : XIII. 33

Bistonis, Thracian : XVI. 346

Bistonius, Thracian, from the Bistones : II. 90

Boreas : XIII. 15; XVIII. 39, 209; XXI. 42

Briseis, the Mysian captive loved by Achilles, from whom she was taken by Agamemnon to replace Chryseis, his own love, an act which caused the Wrath of Achilles. She writes to reproach her lover for not claiming her : III. 1, 137; XX. 69

Busiris, tyrant of Egypt, who sacrificed strangers to his god : IX. 69

Calyce, mother of Cycnus : XIX 133

Calydon, home of the famous boar, in Aetolia : XX. 101

Canace, daughter of Aeolus, guilty with her brother Macareus, whose deep love she returns. Discovered by her father, and bidden to take her own life, she writes Macareus of her fate. The subject is unpleasant, but the letter one of the best : XI., title

Carthage : VII. 11, 19

Cassandra, sister of Paris, a prophetess : XVI. 121

511

INDEX

INDEX

INDEX

Pasiphae, wife of Minos, mother of Ariadne, Phaedra, and the Minotaur : IV. 57

Pegasis, fountain-nymph, a term applied to Oenone : V. 3; of Pegasus, a Muse : XV. 27

Pelasgias, Greek : IX. 3

Pelasgis, a descendant of Pelasgus : XV. 217

Pelasgus, king of Argos : XIV. 23

Pelasgus, the adjective : XII. 83; XVII. 239

Peleus, husband of Thetis and father of Achilles : III. 135

Pelias, of Pelion, a mountain in Thessaly : III. 126; XII. 8

Pelias, usurper of Iolcus, uncle of Jason : VI. 101; XII. 129

Pelides, son of Peleus, Achilles : VIII. 83

Pelopeius : VIII. 27, 81

Pelops, son of Tantalus and father of Atreus and Thyestes : VIII. 47; XVII. 54

Penates, household deities : III. 67; VII. 77

Penelope, wife of Ulysses, who was absent ten years at the siege of Troy, and did not reach home for ten years more. Her letter is written not long after the fall of Troy : I. 1, 84

Penthesilea : XXI. 118

Pergama, Troy : I. 32, 51; III. 152; XVII. 205

Persephone, daughter of Ceres : XXI. 46

Perseus, son of Jove and Danae : XV. 35; XVII. 153

Phaedra, daughter of Minos and wife of Theseus, of whose son Hippolytus, a chaste devotee of Diana, she is enamoured. Her letter is a declaration of passion : IV. 74, 112

Phaon, legendary lover of Sappho : XV. 11, 90, 123, 193, 203

Phasiacus : XII. 10

Phasias, daughter of the Phasis, Medea : VI. 103

Phasis, a river near Colchis : VI. 108; XVI. 347; XIX. 176

Phoebe, sister of Helen : VIII. 77

Phoebe, Diana, the moon-goddess : XV. 89; XX. 229

Phoebeus, of Phoebus Apollo : XVI 182

Phoebus : I. 67; X. 91; XI. 45; XIII. 103; XV. 25, 165, 181, 183, 188

Phoenix, envoy to Achilles : III. 129

Pherecleus, of Phereclus, who built the ships in which Paris sailed to carry away Helen ; XVI. 22

Phrixus : VI. 104; XII. 8

Phrixus, who, with his sister Helle, escaped through the air on the golden ram from Ino, their stepmother. Helle having been lost in the waters afterwards called the Hellespont, her brother arrived in Colchis, married King Aeëtes' daughter Chalciope, and sacrificed the ram to Zeus (Jove). Aeëtes hung up its golden fleece in the grove of Ares (Mars), whence it was taken by Jason, whose usurping uncle Pelias had sent him for it in the hope that he would lose his life : XVIII. 143; XIX. 163

Phrygia : IX. 128; XVI. 143

Phrygius : I. 54; V. 3, 120; VII. 68; VIII. 14; XIII. 58; XVI. 107, 186, 264; XVII. 57, 227

Phryx : XVI. 198, 203; XVII. 200

Phthias : VII. 165

Phthius, of Phthia, a city of Thessaly, Achilles' birthplace : III. 65

Phylaceis : XIII. 35

Phylleides, women of Phyllos in Thessaly : XIII. 35n.

Phyllis, queen of Thrace, who sheltered and loved Demophoon, son of Theseus of Athens. His failure to keep faith and return is the occasion of her letter : II. 1, 60, 98, 105, 106, 138, 147

Pirithous, who, with his friend Theseus, descended to Hades : IV. 110, 112

Pisander, suitor of Penelope : I. 91

Pittheius, of Pittheus, king of Troezen, grandfather of Theseus : IV. 107

Pittheis, daughter of Pittheus, king of Troezen : X. 131

INDEX

Tantalis, a female descendant of Tantalus : VIII. 122

Tegaeus, of Tegea, a town in Arcadia : IX. 87

Telemachus, son of Ulysses : I. 98, 107

Telamon, a Greek hero at Troy : III. 27; XX. 69

Tenedos, an island in the Aegean : XIII. 53

Tenos, an island in the Aegean : XXI. 81

Teucer, son of Telamon, and brother of Ajax : III. 130

Teucri, Trojans : VII. 140

Teuthrantius, of Teuthras, father of Thespius, king of Thespia : IX. 51

Thalia, a Muse : XV. 84

Thebae : II. 71

Therapnaeus, of Therapne, a town in Lacedaemon : XVI. 198

Theseus, the great hero of Attic legend : II. 13; IV. 65, 111, 119; V. 127, 128; X. 3, 10, 21, 34, 35, 75, 101, 110, 151; XVI. 149, 329, 349; XVII. 33

Thesides, Hippolytus : **IV. 65**

Thessalia : VI. 1

Thessalicus : IX. 100

Thessalis, Thessalian : XIII. 112

Thessalus : VI. 23; XVI. 347; XVIII. 158

Thetis, a sea-nymph, mother of Achilles : XX. 60

Thoantias, Hypsipyle, daughter of Thoas : VI. 163

Thoas, father of Hypsipyle : VI. 114, 135

Thrace : II. 84

Thrax : II. 81; XVI. 345

Threicius : II. 108; III. 118; IX. 89

Thressus : XIX. 100

Thybris : VII. 145

Tiphys, the helmsman of the Argonauts : VI. 48

Tisiphone, one of the Furies : II. 117

Titan, the sun : VIII. 105; XV. 135

Tithonus : XVIII. 111

Tlepolemus, a Greek (Rhodian) prince in the Trojan war, slain by Sarpedon : I. 19, 20

Tonans, the Thunderer : IX. 7

Trinacria, Sicily : XII. 126

Triton, a sea deity : VII. 50

Tritonis, of Pallas Athena : VI. 47n.

Troas, a Trojan woman : XIII. 137; the adjective : XIII. 94; XVI. 185

Troezen, to the south of Corinth : IV. 107

Troia : I. 3, 4, 24, 49, 53; V. 139; VIII. 104; XIII. 71, 87, 123; XVI. 92, 107, 295, 338; XVII. 210

Troicus : I. 28; VII. 184; XVII. 109, 160

Tros, a Trojan : I. 13

Tydeus, brother of Deianira : IX. 155

Tyndareus, father of Helen : VIII. 31; XVII. 54, 250

Tyndaris, Helen, daughter of Tyndareus : V. 91; XVI. 100, 308; XVII. 118

Typhois, of Typhoeus, a Giant buried under Aetna : XV. 11

Tyrius : VII. 151; XII. 179

Tyro, loved by Poseidon, and mother of Pelias and Neleus : XIX. 132

Tyros : XVIII. 149

Ulixes, prince of Ithaca, hero in the Trojan War : I. 1, 35, 84; III. 129; XIX. 148

Ursa, the Bear : XVIII. 152

Venus : II. 39; III. 16; IV. 49, 88, 97, 102, 136, 167; V. 35; VII 31; IX. 11; XV. 91, 213; XVI. 35, 65, 83, 140, 160, 285, 291, 298; XVII. 115, 126, 131, 141, 253; XVIII. 69; XIX. 159

Xanthus, a river of the Troad : V. 30, 31; XIII. 53

Zacynthos, an island near Ithaca : I. 87

Zephyrus : XI. 13; XIV. 39; XV. 208

INDEX

II. AMORES

INDEX

INDEX

INDEX

PRINTED IN GREAT BRITAIN BY FLETCHER & SON LTD, NORWICH

THE LOEB CLASSICAL LIBRARY

VOLUMES ALREADY PUBLISHED

Latin Authors

AMMIANUS MARECLLINUS. Translated by J. C. Rolfe. 3 Vols.

APULEIUS: THE GOLDEN ASS (METAMORPHOSES). W. Adlington (1566). Revised by S. Gaselee.

ST. AUGUSTINE: CITY OF GOD. 7 Vols. Vol. I. G. E. McCracken. Vol. II. W. M. Green. Vol. III. D. Wiesen. Vol. IV. P. Levine. Vol. V. E. M. Sanford and W. M. Green. Vol. VI. W. C. Greene.

ST. AUGUSTINE, CONFESSIONS OF. W. Watts (1631). 2 Vols.

ST. AUGUSTINE, SELECT LETTERS. J. H. Baxter.

AUSONIUS. H. G. Evelyn White. 2 Vols.

BEDE. J. E. King. 2 Vols.

BOETHIUS: TRACTS and DE CONSOLATIONE PHILOSOPHIAE. Rev. H. F. Stewart and E. K. Rand.

CAESAR: ALEXANDRIAN, AFRICAN and SPANISH WARS. A. G. Way.

CAESAR: CIVIL WARS. A. G. Peskett.

CAESAR: GALLIC WAR. H. J. Edwards.

CATO: DE RE RUSTICA; VARRO: DE RE RUSTICA. H. B. Ash and W. D. Hooper.

CATULLUS. F. W. Cornish; TIBULLUS. J. B. Postgate; PERVIGILIUM VENERIS. J. W. Mackail.

CELSUS: DE MEDICINA. W. G. Spencer. 3 Vols.

CICERO: BRUTUS, and ORATOR. G. L. Hendrickson and H. M. Hubbell.

[CICERO]: AD HERENNIUM. H. Caplan.

CICERO: DE ORATORE, etc. 2 Vols. Vol. I. DE ORATORE, Books I. and II. E. W. Sutton and H. Rackham. Vol. II. DE ORATORE, Book III. De Fato; Paradoxa Stoicorum; De Partitione Oratoria. H. Rackham.

CICERO: DE FINIBUS. H. Rackham.

CICERO: DE INVENTIONE, etc. H. M. Hubbell.

CICERO: DE NATURA DEORUM and ACADEMICA. H. Rackham.

CICERO: DE OFFICIIS. Walter Miller.

CICERO: DE REPUBLICA and DE LEGIBUS: SOMNIUM SCIPIONIS. Clinton W. Keyes.

CICERO: DE SENECTUTE, DE AMICITIA, DE DIVINATIONE. W. A. Falconer.

CICERO: IN CATILINAM, PRO FLACCO, PRO MURENA, PRO SULLA. Louis E. Lord.

CICERO: LETTERS to ATTICUS. E. O. Winstedt. 3 Vols.

CICERO: LETTERS TO HIS FRIENDS. W. Glynn Williams. 3 Vols.

CICERO: PHILIPPICS. W. C. A. Ker.

CICERO: PRO ARCHIA POST REDITUM, DE DOMO, DE HARUS-PICUM RESPONSIS, PRO PLANCIO. N. H. Watts.

CICERO: PRO CAECINA, PRO LEGE MANILIA, PRO CLUENTIO, PRO RABIRIO. H. Grose Hodge.

CICERO: PRO CAELIO, DE PROVINCIIS CONSULARIBUS, PRO BALBO. R. Gardner.

CICERO: PRO MILONE, IN PISONEM, PRO SCAURO, PRO FONTEIO, PRO RABIRIO POSTUMO, PRO MARCELLO, PRO LIGARIO, PRO REGE DEIOTARO. N. H. Watts.

CICERO: PRO QUINCTIO, PRO ROSCIO AMERINO, PRO ROSCIO COMOEDO, CONTRA RULLUM. J. H. Freese.

CICERO: PRO SESTIO, IN VATINIUM. R. Gardner.

CICERO: TUSCULAN DISPUTATIONS. J. E. King.

CICERO: VERRINE ORATIONS. L. H. G. Greenwood. 2 Vols.

CLAUDIAN. M. Platnauer. 2 Vols.

COLUMELLA: DE RE RUSTICA. DE ARBORIBUS. H. B. Ash, E. S. Forster and E. Heffner. 3 Vols.

CURTIUS, Q.: HISTORY OF ALEXANDER. J. C. Rolfe. 2 Vols.

FLORUS. E. S. Forster; and CORNELIUS NEPOS. J. C. Rolfe.

FRONTINUS: STRATAGEMS and AQUEDUCTS. C. E. Bennett and M. B. McElwain.

FRONTO: CORRESPONDENCE. C. R. Haines. 2 Vols.

GELLIUS, J. C. Rolfe. 3 Vols.

HORACE: ODES AND EPODES. C. E. Bennett.

HORACE: SATIRES, EPISTLES, ARS POETICA. H. R. Fairclough.

JEROME: SELECTED LETTERS. F. A. Wright.

JUVENAL and PERSIUS. G. G. Ramsay.

LIVY. B. O. Foster, F. G. Moore, Evan T. Sage, and A. C. Schlesinger and R. M. Geer (General Index). 14 Vols.

LUCAN. J. D. Duff.

LUCRETIUS. W. H. D. Rouse.

MARTIAL. W. C. A. Ker. 2 Vols.

MINOR LATIN POETS: from PUBLILIUS SYRUS TO RUTILIUS NAMATIANUS, including GRATTIUS, CALPURNIUS SICULUS, NEMESIANUS, AVIANUS, and others with "Aetna" and the "Phoenix." J. Wight Duff and Arnold M. Duff.

OVID: THE ART OF LOVE and OTHER POEMS. J. H. Mozley.

Ovid: Fasti. Sir James G. Frazer.

Ovid: Heroides and Amores. Grant Showerman.

Ovid: Metamorphoses. F. J. Miller. 2 Vols.

Ovid: Tristia and Ex Ponto. A. L. Wheeler.

Persius. Cf. Juvenal.

Petronius. M. Heseltine; Seneca; Apocolocyntosis. W. H. D. Rouse.

Phaedrus and Babrius (Greek). B. E. Perry.

Plautus. Paul Nixon. 5 Vols.

Pliny: Letters, Panegyricus. Betty Radice. 2 Vols.

Pliny: Natural History.
10 Vols. Vols. I.–V. and IX. H. Rackham. Vols. VI.–VIII. W. H. S. Jones. Vol. X. D. E. Eichholz.

Propertius. H. E. Butler.

Prudentius. H. J. Thomson. 2 Vols.

Quintilian. H. E. Butler. 4 Vols.

Remains of Old Latin. E. H. Warmington. 4 Vols. Vol. I. (Ennius and Caecilius.) Vol. II. (Livius, Naevius, Pacuvius, Accius.) Vol. III. (Lucilius and Laws of XII Tables.) Vol. IV. (Archaic Inscriptions.)

Sallust. J. C. Rolfe.

Scriptores Historiae Augustae. D. Magie. 3 Vols.

Seneca: Apocolocyntosis. Cf. Petronius.

Seneca: Epistulae Morales. R. M. Gummere. 3 Vols.

Seneca: Moral Essays. J. W. Basore. 3 Vols.

Seneca: Tragedies. F. J. Miller. 2 Vols.

Sidonius: Poems and Letters. W. B. Anderson. 2 Vols.

Silius Italicus. J. D. Duff. 2 Vols.

Statius. J. H. Mozley. 2 Vols.

Suetonius. J. C. Rolfe. 2 Vols.

Tacitus: Dialogus. Sir Wm. Peterson. Agricola and Germania. Maurice Hutton.

Tacitus: Histories and Annals. C. H. Moore and J. Jackson. 4 Vols.

Terence. John Sargeaunt. 2 Vols.

Tertullian: Apologia and De Spectaculis. T. R. Glover. Minucius Felix. G. H. Rendall.

Valerius Flaccus. J. H. Mozley.

Varro: De Lingua Latina. R. G. Kent. 2 Vols.

Velleius Paterculus and Res Gestae Divi Augusti. F. W. Shipley.

Virgil. H. R. Fairclough. 2 Vols.

Vitruvius: De Architectura. F. Granger. 2 Vols.

3

Greek Authors

ACHILLES TATIUS. S. Gaselee.

AELIAN: ON THE NATURE OF ANIMALS. A. F. Scholfield. 3 Vols.

AENEAS TACTICUS, ASCLEPIODOTUS and ONASANDER. The Illinois Greek Club.

AESCHINES. C. D. Adams.

AESCHYLUS. H. Weir Smyth. 2 Vols.

ALCIPHRON, AELIAN, PHILOSTRATUS: LETTERS. A. R. Benner and F. H. Fobes.

ANDOCIDES, ANTIPHON, Cf. MINOR ATTIC ORATORS.

APOLLODORUS. Sir James G. Frazer. 2 Vols.

APOLLONIUS RHODIUS. R. C. Seaton.

THE APOSTOLIC FATHERS. Kirsopp Lake. 2 Vols.

APPIAN: ROMAN HISTORY. Horace White. 4 Vols.

ARATUS. Cf. CALLIMACHUS.

ARISTOPHANES. Benjamin Bickley Rogers. 3 Vols. Verse trans.

ARISTOTLE: ART OF RHETORIC. J. H. Freese.

ARISTOTLE: ATHENIAN CONSTITUTION, EUDEMIAN ETHICS, VICES AND VIRTUES. H. Rackham.

ARISTOTLE: GENERATION OF ANIMALS. A. L. Peck.

ARISTOTLE: HISTORIA ANIMALIUM. A. L. Peck. Vols. I.–II.

ARISTOTLE: METAPHYSICS. H. Tredennick. 2 Vols.

ARISTOTLE: METEOROLOGICA. H. D. P. Lee.

ARISTOTLE: MINOR WORKS. W. S. Hett. On Colours, On Things Heard, On Physiognomies, On Plants, On Marvellous Things Heard, Mechanical Problems, On Indivisible Lines, On Situations and Names of Winds, On Melissus, Xenophanes, and Gorgias.

ARISTOTLE: NICOMACHEAN ETHICS. H. Rackham.

ARISTOTLE: OECONOMICA and MAGNA MORALIA. G. C. Armstrong; (with Metaphysics, Vol. II.).

ARISTOTLE: ON THE HEAVENS. W. K. C. Guthrie.

ARISTOTLE: ON THE SOUL. PARVA NATURALIA. ON BREATH. W. S. Hett.

ARISTOTLE: CATEGORIES, ON INTERPRETATION, PRIOR ANALYTICS. H. P. Cooke and H. Tredennick.

ARISTOTLE: POSTERIOR ANALYTICS, TOPICS. H. Tredennick and E. S. Forster.

ARISTOTLE: ON SOPHISTICAL REFUTATIONS.
On Coming to be and Passing Away, On the Cosmos. E. S. Forster and D. J. Furley.

ARISTOTLE: PARTS OF ANIMALS. A. L. Peck; MOTION AND PROGRESSION OF ANIMALS. E. S. Forster.

ARISTOTLE: PHYSICS. Rev. P Wicksteed and F. M. Cornford. 2 Vols.

ARISTOTLE: POETICS and LONGINUS. W. Hamilton Fyfe; DEMETRIUS ON STYLE. W. Rhys Roberts.

ARISTOTLE: POLITICS. H. Rackham.

ARISTOTLE: PROBLEMS. W. S. Hett. 2 Vols.

ARISTOTLE: RHETORICA AD ALEXANDRUM (with PROBLEMS. Vol. II). H. Rackham.

ARRIAN: HISTORY OF ALEXANDER and INDICA. Rev. E. Iliffe Robson. 2 Vols.

ATHENAEUS: DEIPNOSOPHISTAE. C. B. GULICK. 7 Vols.

BABRIUS AND PHAEDRUS (Latin). B. E. Perry.

ST. BASIL: LETTERS. R. J. Deferrari. 4 Vols.

CALLIMACHUS: FRAGMENTS. C. A. Trypanis.

CALLIMACHUS, Hymns and Epigrams, and LYCOPHRON. A. W. Mair; ARATUS. G. R. MAIR.

CLEMENT OF ALEXANDRIA. Rev. G. W. Butterworth.

COLLUTHUS. Cf. OPPIAN.

DAPHNIS AND CHLOE. Thornley's Translation revised by J. M. Edmonds: and PARTHENIUS. S. Gaselee.

DEMOSTHENES I.: OLYNTHIACS, PHILIPPICS and MINOR ORATIONS. I.–XVII. AND XX. J. H. Vince.

DEMOSTHENES II.: DE CORONA and DE FALSA LEGATIONE. C. A. Vince and J. H. Vince.

DEMOSTHENES III.: MEIDIAS, ANDROTION, ARISTOCRATES, TIMOCRATES and ARISTOGEITON, I. AND II. J. H. Vince.

DEMOSTHENES IV.–VI: PRIVATE ORATIONS and IN NEAERAM. A. T. Murray.

DEMOSTHENES VII.: FUNERAL SPEECH, EROTIC ESSAY, EXORDIA and LETTERS. N. W. and N. J. DeWitt.

DIO CASSIUS: ROMAN HISTORY. E. Cary. 9 Vols.

DIO CHRYSOSTOM. J. W. Cohoon and H. Lamar Crosby. 5 Vols.

DIODORUS SICULUS. 12 Vols. Vols. I.–VI. C. H. Oldfather. Vol. VII. C. L. Sherman. Vol. VIII. C. B. Welles. Vols. IX. and X. R. M. Geer. Vol. XI. F. Walton. Vol. XII. F. Walton. General Index. R. M. Geer.

DIOGENES LAERTIUS. R. D. Hicks. 2 Vols.

DIONYSIUS OF HALICARNASSUS: ROMAN ANTIQUITIES. Spelman's translation revised by E. Cary. 7 Vols.

EPICTETUS. W. A. Oldfather. 2 Vols.

EURIPIDES. A. S. Way. 4 Vols. Verse trans.

EUSEBIUS: ECCLESIASTICAL HISTORY. Kirsopp Lake and J. E. L. Oulton. 2 Vols.

GALEN: ON THE NATURAL FACULTIES. A. J. Brock.

THE GREEK ANTHOLOGY. W. R. Paton. 5 Vols.

GREEK ELEGY AND IAMBUS with the ANACREONTEA. J. M. Edmonds. 2 Vols.

THE GREEK BUCOLIC POETS (THEOCRITUS, BION, MOSCHUS). J. M. Edmonds.

GREEK MATHEMATICAL WORKS. Ivor Thomas. 2 Vols.

HERODES. Cf. THEOPHRASTUS: CHARACTERS.

HERODIAN. C. R. Whittaker. 2 Vols.

HERODOTUS. A. D. Godley. 4 Vols.

HESIOD AND THE HOMERIC HYMNS. H. G. Evelyn White.

HIPPOCRATES and the FRAGMENTS OF HERACLEITUS. W. H. S. Jones and E. T. Withington. 4 Vols.

HOMER: ILIAD. A. T. Murray. 2 Vols.

HOMER: ODYSSEY. A. T. Murray. 2 Vols.

ISAEUS. E. W. Forster.

ISOCRATES. George Norlin and LaRue Van Hook. 3 Vols.

[ST. JOHN DAMASCENE]: BARLAAM AND IOASAPH. Rev. G. R. Woodward, Harold Mattingly and D. M. Lang.

JOSEPHUS. 9 Vols. Vols. I.–IV.; H. Thackeray. Vol. V.; H. Thackeray and R. Marcus. Vols. VI.–VII.; R. Marcus. Vol. VIII.; R. Marcus and Allen Wikgren. Vol. IX. L. H. Feldman.

JULIAN. Wilmer Cave Wright. 3 Vols.

LIBANIUS. A. F. Norman. Vol. I.

LUCIAN. 8 Vols. Vols. I.–V. A. M. Harmon. Vol. VI. K. Kilburn. Vols. VII.–VIII. M. D. Macleod.

LYCOPHRON. Cf. CALLIMACHUS.

LYRA GRAECA. J. M. Edmonds. 3 Vols.

LYSIAS. W. R. M. Lamb.

MANETHO. W. G. Waddell: PTOLEMY: TETRABIBLOS. F. E. Robbins.

MARCUS AURELIUS. C. R. Haines.

MENANDER. F. G. Allinson.

MINOR ATTIC ORATORS (ANTIPHON, ANDOCIDES, LYCURGUS, DEMADES, DINARCHUS, HYPERIDES). K. J. Maidment and J. O. Burtt. 2 Vols.

NONNOS: DIONYSIACA. W. H. D. Rouse. 3 Vols.

OPPIAN, COLLUTHUS, TRYPHIODORUS. A. W. Mair.

PAPYRI. NON-LITERARY SELECTIONS. A. S. Hunt and C. C. Edgar. 2 Vols. LITERARY SELECTIONS (Poetry). D. L. Page.

PARTHENIUS. Cf. DAPHNIS and CHLOE.

PAUSANIAS: DESCRIPTION OF GREECE. W. H. S. Jones. 4 Vols. and Companion Vol. arranged by R. E. Wycherley.

PHILO. 10 Vols. Vols. I.–V.; F. H. Colson and Rev. G. H. Whitaker. Vols. VI.–IX.; F. H. Colson. Vol. X. F. H. Colson and the Rev. J. W. Earp.

PHILO: two supplementary Vols. (*Translation only.*) Ralph Marcus.

PHILOSTRATUS: THE LIFE OF APOLLONIUS OF TYANA. F. C. Conybeare. 2 Vols.

PHILOSTRATUS: IMAGINES; CALLISTRATUS: DESCRIPTIONS. A. Fairbanks.

PHILOSTRATUS and EUNAPIUS: LIVES OF THE SOPHISTS. Wilmer Cave Wright.

PINDAR. Sir J. E. Sandys.

PLATO: CHARMIDES, ALCIBIADES, HIPPARCHUS, THE LOVERS, THEAGES, MINOS and EPINOMIS. W. R. M. Lamb.

PLATO: CRATYLUS, PARMENIDES, GREATER HIPPIAS, LESSER HIPPIAS. H. N. Fowler.

PLATO: EUTHYPHRO, APOLOGY, CRITO, PHAEDO, PHAEDRUS. H. N. Fowler.

PLATO: LACHES, PROTAGORAS, MENO, EUTHYDEMUS. W. R. M. Lamb.

PLATO: LAWS. Rev. R. G. Bury. 2 Vols.

PLATO: LYSIS, SYMPOSIUM, GORGIAS. W. R. M. Lamb.

PLATO: REPUBLIC. Paul Shorey. 2 Vols.

PLATO: STATESMAN, PHILEBUS. H. N. Fowler; Ion. W. R. M. Lamb.

PLATO: THEAETETUS and SOPHIST. H. N. Fowler.

PLATO: TIMAEUS, CRITIAS, CLITOPHO, MENEXENUS, EPISTULAE. Rev. R. G. Bury.

PLOTINUS: A. H. Armstrong. Vols. I.–III.

PLUTARCH: MORALIA. 16 Vols. Vols. I.–V. F. C. Babbitt. Vol. VI. W. C. Helmbold. Vols. VII. and XIV. P. H. De Lacy and B. Einarson. Vol. VIII. P. A. Clement and H. B. Hoffleit. Vol. IX. E. L. Minar, Jr., F. H. Sandbach, W. C. Helmbold. Vol. X. H. N. Fowler. Vol. XI. L. Pearson and F. H. Sandbach. Vol. XII. H. Cherniss and W. C. Helmbold. Vol. XV. F. H. Sandbach.

PLUTARCH: THE PARALLEL LIVES. B. Perrin. 11 Vols.

POLYBIUS. W. R. Paton. 6 Vols.

PROCOPIUS: HISTORY OF THE WARS. H. B. Dewing. 7 Vols.

PTOLEMY: TETRABIBLOS. Cf. MANETHO.

QUINTUS SMYRNAEUS. A. S. Way. Verse trans.

SEXTUS EMPIRICUS. Rev. R. G. Bury. 4 Vols.

SOPHOCLES. F. Storr. 2 Vols. Verse trans.

STRABO: GEOGRAPHY. Horace L. Jones. 8 Vols.

THEOPHRASTUS: CHARACTERS. J. M. Edmonds. HERODES, etc. A. D. Knox

THEOPHRASTUS: ENQUIRY INTO PLANTS. Sir Arthur Hort, Bart. 2 Vols.

THUCYDIDES. C. F. Smith. 4 Vols.

Tryphiodorus. Cf. Oppian.
Xenophon: Cyropaedia. Walter Miller. 2 Vols.
Xenophon: Hellenica. C. L. Brownson. 2 Vols.
Xenophon: Anabasis. C. L. Brownson.
Xenophon: Memorabilia and Oeconomicus. E. C. Marchant.
Symposium and Apology. O. J. Todd.
Xenophon: Scripta Minora. E. C. Marchant and G. W.
Bowersock.

IN PREPARATION

Greek Authors

Aristides: Orations. C. A. Behr.
Musaeus: Hero and Leander. T. Gelzer and C. H.
Whitman.
Theophrastus: De Causis Plantarum. G. K. K. Link and
B. Einarson.

Latin Authors

Asconius: Commentaries on Cicero's Orations.
G. W. Bowersock.
Benedict: The Rule. P. Meyvaert.
Justin–Trogus. R. Moss.
Manilius. G. P. Goold.

DESCRIPTIVE PROSPECTUS ON APPLICATION

London   WILLIAM HEINEMANN LTD
Cambridge, Mass.   HARVARD UNIVERSITY PRESS